Oaklayne,

The Reconstruction

By

Karen C. Shriver

and

Maurine R. McCullah

ISBN: 1453897402
ISBN-13: 978-1453897409

Acknowledgments

Maurine McCullah passed away before she could finish this sequel to her earlier book, <u>Oaklayne, A Civil War Saga</u>. She produced an outline and had just begun writing a few of the more dramatic scenes of <u>Oaklayne, The Reconstruction</u> before she went to be with the Lord December 20, 2011 at the age of 93.

Maurine's family would like to express profound appreciation to Maurine's friend, Karen Shriver, for the many long hours spent doing research and lovingly contributing her creative expertise to the completion of this book. We are sure Maurine would be very pleased with the end result.

Many thanks as well to Chadna Kelley, Steve Baker and Wendy Parnell who collaborated in the editing and formatting effort.

Karen Shriver would like to especially recognize Wendy Parnell's extraordinary contribution as Editor of this work. Wendy's skill is evident in the way she seamlessly blended the very different writing styles of two authors into this single, compelling tale.

Chapter 1

MAY 1865

Lisa turned to bid a final farewell to Captain Andrew Abbott. A tall young man with bushy red hair and a ruddy complexion, Andrew was a well-spoken southern gentleman. He had been shot several times while attempting to drag one of his wounded men to safety. Captain Abbott was Lisa's favorite of the injured men she had rescued from the Yankees, as they invaded Richmond. Leaning on a crudely fashioned crutch, the soldier was trembling as much from emotion as weakness, when he took Lisa into his arms to bid farewell.

She stepped back from his embrace, sobbing and wiping tears from her face. How could she leave these men? But, she had thoroughly thought the matter through, and felt she had no choice. She was supposed to meet her husband Goddard here in Manchester, Virginia, but he had never arrived. What has become of him?

She knew she had to find Goddard. Since there were no horses available in the area, her only alternative was to start walking. She hoped she would eventually meet someone along the way who would allow her to ride along in their wagon or buggy.

The last time she saw Goddard was in Richmond when Sherman was approaching. He sent her to Manchester with several wounded Rebel soldiers, promising to meet her there. From rumors she had heard, she expected to be able to cross the Mayo Bridge into Richmond...that is, if she could just get there. She carried with her only a well-worn shawl and the reticule she had when she left Richmond. She also had Goddard's medicine bag which he had given her to carry medicinal supplies for the injured soldiers. Now, it held the biggest medicine bottle she could find, filled with water.

Lisa was a petite, young woman, with a deep tan complexion and thick, curly black hair that hung to her shoulders. Under the circumstances, she had not worn any makeup for quite some time, but her cheeks had a natural glow and her lips a light tint of red.

As she walked along the dusty road, her mind traveled to another place and time. She revisited her life with Goddard—their wedding in England when Goddard was still in Medical College; their beautiful

1

home in Richmond; their little four year old son who had died; Angela's birth...and the awful war that was now over. How different their lives would have been if there had been no war. She continued to reminisce about the events in their lives. As she trudged on, she paid little attention to the surrounding territory, nor the few people she met who were traveling south. She seemed to be the only person who was headed north.

As daylight slowly waned, the sun finally dropped below the horizon. After walking alone all day, Lisa saw a campfire burning some distance ahead on one side of the road. Drawing closer, she could see three men standing by the fire, and a couple of women sitting on the ground nearby. The men were talking, laughing and eating, the women just sat quietly.

She watched from a distance, longing for some food and desperately needing a drink of water. Her water supply had proven sorely inadequate several hours before, but did she dare approach these strangers? As she stood there pondering, one of the men caught sight of her, got up and started in her direction. He had an uncouth look about him, his clothes were tattered and dirty, and his hair was unkempt. She was sure he had not had a bath in weeks. And as he came closer, the stench in her nostrils convinced her she was right.

He stopped in front of her and turned his head, shouting boisterously back to the others around the campfire, "Look'a here! We got us some comp'ny."

Turning back to Lisa, he grasped her arm firmly and said, "You travelin' 'lone, Missy?"

Lisa nodded.

"Well", he said, his voice rough and loud, "Come join us. You hungry?" Lisa shook her head and tried to pull away, as she hesitated to join these people she did not know. His grasp stayed firmly on her arm, so she did not have a choice.

"We don' have much, jes' some venison and bread. Looks like yer travelin' kinda' light. Are ya' thirsty?"

"Yes, but my bottle is empty," Lisa replied as she showed him the container. "And I would really like a drink of water."

"Water?" Again, the boisterous laugh. "We got somethin' much better 'n water, Gal. How 'bout a drink of home brew?"

"No thank you, I prefer water."

She was now strongly wishing she had not stopped, but just walked on by herself. Yes, she was hungry and thirsty, but she had a peculiar feeling about these people, and she was fearful of this man who held her arm so firmly.

2

But the man would not take "No" for an answer. He reached around her, took hold of her other arm also, and led her into the light from the fire.

"My aren't you a purdy li'l thing," he said as he looked her up and down with a hungry eye. Continuing, he turned to one of the other men. "Don't you think we should take this one with us? She otta' have some protection out here, don't 'cha think? Why, a li'l gal like this might get hurt, all alone out here!"

Lisa tried to get free, but his grasp was very firm on her arms, now. He put his face close to hers and in a coaxingly soothing voice, his breath with a strong odor of fermented drink, he said, "Here, honey, don' 'cha try to git away. Now that yer here, we'll have a lady fer each of us. We'll have us a great time, you'll see."

Turning to the third man, Jake motioned toward a jug on the ground. "Pour this li'l lady a cup of home brew, Marty. I'll help her drink it, and then she'll feel much better."

As Marty rose to pour a cup of the strong drink for her, Lisa began struggling frantically to get out of the grasp of this vermin of a man who had hold of her arms. She was now terrified, but when she tried to pull away he only tightened his grip.

Gritting her teeth to keep her voice steady as she wrestled to free herself, Lisa said, "If you will just give me a little water, I will get on my way and not bother you further." She reached way down inside herself for the strength to resist his grasp, but he now had a very firm grip on both arms behind her back, and propelled her to a spot nearer the fire.

"You jes' sit right down here, Girly," he repeated a bit more testily, then forcefully pushed her down to a sitting position on the ground, beside one of the other women.

"No purdy lady should be travelin' 'lone out here, right, Judd?" her captor continued as he turned toward the other man, and took the cup of whiskey he had poured from the jug.

"Right, Jake." The man answered with only two words, but it was very obvious that the one who held her arms was in charge, and the other two men would agree to anything he said. Neither of the women made any attempt to help her. They just sat, watching.

Now Jake turned to the other men and said, "Come on, y'all hold her, while I get her to drink this."

As he loosened his grip to hold her arms with one hand, he reached for the cup from Marty. As he did so, Lisa kicked at him with all the force she could muster. She knew she had hit a vital spot when Jake yelped and slouched over. Then the other men seized her, while the enraged Jake grabbed the cup, held her by the cheeks and forced her

3

mouth open. He poured the liquid in the general area of her mouth, choking her and slopping the smelly liquid all down the front of her blouse.

Jake turned toward his male companions, as Lisa started to rise to her feet. But, she was immediately pushed back to a sitting position with a hand roughly placed on her shoulder. Then a softer hand slid over her hand, where she had placed it on the ground to help in her attempt to stand again.

"Don't try it," a voice whispered beside her as she turned and looked at the woman sitting there. "It's no use. They'll just beat you until you give up."

Lisa thought back to the time in the cemetery in Richmond when she had been accosted by two men and was able to escape by outsmarting them. The men were continuing to pass the jug between them, as they staggered around congratulating one another on their conquest of a new woman for their harem. Since they seemed distracted, she decided to take advantage of their inebriated condition and just be as still as possible. Perhaps, she could quietly get away after they pass out in a drunken stupor. She would walk all night, if necessary, to put distance between herself and this group of ruffians. If her plan worked, they would not know where she had gone, or where to look for her.

She was grateful she had been deposited close to the fire. She wrapped her shawl tightly around herself and laid down on the damp ground very quietly, trying not to draw attention to herself, while absorbing the warmth from the waning cooking fire. The men eventually got quiet and the other women got into one of the wagons. Soon she heard snoring, evidence that at least one of the men was soundly asleep on the other side of the camp. While she tried to decide if she could safely move, Lisa heard the distant sound of a wagon and horses on the trail.

Why would anyone be traveling this late at night? Perhaps it is a delivery wagon and I could get a ride. Anything would be better than this!

The fire had died down, but moonlight filtering through the trees provided enough light for her to see the way back to the road. The forest was alive with the sounds of the night, so Lisa quietly rose and started to walk as quickly, but silently as possible, back toward the trail. But, when she stepped on a twig, it broke with a crack and the noise aroused Jake. He jumped to his feet, and came running after her. She ran as fast as she could toward the trail and the oncoming wagon. A very muscular young black man, hearing her shouting and running toward him, jumped down from the wagon and started toward her.

4

As soon as she reached him, he put his arm around her and pulled her close to him in a gesture of safety. Then the man asked, with a voice that sounded like it came from deep down in a well, "What's happenin' here? Why's a purdy li'l lady like you out here at night, alone on dis here dark road?"

Lisa only had time to gasp, "Help me!" as she clung to him.

Now Jake clumsily crashed against the wagon, and said, "Get out of here, Blackie, and leave my woman alone." He reached for Lisa, but the big black man held her tightly.

Lisa pleaded, "Please, help me! I'm not his woman! This man has been holding me against my will."

"Why yo' do that to the lady?" asked her protector, pushing the white man away from the wagon easily, as if he was merely a rag doll. The attacker lost his balance and almost fell.

As he staggered to retain an upright position, Jake shouted at the man who was still defending Lisa. "Ain't none o' yer business, Blackie."

"Ah say it is, if'n she don' want to be held," the big man replied firmly. "Yo' go on, git outta here. Ah'll take the little Missus wit' me." Then the big man reached and picked up a Henry repeating rifle from the seat of the wagon and aimed it at the drunken man.

Jake suddenly realized he had not picked up his gun when he left to chase after Lisa. Now he was at a distinct disadvantage. He was smaller than this big black man, and he had no weapon.

Holding the rifle, pointed toward Jake, the big man turned to Lisa, and asked, "Would 'ya like to 'cump'ny me an' my fam'ly? We's a goin' into Richmon', to see if they's anythin' left o' our home there."

She did not hesitate for an instant, but answered, "Yes, please. I would very much like to go with you and your family."

"Jes' get in th' wagon, then, Missy. I'm sure mah wife and daughters will 'njoy yer cump'ny."

He pulled back the blanket that was drawn across the front of the covered wagon. Giving Lisa a hand up into the wagon, he said, "My name is Moses. You bes' git in here wit' my wife, Martha, an' rest a spell."

All this time Moses watched Jake like a hawk. He now turned back to him. Squinting his eyes for emphasis and speaking in a threatening tone that was slow and emphatic, he said with his deep voice booming, "Don't foller us or try to git the little missus back. Yo' will have me to battle wit', if'n yo' does." Then, he climbed up onto the seat of the wagon and gave the team a sharp snap of the reins, to start them on their way at a trot.

5

Lisa was welcomed into the wagon by the man's wife who had been awakened by the ruckus outside. The two daughters remained sound asleep, so Lisa smiled and squeezed the woman's hand as it was extended to her, suggesting in a whisper that they wait until morning to get acquainted.

Lying down on the wagon bed, Lisa covered herself with her shawl and closed her eyes, as a feeling of safety enveloped her. But sleep was long in coming, her mind traveling back again to her life with Goddard. Their love for each other had sustained them through so many trials, even the hardships of war and the death of their son. Oh, how she missed him.

When she reached Richmond, she would start looking for him first at their home, although from the rumors she had heard, all of Richmond was in a shambles. However, there was just a chance that their house had been spared by some miracle. She would next go to Chimborazo Hospital, and then to other hospitals, wayside homes, any place still standing where someone might be able to tell her if Goddard was alive or dead. And Angela? Did Goddard get to Naomi's house before it was destroyed? Had Naomi and her family already left the house and taken Angela with them? Where would they go? And how could she search for them? Lisa would not recognize the child even if she saw her face to face, for it had been three years since she had last seen her baby girl.

Chapter 2

The next morning, Lisa awoke, after a few hours of fitful sleep. The delicious smell of meat frying and the distinct feeling of hollowness in the pit of her stomach reminded her of how painfully long it had been since she had eaten. Martha was still sleeping, as were the two young girls. Lisa climbed quietly from the wagon and found Moses frying several small pieces of rabbit over the fire he had built. On a metal tray across one side of the fire was a large tin can filled with steaming coffee. As soon as he realized Lisa was awake and emerging from the wagon, Moses dipped a cup of coffee and handed it to her.

"Did yo' sleep, Ma'am?" he asked, reminding her immediately of his remarkably deep voice.

"Good morning, Moses. Yes, thank you, I did sleep, but not very soundly after having such a fright. Were you able to stop driving the wagon long enough to get any sleep?"

He nodded, "Yes, Ma'am. Ah'll be jes' fine."

"Thank you again for coming to my aid last night," she continued. "I was in a desperate situation, and I am so grateful you came along just when you did."

"God was directin' ma' way, as He usual do, Missy," he smiled as he rose and slightly bowed toward her from the waist in a gesture of gallantry. "So glad ta' be of assistance, Ma'am."

Lisa smiled, but did not respond. In her preoccupation, she just continued with her own thoughts as though Moses had not spoken. "Can you help me get the rest of the way to Richmond? I must search for my husband there. He was to meet me in Manchester, but he never arrived."

Moses nodded. "Yes, Ma'am, we sho' can take yo' right into Richmon' to whereva' yo' wants to go. But why yo' out here by yo'self?"

Setting her cup of coffee on the tailgate of the wagon, Lisa extended her hand and said, "I am sorry, Moses, my name is Lisa Layne. My husband is one of the doctors at Chimborazo Hospital in

Richmond. My father-in-law was Senator Mason Layne—you might have heard of him."

Moses nodded, and took her small proffered hand, holding it in his huge right hand, while patting it with his other one that still held the fork for turning the meat. "Yes, Ma'am, Ah believes Ah's heared talk o' Senata' Layne."

Lisa nodded. "Everyone loved Senator Layne, except the Yankees up north, of course." She smiled, and continued as her features began to reveal her grief. "He died from a bullet wound at Chimborazo Hospital, while my husband was attempting to save his life." She looked at Moses as tears filled her eyes. He nodded sympathetically.

In his strong dialect, Moses explained to Lisa that he and Martha both belonged to Warren Callahan from early childhood. Since the war ended, the Callahan Plantation could not afford to pay their former slaves to work. So Mr. Callahan sent them away to find work elsewhere. Before they left, he gave them the wagon, the team and the Henry rifle for protection. He warned Moses to keep the rifle concealed and only use it in an emergency, because black men are not allowed to have guns in their possession.

Moses had not been able to find any employment, so they were going to travel north to see if they could find work in Yankee country. But, first they planned to stop by the Callahan Plantation near Richmond to see if Mr. Callahan was okay.

Just then, his wife pulled back the front blanket on the wagon and came to the edge of it. Moses immediately went to her, and holding his arms up toward her, lifted her easily from the wagon, and set her feet on the ground. He leaned over and kissed her tenderly on her forehead. Lisa was impressed by the way the woman carried herself. She was a tall, well-built woman, graceful and strong. Her hair was neatly pulled back into a bun. Her face was friendly, and her smile was warm and genuine.

"Good morning, Miss," she said, as she put her hand out to Lisa. "My name is Martha. Did I understand you to say you are married to one of the Layne boys?" Her speech showed that she had been educated.

"Yes," Lisa answered. "My husband is Dr. Goddard Layne."

"Do you have any children?"

"Yes," Lisa answered. "We had a beautiful little boy, Goddard, Jr. He died of a fever when he was about four years old. We also have a little girl who is now three years old. My husband went to get her when we were told to evacuate Richmond. I worked with Goddard during the war as a nurse in the hospital. He sent me to escort a group of wounded

8

men from the hospital to where he was to meet us across the James River in Manchester. But I haven't seen him since that day. I'm hoping to find him and our daughter when I get back to Richmond."

She thought it best to not mention how long it had been since she had seen Angela.

By this time the two little girls were awake, and Martha set about to feed them some breakfast. When everyone had eaten their fill, Moses put out the breakfast fire and packed the gear in the back of the wagon, so they could continue on their way toward Richmond.

Lisa and Martha visited, as they rode together in the wagon. Sometimes they got out for a while and walked beside the wagon, as they talked.

"Moses and I were purchased together by Mr. Warren Callahan many years ago from a slave market in Savannah. We were just small children at the time, and unrelated," Martha explained. "Our parents lived much harder lives, working the cotton fields in the Deep South, suffering a lot of cruel abuse by their owners. We have been told that they all died at a very young age. Their owner, like most of the owners in the Deep South, believed it was cheaper to work a slave until he died than it was to feed and shelter him. So, though we both sincerely missed growing up with our parents, Moses and I have always known that the Lord blessed us when Mr. Callahan bought us and moved us here to Virginia. Mr. Callahan's plantation is just east of Richmond. Do you know the Callahan's?" she asked.

Lisa shook her head, indicating that she did not.

Martha continued, "We lived on the Callahan plantation for most of our lives. Both Mr. and Mrs. Callahan treated us well, and we were happy there. I worked in the big house, where Mrs. Callahan taught me to read and write when I was very young. She had something wrong with her eyesight that she knew was getting worse, so she wanted me to be able to read the Bible to her when she was unable to see well enough to read alone any longer. She had to be very careful not to let anyone know she was teaching me to read. Slaves were not allowed to read for fear we would learn how to resist our owners or learn how to escape.

"Our two young daughters were born there. They are Leah, who is 10 years old and Dinah is 12 years old." The girls sat quietly on boxes in the back of the wagon, dangling their feet and watching the countryside pass by.

"Moses and I were very excited, along with all the other slaves, when Mr. Lincoln set us free. But, now we wish we had never left and gone out on our own. Moses cannot find work, with everything being so chaotic everywhere. We are afraid to go back to the Deep South, that's for sure! We've heard too many horror stories from friends and family. When we were very young, we determined to never go there for any reason...ever. We will go north if we must, but rumors say it isn't any better there...who knows. There are just too many freedmen looking for work. So many of them have become criminals to feed their families...but not my Moses. He is a good man.

"Well, enough of my ramblings...Tell me more about what brought you to be on the trail alone last night, Lisa?" Martha questioned.

"Well," Lisa began, "as I said before, when the order was given to abandon Richmond because the Yankees were invading, Goddard ordered me to gather together all the wounded soldiers who could walk, and take them across the James River to Manchester. He left to go and get our daughter Angela, promising he would catch up with me along the trail or in Manchester. He said we should urgently keep going until we were far enough into Southern territory that the injured men would be protected. Everyone at the hospital felt the Union troops would undoubtedly kill every Confederate soldier they could find when they rolled into Richmond.

"I followed his instructions and gathered together about twenty soldiers that I thought could make the trip. We started walking south since there was no transportation available." She paused. "It was hard to leave the rest of the wounded behind."

"But," Martha interrupted, "I don't understand why your husband didn't go with you? Surely he knew that even a doctor would face serious danger when the Union soldiers arrived."

Lisa nodded. "I knew in my own mind that Goddard was more concerned about getting me and Angela out of the area than he was for the soldiers. But he also knew I wouldn't go on ahead of him without a good reason. He knew how much I loved those boys."

Martha nodded her head in agreement. "But why didn't you wait for him, and the two of you go together? Surely a few more minutes waiting to leave would not have hurt anything." Martha was spellbound by the story that was unfolding to her, remembering back to when she and Moses ran from the Richmond area with their girls, as the Union Army approached.

Lisa explained, "He went to find our three year old daughter, not knowing how much trouble he would run into. He insisted that I go on ahead and he would meet me in Manchester on the other side of the James River. I thought he would be there in a matter of hours after me, but he never arrived." Her voice broke as she finished the sentence.

10

"That was some time ago, Martha...I'm afraid of what may have happened to him."

Lisa struggled to gain control of her emotions. "Those men and boys were so valiant, trying the best they could to keep up a fast enough pace to finally reach safe territory. After a number of miles of stumbling, falling, getting up and going on, one of the young men with only one leg and a crutch, could go no further. He sat down at the side of the narrow road, the heels of his hands on his forehead, tears in his eyes.

"Please go on without me, I'm only slowing you down."

Lisa continued, "I tried to console him and assure him there was a hamlet just ahead that we could see over the hill. I pleaded with him to walk only that far. Her voice broke. I promised that I would help him. But he just shook his head and sat there, his crutch at his side, his head in his hands. He had given up."

Lisa started to sob violently, and Martha realized what an ordeal this petite young woman must have endured. Her arms naturally reached around Lisa in a gesture of compassion, and Lisa's head rested easily on her shoulder.

After regaining her composure, Lisa raised her head and continued, "Another of our wounded, a man with only one arm, came to that boy's side knelt down, saying, 'Don't quit now. If I could, I'd carry you the rest of the way...but, as you can see, I have only one arm. Tell you what, if you help me and I help you, I think we can do this together, what do you say?' Then, with his one good arm under the arm of the man with only one leg, they both made it all the way to Manchester."

Lisa had always been resourceful, and for their sake, showed only confidence and hope to the men, in spite of her discouragement. When they arrived in Manchester, she eventually found food and shelter for them in a corner of the city park. People of the town had been good enough to share their meager food rations with these men who had fought so gallantly for the Confederate cause. Some even took the younger injured boys into their homes until they were healed enough to travel on to their own homes."

Now, Lisa began to regain control of her emotions and looked into Martha's tear filled eyes. Still sobbing a bit, Lisa asked, "What will happen to them, Martha? If they are ever able to get back to their home towns, will they be accepted? Will their families still be there? Can they find any kind of work to do to support themselves?"

For a few minutes, there was silence between Lisa and Martha. Moses, who had listened to all this conversation between the two women now sat, grim-faced and silent. He too realized what Lisa and

11

so many Confederate soldiers had endured in the last few days. His master had refused to let him enlist in the Army, because he was needed too much at home in the fields.

Finally, Martha lifted Lisa's chin, and asked, "What about your little girl? Maybe your husband just changed his plans for some reason to keep her safe, and you'll find them both in Richmond?"

Lisa shook her head.

"I don't think he would have any trouble getting Angela to go with him. And he promised to meet me in Manchester, so I'm sure he would not have decided to stay in Richmond."

Martha frowned. "Why would your little girl not want to go with her own papa? I do not understand..."

Caught in a slip of the tongue, Lisa had never before told anyone her dark family secret. Her whole life long, she always explained her black eyes and darker complexion by telling people that she was of New Orleans Cajun descent. She didn't want anyone to know the truth about her ancestry. Now, suddenly, she had a very strong urge to tell Martha all about herself and her daughter, Angela.

Swallowing hard and taking a deep breath, Lisa began, "Most of my life, I've carried a dark secret."

Martha just looked at her with no response, waiting for her to continue.

"You see, my grandmother was a black woman," she admitted aloud for the first time in her life, "and a white man fathered my mother. She had a dark complexion, but some white features and eventually married a white man. When I was born, I was much lighter skinned than my mother, enough so that she immediately began calling me her 'little Cajun girl'." Lisa drew in another long, deep shuddering breath before continuing.

"When I married Goddard, I did not tell him or his family of the black blood in my family. Everything was fine, and I was accepted by the white people without question. Soon Little Goddard was born and we were a very happy family."

"Then, three years ago, little Angela was born...a 'throwback' baby, with black skin and some obvious Negro features." Lisa sobbed as she caught her breath, "Goddard was horrified, thinking I had been with a black man and didn't tell him. That is when I had to explain my heritage to him.

"We both knew that the Layne family would be embarrassed by such a child. And Goddard, who was just starting his medical practice in Richmond, would probably lose patients if he had a black child. So, we talked about it, and reluctantly decided to give our little baby

12

Angela to Ruth, a housemaid of the Layne's. Ruth took Angela to her daughter, Naomi, who agreed to nurse Angela and raise her as her own child. She already had a little girl of her own that was born that same month. She promised to never let anyone know who Angela really was.

"At first, Naomi regularly brought Angela to our home for me to see her, until she was about three months old. But, each of those meetings was torture for me. I knew that I could not continue to be a part of her life, because I could not let her know I was her mother. That would not be good for Angela...she would not understand. I have never once seen her since that time."

As Lisa sat, still sobbing, Martha just rubbed her back and said nothing.

Lisa swallowed hard, struggling to gain control of her emotions. "The Yankees were coming, so Goddard went to find Angela at Naomi's house. She lives on a plantation that is located outside of Richmond..." Here she broke into deep sobs again.

Martha, with tears in her own eyes, continued holding Lisa, and began to sing very softly, "Nobody knows the trouble I've seen, nobody knows my sorrow. Nobody knows the trouble I've seen, Glory hallelujah! Sometimes I'm up, sometimes I'm down, Oh, yes, Lord. Sometimes I'm almost to the ground, Oh, yes, Lord..."

The road into Richmond was very busy. Buggies, wagons, people walking and riders on horseback plodded along at a slow speed, holding their place in the movement. Anyone who tried to get ahead was pushed out of place, and another section of the crowd went on through. When Richmond began to come into view across the river, the vast crowd of travelers gasped, and then became silent, as they viewed the extensive devastation from the evacuation fire.

Moses drove the wagon across the make-shift bridge that had been erected to replace the burned-out Mayo Bridge. Lisa stood up and moved into the wagon seat beside him. The stench of the smoldering ruins that had once been a thriving metropolis was overwhelming, making her want to cover her nose and mouth. She could not believe her eyes. The gray hulks of the once beautiful buildings looked like giant tombstones in a lonely unkempt graveyard. It was a horrid and shocking sight.

Moses stopped the horses and wagon. He got down, and turned to reach up to help her down. As she reached the ground, she began to speak, "I'll just walk the rest of the way to our house, Moses. I have no idea what I will find, but I'll start there. If the house is still standing,

perhaps I can see if Goddard is there and continuing to work at the hospital. If the house isn't there, I'll just go on to Chimborazo Hospital and ask about him. Maybe they can help me find him."
Moses objected, fearing that Lisa would not be safe on her own. He turned to Martha and asked, "Wha' yo' think, Hon'? Should Miss Lisa be runnin' roun' by ha' se'f?"
Lisa turned to look at Martha for her response.
"Well," Martha began slowly, thinking as she talked, "We need to go on to Mr. Callahan's Plantation to check on him. If Miss Lisa can find a place to stay here...a hotel room...a friend maybe? I think we should stay too, just until she finds her husband or learns something about his whereabouts. Then we can go on, after we are sure that she is at least safe from harm."
Moses suggested that Lisa just stay with them in the wagon, where he could keep an eye out for her safety himself.
"No," Lisa shook her head, and turned back to Moses. "I'll be alright here. Richmond is my home. I know people here, and I know my way around. I can look for my family at the house, and then walk to Chimborazo Hospital; then I will decide what to do from there. You've been wonderful to me, but I don't want to hold you up any longer. You get on your way. Check with the Callahan's first, maybe they will have work for you. If they cannot help you, I agree that you should go on north. You'll be in Union country in a few more days, and you can begin to look for work there.
"Again, you've been so wonderful to me, and I will never be able to thank you enough. I just don't know how I would have ever made it to Richmond without you." She put her arms around Moses and hugged him, then turned to Martha, hugged her, and knelt down to the girls.
"I'm sure the two of you will grow up to be fine young ladies. I know your parents are very proud of you both." Both girls smiled broadly and giggled shyly, as she gave each of them a hug. Then she turned to Moses and Martha and said, "My time with all of you will always be one of my fondest memories. Be careful, and if you come back this way, look me up."
She turned and walked away, so they would not see her tears or the fear on her face, as she realized she was now alone again. She could hear Moses telling Martha that he did not like leaving her behind. Martha agreed, but thought they needed to honor her wishes.
Lisa stopped on Franklin Street in front of what had once been the home that she and Goddard loved so much. It was now just a pile of rubble. The sight of something that had once been so beautiful brought tears to her eyes again. It was a grim reminder of what was left of her

14

life now. Then she visualized the day Goddard carried her over the threshold into their new home for their first night together, and smiled.

It was almost dark, and Lisa had no place to stay for the night. Hesitant now to risk involvement with any more strangers, after her harrowing experience on the trail, she got busy and cleared off a sizeable piece of one of the fallen walls she found in the rubble of what had once been her home. It was grimy, heavy and hard for her to manage, but it was also smooth and large enough for her to prop at an angle inside the brick foundation, forming a small triangular shaped refuge that would offer her some protection from the elements, and obscure her from the view of any passerby with other-than-honorable intentions.

It would be dark in a few more minutes. She would just lie still and stay very quiet in her makeshift shelter. She lay down in her new "home" and covered herself with her shawl. Shivering more from fright than from the cold, she thought back over the events of the last few days. Then, adding her search for Goddard and Angela to her thoughts, in spite of her fear, she finally dropped off to sleep.

Chapter 3

MAY 27, 1865

Adam Layne was exhausted as he finally arrived at Oaklayne Plantation. He was so grateful to have recently been reunited with his 14 year old son, Randy, whom he had earlier feared was lost in the war. Randy and his friend Benjy, a former slave who was also 14 years old, had run away from home together and joined the Union Army less than a year before the war ended.

Adam did not hide his concern for the boy when confronted with the dreadful realization that his son was blinded in battle by a bullet to the head. Grateful beyond words, Adam had been told that Benjy saved Randy's life by covering him with his own body to prevent further injury. Then Benjy carried the larger Randy on his back quite a distance, until he found help. Benjy had saved Randy's life, but the medical profession had been unable to save his eyesight.

The three of them rode along in the wagon with Adam's chestnut horse tied on behind. When they arrived in front of the ruins of the old mansion, Benjy gasped, "Oh, Massa Adam! What happen 'ta yo' big house? It's gone!"

Adam put his arms around both boys, looked at each of them intently and said, "I know this looks like a big mess. But what really matters now, is the people we love that are still alive after such an ugly war. God will help us make something beautiful of this pile of rubble...you will see."

Just then the door slammed on one of the out-buildings, and they heard a squeal of joy from Sara Ella, "I don't believe it! Praise God, they're alive!" She was running toward the wagon, as fast as her skirt would allow.

Emma Lou came running, right on her heals, yelling, "That's my boy! Ah dun' tol' y'all he be back one day!" Running with her arms outstretched, she lost her balance and fell. Benjy reached her side and helped her to her feet, giving her a big bear hug. With tears running down her cheeks, she kissed him again and again, as he lifted her off the ground in complete abandon.

Then she held him at arm's length and said in a mock scolding tone, "Benjy, how could yo' treat yo' Mama dis away, makin' me wear out ma' knees a'pray'n and a'cryin' for yo wayward soul? Ah's of a min' to whup yo behin'!"

Adam got down hurriedly from the wagon and rushed toward Sara Ella's open arms. He picked her up and twirled her around like a rag doll. Then she broke free and ran to the wagon where Randy remained seated, looking blankly straight ahead.

"Would somebody please tell me what is going on!" Randy yelled. "Is that you, Sara Ella?"

She quickly shot a look of confusion and alarm at Adam, who nodded his head in affirmation. "Randy is blind, Sara Ella."

Coughing to disguise her shock and dismay, Sara Ella quickly climbed into the wagon and embraced Randy warmly, tears coming to her eyes. She was glad to have this joyful reunion to camouflage her tears of sorrow over Randy's loss.

"Well, all of this crying, hugging and laughing is music to my ears," she said.

"I know, I'm about to burst with joy, myself," Adam said, helping Randy down from the wagon. "The Lord has blessed this family with the safe return of our boys. And now that we are home, life is just about as perfect as it can get!"

Sara Ella, a school teacher Adam met during the war while stationed at Harper's Ferry, had utterly stolen his heart. She later rescued him from Andersonville Prison, and took him home to Oaklayne, where they were shocked to find the plantation in dire ruin. After a short time of recovery from his wounds and the treatment he received at Andersonville, Adam left Sara Ella behind and traveled further north to meet with President Lincoln in Washington City to report important news on the war. Adam and Sara Ella were determined to be married, as soon as possible.

Adam, now a retired Union Army General, was taken to Andersonville Prison during the war after he was assaulted by catch dogs in a failed attempt to escape from another Confederate prison. The dogs attacked him and ripped open one leg. He lost a lot of blood, then the injury became so infected that he was eventually unable to walk.

He was a tall, slender man, like his father, with dark brown, wavy hair. Adam's brown eyes flashed when he talked, and he had an infectious smile. His injuries, however, would cause him to walk with a limp for the remainder of his life.

Ownership of Oaklayne Plantation had passed to Adam when his father and mother died during the war. It was now his responsibility to rebuild the plantation, including the mansion and the many out-buildings that were necessary to the operation of the plantation. He hoped to hire freedmen who had worked for his father before the war and had already proven themselves to be hard workers.

Looking at the ruins before her, Sara Ella exclaimed, "Adam, every time I step back and look at it again, it takes my breath away. It's hard to believe that all of this rubble was once so magnificent and beautiful. I'll never forget the elegant spectacle, when your lovely sister Laura came down the staircase on her wedding day, dressed in her Grandmother's wedding gown. I sure wish we knew what happened to her, Adam. What a tragedy to hear that her husband Hamilton was killed while on that reporting assignment for the New York Times. I guess she must have been with him that day, but no one seems to know for sure."

Adam sat, staring off into space. "There are so many loved ones yet unaccounted for, dear. We'll just have to keep praying and hoping they are okay, and that one day we will see them again. We're going to rebuild and restore everything back like it was, Sara Ella, as much as possible." He reached over and put his arms around her, pulling her close and staring deeply into her big beautiful brown eyes. "Yes, you will see." Turning, he looked around as if to imagine, "This place will be grand again."

Chapter 4

JUNE 3, 1865

Breathing heavily from exertion, Adam turned to Nathaniel and said, "Go ask Tom to bring three or four strong men with him to help us get this wagon loaded again."

Nathaniel, a middle-aged freedman that Adam had known all his life, was formerly his father's lead slave. The two men spent the morning struggling to get a wagon out of the mire that had once been loaded with several large logs from the far side of the plantation. Much to their dismay, two of those logs had rolled off the wagon onto the ground in the process. Fortunately, the Layne family lumber mill had not been destroyed during the war, so they were taking the raw wood to the mill to be sawed into lumber for construction.

After finally freeing the wagon from the mud, Adam and Nathaniel tried to lift one end of the smaller of the big logs to load it back on the wagon, but found it was much too heavy for them to handle alone.

Adam wiped the perspiration from his brow and said, "Guess we are going to need some help, Nathaniel. Go get Tom and some other men to help us with this thing."

"Yes, sah', Mr. Adam. Ah'll tell Tom to come in a hurry. Yo' know, night's gonna' git here pretty soon, an' then it'll be too dark to git that bigger log back on that there wagon, without the loader from up at the fellin' area." Nathaniel loved to talk.

"I know, Nathaniel," Adam answered sternly, his exasperation with their problem showing. "Better get moving!"

"Yes, Sah', Mr. Adam" Nathaniel replied, still acting like a slave answering his master, yet he knew he was a free man. It was clear to anyone who cared to notice, how much he loved and respected Adam.

"Go on, now!" Adam motioned with his hand as though brushing something from his sight.

Tom was Adam's life-long friend. Born on the plantation at about the same time, the two boys grew up playing together as children. Tom was the son of slave parents, Adam the son of the plantation owner. As they grew into adulthood, Tom became Adam's house boy. When Adam joined the Army, Tom went with him as his personal attendant. So there was a great bond of friendship and understanding between the two men. Now, Tom was a freedman, working for a good wage on the plantation. He remained, as always, Adam's closest friend.

Nathaniel had been Mason Layne's right hand man, a slave of Oaklayne for many years. Adam was fortunate to have two such faithful men to help him rebuild Oaklayne back to the beautiful plantation it had been just a few years ago, before the war. Purchased as a young man, Nathaniel had been on the plantation all of Adam's life. Adam relied heavily on Nathaniel's knowledge, experience and maturity.

Nathaniel started toward the fenced area where they kept their livestock until barns could be completed, moving as quickly as he could. He knew that Adam's bad leg was causing him a lot of pain, which it often did when he over used it. After Nathaniel was out of sight, Adam sat down on one of the big logs, rubbing his hands over the old wound and waited impatiently for Nathaniel to return with help. "Blast this leg! Guess I should be glad it isn't worse than it is…at least I still have it."

Earlier in the day he had assigned Tom to supervise the few former slaves who were working to clear the area where the mansion previously stood. The area was covered with charred timbers, broken glass, bricks and shattered pieces of the furniture that had once graced the halls of his former home. They would rebuild the mansion on the old foundation, with the same floor plan as the original manor home that Adam's great-grandfather, George Layne, built more than a hundred years prior, when he was a young man. They did not have the original plans, so Adam did not know where to start to build it back the same as before. But, the home he grew up in was the only dwelling he could imagine standing in that spot on the Oaklayne property. He had lived there most of his life. He felt sure that the foundation, still there in the ground under the rubble, would give them at least the outer dimensions of the structure. That would be a good start.

Temporary housing for the family and the three former slaves consisted of two small slave cabins that survived the war and a roughly and hurriedly put together frame building that Nathaniel and Tom had constructed while Adam was in Washington City. The new structure was large enough for several sleeping rooms above a kitchen that included an eating space and a small relaxing area on the first floor. However, everyone living there was always either working, sitting at the table eating, or sleeping most every hour of each 24-hour day, so the relaxing area was scarcely used.

The horse and cattle barns, tobacco sheds, hay barns, storage barns and smaller buildings that held the forge, chickens and pigs, were in urgent need of attention. Almost everything had been destroyed in the fighting that had raged across the plantation during the War Between the States. Sara Ella and Emma Lou were living in one of the cabins together, with Adam and Randy in the other. Tom, Nathaniel and Benjy slept on straw pallets in the rooms above the kitchen of the Temporary Building.

Emma Lou suggested that she also move to the Temporary Building when it was finished, to give Sara Ella a cabin to herself. But, Sara Ella would not hear of it. She felt that the Temporary Building's sleeping rooms did not offer a lady enough privacy. Emma Lou was grateful for the special consideration. Her love for this gracious lady that Adam soon planned to marry was growing sweeter every day.

As Adam sat there waiting for Nathaniel, his mind would not rest. *I don't have time to just sit here and do nothing.* He was clearly frustrated. There was so much to be done, and he didn't seem to be making much progress. *At least we have a roof over our heads, such as it is.*

But, I really need to be getting back to Andersonville to find Richard. I don't even know if he survived…that was such an awful place. The guards could very likely have taken it out on him when they discovered I was gone. I didn't like leaving him behind when Sara Ella bought my freedom, but I really didn't have any choice. I had to get to Washington City to report to the President. Sara Ella used every penny she had to get me out, so I probably would have jeopardized everything if I had gone back inside after him at the time. I owe Richard my life, and I'll not rest until I know what happened to him. But, leaving here to go and do that will take weeks, possibly months, and my family is counting on me to make some sense of this mess here. That's going to require that I locate the right materials and skilled laborers to do the work. I don't mind admitting that I don't even know where to begin…

Then, there's also Randy…I need to hire someone to help him learn how to live as a blind person in this world…

And on top of all that, apparently my country still needs my services, or Secretary Stanton would not be pressuring me to return to Washington City to meet with him…wonder what that's all about? Maybe, Sara Ella and I could be married in Washington City, either before or after I meet with Stanton? I'll have to present that idea to her and see what she thinks.

Adam sighed deeply, then looking heavenward and prayed, "Lord all of my life I've either ignored you entirely or blamed you for my problems. I am so sorry for my insolence...my heart is clearly full of sin, Lord. Please forgive me.

"I have so much to be thankful for...I can see that You have been with me all along. You have been my comforter in sorrow, and my strength and wisdom when I have been overwhelmed in difficult situations. Lord Jesus, I know I do not deserve your grace. I've never felt your presence more than when you let me find Randy in such an improbable place and bring him safely home.

"I have always needed your help, Lord, but never more than today. Please give me direction as to where to start...guide my steps so that I may lead my family well and honor You with my life..."

Suddenly, Adam heard voices, coming up the trail from the mansion area, to where he was waiting. He rose to his feet, and saw that there were several men trotting toward him on foot. There was Nathaniel, Tom, three more black men and a white stranger that he did not immediately recognize—but, as they moved closer, he realized it was...

"Oscar! Oscar Baynes!" Adam shouted. He completely ignored the pain in his leg and ran as fast as he could toward the men and grabbed the white man by the shoulders, nearly knocking him down. They hugged each other and everyone laughed boisterously.

Tom was somewhat out of breath from running, but knew Adam would be pleased to see his old school friend from West Point.

Adam could feel Oscar chuckling, and leaned back to look him in the face.

"Oscar!" he exclaimed. "How are you, my dear friend?" as he affectionately slapped him on the back.

Oscar grinned and answered, "I'm fine, now that I'm finally here! It was quite a journey from Washington City. I'll tell you all about it when we have time." Then he changed the subject and said, "Nathaniel says we need to get this wagon up to the lumber mill before dark. How can I help?"

Adam suggested, "Here, you take the reins and hold the horses, while the rest of us try to get these big logs back on the wagon. I hate to have to leave them here, but I guess that's what we'll have to do if we can't lift them back onto the wagon. We need to get them over to the mill. Every available piece of wood is priceless these days."

"Both logs are huge, Adam," Tom muttered under his breath, as he looked at the bigger one of the timbers, laying there on the grass.

"Maybe we should do what we can to cut them up some, before we try to load them?"

"I would rather not cut them here, because we would lose a lot of good wood doing that," said Adam.

Oscar stood with his arms folded across his chest, surveying the situation. Then, with a twinkle in his eye, and a grin lifting the corners of his mouth, he spoke, "How about if we unhitch the team from the wagon and let the horses do all the heavy work for us. That way, all we have to do is lift one end, enough to wrap that chain around it."

Adam smirked and asked, "Where were you earlier today, when Nathaniel and I were struggling with these monstrous logs? I knew you'd be good for something, someday, Oscar," Adam replied with a chuckle. Nathaniel and Tom giggled like little boys, and the other men joined in the merriment. They had not seen Adam this cheerful since he had returned to Oaklayne. Adam had not heard these men enjoy themselves this much in a very long time!

Then, suddenly Oscar put his fingers in his mouth and let fly with a very loud and long whistle. Almost immediately, eight trail-toughened young men rode up on horseback in a cloud of dust.

While Nathaniel began to unhitch the horses from the wagon, Oscar put his arm around Adam's shoulders and gestured toward the men on horseback. "Adam, meet some of the best soldiers of the U.S. Army Corps of Engineers. We've built and re-built bridges, forts, fortifications and whatever the Union needed during this awful war." Then turning to the men he said, "Men, please give these men the assistance they require, while Adam and I go back to the house and talk. It shouldn't take you long to get those big logs to the saw mill."

"Yes sir, Colonel Baynes. We'll have this taken care of right away, sir."

"Colonel! I'm impressed," Adam said. Nathaniel and Tom sighed with incredible relief.

"And, how are things with you, Adam?"

"Hey, Mr. Adam," Nathaniel winked at Oscar, "do yo' think we could keep yo' frien' here at Oaklayne fer awhile? He 'pears to have his mind all put togetha' real good an' he come with an army of help!" He laid his head back and laughed loudly.

"Well," Adam replied, "We'll keep him here just as long as we can, how's that?" He chuckled and put his arm around Oscar's shoulder, patting his back.

As he was speaking, they heard the supper bell ring from the house. Adam pulled his watch from his pocket and looked at it. "Goodness!" Adam exclaimed. "It's already supper time."

Turning to Nathaniel, he asked, "When you're finished loading those logs, can you men take the wagon on up to the lumber mill, while I take Oscar down and introduce him to Sara Ella and Emma Lou? Then he stopped, and with tongue in cheek, a solemn look on his face and a tone of sarcasm, he said "Oh, I just realized that with all of these extra men here there won't be much supper left if you aren't there when Emma Lou serves it. Oh, well...sorry...you know how she is..." He smiled, patted Nathaniel on the back again and continued, "But I'll make sure she saves a little for you...you men deserve something to eat this evening, after working so hard."

"Yes Sah', Mr. Adam, we sho' do. We'll hurry." Nathaniel knew Adam's love for kidding him.

"I thought that might hurry you along a bit, Nathaniel. See you at the house," said Adam.

"But yo' knows Emma Lou'll take care o' me. She always do." Nathaniel always had the last word.

Adam took hold of Oscar's arm, and they started to trudge back to the Temporary Building. Oscar leaned toward Adam and offered, "Adam, we brought plenty of food with us, since we didn't know for sure what we'd find when we arrived."

"We will mention that to the ladies," said Adam. "Emma Lou and Sara Ella always fix way more than we need, so between what we already have and what you brought, I am sure there will be plenty for everyone."

As they walked, Oscar remarked, "Adam, I was surprised to see you still have slaves. These men call you Mr. Adam, and treat you like you are their master. I thought they were all freedmen."

"True, Oscar. They are freedmen, but they didn't want to leave here when the war was over. So I told them they could stay and I would give them a place to live and food, plus pay them to work for me. It has worked very well for them and for me. They are great workers, trustworthy and happy just being here, where they know their employer. And, of course, I've got plenty of work to keep them busy. They have always called me Mr. Adam, so," he shrugged his shoulders, "it's just comfortable and customary for them to continue, I guess."

Oscar nodded. He could not imagine what it must be like for the newly freed black men, having to go out into the free world to find a way to support their families, among people they do not know, especially the ones who had been well treated by their masters. There were so many crooks, waiting to take advantage of these men and their lack of experience with white scoundrels.

As the two men approached the house, Sara Ella was standing at the door with her arms folded across her chest, Emma Lou standing just inside the house behind her.

"Come on, Oscar. There's someone I want you to meet." Adam took Oscar's arm and they hurried on ahead to greet the ladies.

"Oscar, this is my fiancée, Sara Ella Gary. Sara Ella this is Colonel Oscar Baynes of the US Army Corps of Engineers. We went to West Point together. Oscar was smarter than me and earned an engineering degree while we were there...," Adam said with a boyish grin.

"Adam, you were always the best at everything you ever tried, so don't talk about me being smarter than you!" Oscar scolded.

"Oscar, Sara Ella and I plan to be married before long. She wants to wait until after the Episcopal Church has been restored enough to have a wedding there, but I don't know if I can wait that long." Adam smiled at her with a twinkle in his eyes, and continued, "It could take *years* for the church to be ready!"

Sara Ella looked at him, smiled, and answered teasingly, "Guess you'd better pray it doesn't take that long, then." Turning to Oscar, she continued. "Thank you for coming by the plantation to see us. I've heard Adam speak of you before, so it is good to have this opportunity to meet you." Turning to Adam again, she continued, "Now, you men get washed up and ready to eat."

Before turning to go to the wash basin, Adam introduced Emma Lou. "And this is one of our long time housemaids, Emma Lou. She is Benjy's mother, you'll meet him later. Benjy saved my son Randy's life. There's just so much to tell you about!"

Emma Lou offered her hand, nodded her head slightly, and said simply, "Colonel Oscar," as they shook hands, "welcome to Oaklayne." She turned and went back to the kitchen.

Adam turned to Oscar and asked, "So, what brought you here to Oaklayne? I'm so surprised to see you. I heard some stories about the work of the U.S. Army Corps of Engineers during the war, but we never had a reason to cross paths with any of you in the field."

"Well," Oscar began, "it's the strangest thing. You see, I was attending the spectacular review that Secretary of War Stanton designated to display the might of the nearly 200,000 Union troops around Washington City on May 23rd, when right out of General Grants viewing area, low and behold, you came bounding down the stands, pushing Generals and dignitaries out of your way and running right into the middle of that parade! I watched you run down the street through the crowd and then disappear. Well, I have to tell you, I couldn't get that scene out of my mind since then.

"When we were released from service, these men wanted me to lead them into the destruction in hopes of finding some work rebuilding the South. That's when I decided to look you up and see what that spectacle I witnessed in Washington City that day was all about. I have lots of fond memories of the mischief we got into when we were in school together, so I figured I must have missed out on something really good from the looks of it!"

"We did have some good times, didn't we...," Adam responded.

"It sure smells wonderful in here, ladies...can we eat now?" Adam called out as he winked at Oscar.

"We'll eat when Tom 'n Nathaniel gets here, Mr. Adam," Emma Lou said with authority in her voice, looking over her shoulder at him. "Ah' fixed ma' special co'n bread that Nathaniel likes sa' much, and he'd be a heap upset if'n Ah' was to give it to yo' when he ain't here. Yes, Sah...a heap upset he'd be!"

Adam just looked at her, smiled, and in a teasing tone said, "You can't blame a man for askin' now can you? Since we can't eat yet, come out front with me and sit down, Oscar. We can talk until they see fit to serve us supper. Tell me about your family and that pretty sister of yours."

It was apparent to Oscar that Adam was changing the subject instead of answering his questions about the parade episode, so he relaxed and started explaining about the circumstances of his own life. "I went home right after the war, Adam. My Father passed away while I was gone and my Mother moved in with my sister Lori and her new husband Ronald (guess that answers your question about my pretty sister, huh).

"Well, the old plantation home that I grew up in was completely destroyed by mortar fire, but the larger house that Lori and Ronald live in now, had been spared. You know me, I came charging in wanting to rebuild the old home place, but since Ronald is now managing the plantation, I could see that I was just in the way. So, I rounded up these men and started south to find work. But, that was right after going to that Union troops review in Washington City where I saw you in the crowd. I'd still like to know what that was all about...that is, when you are ready to tell me."

Adam was too emotional to talk, as he thought about that day in Washington City when he saw Randy and Benjy in the crowd, but knew they did not see him. He was still physically very weak from his stint in Andersonville Prison, but that didn't stop him from using every ounce of strength that remained in his frail, pain-racked body to run to Randy's side. That is when he learned that Randy was blind. As they sat in awkward silence on the ground in the shade of a huge live oak tree, Oscar changed the subject.

"I've been looking over the situation here since we arrived, Adam. This is sure not the Oaklayne you described to me when we were at West Point! Have you always lived in such deplorable conditions, or is this some kind of new method of plantation management?" Oscar hoped to lighten the discussion with a weak stab at humor.

"Oh, it sounds like you don't like it like this...you always were picky," Adam quipped back at him.

"Seriously, Adam, do you realize the magnitude of the reconstruction project you have ahead of you to rebuild this place? This will be a complex undertaking with many challenges, Adam...not a job for the fainthearted! For instance..."

Oscar's comments were interrupted when he noticed Adam's countenance brighten, as he saw two young men walking toward the house. Randy and Benjy were coming back from their walk down to the James River. The way they were walking together, Oscar immediately noticed that one of them was blind. "Who's the young blind man?" Oscar asked.

Adam looked at him with a saddened expression and answered, "The young blind man is my son Randy and the young man with him is Benjy, Emma Lou's son. They are the same age and grew up together.

"When Sara Ella and I arrived here from Andersonville, Randy wasn't here, nor was his young friend, Benjy. No one knew where they were, but they had both disappeared from the plantation at the same time. Everyone thought the boys had been taken by the Confederate Army when they passed through the area at about that time. We later learned that wasn't the case...those boys ran away that day and joined the Union forces.

"When you saw me running out through the parade at the Grand Review of the Union Army in Washington City, I had just caught a glimpse of Randy riding in the back of a wagon up ahead. I knew I might never find him again if I didn't get to him right away. I didn't know he was blind until I reached the wagon." Adam's voice shook, and he swallowed hard before continuing, "He took a shot to his head. If Benjy had not been with him, he would have bled to death on the battlefield. Benjy actually picked Randy up and carried him on his back to safety, even though Randy is bigger than he is. When I found them in Washington City, I brought them both home to Oaklayne."

Both men sat quietly, taking in the intensity of the moment, until Oscar finally asked, "How were they able to get into the Army in the first place? They're just kids now, so they would have been too young for sure back then."

"Randy told me that they lied about their age. They told the authorities they were sixteen and had the permission of his father, General Adam Layne, who understood that his son wanted to 'follow in his father's footsteps'. The Union needed troops so badly, I'm sure they didn't scrutinize the situation much."

Oscar shook his head, "The things that children do..."

Adam nodded, but continued, "They are both young adults now. The war certainly made them grow up in a hurry. I really need to find a school around here, or at least someone competent to teach the blind. Randy will need to learn some skills to help him get along better. I'm hoping he will be able to continue his regular education, but I'm not sure if that is even possible.

Nathaniel and Tom came puffing down the trail to the house. Emma Lou, who had been watching for them, called out, "Supper in five minutes. Y'all git washed up now."

Following Adam's simple prayer at the supper table, Sara Ella told Oscar about their courting days at Harper's Ferry, their first engagement and the subsequent break up, when they regrettably went their separate ways for a time. Then she told how she learned from her brother, Willie, that Adam was in Andersonville Prison, and how she enlisted her brother's help to bribe Adam's way out of there. She had a hard time putting into words how frightened she had been that night when she went to the prison and snatched him out.

Everyone enjoyed a wonderful meal of stewed chicken and vegetables. Emma Lou had skillfully stretched the meal to accommodate their unexpected guests by adding rice that had been salvaged from the cellar at the plantation house and extra delicious, warm, buttery corn bread that she made "especially for Nathaniel".

After supper Adam and Oscar went to look over the ruins of the mansion. Oscar was impressed with what was left of the original foundation and remaining walls.

"Adam – this is amazing! Do you realize how advanced the design of this structure was for the time it was constructed?"

"Frankly Oscar, I don't have any idea. I freely admit that I'm completely overwhelmed. I don't even know where to start. Besides finding the people and supplies for the work of rebuilding the plantation, I also need to make a trip to Washington City on business...and get married...and find someone to teach Randy."

"But, the most pressing thing of all is that I urgently need to go down near Macon, Georgia and find my friend Richard Moreland. He saved my life while I was in Andersonville Prison, and I don't yet know if he even survived the war.

"I'm so weighed down with concerns right now that I finally fell on my face earlier today and asked the Lord to help me...and I think He answered my prayer by sending you!" Adam had never talked about the Lord to anyone except Sara Ella before, so it felt strange to him to tell Oscar about his prayer.

"Oscar, would you consider staying here to manage the rebuilding of the plantation for me? I would compensate you well. My grandfather left me with plenty of funding for all that will be needed for the entire project. Money should not be a problem. I trust you to be the knowledgeable and skilled expert I need...but more than that, I know you will be honest and take good care of me and my resources. If I know you are handling this enormous responsibility, I can focus on these other pressing matters."

"I was hoping you'd say that Adam," Oscar said with a grin. "I'd love to take on this challenge! Can't think of anything I'd rather do, in fact!"

"I'd also like to suggest that you let me pick a couple of my best men to go after this Richard Moreland for you and bring him back here...or come back with news of what happened to him, at least."

"That's an excellent idea!" Adam exclaimed. "I'm dumbfounded...are you accustomed to being the answer to someone's prayer? It would be fantastic if you can do all this for me. What a relief!"

Oscar put his hand on Adam's shoulder as a gesture of comfort. "Now, tell me about this Richard Moreland, Adam."

Adam couldn't help but shudder as he thought back to his time with Richard at Andersonville Prison. Very somberly he began, "Have you heard about Andersonville, Oscar?"

"I've heard enough to know that it's not a place I'd ever want to be," Oscar said.

"That's an understatement. The stench of death and decay was so strong it was hard to breathe. People were dying all around me from hunger and disease. I was seriously wounded with infected dog bites that I received when I tried to escape from the Confederates earlier. I'm sure I would have died if Richard had not stayed by my side, boiling rags for bandages and keeping my wounds as sterile as possible in incredibly filthy, mucky conditions. He never gave up. When Sara Ella rescued me, I promised myself that I'd go back after Richard as soon as humanly possible."

"Andersonville Prison is near Macon, right?"

"Yes it is, and that is quite a long ride from here. I'm sure that Richard would have been released after the war…that is, if…if he survived…but, he may be hard to find, and he will be in very fragile health if he did survive."

"Well, my men are young and tough. You can give them whatever information and instructions you'd like. They will do exactly what you command, and I can certainly vouch for their compassion and sensitivity. If Richard can be found, they will find him, and bring him back here safe and sound."

"I…uh…Adam began to lose his composure as tears pool in his eyes. Are you really Oscar Baynes, my friend? Man, you sure seem more like an angel to me right now…"

"Hey, no problem, I'm just glad to be able to help in some way." Looking again at the ruins, Oscar remarked, "Oh, Adam, what a treasure you have here! This dwelling was built using designs developed for modern forts. How did they know back then how to stabilize the brick walls using triangulated designs, where the fireplace chimneys are an integral part of the structure, bracing the exterior walls?

"It is incredible how much of the original walls are left standing, considering the barrage those unions' unleashed on it! Look at how the interior brick walls served as firewalls—nearly a quarter of the wood interior framework remains. We simply must rebuild this, Adam! We must preserve this wonderful design. We can also add a few new features based on the war experience." The more he studied the ruins, the more fascinated and thrilled Oscar became. By the time he stopped talking, he was visibly giddy with excitement.

"Looks like a pile of rubble to me," said Adam. "They say that one man's trash is another man's treasure—guess that is literally true in our case!"

Walking on part of the foundation, Oscar moved some debris for a more careful examination. "Well, the foundation appears to be intact. Much of the exterior walls and chimneys remain, and most of the bricks are unbroken," Oscar explained. "In fact…now, that is interesting—why aren't the bricks shattered? Most remain in one piece and are reusable. I need to understand that…" Now he was in another world, completely ignoring Adam and the rest of the world around him…all that mattered to him was this magnificent pile of rubble that he wanted to put back together, even better than before.

Oscar tripped over a board and stumbled as he made his way closer to one of the six triangular shaped chimneys. "How curious...," he mused as he studied the design. He noticed that the long side of the triangle was a part of the exterior wall, and that the other two sides had fireplaces on them, each facing an interior room. The interior point of the triangle continued sixty feet, across the building to another chimney on the opposite wall. This brick wall extended to the top of the second story, forming a fire wall and dividing the house for protection in case of a fire. While much was destroyed and charred, enough remained for Oscar to observe the impressive uniqueness of the design.

"This is interesting, Adam...," Oscar commented. "There is a small doorway in this part of the back room chimney, and there appear to be stairs going down into the lower level. Why? There does not appear to be any other access to that area."

Oscar stepped back, surveying the remains. Clearly perplexed he sought to understand what the designer intended when he devised the plan. There was far too much rubble to fully understand the details of the layout. He didn't understand yet why the foundation under the fire wall was far wider than it needed to be to support that interior barrier.

"Why would there be steps going down into an isolated space bounded by the two fireplaces and the exterior wall. Why is the foundation for the fire wall so wide—eight feet, or maybe nine? Why?"

"Adam, do you have the original plans for this remarkable dwelling?" Oscar asked. "A look at the plans would answer a lot of questions and help us reconstruct it."

"No, I don't know where the plans are, Oscar," Adam responded. "Do you really think it can be rebuilt? If you can return this mound of rubble to even a livable home, I would be forever grateful."

"Look Adam, you leave this little undertaking to me. My boys and I have overseen rebuilding projects much more massive than this. Did you hear about the condition of Fort Macon in North Carolina after the Union took it from those Johnny Rebs? It was so bad that the walls adjacent to the magazine were cracking from so many hits by Parrott guns. It is truly amazing that it didn't fall and cause the gunpowder magazine to explode. I'm telling you, Adam, that entire structure was nearly annihilated. I don't mean to brag, but we were the ones who reconstructed it so the Union Army and Navy could have protected use of Beaufort Harbor for the remainder of the war. So, we are not intimidated by this challenge. If you have the funds, my boys and I can rebuild it better than ever!"

"I don't know what to say...I would be so grateful...thank you so much..." Adam stammered for words.

Oscar rubbed his hands together, clearly enthused about getting started right away. "Well, okay then. Would you mind if my men and I immediately begin to carefully sift through all this rubble to see what we can save to be reused and then burn what is completely destroyed? Once we get it cleared out we can work on drawing up new building plans."

"But, we haven't even agreed upon the terms! How do you know if I will make it worth your while to go to all this trouble?" Adam teased.

"I'm not worried about that. If you don't pay me enough, I'll take it out of your hide!" They laughed and laughed, both men knowing that they needed each other. After so much heartache, having hope felt very good to each of them.

Chapter 5

Lisa woke up early in the morning, with her stomach growling fiercely. She didn't have any food to quiet the monster that she knew had begun to eat her alive from the inside out. Wearily, she began to walk toward Chimborazo Hospital, hoping she could find something to eat and drink along the way. *Maybe, someone at the hospital will know something about Goddard,* she thought.

She stopped at a roadside vendor who had some jerky for sale, as well as some raw, home grown fruit and vegetables. They were not at all fresh, but were still edible. The price was exorbitant, but she had no choice but to pay. She asked the man if he had anything she could drink.

"If you have something to put it in, little lady, I have some clean water I can spare."

She smiled and nodded graciously, pulling her medicine bottle from the pocket of her skirt. He poured a small amount of tepid water into it, being very careful not to spill any of the precious liquid. Lisa thanked him, and walked away hungrily biting into a raw potato.

As she approached Chimborazo Hospital, she was astonished by what she saw. There were still broken out windows and one corner of the building had been hit by a small volley, leaving a hole in that area of the structure. Though the building was in disrepair, people were still coming and going through the doors as if nothing had happened there.

She walked around to the Emergency entrance and went through the unguarded door. The strong odor of alcohol and death greeted her, flooding her mind with memories that were not at all welcome thoughts.

At the front desk sat a woman in nurse's uniform, but Lisa did not recognize her. As the woman looked up from her paperwork, she asked in a cheery voice, "Can I help you, Ma'am?"

Her heart pounding rapidly, Lisa asked, "Yes, can you tell me if Dr. Goddard Layne is still working here at the hospital?"

The woman looked at Lisa blankly, hesitated a moment, then said, "I am not acquainted with Dr. Layne, Ma'am. But, I'm new here. Would you like to speak with the Director of Staff?"

Lisa nodded and said, "Yes, please."

They walked toward the wing where the operating rooms are located. Lisa was very acquainted with this part of the hospital, because of her work assisting Goddard in surgery during the war. She started feeling sick to her stomach, as she thought about all the human suffering she had seen in that place.

Her heart began beating much faster, as the woman pushed open the door. Looking into the room, she announced, "This lady is inquiring about a Dr. Layne. Can you help her? I don't remember meeting anyone by that name since I've been here."

The older man with a darker complexion and commanding brown eyes was also unknown to Lisa. He nodded to the woman and said "Thank you, Nurse. You may go. I'll talk to her." Turning to Lisa, he said, "Come in, dear. Are you related to this Dr. Layne you are looking for?"

Lisa's heart sank as she realized that the whole staff of the hospital must have changed since she left weeks ago. She nodded, but was unable to utter a word.

The doctor pulled out a chair and motioned his hand toward the seat. Kindly, he said, "Please, sit down, Ma'am. I'm Doctor Barton. I was put in charge here by the Union forces. Now, did you say you are Dr. Layne's wife or just a family member?" he asked again.

Lisa nodded, swallowed the lump in her throat and nodded again, then said, "I am Lisa Layne, his wife. I was a nurse at this hospital during the war, working at my husband's side with the injured soldiers. I helped evacuate a group of them before the Union forces arrived. Dr. Layne was to follow and meet me in Manchester." Her voice broke as she added, "He never arrived, so I'm trying to find him."

"Do you have any identification, Mrs. Layne?"

Again, she nodded, picked up her reticule from where she had laid it beside the chair, pulling her hospital pass from it. She handed it to Dr. Barton and said, "Can you tell me if Dr. Layne is on duty today?"

He glanced at the pass, nodded and handed it back to her. Pulling a chair up beside her, he reached over and put his hand on her arm. Then in a very soft voice, he said, "Dr. Layne was brought in here after the accident, as I understand. I was not on staff here when the Union Army entered the city, but I was told about him by a doctor who was on staff here at the time. Your husband had apparently been run over by a wagon and trampled by a horse. He was still alive when he arrived, but died on the operating table, while a team of surgeons tried their best to save his life. I'm so sorry."

34

Lisa looked at the man in disbelief and broke into sobs, shaking her head. "But, that's impossible! He promised he would meet me in Manchester with our little daughter, but he never came."

"Daughter?" He shook his head. "There was no little girl with him when they brought him in. I'm sure I would have been told if there had been a child with him. He had a Chimborazo shield on his shirt, so they knew he was a staff member here."

Lisa dropped her head into her hands, and said brokenly, "Oh Goddard, you cannot be dead! What will I do without you? And Angela...please, she cannot be dead, too! I cannot bear it!" She sobbed uncontrollably.

Doctor Barton shook his head, but said nothing. He pulled Lisa's hands gently from her face and looking in her eyes, said, firmly, "Mrs. Layne, your husband is dead, that much I know for sure." He continued, "I am not sure if there is a record of where his body was buried, but I will have what records we have checked thoroughly for that information. You know, there was complete pandemonium around here at that time, so I can offer no guarantees."

Lisa nodded, and through her tears, asked, "If Goddard is dead and Angela was not with him when he was brought here, where could she be?"

The doctor just shook his head. He could not answer her question. He walked to the door, and called, "Nurse."

When the nurse appeared, Dr. Barton said, "Nurse, Mrs. Layne has suffered a terrible shock. Please bring her some water right away."

The nurse disappeared, but was back in just a moment, following the doctor's orders.

Lisa sat there until she finally stopped sobbing. The staff moved her out of Dr. Barton's office to a bench in the hallway, where she was allowed to stay until she could pull herself together. She slept there for several hours.

When she was finally able to leave, she told the nurse, "Well, now I can stop looking for my husband and concentrate on trying to locate my daughter. Thank you again. I will be back later to see if Dr. Barton has found any record of where Goddard is buried. So many men died in this awful war and are forever lost to their families...God only knows where he is, I'm sure."

Lisa turned and left the hospital alone. She was completely exhausted, feeling as though her melancholy thoughts and overwhelming sorrow were the only things she had left in the world. *I have no idea what to do without Goddard...I simply cannot go on without him. I am so very tired...I think I will just sit down here on this bench for a while...*

Awakened with a start by the noise of hammering, Lisa was surprised to find herself in a tastefully decorated bedroom with high ceilings that were embellished with ornate crown moldings. Then she realized she was lying in a stately Victorian mahogany bed that was covered with fresh smelling, clean white sheets. She turned her head to see a huge Victorian wardrobe that matched the carving on the bed. Without lifting her head from the pillow, she quickly surveyed the rest of the furnishings in the room, and was very grateful, when her eyes came to rest on Martha getting up out of a rocking chair on the other side of the bed.

"Lisa! I am so pleased to see that you are finally awake."

"Where am I, and how did I get here? Is this a dream?"

Martha laughed softly and said, "No, dear, it is not a dream. You are at the Callahan Plantation. Moses and I went looking for you yesterday and found you lying on a bench in front of the hospital."

Rising up in bed, Lisa said, "So, Mr. Callahan did have work for you, and you can stay here in Virginia?"

"Well, Mr. Callahan said we can stay as long as we want, but he has no work to give us, because he has no money. He lost everything in the war, except what is left of this home."

"I do not understand...what does that mean, Martha?"

Gently encouraging Lisa's shoulders back down onto the pillow, Martha said, "All of your questions can wait, my dear. Right now you are in desperate need of rest and nutrition. I have been spooning little sips of water into your mouth while you were so groggy, but now I am going to get you a bowl of soup. You need something nutritious if you are going to get your strength back."

"Thank you Martha, it seems that you and Moses are always rescuing me."

When Martha left to go get the soup, Lisa heard the same hammering sound again that she had heard earlier. Weak as she was, she raised up to look out the window beside her bed. Curious, but unable to see anything from the bed, she slowly got up and made her way carefully over to the window to investigate, but was still unable to satisfy her curiosity. She discovered that she was dressed in a simple night gown, and found the matching night wrapper draped across the end of the bed, so she put it on over her gown. Slowly, she walked toward the door.

36

When she looked into the long hallway outside her room, she saw a door across from her and then two more doors across from each other to her left and another door down at the end of the hall. When she looked to her right she saw some rough cut boards with a homemade door and wooden turn latch.

"Interesting...wonder what on earth...?" Lisa thought, "There is some kind of very bright light shining through those cracks around the outside of that door. Could I be dreaming? Perhaps, I have died, and Heaven is on the other side of that door?"

Lisa opened the odd door, and was immediately blinded by intense sunlight. As she stepped forward and started to raise her arm to shade the sun, she heard a loud crash and Martha yelling, "Stop, Lisa! Do not move. I will be right there!"

Lisa froze, continuing to lift her arm to protect her eyes. As her vision adjusted to the bright sunlight, she suddenly realized that she had literally, almost walked into Heaven! She was standing on the second board of a small, crudely constructed landing that was only two boards wide and led to a stairway on her left. In front of her was nothing but space and a 14 foot drop to the ground below! Lisa panicked, but was so weak, she was wobbly, as she stepped back from the precipice. Martha reached out to steady her, leading her safely back to the bedroom, scolding her along the way for getting out of bed.

"Lisa, I am so sorry that I did not explain the situation here, but I had no idea you would wander into danger like that! I am so thankful that the Lord guided my steps so that I would see you just when I did. Are you sure you are okay?"

"Yes, I think so...but I do not understand. What is going on here?" Lisa questioned.

"Well you see, half of this beautiful Callahan mansion was destroyed in the war. Oddly enough, the stairway on this side survived, but, as you have seen, the balcony that led from the stairs to the bedrooms is completely gone. Most of the walls of the entry hall are standing, except for the far wall on the east side from where the sun was shining in. Some people from church are working hard to rebuild that east wall for Mr. Callahan, but regrettably, he does not have enough money to rebuild the entire house back like it was before."

"It sounds like he has a challenge ahead of him. What did you mean by saying that you can stay, but he cannot pay you?" Lisa responded.

Martha walked over to the window and looked off into the distance as she answered, "When we came down the lane and got close to the house, Mr. Callahan came running out to greet us. He hugged everyone warmly, as he choked back tears of joy.

"When he asked us if we had found work, we told him that we had not and hoped that he would have work for us here. His countenance fell as he said that he had no jobs, because he cannot pay. Before the war Mr. Callahan was a wealthy man, but Confederate money is worthless now. He is a kind and generous man, so he helped all of his former slaves, the way he helped us when we left. We also know that he has helped all his neighbors as much as possible. But, there is nothing left, now. The best he can do for us now is to give us a place to live for as long as we want. But, under the circumstances, we will have to find work somewhere else.

"Now I need to go and get you some more soup, and then clean up the soup that I spilled on the floor when I saw you about to fall to your death. Now, please stay put this time, and I will be right back."

"Thank you again, Martha," Lisa said. "I will follow your orders this time. Frankly, I am afraid to do otherwise." she said with a weak laugh.

Martha continued, "Mr. Callahan asked me if you would be strong enough after you finish your soup for him to visit with you, briefly. I told him I would ask you. Would you like a visit from him?"

"Of course, Martha. He has been most hospitable, having given me this fine room and bed. I would love to meet him...and what about Mrs. Callahan...Is there a Mrs. Callahan?"

"It pains me so to say that Cora Callahan did not live through the war. When the other end of the house was bombed, she was injured and never recovered," said Martha with tears in her eyes. Then, changing the subject in an attempt to regain control of her emotions, she said, "Now I am off again to get that soup for you."

When Martha returned with a fresh bowl of soup, she made sure that Lisa could manage to feed herself, then turned and left to attend to other responsibilities.

"Mrs. Layne?" a deep melodious voice spoke softly, as the door cracked open.

"Yes, please come in," Lisa responded.

A handsome, tall and slender man with sky blue eyes and silver hair stepped into the room. With grace and humility he said, "My name is Warren Callahan. I do hope you are finding your accommodations acceptable. I know Martha is treating you with every kindness, as is her custom. Do you know of any way that I could make your stay more comfortable?"

"No sir, you have been most gracious to take me in like this. I do not intend to infringe upon your hospitality for very long. I will need to be on my way soon. You see, I must find my little girl, but I do not know where she is..."

"Now, now...don't you be worrying about your little girl right now. You need to get your strength back, for her sake, as well as yours. I am sure you can trust her to God's watchful care, my dear. Please stay here, at least until you are well enough to travel. Besides, it is my pleasure to have you here in my home. I was so very sorry to hear of your husband's untimely death..."

Lisa looked down at her hands, but could not speak. As she lifted her head, Warren saw her tears and the depth of her grief.

"I understand your sorrow, Mrs. Layne. The Lord recently took my sweet Cora, to cherish her in His glorious presence. I do miss her so...but I am comforted, knowing that she is, oh so full of life and love where she is now...my heart is lifted high for her."

"I wish that I could have that kind of peace...Goddard was everything to me...he is the one that kept me going through so many difficulties. Now, I do not know which way to turn," she wept softly, as she shared her heart with this kind gentleman, who appeared to truly care about her dilemma.

"I knew your husband, Mrs. Layne," Warren said. "He was a fine man, that is for sure. You may not know that he actually saved my life a few years ago, not long after he set up his office in Richmond. I contracted pneumonia that winter, and he cured me. It is my pleasure to reciprocate by having you stay here as long as you would like. We are a little short on money around here, but my neighbors have been generously sharing food from their gardens and meat brought in by skilled hunters. With their help, we have planted a garden here on my property that will soon be sufficient for us, with enough extra to share with others. One way or another, you won't go hungry while you are under my roof."

"Mr. Callahan, you are very kind," said Lisa, "and I am very appreciative of your gracious offer. Thank you for the twinkle of hope you have brought to me today."

"You are more than welcome, my dear."

After sleeping soundly the rest of that day and through the night, Martha brought Lisa a hot breakfast of scrambled eggs, bacon and biscuits. After eating her fill, she was feeling enough stronger that she wanted to get up and dress. Obviously, Martha had anticipated this, because Lisa discovered her red dress had been cleaned and mended, along with her under garments, and they were neatly folded on the trunk at the end of her bed. There was also a wash basin with a pitcher of water on her dresser. After washing and dressing she hugged herself and said out loud, "I feel cleaner than I have felt in over a month!"

"Good morning, Lisa," Martha said, as Lisa entered the outdoor kitchen area.

"With these clean and mended clothes, I feel almost normal—at least, on the outside I wish you could find a way to do that for my heart, as well, Martha."

With a smile Martha said, "It will happen soon enough, my dear. You will find the way.

"Do you feel up to helping me prepare a little mid-day snack to feed this crew of carpenters? I hope it will give them strength to carry on until evening."

"I would be pleased to help, but where is the food?" Lisa said as she looked around and saw nothing but some bread.

"Lizzie will be here any minute with some vegetables from her father's garden and a few eggs to boil and mix with them. We will put the mixture on this bread that I made this morning. It's not elaborate, but it should meet the need."

"Who is Lizzie?" Lisa questioned.

"Her name is Elizabeth Jones. She is 10 years old and is one of the children from a neighboring farm. Her father is here helping with the work on that entry hall wall. The Jones family goes to a little church that several families in this area attend, including Mr. Callahan, our family and the families of the other men who are over there working on that wall."

"Hi, Miss Martha!" Lizzie said as she came running into the one room outbuilding, "I've got a bunch of cucumbers, some tomatoes and 6 eggs for us to make something with today. I can't wait until those watermelons get ripe! Yum, yum! Oh!" she stopped, "we've got company!"

"Hello Lizzie," Martha said. "This is Mrs. Lisa Layne. She is going to be helping us today."

"I'm pleased to meet you, Lizzie. Please call me Lisa."

Tall for her age, Lizzie was an energetic girl with long curly chestnut brown hair that had been neatly tied back with a blue ribbon. Her intensely blue eyes were mesmerizing. She looked Lisa over quickly and then blurted out, "You are beautiful, but you're sure not very big!"

Lisa laughed for the first time since she could remember, and said, "Why, thank you, Lizzie, for any part of your observation that was a compliment. You are a beautiful girl yourself! I think that we'll be good friends, what do you think?"

By the end of that week, vital repairs to the Callahan plantation house were finished, and a celebration was under way. Several neighboring families provided a potluck meal outside on the lawn. After dinner, Andrew Delancy began playing his fiddle and some of the men began singing, while the women were clearing the table.

Just then, little Joseph Sheldon came crying to his mother, blood running profusely from a cut to his upper arm. Lisa instinctively grabbed a clean towel and ran over to attend to his wound. The youngster's mother watched with admiration, as little Joseph quieted right down. Lisa spoke to him in a soft voice, while giving instructions to adults to bring her what she needed to stop the bleeding as quickly as possible. Before long, Joseph was treated, bandaged and resting quietly beside his mother. All of the women surrounded Lisa, praising her for her wonderful healing gift.

"Well, I would not call it a gift," she said. "It is what I had to do for years as a nurse, when injured soldiers were brought into Chimborazo Hospital during the war. My husband was a doctor, and he needed help. He told me what to do, and I did the best I could, that is all."

One of the women spoke up and said, "Believe me, Honey, it is a gift from the Lord. I don't care how you got it."

"Yes," they all shook their heads in agreement. Then one of them asked, "Would you be willing to help our families when we need medical attention?"

"Of course," Lisa responded. "As long as I am here, I would be happy to help if I can, with children and adults as well."

Warren Callahan put his hand on Lisa's shoulder and said. "It looks like you have found a meaningful way to contribute to our way of life here, Mrs. Layne. It is great to have you here with us."

Lisa had not been to church since the morning she was with Goddard at St. Paul's Episcopal church in Richmond when the worship service was interrupted by the sexton informing President Davis that Richmond must immediately be evacuated. Painful memories made it difficult for her, but she agreed to go with her new friends the following Sunday morning, because it seemed so important to them.

Going with them was the least she could do, if it would bring them some joy.

Warren and Moses rode in the front of the buggy, while Lisa rode with Martha and the girls in the back. She enjoyed the seemingly endless chatter of the children, their mother chiming in when they occasionally became too noisy. It was a bright, sunny June morning, not a cloud in the sky. She looked down and brushed some imaginary crumbs off her lap, hoping she was dressed well enough for the approval of the congregation.

As they arrived in front of the small rural church, Lisa was surprised to see that the structure had apparently been undamaged by the war. Made entirely of brick, it had brick steps leading up to a wide front porch that was supported by four big white columns. She noticed a small well-cared-for cemetery to the right. Inside the church she saw a beautiful large stained glass window that was arched at the top. The image was of Christ, kneeling in prayer, the sun shining from the upper left corner onto his face. On the left side of the front area was a potbellied wood stove. But of course, the windows were all open on both sides today, giving a refreshing breeze across the pews.

Everyone walked inside together, which seemed very odd to Lisa. Before, slaves had always used a separate entrance and sat in the balcony. But today, at least in this church, no one sat in the balcony.

Annie Sheldon, little Joseph's mother, greeted Lisa with a smile and outreached hand. "I am so glad you came, Mrs. Layne. I would like to introduce you to our Pastor, Reverend Lloyd Long. Pastor, this is Lisa Layne. She is a widow, staying with Warren Callahan for a little while. Lisa is the nurse that I told you about, who took care of Joseph Sheldon's injured arm the other day."

"Hello, Mrs. Layne. How fortunate it was that you were there to help little Joe. I understand that the bleeding was quite a problem! And, we are blessed to have you join us this morning, as well," said Pastor Long.

"Thank you," Lisa said. "It was nothing, really."

Martha introduced her to Robert and Gretchen Turnage, Louis and Claudia Chisholm, and then James and Dorothy Duerson, explaining that James had directed the work to restore Warren Callahan's home back to usefulness. The small choir began to sing, as Martha led Lisa to sit together with her family and Warren Callahan.

Reverend Long walked up to the beautifully carved wooden pulpit and greeted his congregation, "Good morning! Please join me in a warm welcome for Mrs. Lisa Layne, who is here with us today for the first time."

Then, after some announcements, congregational singing and other formalities that Lisa had learned to expect in a protestant church, Reverend Long preached a sermon about Jesus Christ. His message gave Lisa a much clearer understanding of the meaning of Jesus' death and resurrection than ever before. She had always thought that the stories about Jesus she learned as a child were merely historical events, not something that had to do with her, personally. The preacher said Jesus could free her from the penalty of her sin, and give her a new life.

On the way home from church, Lisa was quiet, as she pondered all that the Pastor said in his sermon. And not only that, but her heart was also warmed by the love and respect that was shown to the black people in that little church. How strange it was—having relationships like this in a church or anywhere else, for that matter, was unheard of in the South.

During the prayer portion of the worship service, she was made aware that several of the people in attendance did not have jobs or money. But, everyone contributed in any way they could to the others in the church who had need of their services or provisions. That is how Warren Callahan was able to get his house repaired, before it was damaged further by the elements. She also knew that Warren had given shelter to Moses, Martha and their girls, as well as to herself. She was sure that these people were doing lots more than she would ever know to help one another get through these difficult times.

Later that day, as everyone was resting from the week's labor, she asked Warren, Martha and Moses to help her understand better what she had learned in the sermon that morning. She thoroughly enjoyed the resulting discussion and testimonies from all of them. Just being with these kind, loving people was helping her deal with her loss.

But, despite her growing contentment, Lisa continued to long for her little Angela. She rode with Moses every time he went into Richmond, so she could ask everyone on the streets if they had any knowledge of Ben, Ruth, and Naomi or their two little girls. But, no one knew them, or anyone that fit their description. Lisa became more and more discouraged, as all hope of finding Angela ebbed.

Chapter 6

Tom came running to the lumber mill. Excited and out of breath, he was holding some papers above his head, waving them back and forth.

"I have found them, Adam, I have found them!"

He slid to a stop in front of Adam.

"What have you found, Tom?" Adam asked, reaching for the papers.

"I found the original plans that Mr. Cutler used when he built the mansion for your grandfather!" He was so excited he was actually jumping up and down.

"Let me see, Tom."

"See," Tom said, out of breath from his run up hill to the mill. "Here is Mr. Cutler's signature on one of the pages."

Adam very carefully turned one at a time through the crisp sheets of old yellowed paper, and saw that they were indeed the original plans for the mansion, floor by floor! Some were a bit faded, having been drawn with a pencil. But, with care, all could be read—dimensions, measurements, kinds of wood, brick, metal, windows. One page even had a plan for the oak trees that lined the road leading from the pike to the house.

As he continued thumbing through the document, Adam said, "Tom, this is a wonderful find! How did you know what it was?"

"I was working at the mansion with Oscar and his men. We cleared out an area of debris where the ceiling had fallen in. I was working near the hidden brick stairs down to the secret room in the wall of the fireplace. I lost my footing and fell down on some of that rubble on the stairs. When I looked up, I saw that the whole door to the secret room was still there! It is charred black, but it is still there! I stood up, gave it a powerful kick, and it just popped open! The wall was too damaged to keep holding it shut, I guess.

"Believe it or not, everything in that room was just like your Mama left it. Come and see for yourself! Anyway, as I was rummaging around in there, I ran across these rolled up yellowed papers and pulled them out." He gasped for breath, and continued, "I just knew this was the plans you have been looking for!"

Adam continued examining the plans, page by page, nodding his head in agreement. As he got to the last page, his mouth actually fell open. As he looked at the crest on the top of the page, he drew in a deep breath.

"Tom, did you show this to Oscar?"

"No, I was so excited that I just ran here as fast as I could to show you."

"Come on, he has got to see this," Adam said as he ran as fast as his bad leg could carry him. Tom ran beside him, continuing to tell him about the condition of the newly discovered secret room.

As they came into view of the wreckage of the mansion, Adam called out, "Oscar! Wait till you see what Tom found!"

"What do you have there?"

"It's the original plans for the mansion! "And, not only that," Adam exclaimed, as he pointed in excitement at the crest, "Look, this is an English crest used by the royal family—this is King George III's grant of this land to my great grandfather, George Layne." Then turning to the smaller page behind it, he shouted, "Should I ever need it, this is proof that this land was recorded to the Layne family here in Virginia."

"Tom, please take these documents directly to the house. Be very careful with them. Give them to Sara Ella and tell her what it is. Let her know that Oscar and I will be there as soon as we can get cleaned up to go over them and study them well. I am grateful to you Tom, for finding the secret room. What would I have done without you all these years?" He put his arms around Tom and hugged him.

Tom laughed. "Guess I have saved your neck more than once now!" Adam joined him in laughter.

"Yes, Tom, you have. I will never forget the time we burned down the tobacco shed and you took the blame for it! That counts double, I think. Thank you, again."

After Tom was out of earshot, Oscar asked Adam, "Is it safe for Tom to carry valuable papers like those around? Is he trustworthy?"

Adam smiled, and said, "Oscar, I would trust Tom with my life, actually have numerous times, in fact. We grew up together. He is a wonderful fellow. I could have trusted him to take my gold bricks to the bank, if I had asked him. Yes, I would trust Tom with anything."

"Gold bricks?" Oscar asked with a wrinkle on his brow.

Adam smiled. "Yes, King George III gave my great grandfather five gold bricks, along with these 10,000 acres of Virginia land. George Layne was a shrewd man. He hid those 5 gold bricks away for a future time such as this, when they might be needed. I took those 5 gold bricks with me to the bank in Washington City on the same trip when I found Randy. That is what is funding our livelihood now and this project you are working on."

As they headed back to the Temporary Building, Adam said, "Do you know what this means, finding the plans, I mean? Now you will not have to depend on me to tell you what the place looked like before, and you will not have to draw the plans based on such vague information. That should speed up the process dramatically and allow me to leave and take Sara Ella to Washington City. We can even be married right away, if she will agree to that idea! While I am there, I will go to the bank for more money to get you going full speed on the mansion."

Adam was now encouraged that with Oscar in charge at Oaklayne everything was going to go smoothly. Oscar had already sent his men, Trevor and August, to go find Richard. Adam gave them enough money for their expenses, as well as some extra they might need, should they have to bribe people for information along the way. He was pleased that they were excited, when asked to take on the responsibility of finding Adam's hero for him.

After cleaning up, Adam and Oscar went inside, where Sara Ella greeted them excitedly. "How wonderful that Tom found the original plans for the house!"

"Yes, my love. It is not only the plans for the house and the outbuildings, but also the original deed from King George III for our 10,000 acres."

The two men laid the plans out on the table to examine them more closely. After spending all afternoon going over them, Oscar was visibly impressed. "Wow, you did not tell me the half of how grand this place was. I cannot wait to get started on the construction."

"Well," Emma Lou said, as she stuck her head out of the kitchen, "kin' that wait 'til aft'a suppa'? Ah' needs ta' set the table now y'all."

After supper, when Emma Lou and Sara Ella got up to wash the dishes, the men turned back to the plans that Tom had unearthed earlier in the day. Adam carefully laid each sheet out on the table, and suggested that perhaps they should try not to handle the papers any more than absolutely necessary, because of their fragility. Oscar agreed that was a good idea.

Emma Lou came out of the kitchen area and remarked that the new house should have a kitchen in it. Everyone laughed…that is, everyone except Oscar. He hesitated a minute, then slowly smiled broadly at the thought of a kitchen in the mansion. "Excellent idea, Emma Lou!" He got up out of his chair, rushed over to her, picked her up and whirled her around with her feet off the ground, then planted a big kiss on her cheek. That stunt brought a wooden spoon down on top of his head and roars of laughter from everyone in the room.

"Adam, I agree that we need to add a kitchen as an ell to the dining room, with a warming room in between to keep the kitchen odors and heat away from the dining room. That would be much better than having a separate building for cooking like before, what do you think?"

Adam looked at Tom, and then at Oscar, who looked back at Adam.

"He is right," Adam said. "We should do that. We will put it on the back of the house, so it will not be seen as people come up the drive from the pike."

Tom shook his head. "That is not good, Adam. That puts the kitchen right by the veranda on the James River side of the house. You don't want that."

Oscar intervened. "Adam, instead of an ell, I suggest you put it on the end of the mansion. It would make an attractive wall on the drive way side. Add the kitchen and warming room in such a way that the walls of the mansion will still be straight, not jutting out somewhere, announcing that a room has been added on."

"That is a good idea, Oscar. Thank you. We will add it on the end that is nearest the barns, making the mansion some twenty feet longer but keeping the width the same. That should be enough, don't you think?"

Oscar nodded. "We will put a fire wall between the kitchen and the house, so if there is ever a kitchen fire, it will be contained in the kitchen."

"Thank you again, Oscar. And many thanks to you Emma Lou! Please do incorporate that idea into the new plans." Emma Lou glowed all over, very pleased to have contributed something meaningful to the project...not to mention her personal joy about not having to go out in the weather to carry supper to the big house all the time.

Oscar asked, "Where are we going to get the English walnut for Steven's carving work, Adam? He needs English walnut, because of the tighter grain, you know. That will need to come from overseas, will it not? If you did not have your own lumber mill, I doubt you could find enough lumber to build the house according to these plans. Everyone in the south will be needing lumber."

Adam frowned and added, "We cannot get the furnishings we will need here, either..."

For the first time Nathaniel spoke, although he had been listening intently to everything that was being said. He told Adam about going with his Father, Mason Layne, during the war to Charleston to see a blockade runner. Mason hired the man to take a load of tobacco to England and sell it to buy foodstuffs and other supplies that were urgently needed for the survival of the plantation. The blockade runner's name was Matthew Wythe. Nathaniel thought he might have survived the war and be available to go to England again for supplies.

"Capt'n Wythe live on the Batt'ry in Charleston, Adam. Yo' could go an' see if'n he could he'p again."

"Great idea, Nathaniel!" Adam said. "I have been concerned about where to go to get the kind of building materials and supplies we will need. Nathaniel, you have always been a great asset to this family. I was so impressed with your initiative and the way you had the saw mill working by the time I got home with Randy. And, the way you manage the men operating the lumber mill, as well as those who are felling and moving the trees is extraordinary. I want you to know that I appreciate you...always have."

Oscar whistled a little trill and shook his head. "You are quite a fellow, Adam Layne!" And he slapped his friend on the back.

Adam smiled.

Chapter 7

"What are you slowing down for?" August called out to Trevor. "I thought we had decided we were going to ride hard to get there. We need to find Richard Moreland, before he hightails it out of that Deep South country for a friendlier climate in Union territory."

"Oh, stop complaining, August. We been traveling most of the day, with only one break to take in some of them great vittles that Emma Lou packed for us. That woman can sure cook! Besides you know we can't push these horses too hard. We will have to ride at least two weeks, just to get there. And, in case you hadn't noticed, there are some dark clouds rolling in over there in the west. I'm thinking we need to be looking for a good campsite, with some water for our canteens and these horses. It sure would be better to get set up before the storm hits. Besides, I'm sure looking forward to getting into some more of them vittles."

Tilting his head back to see the sky from under the brim of his hat, August remarked, "Hm...I had not noticed them clouds. You could be right. Maybe we should turn in a little early tonight so we can get an early start in the morning."

Chapter 8

All morning Oscar and Adam perused the plans and deliberated on what materials would be needed right away. "Adam, why did you not tell me about this secret room? That explains a lot of what I observed when we were looking at the foundation."

"I am sorry; I can see that it would have been better to have enlightened you, under the circumstances. It's just that—it was instilled in me from a very young age to never mention the secret room to anyone for any reason. I guess old habits are hard to break. Besides, my mind was just somewhere else when you were going on and on with all that technical jargon. It is exciting to see you impressed with things like the foundation though, which I obviously had no idea about."

Adam turned to Sara Ella, who had been coming in and out of the kitchen helping Emma Lou, and said, "You know, Honey, Oscar handling this construction for me is going to save us a lot of time. We may have a home of our own before you know it! And that means we may need to be married sooner than you think!" He cracked a silly boyish grin her way.

She responded with a mocking flip of her hair, a tilt of her head and her nose in the air, as though she was not interested in the slightest. Then she answered, "It sounds as if you might be in some sort of hurry, Mr. Layne," reaching over and gently patted his cheek in jest.

"Seriously, Sara Ella" Adam said as he took both of her hands in his. "How long do you think it would take to pack your bags?"

"What are you saying," she said with a catch of breath.

"Well it seems to me that you and I are no longer needed around here. Trevor and August are on their way to get Richard Moreland, Oscar and Tom have a crew busy doing cleanup work, with plans to start construction right away, and Nathaniel has the saw mill going full boar. We can hire some additional men, wherever they are needed, and some help for Emma Lou in the kitchen. So, I do not see why the two of us could not leave right away for Washington City. I have business there with Secretary Edwin Stanton.

But before I go...," Adam got down on one knee with some difficulty and clumsiness because of his war wound, and said, "Sara Ella Gary, will you marry me?"

"Adam, oh Adam, yes! Yes, of course I will marry you!!! I thought you were going to put this off forever!"

"I inherited a lovely townhouse in Washington City that my Father and Mother lived in when he was a Senator and Congress was in session. I expect it is in pretty good condition, because Washington City was not hit as hard as other areas. At least, it should be livable.

"We will take the train there, just as soon as we can get packed. If you want, we can take the time for you to shop in the city for a wedding dress and anything else you want for the wedding. I know that being married in Washington City will not be everything you always hoped for your wedding day...your family not being there, and all...but Tom will be with us, and Randy and Benjy could be there. Well, what do you think?"

"Adam Layne, I love you and would marry you anywhere, regardless. Yes, it would be wonderful to have Tom, Randy and Benjy with us. I will go get started putting together some garments that need washed, so I can pack them just as soon as they get dry." Sara Ella's heart was about to burst with joy and excitement. Yes, she had dreamed of having her mother make her wedding dress and her father walk her down the aisle...but, times are such that dreams do not always go the way you originally planned.

That night at the supper table Randy and Benjy were already waiting as all of the others came in. Benjy chuckled and said "Okay, Randy, do it." Then one by one as each person entered the room, Randy correctly identified them, calling out their names as they came through the door.

"What in the world...how is this possible? Benjy, are you somehow telling Randy who we are when we come in?" Adam was mystified.

"Oh no, Massa Adam, Ah'm not doin' nu'thin'. You to'd me to he'p Randy figure things out...well, sir, he jus' learns so fas', Ah' cain't keep up wit' him. Ah' could tell that he was hearin' things real good, betta' than mos' folks. In this here case, Randy knows each o' yo' by the sound yo' makes."

"Randy, this is amazing! I have never seen anything like it." Adam was still not sure it was not a trick of some sort.

"I do not know Papa, but I seem to have a second sense now. I was not aware of it before being blind. I have just been staying quiet around here, keeping out of everyone's way and feeling sorry for myself. I guess I have been listening more than I ever did before. Benjy started noticing and pointing out things I could do that he was not able to do, and then we started trying out some things. It is a challenge, but also kind of fun. It gives me hope—hope that I really needed. Sometimes I get to worrying that I will always be a burden for someone else to carry around—but, I do not want that, Father. When we figure out some more things I can do, we will show you."

Adam had to choke back tears when he turned to Benjy and said, "What a great discovery! Son, thank you for always being there for Randy. I am forever indebted to you."

Everyone was excited for Randy and had lots of questions. They even tried to trick him, testing his ability to recognize them. They had already realized some time back that he always somehow knew who was talking to him.

After the kitchen was empty of everyone except Randy and Benjy, Adam and Sara Ella sat down next to them at the table.

"Boys," Adam said, "Sara Ella and I are leaving right away for Washington City."

"We are going to be married there," Sara Ella interjected excitedly. "And, we want both of you to make our joy complete by coming with us!"

Randy smiled and said, "Well, I would like to see the two of you married—it has been a very long time coming. I am very happy for both of you. I am blind, but I am beginning to realize that not everything needs to be seen with the eyes. So, yes, I would not miss it for the world!"

"Me too," Benjy said. "Ah's happy fo' y'all too, an' Ah wants ta' be there wit' y'all."

"Okay! We'll be leaving just as soon as I can get our clothes washed, dried and packed. I'll start washing in the morning, so you boys—all three of you—bring me your clothes right after breakfast."

"How are we going to get there?" Randy asked.

"Well boys," Adam said "I was thinking that you would enjoy a ride on the train. Am I right?"

"That would be great!" the boys answered in unison.

Chapter 9

The following afternoon, Sara Ella was hanging clothes on the line, when she saw an unfamiliar buggy coming down the road to the house. She stopped what she was doing, and walked to the roadway. She knew it was not one of their neighbor's buggies and could not see the people riding inside, so she just stood there, waiting.

A tall distinguished looking gentleman with silver hair brought the buggy to a halt in front of the house, helping two ladies down. One of the women was small, with long black hair, and the other was a tall black woman with a stately countenance, despite her well-worn garments.

As Sara Ella watched the smaller lady, who was now walking toward her, she suddenly realized who it was! "Lisa!" she cried and hurried to embrace and welcome her.

"Lisa, oh, where have you been? Where is Goddard?" she asked, taking Lisa in her arms again.

Lisa started to cry, as she looked into Sara Ella's eyes, "Goddard is dead, Sara Ella! I came to Richmond to find him, found the ruins of our home and then went to Chimborazo Hospital to see if they could tell me anything about him."

"Oh Lisa, I am so sorry." Sara Ella said, as they both cried together.

Gathering her wits about her, Lisa said, "Sara Ella I want you to meet some very special people who rescued and helped me these last weeks. Please meet Mr. Warren Callahan of the Callahan Plantation outside of Richmond, and my very special friend Martha, who has been a great companion to me and nursed me back to health.

"I am very pleased to meet you both. Please come in." Sara Ella said, as she led the way to the Temporary Building and opened the door. "If you will be seated, I will be right back with some lemonade." As they were entering the relaxation area, Sara Ella asked Mr. Callahan, "How did your plantation fare in the war, sir?"

"Well, it looks like everything is going to be just fine, thank you for asking. I have had a great deal of help from my neighbors and our local church. Martha and her husband, Moses, have been a great help to me, since they returned to the plantation. And, it has also been quite a blessing to have Lisa Layne in my home for the past few weeks," he said with a disarming grin.

Then he continued. "I am happy to see that reconstruction appears to be underway for Senator Layne's plantation. I was so sorry to hear that he and Elizabeth both passed away during the war. They were wonderful people. Now that Goddard is gone, does that mean Adam is doing the rebuilding of Oaklayne alone?"

"Yes, he is. Adam has hired some men with the expertise to build it back like it was before the war, at least as much as possible. Adam will be here this evening, after the sun goes down, Warren. I am sure he will be pleased to see you all, especially Lisa." Sara Ella said, as she looked at Lisa and smiled.

Martha interjected, surprising Sara Ella with her perfect linguistics, "This is wonderful lemonade, Mrs. Layne. Thank you so much for your hospitality."

Mr. Callahan stood, dipped his head to Sara Ella and Lisa as he said, "I am sorry ladies, but we must be going. Please tell Adam that I am sorry we missed him." Then turning to Lisa, he said, "I want you to know Lisa, that my door is always open if I can be of any service to you. Enjoy your family, dear. Thank you, Sara Ella for having us in."

As the buggy pulled out of sight, Sara Ella turned to Lisa and hugged her again, saying, "I am so glad you are here with us, Lisa. Adam will be so grieved to hear that Goddard is gone, as I am. What happened to him? How did he die?"

Lisa looked at the ground to try to keep her composure, as she told Sara Ella her story.

Sara Ella listened to all that Lisa said, but was confused at the mention of "our little girl." What little girl? Was Lisa so distraught that she was mentally disturbed? Sara Ella remembered being told by Emma Lou that a little girl had been born to Lisa and Goddard, but had died in childbirth. Sara Ella said nothing, just let Lisa cry.

When Lisa had regained her composure, she asked, "Lisa, you mentioned Goddard went to get Angela?"

Lisa nodded.

"Angela?" Sara Ella asked again with a question in her voice.

Lisa nodded, and with complete abandon and between sobs said, "Yes, Angela. You know, the little girl we had three years ago, almost four now?" She immediately continued, "Do you know where Ruth is? We gave Angela to Ruth who gave her to her daughter, Naomi, to raise—oh, it is a long story. I will tell you more about it when there is time. But maybe, if I can find Ruth, I can find Naomi and my little

Angela. I have looked everywhere in the Richmond area, but no one seems to know anything about them."

As Sara Ella started to ask another question, Lisa interrupted her. "Please help me, Sara Ella, I have to find Angela." She stood up from her chair, still struggling to keep her composure. Sara Ella held her close and tenderly rubbed her back, as she sobbed uncontrollably.

"All I know, Lisa, is what Emma Lou told me—that Ruth went north with her daughter Naomi's family, as soon as the slaves were freed. That was right before the war ended, when President Lincoln signed the Emancipation Proclamation. She said they hoped to find work somewhere up North. But, I do not remember anything being said about your little girl, Angela." The statement was firm but there was a question in her voice as she finished it. "We have not heard anything from them, so I cannot begin to tell you where to look. I would suggest that we have Adam inquire around to see what he can learn about Ruth's family, and your little girl."

The question was still in her mind. *Angela? We know she died in childbirth. Or, did she?* Now Sara Ella began to question what she had been told about Goddard and Lisa's baby girl dying in childbirth. Why had she been told the baby died, if it was not true? But she said nothing.

Emma Lou came in from the garden and squealed with delight, when she saw Lisa. She clapped her hands and said, "Oh, mercy me! The Lo'd, He don' blessed us ag'in wit' mo' fam'ly that's come home! It's won'erful to see yo' Miss Lisa. Where's Massa Goddard?"

Sara Ella told Emma Lou that Goddard was killed in the war, and promised to explain further later.

"Now, Miss Sara Ella, don' yo' worry 'bout hep'n me in the kitchen. Yo' an' Miss Lisa jes' git yo' self on over to the cabin and freshen up. I'm do'in jes' fine here."

Sara Ella escorted Lisa to her cabin to lie down and rest. She sat in a chair and watched Lisa sleeping restlessly on the bed, and wondered about Angela. Was Angela really alive? Had Lisa and Goddard actually given her to Ruth's daughter to raise? Why would they do that? Why did they not want her? She rubbed her forehead, completely confused. She had so many questions that she hoped Lisa would answer soon.

After a while Sara Ella heard the supper bell ring for the men to come from the lumber mill.

Lisa turned, saw Sara Ella looking at her and said, "Am I really at Oaklayne? It's seems like it was a lifetime ago that I was here before."

"Yes, Lisa, you are at Oaklayne, what is left of it. You mentioned that you had a lot to tell us. Well, we have a lot to tell you, too.

Oaklayne is just now beginning to rise from the dust. Come on, shall we go see what Emma Lou has for us to eat this evening? Adam and the men will be here in a few minutes. Emma Lou rang the supper bell, and they usually make the trip down the hill in a hurry. Tom and Nathaniel are here. Do you remember them?"

Lisa nodded at the mention of both names. Sara Ella continued, "There is a new man, too. His name is Oscar, Colonel Oscar Baynes. He is here with six of the soldiers who served with him in the war. Then there is also Randy and Benjy, of course. Oh, I am sorry to have to tell you that Randy was blinded in the war. Anyway, there will be several of us at the supper table, and those that cannot fit around the table will sit wherever they can. Oh, and Adam has a limp from his time in Andersonville Prison."

The look on Lisa's face changed, as she frowned.

"Andersonville Prison? Adam was there? Oh, how awful...and Randy blind. I am not the only one that has gone through bad times in the last year...I guess everyone has their own story to tell."

Sara Ella nodded, then turned toward Lisa and held out her hand. "Let's be standing in the kitchen when they come in. They will be surprised and so happy to see you."

Randy and Benjy were in the kitchen helping Emma Lou when Lisa and Sara Ella came in, talking.

"Lisa!" Randy said, "I would know that voice anywhere!" He got up and, knowing the way, walked toward the door calling, "Lisa, Lisa!"

"Randy?" Lisa responded. "It is so good to see you. Randy!"

"Emma Lou must have intended to surprise me, because she did not tell us you are here. But, I think I surprised her when I recognized your voice. I would know you in a crowd of 100 people. Oh, I am so glad that you are here!"

They were embracing when they heard laughter. The men were talking jovially, as they left the wash basin and opened the door to come into the kitchen. Adam turned his head to look back at Oscar as he led the group through the door. Oscar followed, then Tom and Nathaniel. As Adam turned to reach for Sara Ella to kiss her, as he usually did when coming in from work, he saw Lisa. His eyes grew larger, and his mouth fell open.

"Lisa! Where did you come from?" Before she could answer, he continued, "We looked for you and Goddard everywhere! No one seemed to know what had happened to you!" He grabbed her and swung her around, her feet coming off the floor. He laughed and put her back on her feet, still holding on to her.

Suddenly he stopped and asked, "Where's Goddard? Where is my little brother?" The smile that had lightened her face as Adam held her suddenly disappeared, when he asked about Goddard.

Quickly, Sara Ella said, "Goddard is dead, Adam. Lisa just found out shortly before coming here to Oaklayne. He was killed in Richmond, attempting to escape as Sherman was invading." She paused, as sadness filled the room.

Then, Sara Ella changed the subject in a feeble attempt to lighten the mood and said, "Adam, please introduce Lisa to Oscar. We will eat when the other fellows have greeted her." She smiled, hugged Adam, and turned to assist Emma Lou with the serving of the meal.

As quickly as Oscar was introduced to Lisa, Tom and Nathaniel greeted her, both squeezing her hand in theirs. They were placed at the table, Tom, Nathaniel, Benjy and Oscar on one side, Sara Ella, Lisa and Emma Lou at the other, with Adam at the head of the table and Randy at the other end.

As always, hands were held to form a circle around the table. Adam returned thanks to God for the safe return of another member of their family, for the amount of work they had done this day, and then for the food they were about to eat. When he said, "Amen", everyone joined together in a second, "Amen".

The food immediately started around the table, and talk started, each, in turn, telling of the events of their day.

When it came Lisa's turn to speak, she looked at Sara Ella with tear-brimmed eyes, and said, "Sara Ella, would you mind speaking for me? If you do not mind, I would rather just listen."

Sara Ella put her arm around Lisa's shoulders and told everyone about Warren Callahan and Martha bringing her to Oaklayne by buggy, relaying Mr. Callahan's message to Adam about being sorry he could not stay long enough to see him. She explained how Martha, her husband Moses and Warren Callahan had been caring for Lisa for the past few weeks.

"What are your plans, Lisa?" Adam asked.

She looked across the table at him, and said firmly. "I'm going to try to find my daughter, Angela."

Suddenly, there was complete silence in the room, as everyone wondered what she meant. It was common knowledge that baby Angela had died as a newborn.

Breaking the spell, Emma Lou got up from the table to bring out a dish of custard pudding for everyone. The dessert was eaten in silence, as each person was lost in thought about what must have happened to Lisa for her to be so confused. Tom and Nathaniel excused themselves and quietly left the table, unable to speak. Then they climbed the stairs to go to bed.

Emma Lou started to clear the table, as Sara Ella turned and took Lisa by the hand, "Shall I get you settled in our cabin for the evening, dear. I know you must be tired."

As the ladies left the room, Adam and Oscar rose from the table and quietly went outside to sit in the darkness for a while, each with his own thoughts. After a short while they came back in the house, as Sara Ella was helping Emma Lou finish the supper clean up.

Adam went to Sara Ella, took her in his arms and kissed her longingly, then said, "Lisa's news gives us all a lot to think about. It is hard for me to fathom that my little brother, Goddard, is dead. I expect Lisa's confusion is based on the same kind of denial that I am feeling. So much tragedy we have all suffered. We need to pray for one another, that we will be able to pull ourselves together and help each other cope. I am glad that Lisa came here to Oaklayne."

Randy and Benjy were still finishing up chores in the kitchen, planning to head off to bed soon. Benjy remarked, "Randy, I wish you could have seen the looks on Adam's and Sara Ella's faces as they embraced tonight. I know they were happy to see Lisa, but her being here means we cannot leave for Washington City tomorrow as planned. So, their wedding is postponed again for a little while longer. I guess we will not be going now, at least not until they know what Miss Lisa's plans are."

Chapter 10

The following morning after breakfast, Lisa asked Sara Ella about Oscar Baynes. The only explanation she had been given was that he had been a Colonel in the Union Army during the war.

"Tell me about Oscar, Sara Ella. Does he have family here in the Richmond area? If not, where is his home? He is obviously a Yankee, which is not an especially endearing quality. But, he seems like a nice enough fellow. Adam sure seems taken with him. What do you think of him?"

Sara Ella answered, "Oscar was a Colonel in the Army Corps of Engineers during the war, so he was mostly involved in construction work, and didn't actually see much combat. He is from the north end of the Shenandoah Valley in Virginia. His family has a plantation there, near Strasburg."

Sara Ella went on telling Lisa about Oscar, but before long she realized Lisa was no longer listening. Since Lisa was obviously preoccupied with her own thoughts, she changed the subject.

"Adam and I are anxious to get married as soon as possible. I would love to have children before I get much older..." She stopped before saying more, remembering that Lisa had just lost her husband, and their son had died a few years back. She did not want to be cruel or sound unsympathetic.

Then her thoughts went back to Lisa's comment about finding their daughter, Angela. I remember distinctly that we were told their little girl baby was stillborn! This doesn't make any sense.

She looked at Lisa wondering, and asked, "Lisa, did you say you need to look for your daughter, Angela? You must be confused, my dear. With all that has happened to you, I am not surprised. Do you not remember, Lisa, your little girl was stillborn."

Lisa turned to her and said, "Sara Ella, it is a long and bitter story." She then told her the secret of the little girl's birth, how they gave her to Ruth's daughter to raise, and their reason for doing so.

When she had completed the story, Sara Ella sat speechless, pondering the seriousness of what Lisa had just shared with her. What kind of mother could give her child away like that? But, at the same time, what kind of life would the child have had if she had not given her away? The situation was clearly a complex one. Sara Ella did not like to think about what she would have done in the same circumstances.

Interrupting Sara Ella's train of thought, Lisa asked, "What are your plans for us for today? I saw you are doing laundry; can I help you fold and put it away? Or, is there something else you would rather I do?"

"No, that is okay, Lisa," Sara Ella said. "I will be helping Emma Lou as she begins preparations for supper, but we can handle things just fine."

"Actually," Lisa said, "I think I will walk around the plantation a bit then. I would like to walk over to the burial ground to pay my respects to Mother Layne and Senator Layne. Then, I may walk up to the lumber mill to see what is going on there. It must be quite an operation."

Sara Ella nodded and said, "Adam's parents are not buried here, Lisa. Do you not remember? Goddard had them buried in Richmond, for there was no way to get a body out here at the time, with the armies facing each other between here and Richmond." As Lisa was reminded, she looked at the floor and slowly shook her head. Then Sara Ella added, "I will warn you, it is a bit of a climb from here to the mill."

"I'll not be gone very long. I just want to get some air and see the operation of the mill. I'll be back in a while." She walked out the door.

As she walked along the way toward the mill, Lisa stopped every little bit to rest and look around. There was a light mist over the meadow, and mourning doves were singing her song. A bright yellow butterfly did its best to cheer her up, but her heart was much too heavy. Would she ever be happy again?

She marveled at the size of the many oak trees growing beside the trail like huge monuments to the stability of life. But in sad contrast, many others of these beautiful trees had fallen in their prime, obviously hit by cannon fire during the war...a stark reminder of her dear husband's death.

When Lisa had visited Oaklayne before she and Goddard were married, she had never had reason to venture up the trail to the mill. As she walked up a small knoll, the mill came into view. Several of the men were busy working at the huge saws, others carrying and stacking lumber as it was cut. The smell of the fresh-cut lumber was very pleasant, but the noise made her uncomfortable.

As she crested the top of the knoll, she heard Adam's voice shout out, "Alright, men, time to take a short break. Get a bit of water and sit down. I will time us. We have five minutes. Catch your breath and be ready to start working again."

Oscar, who was sitting beside Adam and facing her way, shaded his eyes from the sun, smiled and waved at her. As he waved back, Adam turned to see who had Oscar's attention.

"Lisa!" he exclaimed, as she approached the mill area. "What are you doing all the way up here?" As she nodded, he shook his head and continued, "Come, sit down on this pile of lumber with us..." he pointed to a stack of newly cut boards. Lisa sat down on the lumber, Adam on one side and Oscar on the other.

"Adam," Lisa said, "I simply must find Angela. Sara Ella said that she went north with Ruth, Naomi and Ben. Please help me find a way to go look for them."

From across the way Lisa heard someone yell, "Hey, Adam! We all thought that you and Miss Sara Ella was going to Washington City today to get hitched...what happened?"

But, then she heard someone else say, "Shut yo' mouth."

"Is that right, Adam? Were you and Sara Ella planning to leave today? Oh, I am so sorry to barge in at just the wrong time...or just the right time...I'm not sure which it is...I would have been so disappointed if I had gotten here just after you left. But, now I am holding you up, aren't I?"

"No, Lisa, you did not come at the wrong time. Sara Ella and I are so excited about knowing that you are safe and here with us. You belong here. You are family, and we love you."

"Well, I do not want to hold you up a minute longer. What can I do to help here while you are gone?"

With that, Oscar excused himself and went back to work, telling Adam to take as much time as he needed with Lisa.

"First," Adam said, "what is this about finding Angela?"

"Oh, I must find her, Adam. She is the only family that I have left."

"You mean except for all of us here at Oaklayne?"

"Well, yes, but you are not my own flesh and blood."

Then with complete abandon, Lisa told Adam the same emotion-filled story about Angela that she had shared with Sara Ella earlier that morning.

"Lisa, I just cannot see any way to bring Angela back to you. All we can do is pray that Ben will not find work up North, and will eventually come back to Virginia. We can pass the word around, so anyone who hears from them will let them know that we have a place for his family to live and a good job for him at Oaklayne plantation. Do you have any other ideas?"

"No, but I was hoping that you would. I know it sounds unreasonable, but somehow I just have to find her."

"I am sorry that I am not more help, but I will certainly pray for wisdom, and suggest that you do the same."

"Thank you Adam, I know that you would do anything you can for me. But, what can I do now to help you get going on that trip you had planned with Sara Ella?"

"Well, one thing that you could do is go with us to Washington City. Sara Ella told me last night that having you be her maid-of-honor at our wedding would make it complete. She was hoping to talk with you about it today. I will have Randy, Benjy and Tom there for support, and having you there with her would bring her great joy."

"Oh, Adam how can I say no. I know that Goddard would want me to be with you, since he cannot be here. But, maybe I should be looking for Angela, instead..."

"Lisa, 'North' is a very big place. Right now, after the war, anywhere alone is a dangerous place to be. Please search your heart and be realistic about this. I truly think that for you to be reunited with Angela...well, the Lord will have to intervene in a big way. Please go with us to Washington City on the train. We love you, and want you to be a part of our wedding."

"Thank you Adam. Thinking of Angela is what has been keeping me alive, after finding out about Goddard's death. But, I do see the futility of running after her, when I have no idea where to look. It will take me a while to adjust to being without my own family, but being here at Oaklayne with you and Sara Ella has made me feel safe and loved. So, yes. Yes I would love to go with you to Washington City to be Sara Ella's maid-of-honor at your wedding."

"Lisa, I'm so pleased that you will be going with us. But, now that I have shared with you what Sara Ella should have been allowed to discuss with you herself, perhaps you could go back down there and make it easy for her to ask you about being her maid-of-honor. I have overstepped my place this time, for sure!"

"What was that all about?" asked Oscar, as Adam returned to stand beside him at the mill.

"Lisa wanted me to help her go north to look for her little three year old daughter Angela, whom she has not seen since the child was a tiny baby. She has almost no information as to where to begin looking for her. But, I think I convinced her of the unreasonableness of such an adventure. I am relieved that she has agreed to go with us to Washington City, instead."

Chapter 11

"Before I forget, Oscar, there is something that I need your help with right away," Adam remarked, as he returned to work. "As you know, Sara Ella, Benjy and Randy have been helping Emma Lou fix meals every day for the men. When we go to Washington City, she will be very short handed. So, please put a rush on hiring kitchen help for Emma Lou. She will also need help with laundry chores and cleaning, of course. Feel free to hire as many workers as you think it will take. Emma Lou will be a big help with any questions you may have, so please discuss it with her."

"I understand, Adam. You're right, there are so many things being done around here that we don't think about. I will make a point of expressing my appreciation when I talk with Emma Lou about getting her some help."

They continued their work until the supper bell rang, then went to the house for their supper meal. Sara Ella met Adam outside and scolded him, "How could you tell Lisa about being my maid-of-honor! Do you not know that the bride should be the one to do that?"

"I am so sorry, I…" Sara Ella abruptly kissed him mid-sentence and said, "Thank goodness you brought her to her senses about Angela. I am not sure that she would have agreed to go with us to Washington City if I would have asked her on my own, without your help. Did I ever tell you that I love you, Adam Layne?"

After they had eaten, Adam asked Sara Ella, "Is everything packed and ready to take with us to Washington City?"

Sara Ella looked at him and then at Lisa who smiled.

"Lisa, will it take you long to pack?"

"Well, considering that I came here with the clothes on my back, a shawl and my reticule, I don't think that it will take me long at all."

"What about it Randy, can you and Benjy be ready early in the morning?"

"Very much so! We will be ready as early as you would like."

Then Adam said with a grin, "Great, then Lord willing we will be on a fast train to matrimony tomorrow."

Then, putting his right index finger in the air like he just remembered something, Oscar said, "Adam, I need to change the subject for a minute. Earlier, you gave me this list of food and supplies that we will need to get for while you are gone. Well, I have been thinking that we also need some tools and mortar for this construction project before you get back. Do you have the resources available for me to purchase that much?"

"Obtain whatever you need," said Adam, giving Oscar some cash.

After supper Oscar pulled Adam aside and asked, "Okay, Adam. Would you mind telling me what is going on with Lisa?"

"It is a long story, Oscar. Shall we go outside?" Adam whispered.

Chapter 12

"Ah's nev'ah bin on no train b'fore, Massa Adam! Ah's sho' glad Tom is wif' us!" Benjy said, as they were waiting to board the train at the depot.

"Papa", Randy asked, "how long will it take us to get to Washington City?"

"We should be there by this evening, son."

"Boys," Adam said, "there is something I have needed to talk with both of you about. It is important, so please listen carefully.

"Both of you are fine young men now, so I have decided that I should no longer refer to you as boys. I am very proud of you both, and I know that, from here on out, you will do your best to make good decisions in life. I plan to let you decide the direction of your lives, but I will also give you my opinion when I have the opportunity. While on this trip I would like for each of you to consider your future—what is your personal calling in life? Is that fair? Randy?"

"Oh, yes, Papa. I will do my best to make you proud of me, even with my blindness."

"Benjy?"

"Massa Adam, yo' been like a Papa to me, and Ah's mo' grateful than Ah know how to 'spress. Yes Sah', Ah's lookin' fo' my callin', but not 'til Ah's sho' that Randy don' need me no mo'. My first callin' is to him. Ah loves him and yo', Massa Adam. Thank yo' fo' lettin' me be part of yo' fam'ly."

"Benjy, you are a jewel. Thank you for your commitment to Randy and the rest of this family."

"Now that we have established the fact that both of you are men, I think it is time for you to refer to me accordingly. From this time forward Randy, you shall call me Father, not Papa. And you, Benjy will call me Adam, not Massa Adam. Is that understood?

"And another thing, men—what do you think about being called Randall and Benjamin from now on, instead of Randy and Benjy?"

Randy turned up his nose and said, "I get called Randall when I'm in trouble...if it is all the same to you, I would rather just be Randy."

But, Benjy said he liked the idea of being called Benjamin.

Sara Ella squeezed Adam's hand and smiled.

"And, I think it is about time we had some feminine input in this family, what do you think, gentlemen?" Adam asked with a wink.

"Yes Papa...I mean, Father...I agree."

"Yes, sah', Adam, sah'! Yo' sho' is right 'bout that!"

Sara Ella, who had noticed Benjy's intelligence on many occasions, turned and addressed him directly, "Benjamin, son...as you know, I am a school teacher. Therefore, I probably notice schooling in others more than most people do. It is obvious to me that you are a very well educated young man. I asked Adam about this once, and he told me that Randy shared everything he learned with you, as you were growing up together. I am wondering if the slang that you have grown up with is important to you, or would you prefer that I teach you proper English?"

Benjamin hesitated a moment, then stood slowly to his feet in a very dramatic fashion, cleared his throat and answered eloquently, with perfect grammar and diction, "Miss Sara Ella Gary (soon to be Madam Sara Ella Layne), it is with great pleasure that I address you today as Benjamin Layne. I have been in the long and lucrative employ of General Adam Layne, since I was set free by Mr. Lincoln with his Emancipation Proclamation.

"It is true, as you have been informed by my employer, that I have been educated along with my dear friend and comrade Randall Layne. I am fully aware that I am, as you suggested, in need of a great deal more education than has already, by the grace of God, been graciously bestowed upon me up until this time. However, from this day forward, I will use only proper English when addressing you, if that is what you prefer. I am as always at your service, my lady." Then he bowed and kissed the back of her hand, before smiling and taking his seat again.

As everyone broke out in an uproar of laughter, Sara Ella grabbed Benjy and gave him a big hug. "Please, Master Benjamin Layne, accept my most sincere apologies."

"Apology accepted, Madam," Benjamin said with his head held high and a twinkle in his eye.

Chapter 13

"It looks like you have most of what I need here," Oscar said to the shopkeeper. "I see the saws, drills, bores, planes, lathes...and I see mortar over there in that corner...but I cannot find the draw knives. Do you have any of those in stock?" Oscar was like a kid in a candy store, looking at all the tools and supplies the merchant had for sale.

"Uh, yes I think there are some in the back that have not been put out on the shelves yet. Let me go check. We are selling this stuff so fast that we have trouble keeping it in stock. You are in luck though because we just got a shipment in last night, should have them back in the receiving room. I will be right back."

Oscar continued to gather up what he needed and put it out on the counter. "Excuse me sir," he said as he accidentally bumped into a man, as he was backing away. "This place is so full, and..." then looking up he said in astonishment, "Clifford! Clifford O'Riley!"

"That's Sergeant O'Riley to you sir," the man said with a big grin on his face.

"Why, you have not changed a bit! Still that tall, dark, handsome guy, barking out orders! I remember you and your men helping guard the White House during the war."

"That's me, sir."

"Please, just call me Oscar. What are you doing here?"

Clifford removed his hat and said, "Got sent here to Richmond to work these men and clean this place up. Our wheel barrow turned over and one of the handles broke. I sent some yo-yo here to get a new handle, but he didn't come back. He's goin' to be put on KP duty when I find him!"

"When we get through here, let's get some supper together, if you know where we can find something good?" asked Oscar.

"Are you buyin'?"

"Of course, anything for you Sarge."

"Here you go, the storekeeper interrupted. How many of these draw knives do you need, sir?"

Oscar settled up on the supplies that he needed for the plantation house and then let Sergeant O'Riley show him the way to Aunt Bertha's Kitchen at the Mosselman Hotel.

As they were seated, Oscar asked, "What is going on here in Richmond? This place is a mess! It looks like the whole city burned...what isn't burned is otherwise destroyed."

With a serious expression on his bearded face, Clifford said, "The Rebels set fire to everything of value as they evacuated, including the Mayo Bridge, because they didn't want the Yankees to have the city. The fire was completely out of control before the Yankees arrived to put it out. Mostly, they sent me here to do what I can to help keep the peace. Me and my men, we're just trying to help out while we are here, because so many people don't have the money to get things repaired enough to get back in business. Worst of all, at night the looting is terrible. For the most part, it is folks who don't have anything left, not even food. Even those who still have a functional business can't make a go of it though, because nobody has money to buy anything. It's very sad."

"Hello. Gentlemen, my name is Elsie. We are serving pot roast today with green beans and tomatoes. I also just took some fresh rolls out of the oven. What would you like to drink? Oh, in case you're still hungry when you finish your supper, Aunt Bertha made fresh apple pie this morning."

"Well Elsie, everything sounds scrumptious, so we will have two big portions, including a generous piece of that pie for each of us. Do you have some hot coffee?"

"Yes sir, I brewed a fresh pot about a half hour ago."

"That would be great for me, what about you Sarge?"

"Coffee sounds perfect, thank you."

"Coming right up, two suppers, two coffees and two apple pies."

Oscar noticed right away that Elsie's eyes were a lovely hazel green, and they snapped like firecrackers when she talked. Her thick dark brown hair was pulled back in a bun, except for one loose curl that escaped—it bobbed up and down when she walked, teasing him.

Clearing his head with a quick shake, Oscar said, "Clifford, you were telling me about keeping the peace here. What seems to be the biggest trouble you're encountering?"

"It's mostly that so many people are without jobs. They've lost their homes to carpetbaggers, and eventually even run out of food and essentials for their families. Those carpetbagger crooks are coming here, mostly from the north, buying these folks out for a pittance of what their property is worth. People sell out of desperation, so they can buy food and necessities. They think they will surely find work, and then be able to find another place to live. But, when they still can't find a job, it doesn't take very long for their money and supplies to run out. Now, I ask you, how do you lock someone up for stealing food for his family? ...And then how do you appease the struggling family that they stole from? Then, don't forget to throw in the scoundrels that just steal to re-sell things. They actually make a good living doing that."

"I had no idea all of this was going on, Clifford."

"Oh, that's just the tip of the iceberg, Oscar. The worst culprits of all are the Fat Cats that are coming in and buying out all of the small businesses. Then they lower their prices to ridiculous levels, forcing the other merchants to have to sell out to them, because they can't compete and make any money. And, then guess what? More people without jobs...and they didn't get enough money when they sold their business to start over someplace else."

"You can't do this to me Mr. Mosselman!" Elsie said as she burst out the kitchen door. "I've been working here at Aunt Bertha's for you and your wife Mildred for more than four years! You've been wonderful to provide me with food and a room of my own. But I don't have anywhere to go, and there aren't any jobs!"

"Sh-h-h-h, Elsie. Mildred and I have waited just as long as we can," said Jacob Mosselman. "We are in debt over our heads trying to keep the hotel and the restaurant open! But, now we have been made an offer that will at least pay our debt and give us just enough to survive. We are closing both the hotel and the restaurant. I am so sorry, but there is simply nothing we can do."

Elsie flopped into a chair and lifted her apron, put her head in it and wept softly. Then she suddenly pulled herself together, squared her shoulders, lifted her beautiful head, rebellious curl and all, and said, "Thank you, Mr. Mosselman, for all you have done for me." At that she took off her apron, laid it on the table, turned and marched out the front door.

"Uh, excuse me Sarge," Oscar said, "I need to chase down our supper." And Oscar ran out the front door.

"Hey, Elsie, wait up!"

She turned around astonished to hear her name being called.

"You forgot to bring us our supper."

"Did you not hear? I just lost my job!"

"Oh, yes I heard that, but we're still hungry."

"What part of this do you not understand? Or, are you stupid enough to think that I should continue working for no pay, just because you are hungry? I'll have you know that I have very little time to try to find a place to have a roof over my head and...and...and..." she choked back tears.

"I am so sorry, I just wanted you to come back with me and tell me about it. I might have a solution for you."

"What kind of a solution? You need to know that I am not that kind of girl, sir!"

"Suit yourself; I am just trying to help if you're interested."

"Well okay, I guess I could at least hear you out."

"Oscar escorted her back to the restaurant and said as they went through the door, "Now look, you've caused my food to get cold!"

"What! I've caused your food to get cold! What do you mean to blame me?"

"Have you had your lunch today, Elsie?"

"No, I do not...I mean did not...eat until all of the patrons were gone."

"Excuse me", Oscar said to Clifford and Elsie as he went up to the kitchen and knocked on the door. When Aunt Bertha came to the door with red eyes from crying, he said, "May we please have another supper just like the ones we ordered already from Elsie?"

"Oh, yes sir," she said in a squeaky voice. "Please tell her I am sorry they are closing my restaurant. I wish there was something I could do to help her..."

"Thank you very much," Oscar said as he went to sit back down.

"Thank you, sir. Your friend here tells me that you are Colonel Oscar Baynes. Well, Colonel Baynes, that was very sweet of you to buy my supper, but I am afraid that you still do not understand that eating a meal today is not my biggest concern."

"My friend is Sergeant Clifford O'Riley. We've known each other for years. As for your supper, I was thinking that you could pay for it yourself."

Elsie jumped up from her chair nearly knocking it over. "Of all the mean tricks..."

"Sit down, sit down...there you go again, not understanding anything about what is going on. Be a little more patient and listen before you keep jumping to conclusions."

Flopping down in the chair again with a thud, arms crossed firmly across her ample chest, Elsie said under her breath, "It is you who does not understand, Colonel Oscar Baynes..."

"Ah, here is your meal, my dear. Maybe now we can all eat in peace, while Clifford and I catch up. We have not seen each other in a long time. By the way Clifford, I thought it was polite to wait for a lady, before you start shoveling food in your mouth."

"But you were gone when…."

"I know, I know. Now may we eat?"

Elsie started to eat fast, clanking her fork like a field hand at chow time.

"Are you in a hurry, Miss Elsie?" Oscar asked.

"I am, indeed! I've got to get out of here and find a way to pay for this meal!"

At that remark Oscar almost choked and spit out his food, but then started laughing instead.

"So, you think this is funny do you! My life, as I know it, is about to end. My fiancé didn't come back from the war, and now, not only do I not have a job, a place to sleep or a way to pay for another meal, you think it's funny!" she was red in the face and started to cry again, as she jumped to her feet to leave.

"Please, I am so sorry…I've gone too far at your expense. Now if you will listen, I've been trying to tell you that I have a job for you if you want it, and that is how you could conceivably pay for your meal yourself. I will however, be paying for your meal, whether or not you are interested in the job.

"The job is at Oaklayne Plantation, a few miles outside Richmond on the James River. It belongs to General Adam Layne, and I am in his employ to reconstruct the plantation mansion. There are several men working there and we will be hiring more. One of the ladies who had been working there has had to leave, and we are in need of more help, cooking, cleaning and doing whatever needs to be done there.

"You will receive a very good wage and a place to stay, though for now it is very primitive accommodations. You will need to bunk with Emma Lou, the lady who is in charge. I assure you that you will find her delightful. As soon as I'm able to finish my supper and this apple pie, I will be going to pick up food and supplies for the kitchen. When I have finished, I will come back here and ask for you. If you would like to have the job, it would be my pleasure to take you there."

Elsie was speechless and did not remember when she had sat back down in her chair and taken another bite of her food…but, she knew she must have, because she sat there the whole time he was talking with a bite in her mouth and had to swallow before she could answer.

71

"I am so sorry that I misjudged you! I would love to take the job, sir! Oh thank you, thank you...you came along at just the right time. My goodness I have so much to do to get ready and I have to pack as well..."

"Uh hum, now can I finish my supper?" Oscar said with a smile, pleased that this adorable girl with the bewitching curl had accepted his offer.

"Oh, I am sorry again! Here, you can have what is left of mine. I am too excited to eat it. I will be ready when you get back. I promise." And with that off she ran.

"Clifford, now do you think that we can eat in peace?" Oscar said.

"Aw, why'd you have to put that girl through all of that?"

"I just could not help myself, Clifford...she made it so easy!"

Chapter 14

JUNE 9, 1865

As the carriage pulled up in front of the Layne Townhouse in Washington City, Benjamin turned to Randy and asked, "Do you remember what this place looks like, Randy? Oh, it is grand! For starters, there are large balustrades up both sides of the huge mahogany double doors out front...." As they continued walking up the stairs and into the home, Benjamin described everything to Randy in perfect detail. Listening to Benjamin eloquently depict everything that Randy could not see, made everyone appreciate the residence more than ever before.

"Inside here, as you come in, don't forget the foyer has an intricately inlaid marble floor that was done with precision, back when this place was built a long time ago. Then, in the parlor the marble fireplace goes all the way to the ceiling," Benjamin motioned upward with his hands, even though he knew Randy could not see the gesture...he just could not help himself.

"The delicately carved mantle is supported on both sides by columns that have vines and flowers carved on them. There are two big red Chippendale wing back chairs on both sides of the fireplace, with a Queen Ann tea table between them, where your Papa, I mean Father, always sat to read with your Grandfather. Over by the big bay window there is a settee and a small gold Queen Ann chair, with a Queen Ann drop leaf table between them. That gold leaf oil lamp is on that table...the one that we were always warned by your Grandmother not to knock over, remember? Oh, and remember how the colors of blue, red, green and gold are perfectly blended. Your Grandmother certainly knew how to decorate beautifully. Everything is just as she left it. Yes, this place is grand..."

"Thank you Benjamin," Randy said. "You brought back wonderful memories of this place for me. It feels like I should go over to that small Queen Ann chair, extend my hand and feel my Grandmother take it...then direct my other hand to her elbow for me to lead her to the large dining room table, seating her there for a delicious supper." Randy choked back tears, as he remembered his Grandmother, Elizabeth Layne.

"It has not changed since I came here with Laura before Goddard and I were married," Lisa said as she fingered the beautiful heavy tapestry curtains.

"Oh, Adam," Sara Ella said breathlessly. "It is so magnificent! Everything is perfect, and there is no damage at all." She realized that Adam had been watching her, as she ran from room to room, overwhelmed with what she saw, knowing that she had never been there before. So, she put her arms up around his neck to look into his eyes. "We're going to have a wonderful time here. I cannot wait for us to be married.

Now, I know that you are very anxious to go see Secretary Stanton tomorrow. Shall we unpack, so you can leave early in the morning?"

Lisa was standing in front of the big entry table, looking into the gold leaf framed mirror hanging above it and the petticoat mirror at the bottom. She was not at all pleased with what she saw! Before leaving Oaklayne, Sara Ella had sacrificed her best skirt and blouse and altered them the best she could to fit Lisa. But, they could not do anything about Sara Ella's blouse being much too tight across the bosom, and the waist of the skirt was still much too loose. Her own red dress was thread bare, but it was the only thing she had. Her reflection in the mirror would have been humorous to her if she had not been feeling so melancholy.

As she stood there looking at how ridiculous she looked, she wondered...*what is going to become of me? How can I go on without Goddard? If only I could find Angela, perhaps that is the answer...* Her eyes were filling with tears as she stood in her own little world, with the joy, activity and excitement of the others all around her.

Sara Ella caught a glimpse of Lisa and said to Adam, "Would it be alright if I ask Tom to escort Lisa and I to some fine clothing stores here tomorrow? If we had some new clothes to wear, perhaps we could be of assistance in hosting some of your colleagues here at the Townhouse while we are here?"

"Of course, dear! That is a great idea. Tom would you like to spend the day tomorrow with the ladies?"

"It would be my pleasure," Tom replied with a smile.

Sara Ella's organizational skills began to function as she suggested, "Benjy...I mean Benjamin...do you mind staying in Randy's room with him until he knows his way around, then you can move into the room upstairs with Tom? I will stay in the room next door to

Randy's with Lisa until Adam and I get married, if that's okay with you, Lisa. Tom if you do not mind could you take one room in the dormer on the third floor and we will use the other one for guests?"

"Adam does that sound like a good plan to you?" she said, as she saw him grinning at her.

"I am glad to see that you're already taking charge of the house, my dear. My mother would be so proud!"

Secretary Stanton filled the room as he burst from his office and thrust his hand out to greet Adam. He was a large man with dark hair and a beard. "Come in, come in!" The wheeze in his voice as he greeted him reminded Adam that the man suffered from a serious case of asthma.

Pacing back and forth in his office, Stanton was restless as he said, "So much is happening my head is spinning! What a relief to have you here! I've just got to have someone I can trust to help me keep some perspective. I knew that you were a great help to Lincoln, for when you came to see him it always seemed to give him peace. He told me once that you were one of the few that he was sure he could trust. When I asked you to come back here as soon as possible, I had no idea how much I would need you, Adam!"

Adam's cheeks flushed with embarrassment, as he said, "You are giving me way too much credit, sir. I am sure it was Mr. Lincoln's daily prayers that made him such a great man. Each time I came to see him, I gave him my report and then just sat and listened to that great man talk."

"You have no idea what a rare commodity that is around here...listening, I mean. No one here ever listens; they are all talking at the same time. Why, a person cannot even hear his own thoughts, let alone finding the right vision for the future. I do remember though, the role you played in helping Lincoln realize how incompetent Secretary Cameron was. The war may have turned out altogether different if Cameron hadn't been relieved of his duties when he was."

Adam could not help but notice that Secretary Stanton was doing a lot more talking than listening.

He immediately continued, "Things here are really getting out of control. President Johnson ordered the establishment of a military commission to put the surviving conspirators who were involved in Lincoln's assassination on trial, under my supervision, of course. We have now arrested those involved, and we will have them punished soon."

"I remember," Adam said, "you were working on that when I left to go home to Oaklayne."

"Well, you know that Johnson is a Democrat and a pro-Union southerner, right? Well, you may not know that his strong commitment to the Union is the biggest reason Lincoln chose him to run as his Vice President in 1864. Johnson appealed to both sides in the election, and helped Lincoln get re-elected. And, he supported Lincoln while he was in office as Vice President for that month before Lincoln was murdered.

"After Lincoln's death, Johnson said that he was going to continue to govern the same way Lincoln did. He told us to look at his record, which was less moderate than Lincoln's, so we felt comfortable enough with his leadership. He even went out of his way to reassure me, by keeping me on as Secretary of War. As you know Lincoln had appointed me, and that is when you and I started working together. So, I was encouraged when he did not replace me."

The more excited he became, as he was talking, the more the big man wheezed, until it became somewhat hard for him to breathe and talk at the same time.

"It seemed like the logical choice to me," Adam said. "There is not anyone else who could handle the job."

"Well, by the end of May he was already changing course. It is unconscionable, but he immediately pardoned the former confederate leaders. Can you believe it? How can a country survive when they win a war, pardon their enemies and then invite them back to their house? It is ludicrous!" Stanton pounded his desk with the side of his fist and struggled to catch another breath and go on.

Adam broke in and responded in disgust, "Why would he do something like that, with the North being so angry about southern radicals being the ones who assassinated Lincoln, as well as having lost so many of their sons in the war? The North wants strong policies against the South, not pardons!"

"It does not make sense to me," Stanton said, "but some people around here are saying that he did it just so those aristocratic southerners will have to bow down to him."

"It certainly is not what I would have expected of Johnson after he had earlier expressed a totally different approach to governing," said Adam.

Stanton turned and looked out his window, shaking his head.

76

"Adam, I need you to help me think these things through, so I can make rational decisions. You know that I love this country more than anything in the world. It is important to me to do all that I can to promote a strong and healthy nation, and I encourage others to do the same. Will you please come right away whenever I summon you, and make an appearance here any time you are in the city on other business? In other words, I'm asking you to be my personal adviser."

"Secretary Stanton, sir....You and I go way back...." Adam began, but was interrupted.

"Please just call me Edwin, or if you prefer just Stanton, like most everybody else does here."

"Thank you Stanton," Adam continued. "I am humbled by your confidence in me. I would be honored to be of service to you. Of course, I will keep all of our conversations confidential."

"Great, that is great. Now, what other business do you have here in the city?" Stanton said as he sat down in an oversized wing back leather chair and gestured to Adam to have a seat in a matching chair beside him.

As Adam sat down, he grinned somewhat sheepishly, "Well sir, I am here to get married to Sara Ella Gary, a beautiful school teacher from Macon, Georgia."

"Well, it is about time! I am happy for you, Adam. Life is sure lonely without a wife," Stanton said, looking down at his hands, where they rested calmly in his lap. "We have talked about that before, have we not, since both of us have prematurely lost our wives to death in the past. I am so pleased that you have been able to find someone to spend the rest of your life with. Congratulations! I am looking forward to meeting the Southern Belle who has won your heart. When and where is the big day?"

"Well that is the big question. I am afraid I do not know...guess that is not a very good answer for a newly appointed Adviser is it?' Adam said with a smirk.

Both men laughed and agreed to meet again soon.

As Adam was walking back to the townhouse, his mind was churning. Between his troubling conversation with Stanton about the events of late in Washington City and what he needed to do to get married, he could not seem to think straight. Just then, his thoughts were interrupted by someone calling his name.

"General Layne, General Layne!"

Adam turned to see a well-dressed young gentleman who looked familiar, but he could not place who he was.

"I am John Kendall. Remember, you and I met on Lincoln's funeral train. I was a reporter for the New York Times back then, so I am the one who told you the sad news that Hamilton Bromney had been killed in the war. Sorry to remind you of that..."

"Yes, I remember," Adam said. "I am surprised that you recognized me. It is good to see you again, John."

"Thank you," John continued, "We have a common acquaintance that I am on my way to meet with right now. He is the main type setter for the Washington Examiner newspaper here. If you will agree to come with me, I will wait to tell you who it is until you see him. You will both love the surprise!"

As they walked into the newspaper office John greeted the receptionist and said to him, "This is General Adam Layne. I would like to take him in to see Scott, please."

"Sure you can take him back," he said without hesitation.

John and Adam walked back through oceans of cluttered desks, where people were vigorously writing or chewing on their pencils. Some were yelling ideas and commands back and forth across the room to one another. When they arrived in a large room in the back of the building, a man was standing beside a huge machine. John called out over the noise of the machinery, "Scott, look who I have with me!"

Scott looked up, obviously a little exasperated at the interruption, but then beamed as he recognized Adam and quickly extended his hand.

"I do not believe it!" he said. "It is really you!"

"Scott Bryan, I have not seen you since I left Laramie! You were a Colonel in the Union Army then," Adam said.

"General Layne! I'm not surprised that you survived also, sir. And that is a good thing, because you're the best that the military has to offer. Let me turn this blasted machine off so we can hear ourselves think!"

Scott walked around to the other side of the behemoth and shut it off, then continued, "Sir, I've had the thrill of sharing many of our soldiering stories with John here, who wrote me about meeting you on Lincoln's train. I saw that article he wrote...what a tragedy. The next time I saw John I told him all about our working together in Wyoming. Somehow you always seem to come up in our conversations...I will often say, "Well, General Layne would do it this way....""

"Scott, what do you do here at the newspaper and what is this machine?" Adam queried.

"I'm a typesetter, sir. This machine is what prints the newspaper so you can read it. I guess you can tell by looking at me that it can be a kind of messy job," Scott said and laughed. "Pull up a chair where we can visit a little, before I have to get back to work." Then Scott said, "John, tell the General what you have been hearing around town, lately."

"Please call me Adam; it is great to have friends here in town."

"Okay, Adam. What Scott is talking about is the odd things that President Johnson is doing. We were all so sure that he was a strong leader for the Radical Republicans, with the views he expressed shortly after Lincoln was killed. But, now he seems to be siding with the white southerners who want white supremacy. He has pardoned all of their Confederate leaders. It is very strange. The newspapers are really hopping with this story. It makes great news."

Adam was shocked that Scott and John were already privy to what he had just learned from Secretary Stanton. "I am fascinated about how fast you have this information. I would love to keep up with it. Is there a way that we can meet when you have breaking news, so I will know what is going on as soon as you do?"

Scott looked at John, and then John said, "I do not see any reason why not, that is if you're not going to give it to another newspaper."

Adam said, "The only person that I would like your permission to repeat it to, would be Secretary Stanton."

Scott looked at John, then John gave him a one sided grin. "Well, okay, then it is a plan," Scott said. "When we have any breaking political news, we will immediately send a courier to you. If you are back at your plantation at the time, we will send a telegram to be delivered to you immediately. How does that sound?"

"Great! It will be very interesting, keeping up with you, gentlemen! Thanks!"

"Now, I have to get on my way. My bride-to-be is eagerly awaiting my help in planning our wedding. My sister-in-law, the matron-of-honor, will also be offering her counsel. Do either of you have any idea how to plan such things?"

With palms facing forward and head tipped down and to the side, Scott and John laughed heartily, and said in unison, "Not me!"

Adam smirked, "I do not have a clue either, gentlemen..."

Scott said, "I can print your invitations for you, but that is the only contribution I can make. Oh, my wife, Marie, is an excellent seamstress. She works closely with most of the department stores here in the city, so she would probably know who could help with dresses, flowers and such things. She would have a great time helping...uh...what did you say your fiancée's name is?"

"Oh, I am sorry, I do not think I said her name. It is Sara Ella Gary. I know that she will not care about the event being really fancy. But, I want our wedding to make memories that she will always treasure."

"Marie will know exactly what to do, and where to find everything you need," said Scott.

"Great, Scott! ...Oh, I don't believe I just said that!" Adam said laughing out loud. "If you and Marie do not have plans for supper tomorrow night, could you please join us? Marie and Sara Ella could talk about wedding plans."

"We would love to, wait until I tell her, she will be overjoyed, I am sure! Now, where do you live?"

Chapter 15

Just a few miles back, Trevor and August passed by the small railroad town of Tennille, Georgia. As they rode along, they could not help but notice unmistakable signs that Union troops had been through the area on their march to the sea.

One trademark Sherman's men often left in their path was railroad tracks wrapped around tree trunks. What an odd sight to see. The men heated the iron rail until it was soft enough to bend, then they conformed it to the nearest tree, rendering it completely useless to the Rebel troops in the process.

To avoid detection by disgruntled Rebels, they avoided roads and traveled across country. The devastating destruction to land and property the two men observed, took their breath away. As they came up over a rise, just ahead they could see a bridge that had been burned, and some men apparently working to repair it.

Watching from a safe distance, August turned to his brother and said, "Trevor, look at that! They're doing it all wrong. They'll never get that bridge rebuilt, with those joists at that angle! What are they thinking? Someone's going to get hurt trying to cross that sucker, that is, if they ever get it far enough along to use it. I say, we should go help them."

"Oh, no you don't! We need to mind our own business and keep our distance from these Johnny Rebs, so's we can keep our nice short necks short!"

"Hey! What yo' gawkin' at?" one of the men yelled in their direction.

August responded by tipping his hat back on his head in a rather cocky manner, then crossing his leg up over the horn of his saddle, "Just sitting here wondering how on earth you men expect that bridge to hold any weight across it? That is, if you ever get it to the place where you can use it. Why, the way you are going about it, when it is done, it would not hold the weight of my little sister's kitty cat!"

Trevor, always the more cautious of the two brothers, said, his voice low and calm, "Let's go, August...these men do not exactly seem friendly..."

Another of the men raised his hammer and railed, "Why are y'all takin' note o' our bridge, anyway? Ain't y'all some o' them Yankees what burnt this here bridge in the first place?"

By then, Trevor and August were completely surrounded by the dozen or so men who had been trying to fix the bridge.

Raising the reigns of his horse, Trevor said, "We are just passing through. We do not mean no harm. Have a nice day gents."

"They is Yankees! Just listen to 'em talk! And look at them thar' saddlebags!" another man shouted. "Yeah, I'd knowed them purdy black Yankee saddlebags and them Union haversacks any whares."

Another man growled, "Grab 'em boys! We'll show 'em spies what we thinks o' Yankees a snoopin' 'round these parts!"

With that, several men grabbed Trevor and August and wrestled them down from their horses. They threw them to the ground and started kicking and beating them with their fists. Then, standing them back to their feet, the mob continued to beat them and yell, "Curse you, Yankees!"

Someone shouted, "Git a rope y'all! Let's rid this world o' two more 'o them Yankee vermin!"

Then someone else said, "Hey! I say we take 'em to town and let Doc see 'em hang fer killin' Jamie. Him 'n Joy been sufferin' awful, 'count o' them Yankees killin' their son."

When they reached town, dragging Trevor and August behind their horses by ropes tied around their wrists, some of the townspeople came out and joined in the throng. The crowd started chanting, "Yankees! Kill them Yankees!" Someone showed up with a rope that was suitable for hanging, and the heated fury of the mob was heightened further. They came to a stop in front of the livery stable.

Just then, a tall broad shouldered older gentleman with balding hair came out of his office to see the commotion. He quickly called out, "What is all this about killing Yankees, Billy Joe?"

Billy Joe turned, swinging a long rope from between the fingers of his left hand, walked toward the older man and said, "Come on out here Doc, an' you'll see! We done catched us some Yankees snoopin' 'round! We's gonna' teach 'em a lesson. Wanna' watch?"

"I believe I'll do just that," the Doctor said as he closed the door.

Doctor Ralph Fowler and Billy Joe Pritchett approached the crowd, as several men were lifting the two nearly-unconscious Yankees from the ground.

"Whoa, there! What exactly is going on here?" Ralph said, holding up his hand.

"We've done got us some gen-u-ine Yankee spies, Doc," someone said.

"In case y'all hadn't heard," Ralph said, "it's not a crime anymore to be a Yankee. Besides, how do you know they are spies?"

"Oh, y'all should'a seed 'em lookin' at that bridge we been workin' on. What else would they be doin' messin' 'round, hidin' behin' the bushes?" asked Billy Joe.

"Yeah!" another man shouted out, "it's fo' sho' they's spies all right! Look at them saddlebags! An' y'all should'a heard 'em beggin' us to let 'em go in that thar uppity accent. Y'all kin tell they's Yankees, an' we's gonna' git rid of 'em 'fer killin' our people."

"Wait just a minute here men," said the Doctor. "Have y'all listened to what they have to say for themselves?"

Billy Joe raised the rope in the air and shouted so the entire crowd could hear, "No need fo' talkin' now, they's gots to go! We bro't 'em here, 'cause we fig'ered y'all 'd want to see 'em hang fo' killin' Jamie. It's the fault 'o them blasted Yanks, an' we gonna hang 'em fer it."

Ralph motioned with both hands, pushing air toward the ground in a calming gesture and said, "Now, y'all know that we lost as much as any of you did in this war. But, I'd sure like to talk to these men before y'all lynch them. Could you please bring them into my office? After I speak with them, I'll tell you what I learned. Is that fair?"

Billy Joe stomped his foot like a toddler having a tantrum and said, "Aw Doc, we was lookin' forward to this here hangin' right now... But, what about it men, can Doc have his fun with 'em first?"

Someone yelled out, "Yep! Doc deserves that much, on a'count 'o Jamie."

The doctor ran ahead of the men who were dragging Trevor and August, one man on each side, grabbing them up under their arms. As soon as he got inside his office Ralph called, "Joy! Joy, come quickly, I am going to need your help!"

Ralph's wife, Joy, came from their living quarters in the back of the building, just as the crowd of men roughly threw Trevor and August down on the floor.

"There ya' go Doc. Have yo fun wit' 'em, then come git us so'z we can finish our hangin'," said one of the men.

"Thank y'all for bringing them in. I'll come and let you know when I'm ready," Ralph said, hastily encouraging the men out the door.

When the door was shut, Joy ran to help the injured men on the floor asking, "What on earth happened to these poor men?"

"Well", Ralph said, as he was helping Trevor to his feet, "the men who have been trying to rebuild the Oconee River Bridge think that these men are Yankee spies. But, they did not listen to them before they hauled off and beat them up. Hopefully, we can patch them up and find out what they're doing here. Then, maybe we can figure out a way to keep them from getting lynched..."

"Oh, Ralph," Joy cried, "...this war just won't stop! I understand why the men feel the way they do. Why, just a few weeks ago they were being praised for killing Union soldiers! ...and I...even I..." she became rigid to control her emotions, "I am struggling myself, knowing that others like these men killed our Jamie..."

As Ralph and Joy continued to work together to move the injured Trevor and August onto surgical tables for more careful examination, he said, "I know what you mean, Joy. But, I keep telling myself that if the man who killed Jamie had not pulled the trigger first, he would be the one dead instead of our Jamie...and some other parents would feel the way we do."

Then, Ralph pulled Joy close, wrapped his arms around her and said, with a lump in his throat, "We have a choice to make, Joy. Now is our chance to personally put this war behind us...or keep on feeling bitter about the loss of our son. I think that I would like to start remembering Jamie as we knew him before, not as a victim of this awful war."

Joy pulled away from Ralph's embrace, looked into his eyes and with a look of firm resolve said, "Thank you, Sweetheart, I am in full agreement. Now let's see what we can do for these men," as she wiped the tears from her face and started tending to August's wounds.

"Ugh..." August moaned as she swabbed some of the blood from his face. Then he opened his already swollen eyes.

Joy spoke softly to August, "Just be quiet now, young man. I will try to get you cleaned up, so the doctor can check you over. There will be plenty of time for talking later. Just let me know if it hurts when I am moving things around."

Ralph was cleaning Trevor's wounds. He was unconscious for the most part, but occasionally tried to come around. "Joy, when you can get free for a minute, could you please come and watch over this one? I need go get some cooler water to see if that will bring him around."

Joy answered, "Okay, I will be there in just a minute. This one says his name is August and that is Trevor."

"Well, I am really concerned about Trevor here. He cannot seem to stay conscious," Ralph said as Joy came over, wiping the blood from her hands.

"I am here now, so go get that fresh water," Joy said. "August and I are both worried about this young man."

It did not take long for Trevor to wake up, when the doctor washed him down with cool water.

"Well hello, young man!" Ralph said. "We were getting worried about you. I did not find any broken bones, but you are going to have some very large bruises! But, under the circumstances, that is the least of your worries."

Joy spoke up and said, "I do not think these boys are in good enough shape to ride out of here, even if we could get to their horses. They would be seen riding out, for sure."

"You are right," Ralph said. "Men, I know that y'all don't feel much like talking, but you are in a very tight spot here. We are going to have to know exactly why y'all are here in Tennille. You need to start talking fast, because we are running out of time."

Trevor turned his head and looked at August, and then August sat up and said, "This is all my fault. I saw the way them men were bracing that bridge and pointed it out to Trevor. I told him that we ought to go help them men out, but he reminded me that we was in Reb...I mean Confederate country. We was about to ride on, when they grabbed us...you know the rest."

"But, why did y'all come here?" Joy asked.

"Well, we are on our way south to Macon to find a man that was locked up in Andersonville Prison in the war. We are supposed to take him back north for a friend," Trevor said as he struggled to sit up.

"Careful, young man," said the doctor. "Then, I do not understand about the bridge. Do y'all know something about the construction of bridges?" Ralph questioned.

August and Trevor shot a look at each other, started to laugh, but then both doubled over in pain. "Remind me not to laugh ever again," August groaned and then said, "We were both in the Army Corps of Engineers. We done lost count of all the bridges we built and rebuilt during the war. We just stopped when we came upon those men working, because we thought that we might be able to help. They were going about it all wrong."

Ralph looked at Joy and then back at August and Trevor. He was overwhelmed with everyone's total misjudgment of these young men. They only wanted to help when they stopped at the bridge.

"Look," Ralph said, "I am so sorry for what has happened to you here. Many of us here in Tennille have lost family members, homes, and jobs because of the war. Many are having trouble coping with the destruction that Sherman's march through here brought to our community. I am afraid that we're looking for someone to blame, someone we can hold accountable for our loss. I know that's selfish, because this whole country is hurting. But, it is the only excuse I have for our lack of hospitality to strangers. Please forgive us.

"Now, I am going to have to go out there and talk to that angry mob, and try to convince them that they should not hang you. My only hope is to call upon our Lord and Savior, asking Him to intervene on your behalf and soften the hearts of these blood thirsty men."

At that, Trevor and August agreed, realizing the grave danger of their situation. They did not hesitate, but bowed their heads as Ralph prayed, "*Lord I have misjudged these men. Please forgive me and my neighbors here in Tennille, who wish to do them harm. Open our eyes and soften our hearts, Lord. Help us learn from our mistakes, as we heal from this war. Help us to look ahead, with your love in our hearts toward strangers, instead of finding fault and hating others. We know that you answer prayer, so we will trust in you as you resolve this situation in whatever way you see fit. In the name of our wonderful Savior Jesus, who died for our sin, we praise you. Amen.*"

Joy was holding Ralph's hand as he finished praying. She looked into Ralph's eyes, with more respect and love for him than ever before and said, "Praise the Lord that he helped you to make the right decision and do the right thing, dear. I love you."

Chapter 16

"We have hired eleven men now, with the one we just took on today," Oscar said to Nathaniel. "We need to keep these men busy. You are obviously the best man to direct the felling and moving of the trees, as well as the work at the saw mill. I have been impressed with your leadership abilities and knowledge of the equipment, Nathaniel. Together we should be able to prioritize the jobs and decide which man is most qualified to complete each aspect of the work we need done."

"Well, Ah does the bes' Ah kin, Colonel Baynes," Nathaniel said, with some embarrassment evident in his demeanor. Then, rubbing the perspiration from the top of his balding head with his open hand, he shared his observations about each of the new workers. In particular, he mentioned that Dominique was an especially good worker, never complaining and had leadership potential. Also, Ross was obviously very good with problem solving.

"I agree, Nathaniel," said Oscar. "I have also noticed Ross trying new ideas and thinking of better ways of doing things. He does not have the education, but he sure thinks like an engineer. Everyone seems to like both Dominique and Ross, and they both seem to have a good working knowledge of construction. I say, it is time we get organized and make some decisions, what do you think?"

"Yes sah', Colonel Baynes, whateva' yo' say, sah'." Nathaniel stood up and looked as though he wanted to salute. Somehow, Colonel Oscar Baynes always brought that out in people. Nathaniel felt silly for feeling that impulse, especially since he had never even been in the military. And, he knew that a salute was inappropriate in this situation, anyway. So he just smiled and sat back down.

"Now Nathaniel, I wish you would call me Oscar."

"Ah knows dat, Sah, but Ah jes' likes callin' yo' Colonel Baynes betta', if'n yo' don' min', Sah."

"Okay, if you insist." Oscar said with a smile. He did not see any reason to discuss the matter further, so he changed the subject.

Pointing to some notes he had been making, Oscar said, "Here is my list. The very first thing we need to do is fix up one of the two cabins for Adam and Sara Ella to use as a residence, after they return here from their wedding in Washington City. Before he left, Adam asked me to see to that right away. While we are working on the mansion here, Adam will need to spend a lot of time in Washington City. He hopes that Sara Ella will go with him, but they will still need a suitable place to stay when they are here at the plantation. He understands the challenges we will face, but wants us to make the cabin as nice as possible for his new bride.

I think we have hired enough men for now, at least until we get more organized. Next, we have to get that bunk house finished for all of these men to have a better place to sleep. The tents we've been using won't last much longer, and won't keep out the cold this winter. Thank goodness some of the men have homes close by, where they live with their families. We also need to erect a shelter of some sort where we can serve meals to these men. Later, we can enclose it."

Nathaniel shook his head in agreement and reminded Oscar that they will also need to build a barn to shelter the horses and livestock for the winter before long.

"Yes, you are right Nathaniel," Oscar said, as he made a note of it. "For now, I need to focus my efforts on Adam's cabin and then back on the main house. Before Adam went off to get married, I was bogged down with the construction of the bunk house, so I would like to turn the supervision of that project over to Ross. Are you comfortable with having the men following his direction?"

Nathaniel agreed that Ross would be a good choice. He knew he would need to be very careful how he went about overseeing the work of white men, who might be easily offended, under the circumstances, so using a white man for the job made perfect sense.

"Great, then," Oscar said with a smile, "now we are making good progress! I think Ross will need at least two good men to work with him. So, who do you think we should assign to him as a work crew?"

Nathaniel tipped his head to the left and looked off in the distance, thinking, then he said, "How 'bout Norman and Darrell?"

Lifting the index finger of his right hand into the air, indicating he just remembered something, Nathaniel suggested that Oscar keep Steven in mind when it is time to do any fancy woodworking on moldings and trim. He laughed when he told Oscar not to send Steven back to the sawmill, because he kept finding him off somewhere whittling something pretty instead of working.

Oscar laughed aloud and said, "You are right! We'll definitely make that happen. I will take Steven and have him start sketching the intricate trim for the big house. Maybe he will have some ideas for dressing up the cabin, too. I will also take Michael and Brandon to work with me. Perhaps, Elsie will be of some help with making the cabin as pretty as possible with a feminine touch...we shall see. When Ross, Norman and Darrell finish working on the bunk house and the chow hall shelter, I'll bring them over to work with me also. The remainder of the men can work with you, bringing down the timber and operating the saw mill."

Nathaniel suggested they make Dominique the manager of a log felling team, reminding Oscar that he is a black man and some of the white men may not want to work for him. "But, he's the hardest workin' man of the bunch, an' he's smart 'bout them trees."

"If you think he is the best man for the job then make it so," said Oscar.

"Yes sah, Ah does," said Nathaniel. "Ah seed 'im wit' 'em trees, an' he knows how to pick 'em and where t' cut 'em to git's 'em to fall right where he wants. They don' fall on nobody, and they's easy to pull 'em out o' there. Ah 'spect the men'll work fo' him, good as me."

Oscar shook his head in agreement and said, "He sounds like a great choice to me. Who do you think should work under him, and who do you want to work for you at the saw mill?"

"We can put Joseph, Luke, Robert, Odell and Roy workin' fer Dominique in the forest to bring in them trees," said Nathaniel thoughtfully, "...then, Ah'll keep Aaron, Isaac, Vernon and Mathias up at the saw mill. Oh, and dat new man yo' hired t'day...what's his name?"

"Uh, let me see," Oscar said, looking at his notes, "Burt is his name. He will be here tomorrow. I think we can put off building the chow hall until we get that bunk house done, agreed?"

"Yes sah'."

Oscar sat back in his chair and folded his arms, then said, "Shall we call everybody together after breakfast in the morning and assign them to their team? I will pull Ross and Dominique aside this evening at supper to see if they are agreeable to our plans.

"I am excited about this Nathaniel. Now that we have more men, we can start really getting things done around here. I will continue looking for more help, but this is certainly a great start. Thanks so much for your help. I am ready to stop for the evening, how about you?"

"Well Colonel Baynes, Ah sho' hope everthin' goes smooth tomorrow. We been shorthanded, dat's fo' sho," Nathaniel said, and then added, "Oh, an don' fergit, we gonna' need a barn fo' da' animals fo' it gits cold this fall."

Nathaniel turned to leave as Oscar said, "I have it in my notes, Nathaniel."

Oscar could smell coffee brewing long before the sun came up. Since he was awake, he decided to follow that aroma downstairs, where he found Elsie working in the kitchen. She was neatly attired in a light blue dress, with a white apron tied behind her neck and around her tiny waist. Her hair was pulled away from her face and fastened into a bun in the back. He could not help but notice how gracefully she was moving around, getting things ready for a new day. Just then she dropped a skillet that hit the floor with a tremendous clatter.

Oscar cringed, putting his hands over his ears, then said, "Do you have to be so noisy this early in the morning?"

"Oh!" she jumped, "I'm so sorry. I thought everyone was still in bed at this hour. What are you doing here so early?"

"The smell of that coffee drew me down here. Do you think you could spare me a cup, please?"

As she handed him the warm steaming cup, he said, "So, what brings you to the kitchen so early, young lady?"

Elsie looked him straight in the eye as she explained, "Emma Lou keeps us really busy when the four of us are working together in the kitchen, so we keep bumping into each other all day long. I've found that if I get up early and put everything out and organized, then we don't have to climb over each other so much. The kitchen runs much more smoothly that way." That's when he noticed that blasted curl fall loose from its proper place to tease him once again, like it did before.

Obviously mesmerized and a little flustered, Oscar said, "Ahem...well...I'm impressed, with your organizational skills, Elsie."

"Why, thank you, Oscar. It is nice to be noticed." Elsie sat down at a table and patted the chair beside her, motioning for Oscar to sit with her.

Oscar thought "I wonder if she has noticed the way I have been watching her? I had better be careful...at least, now I know how to find her alone, without a crowd around... Huh? Where did that thought come from? I have been ditched once by a woman...I am not going to let that happen again!"

Elsie was chattering away with small talk, then interrupted his train of thought with, "Have you noticed?"

"Noticed what?" Oscar said, as he was startled back to the real world. He realized he had not been listening, just watching her and thinking his own thoughts.

"Jessica and Dominique! Have you not heard anything I have said? That new girl Jessica that you hired last week is sweet on Dominique. And, I am pretty sure he feels the same, seeing the way he watches her during meals."

Just then Emma Lou came bustling into the kitchen. "Good morning, Colonel. Baynes! My goodness, what brings you down here so early?"

"It was the tantalizing aroma of Elsie's coffee. It is well worth coming down early for a cup of this stuff," he said with a grin, holding up his cup.

"She do know how ta make good coffee, Sah', that's fo' sho'! An', did yo' see how Elsie's been settin' up the kitchen fer us gals? She been a mighty big he'p ta' me? Yes, sah', a mighty big he'p."

"Yes ma'am, I have," he said, as Beverly Jean and Jessica arrived in the kitchen to begin their work day.

"Good morning, ladies, I am looking forward to another of your delicious breakfasts," Oscar said, as he bowed with his left arm at his waist, right arm outstretched to his right, palm up, in a gesture of salute to the female gender. Then he quickly hurried upstairs to wait for breakfast to be ready, hopefully before Elsie discovered his vulnerability. *Why does that girl fluster me so much?*

After breakfast Oscar and Nathaniel called all of the men to the front yard to give them their assignments. Lifting his voice, Oscar asked, "Does anyone have any questions about what team you will be with or what you will be doing?" Oscar allowed them a few minutes to respond, when one man cleared his throat as if to attract attention.

"Yes Odell, did you have a question?" said Oscar.

Odell answered, "Yes, sir, I does. Don't make me no neva' min' whar I works, but Ah's had 'sperience pushin' logs through a saw blade if'n yo needs me doin' that, Sa'."

"Thank you, Odell. I'm sorry that I did not get that information from you when you interviewed for the job."

Odell looked pleased to be so important when he said, "Well sa', we's got in'erupted when yo' was askin' me 'bout my 'sperience."

Oscar turned to look at Dominique and asked, "Will it suit you Dominique if, when he gets here, we assign that new man Burt to work with you instead of Odell? I think it would be best for Odell to work with Nathaniel."

"Yes sir. It looks like a good team for fellin' lumber. We'll do a good days work together," Dominique said, as Burt arrived late.

Oscar turned to Burt with a look of disapproval and said, somewhat sarcastically, "Well Burt, it's good of you to join us. Perhaps, you did not understand that we will meet here in the yard every morning at dawn."

"Yeah, well, I got here as soon as I could," Burt said under his breath, with a defensive tone in his voice.

"Excuse me," said Oscar with his hands on his hips, "Our day will start at dawn, so you will need to be here at that time if you want a job here."

"Yeah, whatever you say," Burt said with an insubordinate scowl.

Oscar's first reaction was to fire this man on the spot. He had never had much patience for men like Burt. But he decided to give him a chance to prove himself, primarily because he did not have time to replace him. However, he did not hold out much hope for the man, with the attitude he had shown thus far.

Oscar turned his attention to the gathering of men and announced, "Okay, gentlemen let's head off in our teams and meet back here this evening when the ladies ring the bell. Burt, you are assigned to the tree felling team over there. Dominique will show you how to safely bring down those trees and get them to the mill. Oh, if you have not already, do not forget to fill your canteens with water before you head out."

Burt turned to one of the other men and asked, "Are you on the tree fellin' team? Who is Dominique? If Dominique is supposed to tell me what to do, then who is this Dominique?"

"Name's Roy," the man said, holding out his hand to Burt. "Yes, I'm on the tree fellin' team. I've seen people get killed when one of those big suckers falls in the wrong direction, so we are fortunate to be working for a man that understands the importance of doing this job right. I've been working with Dominique for several days now. He showed me a lot about how to cut them trees so's they fall exactly where they should fall, and where to stand so's they don't fall on me. Yes sir, I'm relieved to be working for Dominique."

"Is that Dominique?" Burt asked, as he pointed to Robert, the only other white man on his team.

"Naw," said Roy, "that big man over there is Dominique."

"You're joshin' me right? There ain't no way that I'm gonna work for no slave!" Burt said growling, as he marched back to the front lawn to find Oscar.

"Colonel Baynes!" Burt was red in the face as he exclaimed, "You're not makin' me work for no slave are you?"

Oscar tried to keep calm as he looked at Burt with a penetrating stare and replied, "No sir, I'm not making you work for anybody. I've merely offered you a good job at a very fair wage. I assure you that Dominique will keep you and the other men safe, as you bring those logs down and into the mill. He is very experienced and qualified to supervise the log felling team."

Outraged, Burt said "I don't believe it! You're tellin' me that I have to take orders from a slave?"

"No, not at all. There are no slaves on these premises. You may work for Dominique, or you may leave if you prefer. At this time, the choice is yours Burt, not mine. But, if you intend to continue this attitude, you will not be welcome here in any capacity."

"I need this job, but I ain't workin' for no slave." By this time Burt was seething, stomping back and forth, and trying to control his urge to beat this Yankee Colonel to a pulp for even suggesting that he would stoop to being a slave's boy! Out of the corner of his eye, he saw that some ladies were standing at the door of the kitchen, watching, and a more mature, well-built black man was hurrying toward them.

"I'll be telling people in these parts what you tried to do to me, Colonel Baynes! Just see if you can get any more help here! You'll see that I'm not someone to mess with!" He yelled as he stormed up the lane to leave.

Nathaniel came up to Oscar and said, "What's dat all 'bout?"

"Well, Nathaniel," said Oscar with a smile, "it seems that Burt has a pride problem."

Chapter 17

Tom laughed, as he helped Lisa up into the carriage. She had just twirled around like a school girl to show him her new crinoline walking gown with its matching bonnet. The gown was a two piece garment made of a soft gray fabric with red piping and red buttons all the way up the center front of the bodice. It featured large pagoda sleeves with shoulder flounces that were set into the eyes of the arms with three large pleats at the shoulder cap. A small stand-up collar was pleated into a ruffle at the neckband. The large skirt was pleated, with a slight train in the back. The bonnet was made of the same gray fabric, piped with red and sporting a large plume of red feathers.

"Isn't it beautiful!" Lisa's voice was melodious, as she reached for Sara Ella to give her a warm hug.

"Thank you so much, Sara Ella! You and Adam are so good to me. I am new all the way through to my skin! Even new shoes! And thank you for the day and evening dresses as well. I cannot decide if I like the blue day dress or the mulberry evening dress the best....or maybe the yellow one...I like them all! Oh, I feel almost as good as I did when I came here with Laura to meet the Layne family years ago." Then her countenance fell and she said, "...I sure do miss her...wonder what has happened to Laura?"

Sara Ella, also looking lovely in her new navy blue walking gown, said "I miss Laura too, Lisa..." Then, changing the subject to brighten the mood again, she hugged Lisa and said, "I know how you feel about the new wardrobe! My old garments were all completely worn out, too. I really needed all these new things." And then, with a wink, she leaned over and said, "Wearing those old clothes made me feel as frumpy as a schoolmarm! Oh, I guess that is because I was a schoolmarm when my mother made them for me!" It felt very good to both of them to laugh aloud at Sara Ella's humorous comment.

Lisa turned her attention to their escort and said, "And Tom, you look quite the dashing gentleman in your new suit as well!"

"I think Emma Lou will be pleased with what we got for her, don't you Lisa?" Sara Ella smoothed her lap as she turned to Tom and said, "Perhaps, tomorrow you can interest Adam in some shopping to find something besides uniforms for himself and new clothes for Randy and Benjamin."

As they started toward home in the carriage, Tom looked around at the busy streets and then remarked, "It's hard to understand how Washington City can be bustling with so much plenty and very little evidence of the war, when Richmond is a pile of rubble, struggling to find enough resources to simply survive..."

"Yes, Tom. The Confederate soldiers burned as much as they could as they evacuated, to keep the Yankees from having the city. The Yankees destroyed or looted anything that remained. What they did not take was carried off by southern scoundrels," Lisa interjected. "I found it very strange when I was in Richmond, looking for Goddard and Angela. Many of the prominent private citizens were there that I had known before, but they were wandering the streets in a melancholic daze. The Negroes, on the other hand were jubilant, having just been given their freedom. The gloomiest were the property owners, who had suffered total losses because of the fire. It was really sad to see the previously poor population obviously excited about the Union occupancy of the city, because of the free help they received. Of course, they were the first in line to offer loyalty to the Union."

Sara Ella choked back tears when she said, "Lisa you have seen so much of the ugliness of this awful war, but, your trials seem to have made you a stronger person. I am sure that the Lord has more great plans for your life." Then she reached out and patted Tom, saying, "Tom, we sure appreciate all of your help today. I hope it was an enjoyable day for you, because we are certainly going to need you some more!"

"Yes, ma'am," Tom replied. "It has been a blessing to watch you two ladies have a good time today and allow the darkness of war to fall away for a little while. Yes, ma'am. I'd be pleased to spend as much time as you want!"

"Well, okay then," Sara Ella said with a smile. "Lisa, when we get home, let's prepare a feast for supper tonight. We need to celebrate our good day! I hope that Benjamin has been able to help Randy feel comfortable finding his way around."

Chapter 18

"Good morning, Scott," Adam said. "It was grand having you and Marie in our home for supper last week. How did you catch a firecracker like Marie? You are one fortunate man! Sara Ella and Lisa love her too, and talk endlessly about spending almost every day with Marie helping them get ready for our wedding. I guess you know by now that our wedding date has been set for June 24th. For the life of me, I do not understand why we cannot get married tomorrow."

Scott smiled as he sat down at his desk in a badly worn chair and motioned for Adam to sit across from him in a straight back wooden chair. Then he said, "From what I've heard, it sounds like Marie's familiarity with shops and resources in the city are helping solve a lot of the scheduling problems for Sara Ella and Lisa. But, I'm sure you were disappointed when they found out that the Episcopal Church is not available for your wedding until August. I understand that both of you are determined to be married in the church, right?"

"Yes, I was disappointed. Sara Ella, though she is a devout Episcopalian, doesn't seem as concerned about the wedding being in the church as I am. Until just a few months ago, I would not have cared one way or the other about being married in the church. But, now it just seems more appropriate to make that covenant with Sara Ella in the church, before my Lord. Besides," Adam said with a chuckle, "I would enjoy seeing some people I know in church for my wedding, who might never come otherwise."

Scott laughed aloud when he said, "Yup, weddings and funerals will bring just about anyone to church."

Adam's expression became a little more serious as he sat back in his chair and said, "By the way Scott, thanks for inviting us to your church last Sunday. Sara Ella and I are excited about having our wedding there. She was a little skeptical at first, because it is a Baptist church and not as formal as she's accustomed to as an Episcopalian. But, the Pastor's message was compelling, and I think she liked being challenged that way.

I was surprised to see some of my old friends there, like Edgar Gray, the Chaplin of the Senate. He and I used to run into each other at the Capitol when I came to visit Lincoln. I thought it was by accident, but now I wonder if it was not more than that. In fact, now I wonder if Lincoln did not put him up to it! Anyway, he would always go out of his way to ask me how I was doing, and never failed to tell me that he was praying for me." Adam looked down at the floor, deep in thought.

Scott broke the spell when he said, "Marie and I were very glad that your family joined us in church."

"Well, so much for all this. Why did you summon me here? Is there some breaking news?" Adam looked anxious to hear what Scott had for him.

Scott leaned forward so he could speak more softly, then said, "I just thought that you might be interested in knowing about an article that will be in the Examiner tomorrow morning. Do you remember a man named John W. Forney, Adam?"

With a chuckle Adam said, "Of course, how could anyone forget? Johnson was drinking with Forney before his inaugural ceremony on March 4th, when they apparently got more than a little carried away. I remember that Senator Zachariah Chandler said, 'Johnson disgraced himself and the Senate by making a drunken foolish speech.' But, our gracious Lincoln told the very upset Hugh McCullough, 'Andy ain't a drunkard.'" Adam was shaking his head as he finished speaking.

"You got that story exactly right, Adam," Scott said. "That is the man I am talking about. Forney's a good friend of President Johnson, and he gave us this article to be printed in tomorrow mornings paper. Take a look..." Scott handed the article to Adam across the desk. "As you can see, he is having us report that Johnson is a 'practical statesman that all earnest loyalists' can trust. I thought you might want to know about this before Stanton sees it."

"Thank you, Scott." Adam knew Stanton would be enraged by the article. Perhaps now, he could present the news to him more softly than if he saw it in the paper with no warning. "Maybe Forney's just trying to make up for having contributed to Johnson's being considered a drunk by nearly everyone."

Scott shook his head in agreement, then said, "You are probably right. Last month Forney put an article in the Philadelphia Press supporting Johnson, also. Let me see if I can find it...I pulled it out to show you...Yes, here it is, look at this." Scott handed the article to Adam, and said, "It bothered me then, because he did it right after Lincoln was killed."

"Oh my," Adam said, as he slapped the paper with the back of his fingers. "This man has no scruples. He said here, about Johnson, 'a sterner and less gentle hand may at this juncture have been required to take hold of the reins of Government.' I'm sure Forney was influenced by that fiery rhetoric from Johnson in the Senate, where he appeared to embrace the southern states theory of 'state suicide'. He said that Congress would have to re-admit the states under their terms, since he apparently believed the south had reduced themselves to nothing more than territories.

"Forney obviously didn't know Lincoln the way I did. Whatever decisions Lincoln would ultimately have made, would have been after lots of prayer and the counsel of many advisers. This President we have now will never hold a candle to Mr. Lincoln, 'sterner' or otherwise. What I don't understand is why Forney is still supporting Johnson now, with the change in direction Johnson seems to be making." Adam turned his attention back to reading the article again.

Scott spoke softly again, "Anyway Adam, I just thought that you might find it interesting to see that Johnson's friend Forney is standing up for him. On the other hand, I've been hearing talk about Johnson wanting to enact 'Black Codes' to restrict the freedmen, even after Chief Justice Chase and some others in the Judiciary insisted on civil rights for freedmen. I do not know if Stanton has heard about that yet, but you might want to ask him about it."

Adam was serious when he said, "Scott, thank you for keeping me updated." He stood up from his chair as he said, "It is amazing that so much happens behind the scenes here in the political realm of Washington City."

Scott got up out of his chair also and said, "Do you have a big day planned, Adam?"

As he turned to leave, Adam offered, "Yes, Scott. I am going to have tea with Sara Ella and a lady named Mrs. Kelley who apparently has some information about a school for the blind for my son Randy. I am personally very skeptical about the whole idea. It seems logical to me that it would be better to have someone come and teach Randy in our home, where he already knows his way around. Randy will be having tea with us also, so it will be interesting to see what he thinks about it. Then, later this afternoon I have a meeting with Stanton."

It did not take Adam long to reach the Layne Townhouse, but along the way he thought more about the idea of sending Randy away to a school. *I nearly lost that boy once, and I cannot imagine him being away from me again. I do not like the idea...it just does not make sense. I will just have to put my foot down and make myself clear on the subject.*

Sara Ella greeted him at the door with a kiss and said, "Adam, you are here at just the right time. I have everything set up, and the tea is hot. Mrs. Kelley will be here any minute."

Adam cleared his throat, puffed out his chest and said, as firmly as he knew how, "Now look, Sara Ella, I just do not think that…"

Sara Ella put up her right index finger and said with a smile, "Hold that thought, Adam…come on in and have a seat with Randy and Benjamin. Again, Mrs. Kelley should be here in a just a little bit. Now, what was that you were saying, Adam? Oh, there is the knock at the door…could you get it for me please, Tom?"

Tom brought the visitor into the parlor and announced her to the gathering.

Sara Ella graciously motioned Mrs. Kelley to a seat and said, "Hello Mrs. Kelley, I would like for you to meet my fiancé General Adam Layne. Adam this is Mrs. Kelley who will tell us more about a blind school for Randy. Does she not look lovely in that hat?"

Adam looked somewhat flustered, but smiled anyway and said, "Uh yes, that is a lovely hat."

Then she turned to the two boys, who stood to their feet, and said, "And this is Adam's son Randy, and his friend Benjamin."

"It is a pleasure to meet you, ma'am," Randy and Benjamin said in unison.

"Uh 'hem…well, let me get the tea. Please help yourself to a scone and I will be right back." Sara Ella said, nervously.

Mrs. Kelley was a small woman with gray hair and kind, hazel green eyes. A very attractive woman, despite her obvious age, Mrs. Kelley was modestly dressed in a sage green walking gown that was trimmed with a delicate lace collar and cuffs. Her city bonnet was sage green with rows of lace that framed her face. "General, I understand that you are Senator Mason Layne's son."

Adam could not help but like this woman. She was clearly very reserved, but not at all unfriendly. "Yes Mrs. Kelley. Senator Mason Layne was my father, and this was his town home."

Mrs. Kelley smiled sweetly and said, "He was a very fine gentleman. I did not always agree with him, but I appreciated him very much."

Just then Sara Ella came in carrying a tray of tea cups and a steaming pot of tea, enough for everyone. "Here we go, let me pour everyone a nice hot cup of tea."

Adam got up to take the tray from Sara Ella and sat it gently down on the tea table.

As Sara Ella picked up one of the tea cups and began pouring, she said, "Now Mrs. Kelley, I am anxious for you to tell Adam and Randy what you told me about the new Perkins School for the Blind in Boston."

Just then, there was a loud rap on the door. Tom immediately entered the parlor and said, "Excuse me, General Layne. There is a young man here with a message for you that he says is urgent."
Adam stood and said, "Excuse me, ladies and gentlemen. I will be right back."
Adam exited the parlor into the foyer, then returned shortly to say, "I am so sorry, but I must leave at once for Capitol Hill. Please, carry on in my absence, Mrs. Kelley. Be sure to give all of the information to my family, so we will be able to discuss the matter further tonight, after I return home. I will see you tonight, Darling," he said as he quickly kissed Sara Ella on the cheek and turned to leave.
Out on the front steps, the messenger said, "I'm very sorry to have interrupted your meeting, General."
"Oh, do not be sorry, young man. You saved me...I am afraid I was about to get myself into some serious trouble," Adam said. Then changed the subject, "So, Stanton wants to see me right away?"
"Yes sir, that's all I know. Have a good day, sir," the messenger said as he turned to leave.
Adam made his way to the Capitol building as quickly as possible. As he was hurrying up the front stairs, he noticed construction work being done high above him to the dome of the structure.
Stanton wheezed and wiped perspiration from his brow with a handkerchief, as he opened the door of his office. "Adam, come in. I am glad that you were able to come so promptly."
Adam shook Stanton's proffered hand as he made his way to a chair. "No problem, it was good timing. By the way, are they ever going to finish working on that dome? They've been working on it for at least ten years."
"Actually, it's been eleven...and, as usual, they say it is only going to be a few more months until they are finished. We have a new architect involved now who replaced Thomas Walter...you remember Thomas do you not?"
Adam shook his head in the affirmative.
"Well the new man is Edward Clark," said Stanton. "I pass him in the hall now and then. Maybe he can get the job done.
"Adam, I have asked you here, because I have been hearing rumors that Johnson is implementing his own Reconstruction policy, while Congress is in recess. His policy apparently has no provisions for black suffrage or freedmen's rights. The conservative democrats, including Seward think that it should be up to the states to handle those problems the way they see fit. Can you imagine? I do not expect that the states that fought to keep them as slaves would be inclined to pass

black suffrage and freedmen's rights, do you? It even sounds like he wants to regulate the freedmen with some kind of codes...let me see...I wrote that down...yes, they are called 'Black Codes'.

"I do not like what is going on here, Adam...something stinks! I have a meeting scheduled with some Radical Republicans that you may know, Thaddeus Stevens, Charles Sumner and Ben Wade. They are also appalled at this development. I wanted to discuss it with you first, before our meeting. Have you heard anything about this?"

Adam was very concerned, cleared his throat and said, "You are not going to like this, but just this morning I learned some things that make it obvious that Johnson's not doing things anything like he had previously indicated he would. Earlier, he led everyone to believe that he was in favor of the freedmen and denounced the secessionists. How can he now be planning quite the opposite? Did not Chase insist that provision should be made for Freedman? I would suggest that you meet with Chase also, since Johnson is ignoring his advice completely. I do not mind saying that I am encouraged, knowing that you are working with men who are standing up for the rights of these freedmen."

Gritting his teeth Stanton said, "We simply must find a way to stop this President Andrew Johnson train, before it is too late!"

Adam rubbed his forehead with his fingers for a moment, then replied, "Is there a way that the pardoned leaders from the south, some of whom I know have been re-elected, could constitutionally not be seated in Congress? We all know that if all of the southern leaders that Johnson has pardoned get their congressional seats back, they could get this thing passed. If that happened, the Democratic White Supremacists will prevail, and the war will have accomplished nothing!"

Stanton sat back in his executive chair with a thoughtful look on his face and scratched his neck with his right hand, then suddenly pulled out his pocket watch and said, "Oh dear, my time is up here Adam, but I think you're on to something. Thank you, for coming by at such short notice. It helps to talk these things over with someone I can trust...to get my thoughts organized and look for workable solutions."

As he walked to the door, Adam said, "By the way, you may be amused to know that John Forney is placing an article in the Washington Examiner tomorrow morning supporting Johnson as a statesman we can trust!"

"Preposterous!" Stanton thundered.

On the way home Adam was uneasy, dreading the discussion with Sara Ella about the blind school idea. "Why did I not just insist she listen to me before? I need to tell her exactly how I feel about Randy going away to school. I do NOT approve...Randy needs to stay home and that's final! It is ridiculous that anyone would think he could find his way in a strange place as large as a boarding school. Benjamin may not always be there to guide him. I will just sit her down when I get there and tell her how I feel. I appreciate Mrs. Kelley's information, but Randy is going to stay home where his loving family will always be there to help him."

As he arrived at the bottom of the front steps of the townhouse, Adam took a deep breath and hesitated, looking up at the beautiful front door. Inside were the people he loved most in the entire world. It crossed his mind that Sara Ella broke their engagement the last time they had a big disagreement. *"I sure hope she will understand my position and support me on this...,"* then he started his ascent up the stairs slowly, with a heavy load on his shoulders.

Chapter 19

Doctor Ralph Fowler closed the door behind him and headed across the street toward the livery stable area. Still a good distance away, he could already hear the angry men who were intent on hanging the young Yankees. These were men he had known all his life, but now they resembled a pack of dogs in a feeding frenzy.

"Look, Doc's comin'!" someone yelled. "Grab a rope!"

Ralph hurried his pace, as the intensity of rage toward the two strangers was getting completely out of control. As he arrived, the doctor attempted to raise his voice over the noise of the throng. But, it soon became obvious that they were not particularly interested in hearing what he had to say.

Nevertheless, he persisted until he finally yelled at the top of his lungs, "Men! Aren't you interested in hearing their story, so that you will be able to tell it to your grandchildren? Come on, now! Calm down and go inside."

"Naw, we're ready for this hangin', ain't we men?" Billy Joe yelled.

"Yeah!" the fury of the crowd was not diminished, as they pushed Ralph aside and headed toward his office to get their hands on the Yankee spies.

"Wait! Listen to me! Let me tell you why those boys are here! It is not what you think!" Ralph was trying to tell them, but no one was listening.

Billy Joe led the pack as they pushed Ralph aside and forced their way through the door. Joy was frantically pleading with them, as they half carried, half shoved Trevor and August out into the street.

"Where we gonna' hang this here rope from?" Billy Jo shouted over the fray.

"Over the livery stable door! That should do it," Jimmy hollered.

"Yeah," someone called out, "We'll hang 'em Yanks one at a time, so the other one can watch! Then they'll know some o' how we feel 'bout losing our kin down here. Wish we could find more of 'em, so they can pay back what they done."

Trevor was beginning to stumble, and Ralph knew that he was about to lose consciousness again. He and August had both been beaten up badly earlier, and had lost a lot of blood.

Ralph called out as loud as he could, but the men were so intent on their mission to hang these Union soldiers that he was completely ignored. At that point Trevor collapsed.

One of the men said, "Someone go get some water! It ain't gonna' be as much fun to hang this one if he's out cold."

Since Billy Joe had been drinking heavily by this time, it was difficult for him to position the rope for the hanging. So, Johnny offered assistance until it was in place, then said, "Now, find us a box or somethin' for 'em to stand on, so's we get this rope 'round their Yankee necks!"

"Over here!" someone called out from inside the stable.

"Hurry up wit' that wat'a! We needs t' hang this one firs' 'for he dies. His buddy kin watch 'im die!" one man growled.

Trevor shook his head as someone threw a bucket of water in his face. The men cheered and said, "Grab him quick, before he passes out again! Two men drug him over to the box. But, they were having trouble holding him, while they were putting the rope around his neck, because he was so weak and faint. Ralph kept yelling, trying to get in front of the crowd...but, it was hopeless...he could never get through.

"Okay, it's on there now!" one of the men holding Trevor yelled. "Now, stand back y'all, so's ever body can see us let go of him and kick this box out of the way."

They stepped back and yelled, "Let him go, let him go!"

Suddenly, a tremendous boom sounded from inside of the stable. Pieces of wood splintered and horses reared and snorted, as they kicked and jumped with fright in their stalls. The mob of men fell absolutely silent.

Then, coming out of the dim light of the stable, the men heard the unmistakable mechanical cocking sound of a big gun. Joy Fowler walked out into the light, holding a Spencer rifle that was pointed directly at the men who were supporting Trevor's limp body.

One man exclaimed, "Watch out ya'll! That's Ralph's repeat'n 56, so she's got 6 rounds left!"

Slowly and deliberately, but loud enough for every ear to hear, Joy said, "If either of you men wiggle your big toe before that rope is off of that young man's head, it will be y'all's grave we will be digging! Do you understand me? Now, we are all friends here, so it pains me terribly to be pointing this rifle at y'all. But, do not make the mistake of forgetting that I am a very good shot! If I miss one of these men I am aiming at now, I am afraid that my bullet will go directly into your lynch mob. I will not be responsible for how many are killed or maimed with one shot! So, I would recommend that all y'all encourage these folks to do exactly what I have said. Ralph, if you are still out there, please come up here and reason with these folks! They surely do not know what they are about to do."

Ralph pushed his way to the front of the crowd, as he greeted some of the men and then turned to address them. "Gentlemen, I am afraid that we were about to do something that we would forever regret. These men are innocent and I think that I can prove it, if you will but give me a chance."

"We already know that they're Yankee spies, Doc. How can they be innocent? They killed our brothers, fathers and sons."

"I know how you feel, and so does Joy. We miss Jamie every day, so we can relate to how you feel. But, hear their story and I will show you how we will know if they are telling the truth. August, are you strong enough to sit on this box and tell these men what y'all told Joy and me about why you are here?"

Ralph helped August up and steadied him as he sat on the box.

"Doc, please help Joy with Trevor, and I will do my best to explain," August said weakly.

Then through lips that were mangled beyond recognition and with one eye swollen completely shut, August said, "I told the Doctor...cough...that it was all my fault...cough. Trevor said we should keep on moving and mind our own business..." He stopped to catch his breath.

"You see, we was both in the Army Corps of Engineers during the war." He coughed again, and then said, "We tore down, then built back, a lot of bridges in our time, as well as forts and such...cough...when we saw you men working on that bridge outside of town, it looked to me like you could use some direction, if the structure was going to be strong enough to support wagons with heavy loads going across it. Trevor said you probably would not appreciate our help, seeing as we are Yankees. But, I was arguing with him when you saw us. I am sorry that we barged in on your business. Trevor was right, and I should have listened. I am the one that caused all this trouble." August fell forward, holding his stomach, and Ralph quickly steadied him.

Billy Joe was the first one to respond, "Is that it? Do you means to tell us that y'all believe a crazy story like that?"

Ralph answered before the whole mob got excited again. "No, that is not the whole story. There is more. But, before I tell you the rest, I want y'all to understand that I know a sure way to prove if their story is true, or not. I know you people well enough to know that you would not want to murder innocent people who are on a mercy mission. If their story is true, I want you to put yourself or your son in their position right now, and consider what the right thing to do here is?"

All was quiet for a moment, then Johnny raised his voice and said, "Oh, come on Doc...we need to just hang these spies and have it over with!"

Then Mr. Collins spoke up for the first time and said, "Shut up, Johnny. I want to hear this out, and see how Doc thinks he can prove they are innocent."

Doc continued, "Another thing I want you to think about while you're listening is this: Do any of y'all recall staring down the barrel of a gun at either one of these young men during the war? And if you did, would you have tried to pull the trigger before they did?"

Someone shouted, "You bet I'd pull the trigger first! That Yank'd be deader than a doornail!" That brought out hoots of laughter from the crowd.

Then, Doc quieted them down again and said, "Would you expect him to just stand there while you shot him?"

Billy Joe said, "Doc, what is your point?"

Doc threw up his hands and said, "I am just trying to help you see that it was a WAR we been fighting for these past many years. And if the Yankees had not killed my Jamie, I know that he would have killed them. It was war, so who ever pulled the trigger first and best is the one that lived—and the other man died.

"But, now the war is over. We cannot just keep on killing and hating. It is time to be free of the bitterness, especially toward those who have experienced the same misery on the other side. All of us are trying to put this war behind us, so we can get on with our lives.

"I am just saying, perhaps we could learn something from these men that would help us with that bridge. After all, they are engineers, and we desperately need that bridge, gentlemen. I do not know any other engineers, do you?"

From in the middle of the mob a man said, "You've got my attention Doc. I know that I, for one, am fed up with all of the sadness and bitterness that I've been holdin' onto. If you can prove that these Yanks are legit', it would be a relief to end this war in my heart right here and now. What about the rest of you men?"

Doc sighed and relaxed somewhat, then said, "Thank you, Martin. Now, let me tell y'all why these men came here. Trevor and August are on their way to Macon, Georgia to find a man that was in Andersonville Prison and take him back north to Virginia with them."

"Oh, man! There ain't much chance o' no man from Andersonville travelin' anywheres. These boys 'r gonna' be disappointed, that is if'n the man ain't dead already," another man interjected.

"But Doc, you ain't told us how we can prove any o' this story you done tol' us," said Johnny.

Doc stood up straighter and declared, "If Trevor and August are willing and if y'all can swallow your anger long enough to give it a chance, there is a way. And, in the process, the desperate situation of this town and the outlying settlements will be greatly improved."

"That seems unlikely," one man murmured.

Doc ignored the man's negative comment and continued, "This is the deal I am proposing: First—if the man who has been in Andersonville Prison is still alive, he will be in desperate need of medical attention if he is going to be taken as far north as Virginia. Second—Tennille is in desperate need of a bridge to regularly carry wagon loads of goods and supplies to and from Macon. Thus far, we have been unsuccessful on our own. This town will die soon if we remain isolated like this much longer."

"What are you suggesting, Doc?" August groaned.

"Well August, where in Virginia are y'all planning to take this man who was in Andersonville?"

"His name is Richard, Richard Moreland. We need to take him to Oaklayne Plantation near Richmond, Virginia," said August.

"Okay, August. If you would let me go with you to Macon to help find this man, then I will ride back with you up to Virginia. If the man is alive, we will probably need to take him in a wagon. I can tend to his medical needs and hopefully, keep you out of trouble in these southern towns."

"That sounds all well and good," August said, holding his throbbing head. "But, what about Trevor? I am not going anywhere without Trevor."

"Trevor would need to agree to stay here, and after Joy helps him recover from his injuries, show these men how to rebuild this bridge properly?" Doc answered.

Then he turned to the crowd and said, "Do you not see? If August and I find Richard Moreland and take him to Virginia, and Trevor proves to know how to successfully rebuild that bridge, then we will know that everything they told us is true. And, if it is true, we will have helped them and they will have helped us...everyone wins!" Doc smiled and raised his arms up in the air in a gesture of hope.

A low murmur began to spread through the crowd. To prevent the mob frenzy from re-igniting, Doc suggested, "I tell you what...y'all go on home and talk to your friends and family about this idea. Joy and I will take these young men back to my office and attempt to patch them up enough to see if they will agree to our plan. It will probably be difficult for them to agree to Trevor staying here, after the welcome we gave them. So, y'all might want to talk to the Almighty about that...I expect, He may need to intervene for us."

The crowd started to break up, and men began to shuffle away a few at a time. Most of them were grumbling, but others tried to reason with and push along the few who were loud and intoxicated.

"We'll see y'all in the morning gentlemen," Ralph called after them.

As Doc was helping him to his feet, August said, "I have got to hand it to you, Doc...that was very ingenious! Now, how are you going to get Trevor and me out of here before morning? He is in a bad way, and I do not want him near Tennille, Georgia ever again!"

Chapter 20

"Okay men, there's the dinner bell! Let's go, I'm starved!" Brandon said.

"And, do not forget that we have a meeting planned for after dinner, gentlemen," Oscar quipped, and then turned to Brandon and continued, "that is, before you get started picking on that guitar of yours. Looks like you would get tired of playing that thing incessantly like you do."

Brandon responded, "Oh yeah, thanks for the reminder...I almost forgot 'bout the meetin'. I been thinkin' 'bout goin' over to Aaron's house...you know, that new guy, Isaac's father? Aaron says he's got a guitar, a mandolin and some drums. I'd love to sit around and play music with him for a while."

Michael spoke up and said, "When you go, can I go with you?" Michael, loved to sing when Brandon played his guitar.

"Sure, that would be great!" replied Brandon. Then Brandon and Michael started toward the chow hall together.

As the men who had been working on the big house approached the water basins next to the new chow hall, they could see the men coming down from the mill, along with the men who brought in a load of trees earlier in the day.

Oscar raised his voice over the noisy dinner and questioned, "Did any of you men run into trouble again today, trying to get here?'

"Well," Vernon said, "them ruffians don't mess wit' me so much now, since the men been walkin' me here of a mornin'. But, they's been follerin' me home, so done seed whar' Ah lives."

Dominique glanced quickly, and was relieved to see that Jessica was busy enough to not hear him, so he added in a low voice, "They's follerin' me too, but ain't tried to hurt me none, so far. They yells awful things at me, callin' me names and such, though."

Luke spoke up and said, "My missus and chil'un is mighty scar't when them rascals is sneakin' 'round my house at night...especially, after the way that bunch of 'em beat me up on the way home that first day. I missed morn' a few days o' work 'cause o' that."

"You have all been brave men to keep coming anyway," Oscar said proudly.

One of the men commented, "Well sir, if'n we didn't come, we couldn't feed 'r fam'lys."

"Let's put our thinking caps on, and see if we can come up with some answers to address this situation. Come on, what do you think men?"

"Ah thinks y'all ought t' foller behind a bit, an' shoot anyone yo' sees follerin' us," Henry said in half-jest, since he had to walk home, too.

Oscar laughed, but didn't completely dismiss the idea, then said, "Perhaps we can be a little more creative than that...any other ideas?"

Michael, one of the army men who rode in with Oscar said, "Hey, do you guys remember when our unit was in Kentucky that time? We was sittin' ducks, fixin' those tracks out in the open like that. We just knew them Johnny Rebs was gonna' sneak up out of the bushes and wipe us all out? You remember, don't you?"

Steven snickered, "Yeah, and when they did show up, we engaged them to defend ourselves! Brought more of them Rebs down than there was of us that day...and we didn't leave nobody to go get help, either."

"Do you remember what we fixed up in them bushes to alert us ahead of time that the enemy was approaching? That secret alarm system we figured out then could help us now, couldn't it? If we rig up alarms at each of these men's houses, they would have plenty of warning to defend themselves if anybody came snooping around outside. It'd be over before the perpetrators ever figured out what happened!"

"And, we can continue to split up and walk the men home and back in groups each day, like we've been doing." Brandon added.

"Now you're talking!" Oscar said. "And, since we are having this meeting tonight, that should confuse them a little, too. You are all going to be late heading home today, so you probably messed up their plans for tonight. But, if we do what you're suggesting, Michael, you men will be out most of the night rigging up all those alarms. Are you sure you want to do that?"

The room erupted with a rumble of indistinguishable chatter, as everyone spoke up at once to express wholehearted determination to do what they can to put an end to the problem.

Brandon stood up and raised his voice saying, "Colonel, we are all sick and tired of the delays and interruptions this bunch of bullies are causing. They are slowing down our progress, and it is time for us to do whatever is necessary to stop them. It is wrong what they are doing to these men who are just trying to do their jobs, so they can feed their families. We are better men than they...just let us prove it!"

Everyone cheered as they shook their fists in the air and made affirmative remarks.

"Okay, then," said Oscar. "Under the circumstances, feel free to come in late in the morning. That should confuse the ruffians even more, and let you make up at least an hour of lost sleep. Then let's start staggering work hours every day. Hopefully, doing these things will help the situation, at least for a while. Then, next time I go to Richmond, I will ask Sergeant O'Riley if he has any other suggestions."

The men were jubilant, all talking at once. The soldiers were thrilled with the challenge, and the men who lived off of the plantation were grateful for their help.

Oscar stood to his feet and motioned for the men to quiet down, then interjected, "Well, it sounds like we have a good plan to solve that problem, so let's get on with our meeting. After we clear off the table and carry our dirty dishes over to the wash tub for the ladies, I would like us to group into our work teams to discuss work issues. Please feel free to express your ideas and any constructive criticism you may have about the way things are being done. We want to be efficient as well as safe, as we pursue perfection on the job around here. Nathaniel and Brandon, I need you men to stay after the meeting, please."

"Oh, come on!" Brandon said, sarcastically, "and miss the fun tonight?" Everyone knew that this kind of "night out" was not his thing, though he was actually the one that designed the secret alarm system they used in Kentucky during the war.

Everyone laughed lightheartedly.

"Before we get started," Oscar said, ignoring Brandon's remark, "Ross, I would like to congratulate you, Darrell and Norman on the fantastic work you did on the bunk house and chow hall." While everyone applauded, Oscar continued with, "I am sure you will be a tremendous asset to me, working on the mansion."

"We couldn't have done it without the good work of the men on the other two teams, sir," Ross responded, as Darrell and Norman nodded in agreement. "'T'was a team effort, and I'm glad it came out so well, Colonel."

Oscar motioned for everyone to break up into teams and begin, as he turned to Steven and said, "Do you have any sketches you would like to pass around of the fancy trim work for the mansion, so we can all see what you are suggesting for the finer touches? This is going to be a grand home when we are done with it, so we do not want to overlook the details that will make it magnificent!"

111

Steven opened his sketch book and dazzled everyone on the mansion team with his creative eye and artistic ability. He had fashioned beautifully ornate, but practical, trims and architectural features.

Oscar changed the subject when he said, "Darrell and Norman, you are also artists with those old bricks! I am amazed. It is almost impossible to tell where you are piecing them in with the original Oaklayne bricks that were still standing. I know that the lathing is a long way off, but be sure and let me know in plenty of time how much plaster you will need.

"Michael do you have plans yet for where the tubing will be placed for the gas lamps throughout the house? I would like to look at those. It will not be long until you can start running some of that tubing through the framework that Brandon has already constructed. By the way, I really like your ideas for maximizing ventilation in the summer and optimizing heat in the winter.

"Brandon, you have captured the essence of the incredible original framework design reflected in the plans of this remarkable home. You and Michael are doing a superb job fitting your work to the old foundation and what is left of the original structure. I would like for you to meet with Nathaniel to go over the sizes of the structural beams you will need next."

"Ross, you've been a big help coming up with extraordinary solutions to some unusual situations we've encountered. I want you to know that I am very pleased with your oversight of each part of this project. You have been very organized and have kept me up to date well, so I can figure out what materials will be needed next and have things ready for you when you need it."

Elsie was suddenly overcome with the intense desire to tickle Oscar's foot, when she entered the relaxing room and saw him sound asleep there in the big chair. He resembled a rag doll, with his head hanging down and flopped over to one side. As usual, she was the last one to finish up in the kitchen, and simply couldn't resist the urge. She quietly tiptoed toward him, but as she reached out to touch his foot, she accidentally tripped over his boots and landed with her full weight in his lap!

Oscar, rudely jarred out of a deep sleep, jumped up as if he had been tackled by a troop of Johnny Rebs! In the process, Elsie was dumped to the floor on her backside. Then Oscar proceeded to trip over her skirt and landed face down, right on top of her!

"Get off of me!" Elsie screamed, as the weight and shock of having him on top of her gave her a fright.

The thunder of men coming down the steps, falling over each other, as they hurried to Elsie's rescue, caused them both to look up from their inopportune positions, as men piled up at the bottom of the steps, with confused expressions on their faces.

"What on earth is going on?" Oscar exclaimed.

"That's what we'd like to know!" Nathaniel's voice boomed as he stood there in his long johns.

Ross was right behind him with his revolver ready for action.

Then, unable to contain herself, Elsie began to giggle and then belly laugh uncontrollably.

"I was only...," she was trying to explain, but could not stop laughing.

"Now, see here Elsie! I said, what is going on here?" Oscar said with a very confused expression.

"I just wanted to.....tickle....please, wait a minute...until I...get untangled from your legs...," she said, all the while still laughing.

"Miss Elsie, is yo' okay? Yo' don' scar'd the daylights out o' us," said Nathaniel as he helped her to her feet.

She sat down, trying to regain her composure, as all of the men were staring at her. "It's okay, everyone. I can explain. You see, when I came out of the kitchen and saw Oscar asleep over here, I couldn't resist tickling his foot. No big deal, except that I tripped over his boots and landed in his lap! Then he jumped...and, well you know the rest."

Ross could not contain his laughter, which became contagious to everyone, as he said, "I am disappointed in you, Oscar!"

By this time, Oscar was blushing like a school girl when he said, "I did not mean to..."

"That's what I'm talkin' about, man! You had this pretty little filly right there in your lap, and what did you do...you dumped her in the floor!"

Then everyone roared with laughter, while Oscar stood staring at Elsie with a questioning look on his face that she could not read. She had the strangest feeling, right after landing in his lap...the instant before he bolted up...it was if.... she belonged there.

"Well, gentlemen, I think I have entertained you well enough for now, so I will bid you a good night," Elsie said, as she quickly headed out the door with her head held high, the men staring after her.

113

Chapter 21

Adam sat, stunned. How had this happened? As a Major in the Army at Laramie, he had very successfully lead troops into battle. For President Lincoln, he had risked his life, working undercover, exposing Union soldiers who were illegally dealing arms to the Confederates. As a Union General, he was Lincoln's Adviser...and now, as a civilian, Secretary Stanton's Adviser. So, how is it that he had failed so miserably in this battle?

He had been resolute in his plan. He was sure that he approached it with integrity, considering everyone's best interests. So why had he failed? It seemed to him that he had lost everything he ever cared about. He sat with his head in his hands, clearly a defeated man. This was not supposed to happen, but...

"Are you ready to go, Father?" Randy said as he walked into the room. "You are here are you not? Oh yes, I can hear you breathing. Are you okay? Is something wrong? "

"Uh-hem," Adam tried to clear the lump in his throat. "Yes son, I am fine...just trying to resolve the issues."

Randy walked confidently over and sat down in the wing back chair across from his father, as if he were not blind at all, and said, "Father, do you not understand? I am not a little boy anymore. I am a man now, and I have to do this. I will not remain like a little puppy, being led around from place to place. I must learn to be productive, contributing to society. I am excited about this adventure, and simply must take advantage of it. I wish you could understand.

"I also want to make you proud of me, Papa. I know that you love me, and do not want anything to happen to me. But, even if I still had my vision so I could see the risks I am facing, I would still have hazards to deal with in life. Please let me go with your blessing and encouragement, so I can be all that I am able to be and more, with the Lord's help."

Adam sat quietly for a spell, collecting his thoughts and trying to control his conflicted emotions. "Randy, what you are asking is the hardest thing that I have ever had to do. I so much regret all of those

114

times in the past that I had to leave you with your Grandparents, because duty called. I wish now that I had stayed with you, but..."

"Yes Father, I know...but please understand that what calls me now is the same thing. I am so proud that you served our country and made such a difference. It is because of you and men like you that my best friend, Benjy, and those like him are free men today. That is also why I do not want him to go with me. Benjamin must find his own way too. He has too much to offer to spend his days looking after me. Me going away to this blind school will give Benjamin his chance to make a difference, too."

Adam reached over and placed his hand on his son's leg, then resolutely stated, "Randy, no father who ever lived is more proud of his son or has more pain in letting him go than I do. You are more courageous than any man I know, son. I also understand that you have to leave, whether or not I give my blessing. But, I have to admit that my pride in you overwhelms me to give my blessing, against my better judgment. I am confident that you will work hard at that school with the determination for excellence that you have always shown in the past. Please, do the best you can to find ways to communicate with us as often as possible. Maybe then, I will be better able to bear your absence."

Randy rose and reached out his hand to Adam saying, "Thank you, Father." When Adam stood and grasped his son's hand firmly, Randy threw his arms around his father and they embraced long and unashamedly.

Just as the two men moved apart, Lisa came in the door and said, "Are you ready to go, Randy?"

"I am," he said with authority and enthusiasm.

"Lisa, I do not know how to thank you for escorting Randy on this trip. I understand why he doesn't want me or Benjamin to go...and he is probably right. Anyway, I do appreciate your offer to accompany him to Boston. This should be plenty of money for anything that you may need along the way." Adam handed her a generous amount of cash.

Sara Ella and Benjamin came into the room to say their good-bye's, each hugging Randy in turn.

Adam could not help but make one last attempt at softening Randy's resolve when he said, "Randy, I sure would like to go with you to the depot. I promise that I will let you go...please...may I at least see you get safely on that train?"

"No, Father. I prefer that my parting memory be of these special moments here, without the hustle-bustle at the station. And, it will make it easier for Lisa, as she escorts me. Tom, are you ready with the carriage?"

"Yes Randy, it is my privilege to escort you to the train station."

Adam was clearly frustrated when he said, "Well, do we have the address and everything we need to contact you at the school?"

"Yes, Father. Sara Ella has everything you should need to keep in touch with me there."

Sara Ella reached over and took Adam's hand. She showed him the packet that Mrs. Kelley had given them about Perkins School for the Blind, reminding him that it is in Dorchester Heights in South Boston. Then she said, "Remember, Mrs. Kelley told us that she is available any time we want to go over all of the details of the school again."

"I'm sorry, Randy. I know I am acting like a doting father again," Adam said as he put his arm around Randy's shoulders and escorted him down to the carriage.

When Randy and Lisa were seated in the carriage everyone bid farewell again. Adam took Randy's hand one last time and said, "I love you, son...do not ever forget that." Then he nodded to Tom, and the carriage started down the street.

Benjamin felt hollow inside, as he watched his best friend and only reason for living, ride away in that carriage. So, what do I do now? I do not even know who I am, without Randy Layne by my side. I feel as if a vital part of me was just permanently amputated! I am truly free for the first time in my life, what I always wanted, right? At least, I thought I did...but I did not know I would feel so empty... The more he pondered his situation, Benjamin found himself shaking with a terrible uneasiness.

"I think I will go for a walk," he said absentmindedly to himself, not caring if anyone was listening. What difference did it make now that nobody needed him for anything.

Adam watched Benjamin walk off, wondering if he was okay. But, then he was drawn back to his own grief. How am I going to live, not knowing if Randy is okay? He finally came home, but now he is gone farther away than before...will I ever see him again? Lord, please...I cannot lose him again...

They already had their tickets when they arrived at the B&O Railroad Station, so Tom was busy taking the steamer trunks to the baggage destination. Lisa was trying to lead Randy, weaving their way through the crowd toward their train car. Suddenly, a large boisterous man rushed past them in a hurry, pushed his way between them and knocked Randy to the ground. Then the rushing crowd carried Lisa along with them, leaving Randy behind.

"Randy!" Lisa yelled. "Help!" But, she was so small that people kept pushing her on ahead. *Whatever am I going to do!* Just then a big hand reached out and grabbed her. She turned, terrified, but melted in relief, as she saw Tom standing over her, pulling her to the center of the station, where Randy was sitting quietly, as if nothing had happened.

"Oh, Randy! You are okay...", she said as she began to relax somewhat.

"I am sorry, Lisa. Did I give you a scare?" he said with a grin. "Our adventure sure is starting with a bang!"

Lisa looked up at Tom, who shrugged his shoulders. Then she looked back at Randy who did not seem upset at all.

"Okay...okay...I admit it. I was a little frightened, until Tom grabbed me," Randy confessed. "Please Tom, do not mention this little incident to my Father. He is worried enough already."

"Randy, do you not think we should go back and tell your father you have changed your mind, and you would like for me to go with you on this trip?"

"No!" Randy replied, firmly. "I truly want to make this work. Anyway, my Father and Sara Ella need you with them. Again, I ask you to please not mention this at home."

"Okay, I will not mention it, as long as you can both reassure me that you have a plan for staying together in crowds."

"Lisa," Randy said, "I am so sorry you had to be frightened like this. But, if you will work with me, I think I know what will help. You see, I am used to Benjamin keeping me constantly informed of my surroundings."

"I never thought about that being the reason that he talked to you, constantly...I just thought he was a chatterbox. But now it makes sense."

"I am sure that if I had understood the tightness of the crowd we were in, I would have made every effort to brace myself and hold more tightly on to you, while you were holding me."

"Tom, are you willing to follow us for a bit, so we can try again?"

"Sure," Tom said.

Lisa headed for the most congested area she could find. She described everything she saw to Randy, every side step and obstacle in their path. Randy never missed a beat, staying together with Lisa, even when he was jostled and pushed hard in every direction. Now, they felt confident that he was ready. Even Tom was convinced they could handle it, when he helped them both onto the train.

Chapter 22

As Benjamin ambled down the street, contemplating his new life of freedom, he did not notice the scowls on the faces of the well-to-do strangers he was passing.

He overheard someone say, "What is he doing here?"

Then someone else said, "He does not belong here."

But, he was completely unaware that they were talking about him, until he was suddenly surrounded by some well-dressed white men.

"What is the meaning of this, boy? Why are you parading down our street like this? You obviously do not belong here," one of them said.

"Go find your own street to strut down," a young man said, as he pushed Benjamin.

Benjamin threw his arm up to divert a swing from one of them, when he heard someone yell, "Hey! Yo' hasn't run out of them posters ag'in has yo'? An' how'd yo' go an' git in this here trouble? Please, 'scuse us gentlemen. We's a puttin' these here posters up fo' y'all. We'll git right out yo' way, yes sah'," the tall young black man said, as he grabbed Benjamin and shoved him around the corner to safety.

"Are you trying to get yourself killed, or worse?" the young black man said.

"Uh, thank you...I think. This is my first time out in the city alone. I was just in deep thought and forgot my surroundings. Anyway, are we not free men now?" Benjamin did not know what to think.

"Of course, we are free. Mr. Lincoln said so," he said, rolling his eyes in exasperation. "But, these white men still consider us 'separate', you know."

Benjamin was clearly confused, but answered anyway, "I guess I should have realized that, but the people I live with do not treat me like I am 'separate'. My name's Benjamin, Benjamin Layne, by the way. I am here in the employ of General Adam Layne."

"I am Walter Beasley," Walter said with a big grin, "and right now I am putting up these posters. I am pleased to hear that you sound as well educated as I am. That 'throw back language' you heard back there was, of course, for their benefit. It has been against the law for us to be educated, so I did not want to upset them. Surely you know we have to be careful not to let them know we are educated, right?"

"Well I guess I had this grand notion that it would be different now that we are free men," answered Benjamin.

Walter started to laugh, and then said, "You are truly naive, my new friend. There are still many, many rights that we do not have as free men. The means to get an education is one of them. In fact, that is what these posters are about. You know who Frederick Douglass is, do you not?"

"Uh, should I?" said Benjamin.

"Benjamin Layne, I guess you're not as well educated as I assumed. Frederick Douglas is probably the most famous black man who ever lived," Walter said, as he started walking down the street. Then he swelled out his chest and asked, "Can you read?"

"Of course, I can read," Benjamin responded in disgust.

Walter stood erect, indicating the importance of what he was about to say, then proclaimed, "Well, here is the announcement of his coming. It says here that Frederick Douglass is 'an orator, writer, statesman and a leader of the abolitionist movement.' Why, Mr. Douglass has written best seller books, published here in America and in Europe. Some were even translated into French and Dutch. Even before the war, he was the most famous black man in America. You must come and hear the speech he will be delivering in the morning at nine o'clock. I can get you in, if you will meet me at six thirty at that intersection up ahead.

I could use your help with the set-up, in fact. And, if you can stay afterward to clean up, I might be able to introduce you to Mr. Douglass before he goes up to the Capitol to address the Freedman's Bureau."

Benjamin dropped his jaw and said with amazement, "Did you say the Capitol? Do you mean the Capitol of the United States?"

As Walter rolled his eyes again, he said, "Just meet me here in the morning, and you will see for yourself. You've got a lot to learn, my friend. Now, do you want to help me put up these posters, or not? It just might keep you out of trouble. I can show you what streets are safe for you to use."

When Benjamin arrived back home, he found Adam pacing the floor in the parlor. He assumed that Adam was concerned about Randy leaving earlier in the day, until he saw the relief on Adam's face as he came in.

Adam embraced him warmly and said, "Where have you been, young man? It is late, and I was concerned that I had lost you, too. Are you okay?"

Benjamin was surprised, and responded, "I am so sorry, sir. I did run into a bit of trouble, but a new friend helped me out and showed me around. I do not think that will happen again."

Adam sighed in relief, knowing Benjamin was safely at home. But, then his composure darkened a little, as he said, "Benjamin, while you were gone I was chiding myself for not spending time explaining to you how to get along in the outside world without Randy accompanying you. There are some hateful people that are not at all hospitable, and it can be quite dangerous for you out there alone.

I was thinking, perhaps Tom should go out with you to help you learn how to navigate these streets. Both the snobbish white people, as well as some of the trouble making blacks and the desperate new freedman can be a challenge, even for a seasoned veteran like Tom. For that reason you will need to be careful where you go out and in choosing your friends. Do you understand what I am saying, son? You seem to be distracted or preoccupied...what's up?"

"Yes sir, you are right, I am preoccupied. You see, not long after I left here earlier today, a young black man about my age rescued me from a situation, and told me the same things you just said. His name is Walter Beasley. I have to confess, sir...I am confused. Since, we have been freed, why can we not go wherever we want, just like other men?"

"Benjamin, it is really quite complicated. Our government is struggling right now to find answers to your questions, and mine. Freeing the slaves has brought out some unexpected problems. There are some people, like me, who want you to have complete freedom just like white men...but, others want to restrict it. And some, as you can imagine, are angry that your freedom was granted at all. They want to take out their anger on your race. In the middle are some who want to see both sides come to terms with each other, however slowly and gently. That is what Abraham Lincoln was hoping to accomplish before he was killed. For now, you have been freed from slavery...but, there are a lot of rights that white American men have that have not been given to you, yet."

Benjamin looked Adam in the eye and said, "You've always treated me more as a son than a slave, and from the bottom of my heart, and I thank you for that. I know it is not like Randy, of course, but I trust you to want the very best for me, and I honor your advice above all others.

"Please, tell me if you know who Frederick Douglass is? You see, the young man I met on the street is quite taken with this man, and wants me to know him, too. He asked me to go with him tomorrow morning to hear Frederick Douglass speak. Do you think it would be a good idea for me to go? May I?"

"First, I think it would be a wonderful thing for you to hear Frederick Douglass speak. And, you do not have to have my permission to go where ever you wish. I trust you completely, but until we are both comfortable that you know your way around safely, I would appreciate it if you would let me know where you are going and approximately when you will be home. If it is not convenient for you to tell me, please leave a note where I will find it."

Benjamin, nodded his head and said, "Yes sir I will, and thank you for your concern for my safety."

"Good," Adam said, smiling as he continued. "Second, yes I do know who Frederick Douglass is. Your friend has found a great role model! I met Douglass a couple of times when he came to visit President Lincoln about the treatment of black soldiers during the war. And, I had the privilege of hearing him address Congress once. Now, let me tell you, that man is a dazzling orator! If you have the chance to hear him, do not let anything get in your way. It is my understanding that Douglass is supposed to address the Freedmen's Bureau at the Capitol Building tomorrow afternoon. In fact, after you hear him speak tomorrow morning, if you and your friend, Walter, want to eat with me at noon, you can accompany me to the Capitol to hear him address the Freedmen's Bureau." Then as an afterthought, Adam asked, "Did you know that President Lincoln established the Freedmen's Bureau?"

Benjamin was flabbergasted, "Oh my! I do not know what to say! I was stunned when Walter invited me to hear this man's speech in the morning, and now I'm even more astounded to be invited to accompany you to a meeting at the Capitol. I'm so grateful for this opportunity! I am certain that Walter will feel the same way, after the way he talked about Frederick Douglass." He gave in to the impulse to clap his hands, then said, "Thank you so much! Thank you!"

"Benjy...I mean Benjamin...you will soon learn that Mr. Douglass escaped from a harsh slave owner in Maryland, before becoming a leader of the abolitionist movement. He is the most convincing spokesman out there for black suffrage, as well as women's suffrage. His autobiography eloquently describes his slavery experience. I will try to find a copy for you to read. Benjamin, this man has confounded the slave owners, who are telling our leaders that your race is not intelligent enough to take care of yourselves. You and I know Douglass is right, and he is working to communicate that message to the world. His example, and the example of people like you, is hard for them to argue with."

Benjamin shook his head in amazement as he said, "I had no idea that there are people out there who are working so hard for my race. Of course, I have heard some stories from the slaves of other plantations of very bad treatment, and even heard a few at Oaklayne Plantation, when Patrick was the foreman there. But, I never really suffered hard times as a slave, and always felt fortunate to be Randy's friend. Until Randy left, I never had to think about the challenges other black men have faced all of their lives. I guess I do have a lot to learn, like Walter said."

Benjamin had no problem finding his way back to the trysting place, where he met Walter. They had a long walk together to get to the huge church building where Mr. Douglass was to give his speech that morning. Along the way, Walter mentioned that he had come to Washington City with Professor George Vashon, President of Avery College in Pittsburgh. He went on to explain that Professor Vashon was one of his favorite people and had been greatly encouraged by him. Vashon had been invited to Washington City by Mr. Douglass to meet together with him and the Freedmen's Bureau. The meeting had been arranged to discuss the best ways to provide educational opportunities to the freedmen.

It was clear to Benjamin that Walter was elated when he told him that Adam had invited them to attend the Freedmen's Bureau meeting at the Capitol. He could not get over his good fortune, to be able to hear Mr. Douglass speak twice in the same day!

When they arrived at the church, there were dozens of young black people gathered outside. Walter grabbed Benjamin by the arm and pulled him over to where a couple of them greeted him with enthusiasm.

Walter put his arm around a short black man with glasses and said, "Benjamin this is my friend, Ira. He attends Avery College...no...actually, he just graduated, so he thinks he is smarter than the rest of us...." He winked as he made that comment.

"I heard that!" Ira said smiling. "It is nice to meet you, Benjamin."

Then, Walter gestured toward an attractive young black woman and said, "Benjamin, this is, Hallie Quinn Brown. She hopes to be accepted for enrollment to Wilberforce University real soon. You may not know that they are in the process of rebuilding that school after an arson fire last year. Hallie has been told that she has a good chance of being included as one of only a few women students they allow into Wilberforce, once they reopen. Like the rest of us, she is enthralled with Frederick Douglass!"

Hallie smiled and said, "I am glad you are here Benjamin. As you can see, we can use all of the help we can get around here. It is great to have the help of all of these church members. But, we could get a lot more done if we could just convince Walter to stop talking and get to work..."

Walter flashed one of his big trademark smiles and said, "What are you waiting for? Let's get to it!"

To his surprise Walter invited Benjamin to sit with him on the front row. Even more surprising was when the announcer introduced Walter and asked him to come up on stage to sing the special music! Walter proceeded to sing the most beautiful rendition of "Fairest Lord Jesus" that Benjamin had ever heard. He introduced the hymn by pointing out that the words speak of Christ's divine nature, as well as His humanity. As Benjamin listened to the first verse, he heard:

"Fairest Lord Jesus; Ruler of all nature,
O Thou of God and man the Son.
Thee will I cherish; Thee will I honor,
Thou my soul's glory, joy and crown."

Walter's face glowed like an angel, as he finished singing. Before returning to his seat, Walter looked out at the audience and said, "As we ponder the words of that hymn, let us be reminded of the words from John Chrysostom, in his fourth-century sermon:

'I do not think of Christ as God alone, or man alone, but both together. For I know He was hungry, and I know that with five loaves He fed five thousand. I know He was thirsty, and I know that He turned the water into wine. I know He was carried in a ship, and I know that He walked on the sea. I know that He died, and I know that He raised the dead. I know that He was set before Pilate, and I know that He sits with the Father on His throne. I know that He was worshiped by angels, and I know that He was stoned by the Jews. And truly some of these I ascribe to the human and others to the divine nature.'

"For by reason of this, I, Walter Beasley, know that Jesus Christ is both God and man."

When Walter came back to his seat, Benjamin Layne instinctively reached for his hand in true respect.

"Thank you," Walter whispered as he sat down.

Benjamin did not know what to expect as Frederick Douglass, a very dignified black man walked to the podium. People were crammed like sardines into the huge church, filling the aisles and even overflowing out the doors. As Fredrick Douglass began to speak, Benjamin realized he had never heard anyone speak so eloquently. But, it was his humility that drew you into each word he said, as if he cared for every person in attendance. He was talking about equality of all people, not just these black people in attendance, but also Native Americans, as well as recent immigrants and women.

"I would unite with anybody to do right, and with nobody to do wrong." Douglass just said emphatically.

The most powerful thing Benjamin heard Douglass say was, "Knowledge is the pathway from slavery to freedom." Somehow, Benjamin knew that he was talking about true freedom, not just freedom from slavery. He wanted to remember to discuss this with Walter when he got a chance.

Benjamin was elated with excitement when he and Walter met Adam for the noon meal! Adam stood quietly, with his hands clasped in front of him, listening as Benjamin went on and on about Douglass' speech in almost incoherent sentences.

Finally, Adam interrupted, with a wink at Walter and said, "Benjamin, son, would you like to introduce me to your friend?"

Embarrassed beyond measure, Benjamin said, "Oh, please excuse me! I've completely lost my manners. General Adam Layne, please meet my good friend, Walter Beasley. Walter this is General Layne, who has been like a father to me, throughout my life."

"I'm pleased to meet you, Walter. I hope that you are hungry, because you may have to eat Benjamin's food, as well as your own, if he cannot stop talking," Adam said with a laugh, as they sat down.

Joining in the merriment, Walter responded, "I am also pleased to meet you General Layne. Thank you for inviting me to eat lunch with you and accompany you to the Capitol this afternoon. Believe me, sir, I know just how Benjamin feels. This my second time to hear Mr. Douglass speak, and he was just as powerful this time as before. Are you aware that this meeting Frederick Douglass and George Vashon are having with some leaders from the Freedmen's Bureau is about education?"

"My goodness you are certainly up on political affairs, Walter?" Adam said. "No, I didn't know the agenda of the meeting this afternoon."

"Well, I am up on this one, at least. Professor Vashon keeps me informed, and as involved as possible. He keeps telling me that decisions are being made right now that will greatly affect my future and the future of this nation. He says that I need to be prepared to do all

I can to influence others to help my race integrate into society, through ethical, educated choices."

"This Vashon sounds like a wise teacher. I hope I will have an opportunity to meet him. He and Douglas will be addressing the Freedmen's Bureau this afternoon, and that is the meeting that I have invited you to attend with me," Adam said, as he watched Benjamin take the last bite from his plate. He chuckled when he noticed that Walter had hardly touched his.

Benjamin could stand it no longer...he simply must ask his question: "Walter, in his speech, Mr. Douglass said, 'Knowledge is the pathway from slavery to freedom.' I get the fact that he was talking about more than just freedom from slavery, but I cannot help but feel like there is an even greater meaning here. Am I right?"

"Wow, that is deep Benjamin! I am impressed. I have my own thoughts on that, but first I would like to hear General Layne's commentary."

"Well, the only thing I could add, without giving it some thought, is that there are a lot of white men who are not, and never have been, slaves in the same way that you boys have been. They have a great education, and even had all the luxuries that life has to offer, but it does not look to me like they are truly free. It seems we are all slaves to something. I would sure like to hear your thoughts Walter, but I see that we must get moving if we are going to find a good seat at the Capitol."

On the way there, Adam explained that Congress is currently in recess. So, the Capitol is not as busy this time of the year, as in the fall and until about April.

General Oliver Howard, the head of the Freedman's Bureau, under Secretary of War Stanton, started the meeting, stressing the importance of developing a college for the freedmen. He recommended that the first college be a theological seminary to educate African-American clergymen.

Then General Howard introduced Professor George Vashon, the Principal and second black President of Avery College in Pittsburgh, Pennsylvania. Professor Vashon spoke to the gathering about the importance of starting a law school for the freedmen. He stated that there was a great need to train lawyers who would be committed to helping black Americans secure and protect their newly established rights.

Mr. Douglass spent the most of his address to the Freedman's Bureau addressing the importance of lobbying Congress to ratify two new Amendments to the Constitution that were written by some Radical Republicans. The 13th Amendment would give freedom to all slaves including those in the North.

Benjamin's head was spinning with unfamiliar terminology, further convincing him that he did, indeed, have much to learn.

After the meeting, Walter introduced George Vashon to Adam and Benjamin. Professor Vashon introduced General Howard and Frederick Douglass, who, to Adam's delight, recognized him.

Benjamin was completely overwhelmed, and also confounded by how much knowledge his new friend Walter possessed already. He felt a fire burning deep within, wanting to make the world a better place, like these men. They were using knowledge and wisdom to wage a different kind of war for Benjamin's own people. He also had a new appreciation and admiration for Adam, who had accomplished so much good, helping them reach this place. Tonight Benjamin would have a long talk with Adam about his future.

Chapter 23

It was less than a day's ride to Macon, Georgia for August and Ralph. As they loaded up their saddle bags for another day, August laid his arms lazily up across his saddle and mused, "I wish Trevor had been with us to see all the charred black countryside we have been riding through, Doc. It looks like a black desert out there...nothing left...not a fence, a house, or even any animals...no cows, dogs or wild animals, for that matter...not anything. Sherman's march wiped it all out."

Ralph used some sarcasm to recall his own bleak observations of what they saw, when he added, "That's not entirely true, August. Do not forget, we did see some blackened chimneys, where grand manor homes once stood...and do not forget the buzzards we saw circling overhead, occasionally."

August frowned and gave Ralph a one sided half grin, then said, "With my background, it is hard to comprehend the fancy lifestyle the plantation owners led here, just a short time ago. I also do not get the reversed black and white thing they had going on here."

"What are you talking about the 'reversed black and white thing'?" Ralph asked, obviously confused by August's comment.

"You know, everyone usually connects the color black with evil and the color white with good...the old black-hat/white-hat thing. But, this is clearly a case where that connotation was reversed, at least on most of these plantations. The white people were evil, taking advantage of the black folks. So, it seems to me, the whites were acting black. In contrast, the black people submitted like the Bible says we should do...so, the black folks were acting white. Now do you get it?"

Laughing out loud, Ralph shook his head in agreement and said, "Well, I have never heard it put quite that way before, August. But, you certainly have a point! Your way of thinking about it does illustrate clearly that you cannot tell what color a person is by the color of his skin, now can you?"

August swung his leg over his saddle and set his boot in the stirrup, obviously ready to hit the trail. "That is the way I see it, Doc. One thing you said about people here in the South that seems especially rotten to me is how the big plantation owners bought up most of the land, making it difficult for the small farmers to survive. But, now they are reaping what they sowed, like that man we met yesterday who was selling bricks from his burned down mansion, so he could buy foodstuffs from those small farmers he had tried to put out of business before."

The men kept talking, as they made their way down the road toward Macon. Doc said, "You have to understand, August, before the war the dominating slave-holding class made it hard on those small farmers in several ways. Like, they made it difficult to impossible for them to obtain inexpensive tools and goods, and kept them from having any marketplace available to sell their products. Those big plantation owners bought and sold by shipping mostly to European or Northerners, which meant that the small farmers did not even have a way to transport their goods to cities or towns nearby. They completely dominated trade in the South."

August pulled up the reins of his horse, took off his hat and shook off the dust, then said, "Oh no...Thunder has something in his hoof again." He dismounted, pulled Thunder's hoof up and positioned it between his legs with a grunt, then said, "I've got to clean it out, so he does not come up lame." Then he continued, "I understand what you mean about transportation not being adequate, Doc. There sure are not many roads going where we need to go, and the ones that are available, are awful. There, that should do it, old boy." August slapped Thunder on the hip and rubbed the side of his neck before climbing back in the saddle.

Ralph shook his head and declared, "Yep, railroads, highways and canals were all constructed here in the South, entirely for the big plantation owners to ship their crops out and bring in luxury items."

"I had no idea that to such an extent, everything in the South catered to the very rich...it is a terrible thing," said August.

Continuing on with their discussion, Ralph said, "Coming from the North you probably do not realize that most of the population in the south, did not live on a plantation and had no means of getting an education. The wealthy plantation owners controlled the governmental revenues that could have financed public schools, but they didn't want that. Their own children had private tutors or went to expensive private schools, leaving the majority of white Southerners impoverished and uneducated."

August, wrestling his generous head of hair back under his hat, said, "I figured things would be bad for the plantation owners after the war, but I had no idea how rough it was for the working class whites as well as the slaves, even before the war. If slaves were not allowed by law to learn to read and write, then I say their owners were crazy! They could have done a much better job if they were educated...I just do not get it...it does not make sense." "The truth is, they were afraid for them to learn," Ralph explained. "That is the simple answer. You see they thought that if the slaves learned to read and write, they could communicate better amongst themselves and eventually start a rebellion. Or, they could find ways to help each other run away and find their freedom. So, the Southern ruling class passed a law that made it illegal for slaves to read and write. They could not even attend church without a white person accompanying them, nor could they testify against a white person in court or leave their plantation without written permission. Eventually, they passed laws that slave owners were not allowed to free their slaves, even in a will, because 'free blacks are dangerous, they might cause a rebellion.'"

"How did they keep them from running off, anyway?" August asked.

"Well," Ralph answered, "They set up 'slave patrols' made up of young white men. These patrols especially enjoyed bullying and whipping up on any black man they found who was away from his owner's plantation, even if he was carrying permission from his owner. They tended to attack first and ask questions later."

"What was wrong with slaves attending church by themselves?" August asked.

"Boy, you sure do have a lot of questions!" said Ralph, wiping the sweat from his brow. "I say we stop for a bit over there by that creek under those trees, where we can fill up our canteens...mine is getting low. Besides, I have not done this much talking, since Joy wanted an explanation for why I did not come home one night, after I had been hunting and my horse went lame."

August laughed, then queried further, "It sounds to me like there might be more to that story...what..."

"Oh, no you don't," Ralph interrupted. "I think I have answered enough questions for a while."

Trevor was pleased to see that the bridge reconstruction was going very well. At first, he was concerned that these Southern folks would not be willing to follow his instructions. He could tell that they were bright enough to understand what he needed them to accomplish...but, he did not know if they could put aside the fact that he was a Yankee, trying to supervise their construction project. He was pleased to see that some very good men, who were not in the lynching mob that day he arrived, joined in the work. They seemed to provide stability and a level head to the others. They also found good timber just north of Tennille that they were able to use for the trusses. Fortunately, he discovered that some of the men had hidden some good tools from the Union soldiers when they came through.

Joy interrupted Trevor's thoughts, as she brought his dinner and set it down on the table in front of him. "How 'bout some hearty rabbit stew tonight? I shot me a rabbit that was eating my begonias out by the fence...guess he won't be doing that anymore!"

Trevor held up his hands in a defensive manner, while sporting a silly grin and responded, "Uh...you will not need to remind me to be careful where I step out there by your flowers, ma'am!" Then he said, "I gotta' say, that rabbit sure smells good!"

Joy laughed and said, "I hope you enjoy it, young man. Here are some warm biscuits to sop up the gravy."

"I think I got the better end of the deal, compared to August. He is out there on the trail, cooking over a campfire, sleeping on the ground and looking for a needle in a haystack. I have got men working well under my supervision. You served me these great meals to eat, and I have a comfy bed in the boarding house up the street. Maybe, that is worth getting beat up and nearly hanged...or, maybe not. Anyway, I am glad I am not riding down to Macon and back on Lightnin'. August and I are both very thankful for you and Ralph getting us out of that mess."

"Well, I am sorry that it had to happen, but pleased to see how the Lord has used it for His good," Joy answered.

Trevor finished his meal and turned to Joy, "Martin has been telling me about how, during the war, the Confederate General Hardee consulted with General Wayne about further resistance along the Oconee River, where we're working on the bridge. But, General Sherman's Right Wing had already arrived. They destroyed the bridge we are working on, as well as the railroad bridge. They also destroyed miles of railroad tracks in their path, so Hardee ordered a withdrawal through Tennille. Martin said that the last Confederate unit had hardly cleared Tennille, when General Sherman arrived from Sandersville, accompanying his Left Wing, to join up with the Right Wing here in Tennille. This town really was in the thick of the battle!"

Joy looking at her lap and twisted the towel she was holding in her hands, responded, "First, we were over-run with Confederate troops, and then Union Troops. The Union troops destroyed our Depot, the water tank and all of the rail facilities. They burned them down to the ground. Then that bridge you're working on was destroyed by Sherman's Right Wing, and our railroad tracks from the Oconee river and tracks toward Davisboro were destroyed by the Left Wing."

Trevor somberly said, "I am beginning to see why people here are so angry with the Union, ma'am. You sure saw it all in this one little town...I do not even want to know how you were treated. I am so sorry for all that you have been through...worst of all, losing your own son."

"I thought we would never get over it, Trevor," Joy said, "but, you have helped so much, serving us so humbly and professionally. You are winning our hearts, giving us hope that not all Yankees are evil people."

Chapter 24

Randy was excited when he and Lisa reached the campus of Perkins Institute for the Blind in South Boston. He did not know what to expect, but figured this school was his best chance for a meaningful future. He was determined to put everything he had into being successful, learning everything they could teach him.

Lisa set about attempting to describe everything for Randy, as she had learned to do from Benjamin's example. "It looks like a big hotel, Randy. And, it looks like there is a new wing being built on...it is huge!"

"The school is huge, or the new wing is huge?" Randy asked for clarification.

"Both," Lisa said.

"Can you tell what the new wing is for?" Randy asked.

"No, but we can ask when we get inside. Now, we have come to a big door. If you will reach out your right hand, I will direct you to the handle, so you can be a gentleman and open it for me. There is one step up, when you come through the door."

Randy smiled and said, "Thank you, Lisa, for giving me the pleasure of opening the first door to my new life." Then he held out his arm to escort her inside.

After they reached the big open portico inside, Lisa said, "Randy, the entryway is quite large, and straight ahead is a sign that says 'Admissions'. Are you ready?"

"Well, except for the knocking of my knees," said Randy. "I know this is the right place for me so, yes...I am ready."

Randy heard a pleasant voice greeting them, just before they reached the Admissions office.

Lisa whispered, "She is carrying a white cane, and is walking directly toward us."

"Hello! Welcome to the Perkins Institute. My name is Thelma. I heard you come through the front door. How may I help you?"

Randy squeezed Lisa's hand, then with a distinguished smile said, "My name is Randall Layne, but most people call me Randy. This lovely lady with me is my Aunt Lisa Layne. I have come to enroll in this school, so could you please direct us to the appropriate office?" Thelma smiled and said, "Yes, Mr. Layne we are expecting you. Come right this way. Follow the sound of my cane as I tap it on the floor, please."

Randy removed Lisa's arm from his arm, then with a sheepish grin said, "Okay, ma'am, lead the way!" He found himself able to follow Thelma perfectly, and was starting to feel a bit proud of himself, until she stopped suddenly. He bumped into her, and exclaimed, "Oops! Sorry...I knew better...guess I must be excited."

Thelma giggled, and said. "I always do that to first timers, when I stop abruptly. My usual stop, as I will be taking you around the facility, is two quick taps with my cane, like this." She illustrated, so Randy could hear the two taps. "That way we can continue talking, while we are walking. It is one of the first things you will be learning here at the school, Randy."

Randy and Lisa spent the afternoon completing the necessary paperwork, paying the tuition and other expenses. Then Thelma gave them a tour of the school and explained about the new wing. "We are very excited about the new wing! It will be finished soon. Among other things, it will contain a gymnasium, living quarters for school officers, new music rooms, and workshops. We also have purchased a new lot that will soon be a wonderful playground for the children."

Next, Thelma escorted them to Randy's dorm room. Starting from the door to the right, she counted off steps to each object in the room, which were all spaced two steps apart, and then there were two steps to the far wall, which went all the way back to the door.

Randy glowed with enthusiasm when he said, "Thelma this is great! I feel like I already know my way around my room."

Thelma, who was accustomed to new students responding that way, said, "After dinner Brad, who lives on this floor, will show you some tricks to organizing your belongings. But, right now it is time for dinner, and you will need to know how to get there and back...so, pay close attention!"

Randy's excitement was obvious when he said, "Thelma you are a great encouragement to me, especially, knowing that you are blind, too! You seem so happy and confident, knowing your way around so well."

"Who said I was blind?" Thelma asked.

Randy looked embarrassed when he responded, "Well, I guess I just assumed... since you use the cane and all..."

Thelma laughed, "Now see there, Randall Layne, you can see after all! You've learned to reason...that is the first step."

"Randy, this is my queue to head for my hotel," Lisa said with a smile, as they walked out into the hallway. "I am so excited for you. This seems like the perfect place for you to learn what you need to know. Are you comfortable here? Is there anything I can do for you before I leave?"

Randy shook his head and said, "Well, I cannot say I am completely comfortable yet, but I am certain that I am in the right place. Please, tell Father everything you have seen and the potential that is obviously available to me here. Remember to tell him about the library Thelma showed us, where they have books with little bumps on the pages, that I will learn to read. Who knows, perhaps I can even take music lessons here, so I can do a better job playing my drum. And tell him that I love him...and please, thank him for allowing me this opportunity. I intend to do my best here."

"Oh Randy, you are so brave. I am very proud of you." Lisa said, just as a young man walked up to them.

"Randy Layne? Hi, I am Brad Vann. I've been told that you are to reside on my floor. I'm sure we will get to know one another well in the coming months. I will be helping you learn how to find your way to the dining room from here."

Lisa knew Brad did not see her, so she slipped back, whispered good-bye in Randy's ear and squeezed his hand, as she headed for the door.

As the train's wheels went clickity-clack on the rails, Lisa found herself missing Randy. Sure, helping him get around did take every bit of her attention, but at least it made her feel useful for a while. *I was not aware of how much Benjamin did for him all the time. Keeping Randy aware of his surroundings constantly, was a taxing responsibility. I do feel good about the school, though. I guess it is the mother in me that wants to be with him, to protect him...although, I do understand his desire to do as much as he can for himself. But, I also see why Adam is having such a hard time letting him go.*

Just then the train jerked, and she turned her attention out the window, as they pulled into a little town depot. At the station, there were people everywhere. They all seemed to know exactly where they were going and were determined to get there as quickly as possible. *Now that I have finished escorting Randy to school, what is my purpose? Once again, I am lost in a sea of uselessness. Oh, how I miss Goddard. He always found a way to help me feel productive and fulfilled. What will I do now?"* Swallowed up in self-pity, Lisa finally made her way to her sleeping car for the night.

After a few days of exhausting travel, the train finally pulled into the New York Central Terminal. Lisa was scheduled to change trains there, so she busied herself gathering her belongings before disembarking. Without much difficulty, she made her way to the train she would ride for the next leg of her journey.

"Who are those children?" Lisa asked the Porter, as he helped her up into the train car. "It looks like their getting into a baggage car...but, surely not!"

He looked in the direction she was pointing, then answered matter-of-factually, "Oh, ma'am, those children are orphans from New York City who are going west on the train to find families to care for them."

Additional passengers were pushing Lisa onto the train car, so she could not ask any more questions of the Porter about the children, but she wondered whether he understood her question. Surely, his answer made no sense at all.

Lisa changed trains again in Trenton, Pennsylvania, near Philadelphia. As she disembarked, she saw more children lined up like little soldiers on the train platform. She counted about 20 of them, all ages, from babies to teenagers. She could not believe her eyes! Out of curiosity, she watched the proceedings in astonishment. Soon, people started coming forward, obviously examining the children closely, looking at their teeth and then feeling of the muscles in their arms. Lisa felt sick, watching them handle those children like they were nothing more than cattle.

Then her attention was drawn to one boy in particular. Her heart immediately went out to him. He was around 10 years old, and had a terrible cough. It was obvious to Lisa that he needed medical attention. This was more than just a bad cold. The inspecting adults shied away from him, apparently afraid they would catch the malady he was suffering. Lisa could not help herself, so she went up to one of several ladies who were accompanying the children.

"Hello, I am Mrs. Lisa Layne from Virginia. I am concerned about the young boy down there on the end...the one with the bad cough."

"Oh yes, that is Samuel, Mrs. Layne. My name is Mrs. Waters. We thought he had recovered from that cough, before we left New York, but it seems to be getting worse. The town did not bring a doctor to the station this time to look at the children like they usually do, so he has not had any medical attention since we left New York. You know, people want to be sure that the children do not have any diseases when they consider taking them home."

Lisa was appalled at the plight of the children, but tried not to show it when she said, "I am a nurse, Mrs. Waters. Perhaps, I can be of assistance, if I may have a look at him, please."

"Oh, that would be a big help, if you could do that, please," she said, her large frame waddling somewhat, as she walked Lisa down the platform to examine young Samuel. "That would certainly relieve my concern, if you could tell us something we can do for him, poor thing."

"Samuel," Mrs. Waters said, as she walked up to him. "This nice lady is a nurse, and she would like to talk with you."

"Hello Samuel. My name is Lisa Layne. What is your last name?"

The boy coughed, then answered, "Baker, my name's Samuel Baker, ma'am."

"Well, Samuel Baker, I noticed that you have a pretty bad cough. I was wondering how you are feeling? Can you explain to me how you feel?"

The boy looked faint, and his cheeks were much too rosy, but he announced, "I feel great, ma'am. Never better. Just have this pesky little cough now and then. It is really nothing, though."

Lisa smiled and took the boys hand in hers saying, "I am glad to hear it, Samuel." Lisa tried not to show him her concern. "It was great to meet you, young man." Lisa turned back to Mrs. Waters and walked away.

"Well, what do you think?" asked Mrs. Waters.

Lisa spoke gravely, trying to express the seriousness of the situation when she said, "After looking more closely, I am more concerned than I was before. He has a very high temperature, his eyes are glassing over and his skin is on fire. He needs to go to the hospital immediately, or at the very least, he needs to see a doctor."

"Oh, my!" Mrs. Waters was clearly upset. "We cannot do that! The train leaves in just a little while, and I still have to attend to the paperwork for all of the adoptions here. We have a long trip ahead of us. The rest of these children still have to be placed with families. Some of these trains end up taking the children all the way to Texas, Mrs. Layne. Almost all of them end up being adopted out west."

"Do you mean to tell me that there are more trains with orphans than just this one?" Lisa exclaimed.

"Yes, there are thousands of orphaned children in New York alone, ma'am. We are doing our best to find homes where they can be cared for and hopefully loved. They have no hope of a good future if they remain in the city, that is for sure. Most of them would not even survive the filthy streets of New York."

Lisa's heart was breaking for the boy, "I wish I was continuing on this train, so I could tend to him, at least..." She could not stop thinking of how she had lost little Goddard to a fever when he was only four years old. Suddenly, she blurted out, "How old is Samuel?"

Mrs. Waters replied, "We think he's about ten. But, he does not remember his parents, and does not have any family that he is aware of."

Oh my...this boy is the same age that Little Goddard would have been if he had lived. Lisa turned to look back at him again and saw that he also had black hair...and his dark brown eyes reminded her so much of Little Goddard. *If I do not do something, this boy will die, too, just like my baby boy! I simply cannot let that happen...*

"If I take Samuel to a hospital, so he can get the care he needs, what should I do when he gets well?" Lisa questioned Mrs. Waters.

"That is just it," Mrs. Waters said, "We have no provision for that kind of thing. We will just have to take him to the next train stop and hope they have a doctor there who can treat him. But, we cannot leave him behind in a hospital. It is just not possible, ma'am."

Lisa was choking back tears when she pleaded, "But, he must have help, or he could die. Is there not something we can do?"

Mrs. Waters looked Lisa in the eye and bluntly said, "The only way you could help Samuel Baker is to adopt him."

Lisa felt like she had been struck with a lightning bolt. "But, I cannot do that!" she said.

Accustomed to dealing with objections, Mrs. Waters said, "Why not? If it does not work out, you can write to us about it and bring him back here next year. We will take him back and try to place him with someone else," then she turned and walked away.

Lisa felt trapped...not by this woman and her proposition, but by her own heart. *This is crazy! Why does this feel so right? Just moments ago, I had no thought of ever adopting a child...this is moving much too fast...am I feeling this way because I have mourned so for little Goddard, and I miss Angela so much? No, this is not the same...Oh, Lord what shall I do?*

Then, the answer came to her, clear as a bell. She remembered Warren Callahan and the people in the little church in Virginia. When she thought of how those people unselfishly helped each other every way they could, she knew what she had to do.

Running to catch up with Mrs. Waters, Lisa called out, "Wait! What do I need to do to adopt Samuel?"

"Are you serious?" Mrs. Waters said, a little astonished.

Lisa shook her head emphatically and said, "Yes, I am determined to help him. If adopting him is the only way to help, then that is what I will do. In fact, I think that is the right thing for me to do, even if he were not sick!"

"Well, all right then," said Mrs. Waters. "Since you are concerned with getting Samuel to a hospital, you will need to go and get your husband right away."

"I am a widow, Mrs. Waters," Lisa said. "My husband was killed in the war. In fact, I lost my husband and both of my children to that awful war."

"Oh dear, then we have a problem," said the large woman. "Our rules are that these children must go to a household with both a father and mother."

Lisa's heart sank...she spoke softly as she said, "I thought this was the right thing to do for the boy..."

After a brief pause, Mrs. Waters said, "Excuse me a minute, dear. I need to go and speak with the other Agents. I will be right back."

Strangely, Lisa was feeling almost like she had lost another child, when Mrs. Waters came back with a gentleman who introduced himself with his hand extended, "Hello, Mrs. Layne. I am Mr. Gander. We would sure like to help Samuel Baker in this difficult situation. Would you mind answering a few questions? Maybe, we can work something out, but we want to make sure he is left in the best possible circumstances. Do you understand?"

"Yes," Lisa said hopefully, "I will be glad to answer any questions you may have. What do you need to know?"

"Please tell us how did your husband die in the war?" he asked.

"My husband was Dr. Goddard Layne, a surgeon at Chimborazo Hospital in Richmond. I attended him there as his nurse, when the soldiers were brought in from the battlefields. As the Union Army was entering the city, my husband was trampled to death in the chaos. He had already sent me away, leading some wounded soldiers out of harm's way, so I did not actually see it happen. That is what I was told."

"Thank you, Mrs. Layne. I know that was painful, but we want to understand more about you. We have so little time, but we must be concerned for the boy's well-being, you know. Under the circumstances, the other Agents and I have agreed that it is in Samuel's best interests for you to take responsibility for him. We know this is a huge commitment on your part, but from your story it sounds like you have the strength of character to handle it. We also appreciate your gracious heart toward the boy and wish you both the best. He has led a rough life, ma'am. But, I believe you will understand each other well in a short time."

Mr. Gander turned to Mrs. Waters and said, "Please expedite Samuel Baker's adoption papers, so Mrs. Layne can take him to the nearest hospital promptly."

"Thank you so much, Mr. Gander," Lisa replied with tears. "I will take very good care of him, I promise."

After Lisa signed all of the papers, Mrs. Waters brought Samuel to Lisa and announced, "Samuel, this is your new mother, Mrs. Lisa Layne. Mrs. Layne, meet your new son, Samuel Baker Layne."

Chapter 25

"Marie, I am worried about Adam. When I try to discuss the wedding with him, he just doesn't seem interested. I know he misses Randy, but surely he knows that the school is much better equipped than we could ever be to help Randy reach his potential. Adam clearly supported Benjamin's desire to go to school, but I am sure his leaving at the same time as Randy has to have contributed to Adam's melancholy. Those boys have always been together, their whole lives. Perhaps, Adam feels like Benjamin took some of Randy with him when he left."

"Adam will get over it, Sara Ella. Just give him a little time, you will see," Marie tried to console her friend the best way she knew how, but it was obvious that Sara Ella was not really listening.

"If Adam Layne wants to be married, it seems to me that he would want to be involved in the planning. After all, he is the one that has been so adamant about being married in the church. A church wedding requires a lot more planning, especially when important people like he works with every day at the Capitol will be in attendance. Those people are not like the class of people that I grew up with, Marie. I feel so incompetent and inadequate...but, I want everything to be perfectly proper to please Adam. I do not want to embarrass him by doing something wrong. But, whenever I try to share an idea with him, he seems not to care at all.

"He appears to be depressed, Marie. Should he not be happily looking forward to our wedding? Depression is not healthy for a groom, is it?" Sara Ella began to cry.

"I am sorry," Marie said, as she put her arm around Sara Ella. "Did Adam give you that invitation list? Shall we work on that for a while. My boys will not bother us. Dean is down the street at a friend's house, and the younger ones, Sterling and Ross, seem to be keeping each other company well enough for now."

Sara Ella choked back tears as she said, "Please forgive me, for being so negative, Marie. I do not know what is wrong with me...I am not usually like this. You and Scott have been so gracious to open your home to me, when Lisa left to take Randy to Boston. I have grown to love those three boys of yours a great deal. I expect, Adam and I should not have been living under the same roof, even before Lisa left. Thank you for making it possible for us to remedy that situation. Some people might gossip, not knowing of our firm commitment to wait until our wedding."

After addressing envelopes with Sara Ella for about an hour, Marie said, "My goodness, I have to get supper started! You go ahead and finish that batch you are working on, before you come and help. I will get started, and see you in a bit."

When Adam came in the door, Sara Ella went to greet him. As they walked into the parlor to sit a minute, she asked, "Are you hungry?"

Adam paused much too long, processing her question, before he answered, "Not really."

"How can you say that, Adam, after Marie cooked a wonderful dinner for you?" Sara Ella quipped.

"I did not say I do not like Marie's food, Sara Ella...I just said that I am not hungry!" Adam said defensively. "Do not ask me if I am hungry, if you do not want a truthful answer."

"Why are you not hungry?" Sara Ella said with a demanding tone.

"If you really want to know, it is because it is hard for me to sit at the table with this loving family, when I seem to have lost mine," he barked back.

"What do you mean by that? You have me, do you not?" Sara Ella asked cautiously.

Adam looked at the floor and said, "Well, first my son went to Boston, then Benjy moved away. And about the same time, you moved out, when Lisa left. I feel like a man without a family."

Sara Ella softened, put her hand on Adam's shoulder and said, "You have not lost your family, Sweetheart. We will be married soon, and the boys will be back to see us as often as they can, I am sure."

"That is easy for you to say.. After all, it is your fault that Randy left, and Benjy only left because Randy is gone," Adam sulked.

Sara Ella jumped to her feet and stared him down, demanding, "Why is it my fault that Randy left?"

"Well, you are the one that arranged for Mrs. Kelley to come and put the idea in his head to go to that blind school. You knew that I wanted him to stay home and have a teacher come to him. You just do not seem to understand me at all!" Adam was also standing now.

"I do not understand you? So, is that why you do not seem to be interested in our wedding? I have been trying to plan this wedding so that I will not embarrass you and your uppity friends will feel comfortable. But, you have not been any help at all! Is it because I am just a lowly school teacher from the Deep South? Is that why I will never be able to understand you? Is that what this is all about?" Sara Ella yelled, as she stamped her foot, grabbed her skirt tail, turned and stomped up the stairs.

Marie stuck her head out of the dining room, just in time to hear the front door slam and see Sara Ella reach the top of the stairs.

Stanton grabbed Adam's attention, when he mentioned Black Codes again. "Adam, I tell you, Johnson has allowed those rebel southern states to establish Black Codes, giving freedmen subordinate legal status, with second-class civil rights, and no voting rights. The Black Codes of Mississippi and South Carolina actually even stringently limit the blacks' ability to control their own employment! Can you believe it?"

"Why would he do that?" Adam asked. "It sounds like he is still making decisions that are completely contrary to his platform in the election."

"I know...everyone around here is dumbfounded. I have a meeting in a few minutes about it. We plan to put a stop to all of this foolishness, once and for all!" Stanton blustered.

"So, give me your input on the subject," Stanton said.

Adam was caught off guard. He was not sure what to say, so he asked, "Why do you think the southern states passed those Black Codes?" Adam wanted more information, before making any suggestions.

"Well, the southern plantation owners say it is because they fear extensive black vagrancy, which would mean a virtual loss of their essential labor force. But, I am convinced that many of the southern whites simply reject the notion of being considered equal with blacks," Stanton answered.

Adam sat back in his chair, thinking. "Well there definitely has been a great loss of their labor force, and their money is not worth anything now. Nearly all of my father's slaves left the plantation during the war, so I understand the difficulty of trying to develop a new labor force."

"Then, does that mean that you agree with these Black Codes?" Stanton barked out to Adam, pointing his fountain pen at him in obvious disapproval.

"No, of course not! But, you need to realize that the whole South has been devastated, sir. Both blacks and whites are being forced to adjust to some pretty extreme lifestyle changes. Thinking about that gives me reason to ponder my answer long and hard..." Adam was interrupted, as a knock came on the door. It opened, and Ben Wade came in.

"Hello, Ben. I think you know General Adam Layne. Is it time for that meeting we were discussing, Adam? Give me just a minute to get my hat, Ben." Stanton said. The three men shook hands, and then all walked out the door. Adam went left and the other two men turned right.

As he left the Capitol, Adam was very discouraged. He had enough problems of his own, without having to worry about the political issues of a nation in turmoil. Tired and feeling like he would probably never be happy again, Adam was looking down, not watching where he was going, when he literally bumped into Edgar Gray, Chaplin of the Senate.

Embarrassed, Adam said, "Oh, I am very sorry, Chaplin Gray! I have knocked this book right out of your hands," he remarked, as he picked up the book and looked at the cover. "Hmm...Pilgrim's Progress, by John Bunyan. I have not read this book in years."

"It is good to bump into you Adam!" Chaplin Gray said, chuckling and slapping Adam on the shoulder. "I do not know how many times I have read this book over the years, quite a few for sure. Reading it regularly helps me keep my priorities in perspective, along with many other things," the Chaplin mused, as he ran his hands over the cover of the book. "It has been a good friend to me, a really good friend."

The Chaplain clearly had Adam's attention. "It is odd that you should mention priorities. I seem to have lost mine somewhere..." Adam said, rather flatly, looking back down at his feet. "Do you think we could talk sometime? Perhaps, you could help me..."

Edgar Gray smiled warmly, and responded, "Of course, Adam. That is what I do best, listen. And, under the guidance of the Holy Spirit, I do my best to point folks in the right direction."

Aware that Adam was seriously troubled about something, Chaplain Gray steered Adam to a park bench they found along their way. "Actually Adam, I was on my way to see you, so I could pass along a message from Reverend Kilgore. He wanted you to know that the storm that passed through here last night caused a huge tree to fall on the sanctuary. It left a gaping hole in the roof, and there is a great deal of water damage. He thought of you right away, because it cannot be repaired before your wedding day on the 24th."

Adam slumped down on the bench in despair. *What else can happen?* He leaned over and put his head in his hands, then weakly uttered, "After the war was over, I miraculously found my son. That is when I surrendered my life to Christ. Randy had been blinded by a Rebel bullet to his head, so I was most grateful to have him back home!

"Since that time, God has blessed me in so many ways, over and over again. His presence in my life was so real to me...that is, until recently. Now, it is as if God has deserted me, but I do not know why. I feel worse than before, because now I know how wonderful it is to see God working all around me. I do not understand it, or what to do about it. Frankly, I am at a loss..."

Chaplain Gray put his hand on Adam's leg and said, "Adam, do you remember when you read <u>Pilgrim's Progress,</u> the part where Christian, the main character of the allegory, falls into the bog called the Slough of Despond?"

Adam sat back and said, "It sounds familiar, but I do not remember the details. I was not yet a Christian when I read the book years ago."

"Well," the Chaplain explained, "immediately after Christian gets out of the Slough of Despond, the character named Worldly Wiseman attempts to lead Christian astray. But then, Christian finds shelter in Goodwill's house, and Goodwill tells Christian that he needs to go to the Interpreter's home for the help he needs. It is in the Interpreter's home that Christian learns many valuable lessons about faith."

Adam looked confused and said, "I'm sorry, Chaplain, but I just don't follow you...."

"Let's look at your situation another way. I am going to ask you a personal question. You do not have to answer if you do not want to, of course. But it would be helpful for me to know how long it has been since you read your Bible last?" queried the Chaplain.

"Uh-h-h...my father read it to me when I was a boy, and my tutors made me read it a lot when I was a child. But, I have been really busy with lot of really important things..." was all Adam could say.

"Adam, this I know for sure...a Christian neglecting his Bible is much like a man being lost in the woods with a compass in his pocket! You see, if we do not read God's manual for life, how will we know His way? In Bunyan's book, Christian needed to know something he did not yet know. As a new believer, he needed to know precisely, how to get out of the mess he was in. Before he could go to the Interpreter for help, first he needed to have tried to learn something he ultimately did not understand. Interpreters need to have something to interpret, right?

"Look at it this way, Adam, in life, when you first begin to study something new, the subject of law for example, you would naturally seek out someone you trust to help you understand, right? Well, when you first start reading the Bible, it is advisable to find someone, an 'Interpreter' if you will, who's been reading and studying God's Word longer to help you. For example, a man like John Bunyan, the author of this wonderful allegory. That is why I, personally, have read this and many other good Christian books, over and over again. Do you understand, Adam?" The Chaplain asked tenderly.

"I think so," Adam answered.

The Chaplain continued, "Do you recall in the book when Christian and his friend Hopeful took shelter for the night at Doubting Castle? The owner, named Giant Despair, imprisoned and tortured them there, remember? Finally, in their misery, Christian and Hopeful remember that they possess the key of Promise that will unlock any door of Despair's domain. In reality, they were not imprisoned at all, they just thought they were."

"Oh, how I need that key... What do I need to do to find it?" Adam exclaimed.

"That's the thing, Adam. You already possess the key!" the Chaplain announced, with joy. "It is the Promise of Eternal Life that Christ gave you when you trusted Him! You see, Jesus becomes the Key of Promise in the believer's life. When you acknowledge Him as your only priority, as you surrender your life to Him, He will order all the other things in your life, perfectly.

"In the scriptures, there is a story that you have probably read, about an ancient man named Job. After Job had suffered in every possible way, He said, 'I know that my Redeemer lives!' Adam, being a believer doesn't mean you will not have turmoil in your life. But, it does mean that you have hope in the midst of life's trials. Unregenerate man does not have that hope. You can trust God to be faithful as He promised, and that all things work together for good to those who love God.

"Adam, the Christian life is NOT about deciding one day that you will try as hard as you can to please God with your life. The Christian life is a relationship with a person, the person of Jesus Christ. When you surrender your life to Him, God sees the perfection of Jesus when he looks upon you.

"We serve Him and try to please Him, not because that might make Him love us more. We do that in response to His loving us sacrificially, even when we did not love Him at all. Christians read His word to know Him more intimately, because we love Him, not because we have to. He simply cannot love us any more than He already does...or any less, for that matter.

Stop trying to carry the weight of the world on your shoulders, Adam. Just relax and focus your life and your energy on the One who loves you more than you can imagine. He is faithful...you can trust Him with your life and the lives of your loved ones. He will direct your life.

A relationship with the Lord for the true believer is much like a child with his father, Adam. When you were learning how to walk, your father did not expect you to be able to walk like you do today, before he expressed his delight. When you took your first steps, you had no idea how faulty those steps were. You did what came natural, and your father was elated with your growth and development. He did not love you because you could walk perfectly. He loved you even before you took your first step, and regardless of the quality of your walking performance.

But, if you are still walking with the same level of ability several years later, your father would know something was wrong. That is when he would do whatever is necessary to help you learn to walk in an age appropriate way. Not because it is good for him, but because it is good for you."

Looking at his pocket watch, Chaplain Gray said, "Oh! I am late for an appointment, Adam! It is good to see you. I am going to leave this copy of Pilgrim's Progress with you to read. But remember, the most important reading is always your Bible. And, though I certainly do not consider myself an expert, by any means, I would be pleased to visit with you anytime. Just come by my office or send me a note."

Chaplain Gray reached out his hand to Adam and prayed with him, before he went on his way.

Chapter 26

It was about midday on a somewhat dreary day. There were light showers, off and on, but not enough to halt progress on construction at Oaklayne. Suddenly, down the lane at a fast clip, came a buggy, driven by a very heavy set man, with a hard face. Oscar didn't notice the buggy coming until it had almost reached the house, because he was busy, looking at a structural issue on the mansion with Ross and Brandon.

"May I help you?" Oscar asked, as he worked his way over to the buggy across some construction debris.

"I'm here to see Adam Layne," the man demanded.

"I am sorry sir, but Mr. Layne is not here right now. May I help you? I am Oscar Baynes."

"I'm not interested in talking with the work crew," the man said, with a haughty expression. "I am Colonel Herbert Wade Hatfield of the Royal Hatfield Plantation. Tell Mr. Layne that he must report to me at once, regarding a government mandate."

Then, before Oscar could say anything, the man whacked his horse hard on the rump with his buggy whip and proceeded farther into Oaklayne property, past the Temporary and Bunk Houses.

Oscar was startled by the pompously rude man's actions. He had no idea what business the man had, trespassing on Oaklayne in such a preposterous way. Since the only way to exit the plantation by buggy was to come back past the big house, Oscar called his men together to help him form a barricade and challenge Colonel Hatfield when he returned. They watched as the buggy continued all the way down to the river, where the heavy man hoisted himself out of the buggy, and then he walked down to the shipping pier.

"What on earth is he doin' down there?" Darrell asked.

"I can't see good 'nuff from here, can you?" Michael commented.

"Well, it's obvious that he's up to no good," Steven quipped.

Ross gritted his teeth, then made a weak attempt at humor when he said, "Maybe he's fixin to go fishin'..."

Oscar remained quiet, but did not take his eyes off of Colonel Hatfield. The intruder was now walking on the pier, looking into the water and up and down the river, apparently perusing something. With great effort he pulled his heavy frame back into the buggy and headed their way, very slowly, as he seemed to be studying the landscape.

"Men, do not let that man get through here, before I have had a chance to speak with him," Oscar said softly, as the Colonel was approaching.

"Let me pass!" Colonel Hatfield growled, as Norman caught the bridal of the exquisite black gelding that was harnessed to the buggy. The horse startled, causing the buggy to jerk to a stop, almost unseating the portentous driver of the rig.

Hatfield raised his buggy whip in a rage, when Oscar reached out and grabbed it from his hand, looked him directly in the eye, and said sternly, "Colonel Hatfield, you are trespassing on private property. It is my duty in Adam Layne's absence, to advise you that you are not allowed to return to Oaklayne Plantation, for any reason, without the express permission of Mr. Layne, himself. You have no business snooping around this property without authorization. Do you understand me, sir?"

The intruder was red in the face and perspiring profusely, when Oscar handed him back his buggy whip, stepped back from the buggy and said, "Now, I would appreciate it if you would be kind to that horse, as you immediately make your way off of Oaklayne Plantation premises. If you hesitate, I may not be able to keep these men from bodily removing you from that buggy and dispatching your ample backside away from here themselves. So, I would suggest you get a move on, sir."

At the supper table that evening, everyone enjoyed telling his version of the run in with the man in the buggy to those who were not there to witness it.

Oscar laughed right along with the others, but then his countenance became serious, as he said, "All fun aside men, I have a bad feeling about that visit. I cannot put my finger on why it concerns me; it is hard to know what that man was up to. But, just the same, I think it would be a good idea for us to keep particular watch out for anything out of the ordinary. Please let me know right away if you see anything suspicious. I do not want any kind of trouble here, but if trouble comes our way, I want us to be prepared to handle it."

As Oscar carried his plate to the wash tub, Elsie spoke up and said, "I saw that man go trottin' past here in that buggy this afternoon.

He sure was prune-faced! Wonder why he's so angry? Looked like he was fixin' to hit something...or someone."

"Do not be concerned, Elsie," Oscar said, as he lifted her chin up to face him. "I will not let anything happen to you...," Then, as he noticed her eyes getting bigger that blasted curl fell loose from her hair again! He coughed as if to clear his throat, then, looking away, he said, "...or any of the ladies. We will keep a close eye out, but please let me know if you do see anything unusual..."

"Oh yes, certainly," Elsie said, looking back down at the tub. "I am sure that none of the men here would let anything happen to any of us ladies."

What is wrong with me? Oscar thought, as he quickly distanced himself from that mesmerizing curl. *Why am I feeling this way? I cannot seem to think straight when she is around. Elsie has never shown any particular interest in me...except, I am still wondering what falling in my lap, like that, was all about. Was she intentionally trying to cause the men to laugh at me, or did she really just fall? Whatever it was, I still cannot get over it. What a strange mysterious girl."*

As he struggled to sort out his thoughts, Oscar heard a giggle. He looked up to see the peculiar sight of big strapping Dominique, with a dish towel in his hands, standing next to Jessica. He was drying dishes that Elsie handed to him, after she finished washing them. Then, after he was finished, he handed the dish over to Jessica, who stacked it with the others on the table. With each repetition of the procedure, Jessica giggled again.

What is going on around here? Oscar thought, as he turned to walk over to the big house construction site. He brushed sawdust away from the steps and sat down to ponder what Colonel Hatfield might be planning. *What business did he have down at the pier? I wonder...*

Just as Oscar was about to leave, Nathaniel walked up and said, "Could Ah speak wit yo' fer a minute, Sah?"

"Certainly, Nathaniel, have a seat if you don't mind a little sawdust," Oscar said with a smile.

Nathaniel expressed his concerns about hearing from the men that Burt had been seen again, sneaking around in the woods along the road. "Looks like Burt is fixin' to cause mo' trouble, Sah. Yo' tol' us to tell yo' 'bout anythin' odd, so's Ah thought yo' should know."

"Nathaniel, do you think that Burt might be connected with Colonel Hatfield, somehow? I have been sitting here trying to figure out why that man came on the plantation this afternoon. It seems to me that he was not interested in seeing Adam at all. I think he just wanted to look over the plantation. But, why would he do that, Nathaniel? And, why the river?" Oscar appreciated having Nathaniel to discuss the situation with.

Nathaniel did not know, but promised to keep watch and report any further developments that came to his attention.

Oscar ran his fingers through his dark brown curly hair, and said, "Do you think we should have someone stand guard every night, just to keep an eye on things? I hate to do it if it isn't necessary, because it would cost us a lot of man hours away from the construction. But maybe we do not have a choice? What do you think?"

"Well, Sah," Nathaniel answered, "Ah think that's a good idea."

Oscar thought about it for a split second, then jumped up and slapped Nathaniel's back. "I knew I could count on you to help me think this through! Thank you, Nathaniel! You pick the man for the first watch, and we will rotate the job through the work force, changing to a different man every night. If you will tell me who you think should start, I will go talk to him right away. Let's share our plan with everyone we see tonight, so we can all be ready to jump into quick action if we ever hear the supper bell ringing in the night."

Nathaniel said, "How's 'bout Roy, Sah. Lo'd knows dat man could use a rest t'morrow. He loaded some mighty big logs t'day."

"Okay, Roy it is. I'll go talk to him right now. Tomorrow we'll use someone from my crew, and I'll talk to him tonight, too. Thank you again, Nathaniel, for coming to me tonight. Your information may be very important, and you were very helpful in helping me sort out the priorities."

Nathaniel did not try to hide his embarrassment, when he said, "Oh, Ah jes' said what yo' tol' me, b'fore, Sah. Yo's a good man Colonel Baynes."

Roy appreciated the opportunity to rest his weary muscles the next day, and immediately began searching for the best vantage spot from which to observe any unwelcome persons.

"Steven, after that visit from the intruder earlier today and also, learning that Burt has been snooping around after dark, we decided to start posting a guard around here every night. Roy is taking the first watch tonight. Would you mind taking tomorrow night?" Oscar asked.

"No sir, not at all," Steven answered. "I've sorta' missed sleepin' out under the stars. Oh...I didn't mean that I was goin' to do any sleepin', though..." he said as he noticed Oscar's eyebrow rise.

"Well, that is good to know," said Oscar with a grin. "By the way, have you heard anything from that little wife of yours?"

"Not lately, sir," responded Steven. "Her name is Rita Kay, sir. She has light brown hair, hazel eyes and the most beautiful smile you've ever seen. I miss her so much it hurts. I sure hope the money I sent her will help her get a train here from Kansas City, right away. She has been staying with her folks, who moved to Missouri, during the war. I told her I am looking for somewhere for us to settle down together, and I think this area will be a good place. It looks like there will be a lot of work for me here, and I want to find a place for us to live before she arrives. Please, let me know if you hear of anything close by, since working on this project will take us quite a while, sir."

"I will be sure to do that. Perhaps, Clifford O'Riley will have some ideas when I see him next time I go to Richmond."

"How is the Sarge, sir?" Steven asked.

"Oh, you know," said Oscar, "He still barks orders, but he is actually soft as a kitten. Only problem is, his men know it. He does not handle being away from his wife, Patricia, for very long at a time, so I expect that he will be looking for a place to move her here soon, too."

As Oscar turned to leave, he said, "Well, I am going to turn in. Thank you for agreeing to take the watch tomorrow night. But, stay awake! Remember, we are counting on you."

"Oh, yes sir! Yes sir!" Steven said mockingly, and they both laughed.

Oscar opened the door to the temporary house and found Elsie sitting near the kitchen door in a chair, tapping her foot. Her shiny dark brown hair had been let loose to fall over her shoulders. Her enchantingly beautiful hazel eyes, looking particularly greener than usual because of her green dress, glanced up to meet his.

"Uh," Elsie said, a little embarrassed to still be in the Temporary House this late, after the men had already gone upstairs. "Did Emma Lou tell you that we're getting a little low on supplies?

"Yes she did, Elsie." Oscar said simply.

"Oh, well I guess that's taken care of then. She had already gone to sleep when I got finished tonight, and so I could not ask her. Now that I think about it, I guess I could have just waited to ask her about it in the morning. But....well, I am sorry to have bothered you. I will see you in the morning," she said, as she stood up and crossed the floor, walking around him to the door.

Oscar, a little confused said, "Is that all you wanted, Elsie?"

"Yes, she said, as she opened the door and again said, "Good night, Oscar. I will see you in the morning."

After she closed the door behind her, Oscar just stood there, staring at the inside of the closed door, wondering... *What was that all about?*

152

Chapter 27

Late in the afternoon, the sun was shining in the west window of the library, when Walter located Benjamin sitting at a table with a stack of books in front of him. It was obvious that he was engrossed in the particular book he was reading, because he did not even look up when Walter approached.

"What is wrong with your nose, Benjamin?" asked Walter.

Benjamin wiped his sleeve over his nose and mumbled, "I do not know...is it okay now?"

"Are you kidding me? What I am looking at is a much bigger problem than that!" Walter answered with emphasis.

Benjamin put down his book and said, "What are you talking about?"

With a silly grin and mocked relief, Walter said, "Oh, my goodness! Now, it is gone. For a minute there, I thought your nose had turned into a book! I have not seen your nose for several days, you know."

Benjamin rolled his eyes and responded, "Funny, Walter...my nose is just fine, but I am discovering that I am an imbecile. I had previously held to the notion that I was a rather well educated young man, but the books that Professor Vashon told me to read in preparation for my application for enrollment here at Ashmun Institute, are showing me how far behind I am. I have much to learn!"

Walter laughed, "Did I not tell you that the first time we met?"

"Well yes, you did. But, I thought you meant that I had a lot to learn about life...now that I think about it, I guess this is about life. Anyway, it is a much bigger life than I could ever have envisioned. As I am reading, I find myself hungry for more. I am realizing there are things on this table that I have not tasted before, and did not even know existed."

Walter sat back in his chair and said, "I know what you mean. One of my Professors here at the college tells me that the more I learn, the more I will want to know. So, what you are saying is the same thing. I guess you know already that, besides being a teacher, Professor Vashon is also a lawyer?"

"I suppose I should have figured that out. But, I did not realize at first that you are not attending Avery College, where Professor Vashon is the President. That became clear the other evening when you and the Professor joined us for supper, after he addressed the Freedmen's Bureau," Benjamin answered.

"Well I guess that was a little confusing. I should have explained that I met him when he came here to Ashmun Institute to address an assembly about the new Freedman's Bureau that was created by President Lincoln on March 3rd. When Professor Vashon told us that he was going to Washington City to meet with Frederick Douglass and the Freedmen's Bureau, I pleaded with him to take me along. I knew he was traveling with a few Avery students he brought along, so I was able to convince him to include me, also. That's how I came to be on the street that fateful morning to rescue your sorry hide!"

Benjamin sighed, and then responded, "Well, if you had not come into my life that morning, Walter, I would never have known the opportunities that lay ahead for me."

"It was quite a blessing for me also, when General Layne invited us to supper that evening! He seemed to be pleased when Professor Vashon assured him that Ashmun Institute was committed to an equal opportunity education," Walter interjected.

"I was actually surprised," Benjamin said, "that Adam was so fascinated with the discussion. I am glad he was there, because he asked lots of questions that I would never have known to ask. Like for instance, the curriculum, and the location of Ashmun Institute. He seemed relieved that the college is in Oxford, Pennsylvania, which is only about 90 miles away from Washington City. It took us less than a day to get here, coming to Wilmington by train, then the additional 20 miles from there to here by buggy."

Walter added, "General Layne was obviously impressed when Professor Vashon told him that Ashmun Institute had prospered, even before the Civil War, having been started nine years ago."

"Yes," Benjamin said, "I saw Adam's excitement when Professor Vashon told him that John Dickey, the founder of the school, said the Board is considering changing the name of the Institute to Lincoln University. They are going to discuss that at their next meeting. Adam thought the world of President Lincoln, you know."

Walter said, "Yes, I know. If Professor Vashon hadn't offered to take you to Ashmun Institute himself, and recommend you as a student there, do you think he would have let you come back with me?"

"Yes," said Benjamin, "I believe he would have. He was sold on the idea of me going to school here, after he heard you recite the pledge. I have learned it now, too:

> *'We are committed to the elevation of an intellectual elite, divinely ordained, through whom would be exercised on the lower classes among their fellows, the saving grace of God's plan for redemption.'*

"And,

> *'Our mission is to be a citadel of race pride and leadership extending around the world.'"*

Walter was impressed, and responded, "Well I remember that you were so excited you could not even stay in your chair! You kept jumping up and down asking, 'May I go? Please, may I go?' It was clear that the General was not prepared to make the decision so abruptly. Obviously, he wanted what was best for you, but I could tell he was struggling with letting you go. In fact, if you were not black, I would think you were the man's son!"

"Well, Adam is the closest thing I have to a father, Walter. I love him like a father, and want to make him proud of me," Benjamin's voice broke, as he expressed the depth of his feelings for Adam.

Chapter 28

The wind was blowing so hard, it was difficult for August to keep his hat on, especially since he was in urgent need of a haircut. As he and Doc Fowler rode into town, he was surprised that Macon, Georgia was so large. There was not a lot of evidence of the war to be seen, because the fighting was mostly outside the city. There were some people walking the streets, and an occasional horse drawn wagon or buggy. There was an eerie quietness, like a funeral procession might have just passed through town on the way to the cemetery.

August had heard that the Confederate Army outnumbered the Union soldiers two to one, as they entered the middle Georgia area toward the end of the war. But, the Rebel soldiers who attacked were mostly old men and inexperienced boys, so the combat-hardened Union veterans with their repeater rifles made the subsequent battle more like a slaughter.

"This is a rather big city," August exclaimed. "It may be more difficult than I thought to find Richard Moreland, that is, if he is even here. He could be anywhere by now, or even dead. I heard that as many as 100 or more men died every day at Andersonville Prison."

"Well, I'm actually a bit more optimistic than before, since Sherman did not destroy this city. I was really expecting more destruction. The way Sherman's soldiers destroyed everything in their path everywhere else we have been, I wondered if we would even find the home still standing of the family you said we would be looking for here," was Ralph's response.

"I am amazed too," August said looking around. "It is refreshing to see something look somewhat normal. We have seen so many places just wiped off the map, with nothing left but charred black remains. It looks like this town would even be able to ship things down the river, which should help their economy a lot."

"What did y'all say is the name of the family we are looking for?" Ralph asked.

"Gary...the Andrew Gary family...they are Sara Ella's folks. She said her father owns a hardware store on Main Street named "Garrinson's Hardware Store". She suggested that Trevor and I look for

156

her brother Willie Gary, and not try to approach her father, because he is not especially fond of Yankees. So, if we end up needing to deal with her father, perhaps it would be best if you do all the talking, with that southern drawl of yours."

"I do not have a southern drawl," said Ralph sarcastically, with a distinct southern drawl. "Anyway, at least I do not talk so fast I cannot be understood, like you Yankees from up North!"

"I cannot imagine," August said laughingly. "Why would anyone think you have a southern drawl, Doc? It is very clear to me now that you do not. Seriously, though...if we cannot get any help from anyone at the store, I have their home address. We can go there if we need to, and see if Mrs. Gary will help us."

"Well, at least it should not be hard to find that hardware store." Ralph said.

They moved slowly along on horseback, looking over the town, as they searched for Main Street.

Suddenly, Ralph interrupted, "There it is! Garrinson's Hardware Store, just like you said. It is on the other side of the street up ahead."

"I see a hardware store, but that is not the right name. Surely there can't be more than one hardware store on Main Street. Maybe, I had the name wrong?"

"Naw, it's just like you said...see, there on the sign...," Ralph read the sign very slowly, "...Gary and Son's Hardware Store. What did you think the name was?"

"...Oh, neva' min'," August said with a silly pretend southern drawl. "Y'all jes' tawk funny!"

As usual, August led the way into the dimly lit hardware store. He knocked the dust off of his hat and called out, "Hello!"

Startled by a brisk, "Wha' cha' need, son?" from close beside him, August's let his eyesight adjust enough to see a stooped gray haired man stacking some large hinges into a bin.

August said, "Oh, excuse me, sir. I did not see you there."

Ralph bumped into August as he rushed through the door, and said, glaring under his breath, "I thought I was going to do the talking..."

"Sir, I am Doctor Ralph Fowler, and this here is my friend August. We are looking for a young man by the name of Willie Gary. We were told that we might be able to find him here, or that someone here might be able to direct us to him. Do you know where he is, sir?"

"Fred!" the older gentleman called out. Then, turning to Ralph he said, "Fred just talked to his brother Willie this morning. He should know where he is."

"Yeah, Pa. I'm comin'," replied Fred. Then he appeared from behind a tall shelf that was filled with cast iron cookware and oil lanterns. The obviously hunchbacked young man said, "Wha' cha need, Pa?"

"Fred, these men are looking for Willie. Where did he tell you he was going a while ago?" The gray haired man was clearly Andrew Gary, Sara Ella Gary's father.

"Willie said he was fixin' to go help Jim and Ada repair them church pews, Pa. I'll be goin' over there when I get off work this evenin' to lend 'em a hand, especially since Wesley and Cora are gone with Ma. Ila May is there with her youngsters, paintin' the pews. Willie told me it's hard to keep David from wanderin' down to the creek, but Becky Anne's a great help with the paintin'...she's a little older, ya' know. Ila May said Eugene is supposed to get home sometime next week. And Barbara..."

Mr. Gary interrupted, "Fred! All that these gentlemen need to know is, where is Willie? Thank you for your help. Now, get back to work, please." Mr. Gary chided Fred teasingly, rolling his eyes, as he turned back to August and Ralph.

Gesturing with his hands as he spoke, Andrew Gary said, "Well gentlemen, if you go out this door and head south three blocks, then turn right, then go about four blocks and look to your left, you'll see the steeple of the Chapel. It's not far away. You really cannot miss it."

Fred spoke up and said, "Pa, I was just comin' to tell you that Jim's order came in. I'm gettin' ready to deliver it to him. I just saddled Star, so I could show these folks over to the Chapel if you want."

Riding along on his big white mare, Fred talked incessantly. As they made their way together toward the Chapel, he pointed out places of interest in town, like the large Macon City Hall just a little farther down Main Street from the hardware store. Fred mentioned that Macon City Hall was converted to a hospital during the war. He also showed them a nice boarding house that was about halfway down the first side street they had passed. In his opinion, they served the best breakfasts in Macon.

When they arrived at the Chapel, Fred called out, "Jim, your order just came in, so Pa sent me right over with it. I brought along these men who are looking for Willie. Do you know where he is?" Fred questioned.

"Willie's at the Hospital, Fred. You know him, he just can't stay away from there for long. He took off to go over there just a little while ago." Jim informed them.

Ralph reached out his hand to Jim and said, "Thank you so much, Jim." Then he turned and asked, "Fred, the Hospital where Willie is, is it the one at the old City Hall that you pointed out on the way here?"

"The very same," Fred answered.

"Have a good day gentlemen, and thank you for your help," Ralph called out, as he and August turned their mounts to leave. They were relieved to know that Willie Gary was nearby, and had a sense that they were finally close to finding Richard Moreland. At least, they hoped to soon know whether or not he survived Andersonville.

As August and Ralph made their way through the door of the old City Hall Hospital, there was no reception desk, or anyone to greet them. There were rows and rows of cots filled with patients everywhere, even up and down the hallways. They worked their way around the maze of injured men, while inquiring about the whereabouts of Willie Gary.

"May I help you?" The distinctly unfriendly female voice came from behind them.

As they turned around, they were greeted by the sour face of a large woman, carrying a big bundle of clean towels.

"We don't have time for no lookers in here," she scolded them. "State your business and then get on with you."

"Beg your pardon, ma'am," said Ralph. "We were told that we could find Willie Gary here, and....."

"Well, why didn't you say so in the first place!" the woman growled. "Follow me, and be quick about it. I don't have all day."

She led the two men down a long hallway that was lined with more cots of men receiving medical treatment for a variety of injuries and diseases. Ralph found it difficult to walk on by without offering assistance, when it was obvious his services were needed. They eventually passed through a door on the right into a medium sized room filled with hospital beds. Ralph could see that these patients were clearly recovering from various kinds of surgery. Abruptly, the woman stopped and August bumped right into the back of her, sending the towels sailing through the air, landing in a heap on the nearest patient, who was unconscious.

"Of all the stupid...!" she said. As she spun around and glared at the young man, she simultaneously reached to retrieve one of the insubordinate towels. As she did, she lost her balance and slipped, almost falling on her ample backside. But, August's quick reflexes prevented the inevitable when he caught her under the arms and lifted her back to an upright position. She jerked away and grumbled, "There...over there in the corner is Willie Gary. Now, I've got even more work to do, so leave me with it!"

"I would be more than happy to help you fold those towels, ma'am..." August said.

"No! You've done enough already, young man!" she said, pointing over toward Willie. "Get out of my way!"

"Yes, ma'am...if that is what you want." August said apologetically.

Ralph and August saw that there were two men in the corner. One was a strong, healthy man of medium build. He was bent over another very frail, gaunt looking man, sitting in a chair.

As they approached, August said, "Willie Gary?"

"Yes, I am Willie Gary," the healthy man answered. "What do you need?"

As he held out his hand, Ralph said, "Willie, I am Dr. Ralph Fowler and this is August Wyatt. We were sent here to Macon by General Adam Layne to find Richard Moreland, who was imprisoned at Andersonville during the war. We are to escort him back to the General's estate in Virginia."

While Ralph was talking, August noticed tears, followed by a smile, come over the face of the man in the chair. Then after Ralph finished speaking, the emaciated man said, "Willie, when you told me that Adam made it out alive, I told you he would not forget about me.

"Dr. Fowler, I am Richard Moreland. Thank you both so much for coming to get me. I knew if anyone could rescue me, it would be Adam..." Richard was too weak to say any more.

"Adam sent for you as soon as he could," said August. "He wanted to come himself, but was called into service by Secretary Stanton in Washington City. He is there now."

Then August turned to Willie and said, with a smile, "While they are in Washington City, Adam and your sister, Sara Ella, plan to be married."

Willie exclaimed, "Actually, I had already heard about that wedding from Ma, when Sara Ella wrote and told her about it. And, it is about time! She has loved Adam for a very long time. They deserve to be happy, after all they have been through!"

As they began getting better acquainted, Richard said, "I have improved incredibly over the last five weeks or so, since I have been here. They tell me that I probably would not have pulled through if I had not been one of the first ones brought in, thanks to Willie here. I am still not very strong, but that is not my biggest limitation...," he said, as he pulled the lap blanket off of his legs. As they gazed in dismay at Richard's missing right lower limb, he continued, "You see gentlemen, walking is a bit of a challenge for me right now. Riding a horse would be even more of a problem. I am starting to learn to use crutches, but it is a slow and difficult process."

Ralph and August sat down on the side of Richard's empty bed, staring in disbelief at this unexpected complication. Breaking the awkward silence, Doctor Fowler said, "Richard, in time a wooden leg can be fitted on that stump. If manufactured well and properly fitted, you may even be able to get around without a cane." He knelt down and examined the stump further, saying, "Your surgeon did a good job here. I am impressed. May we speak with him?"

"I will go ask Dr. Combs to come and talk with you as soon as he can." Willie said over his shoulder, as he had already started on his way.

In just a few moments Dr. Combs arrived. He followed Willie into Richard's room, with a scowl on his face. "Gentlemen, I understand you intend to take Mr. Moreland back to Virginia. Well, I am sorry to say, that will be quite impossible for at least two or three more weeks.

"When he came in here, his leg was a mess.. It is a miracle he did not die from the infection. The surgery to remove it was done only a little over a week ago. He simply is not strong enough to manage a trip like that. Why, he has just begun to learn how to use crutches. No, I will not let you take him from here now, absolutely not! I am sorry, but it is completely out of the question. Now if you will excuse me I have important surgery to do."

Chapter 29

"Sara Ella," Marie called out, "Look what came to the door for you!"

"Coming!" was the response, as Sara Ella came running from the dining room.

"Oh my, those are for me! I have never seen such a beautiful bouquet! Is there a note?" Sara Ella questioned.

"I am not sure. Bring them over to the window, so we can better see. There, right down in the middle is an envelope," Marie pointed out.

Opening the envelope, Sara Ella stared at the note, her eyes misting over, as she read.

"What does it say?" Marie prodded, "...or is it too personal?"

Sara Ella looked up, handed her the note, and said, "What should I do?"

"Oh, my! What do you mean, what should you do? How often does a man tell a woman he's sorry, and then offer to treat her to dinner at the Willard Hotel? That's the most luxurious dining room in the city! Oh goodness, this says that Tom will pick you up at 6:00! Look at you! It will take every minute we have until then for you to be ready! And that is if I help you! I will start heating the water while you freshen up just the right dress for such an occasion."

Sara Ella just stood there and said, "Wait! Should it be that easy for him?"

"What do you want, Sara Ella? Which is more important to you, your pride or your relationship with Adam Layne? Let me tell you from experience, there is no such thing as a marriage relationship, where you do not have to swallow your pride on a regular basis. It comes with the territory, my dear."

"Marie...," Sara Ella paused, as she shook her head as if to clear it. Then she grabbed the hairpin that was holding up her hair, allowing her beautiful brown hair to fall around her shoulders, threw back her head and laughed like a school girl. Then she grabbed Marie around the shoulders and hugged her warmly, saying, "Thank you, dear! You are a precious friend. Now hurry with that water! I have some fancy dressing to do!"

When they arrived at the Willard Hotel, Sara Ella was seriously intimidated by the elegance of the place. She could not help but wonder if her attire was suitable. She had never seen such opulence and extravagance in one place in all her life!

She had chosen a deep forest green dinner gown made of satin and satin brocade from her newly acquired wardrobe. Marie said it really enhanced her eye color, and she wanted to do anything that helped her look her best tonight! Her gown had a fully flounced skirt with crinolines and a very elegant bodice. Her neckline was square, tastefully low and suitable for the dinner hour, and her three quarter sleeves were fashionably split at the elbows. Marie had done her waist length hair up in the new Coronet style, a thick braid coiled around her head like a crown and pinned, accentuated with a sausage curl to one side and tiny white fresh flowers tucked into the braid. When she left home, she felt good about how she looked, but now she was not so sure. One thing she was very sure of., her corset was extremely uncomfortable!

Adam was waiting and watching for Sara Ella in the lobby when Tom escorted her in. He rushed to her side, took her gloved hand and placed it on his arm, then said, "Thank you Tom. I will take it from here."

"You are welcome. It was my pleasure, as usual, to spend some time with this special lady. Is there anything else I can do for you before I go?"

"No, thank you, Tom. You may go. Have a pleasant evening." Adam said all of that without taking his eyes off of Sara Ella.

Sara Ella considered asking Adam how he could do that, talk with Tom while looking at her. But, she thought he might think she was challenging him, so she held her tongue. She did not want anything to spoil their evening together. Besides, maybe he really was that pleased to see her.

Then as if he had heard her question, he said, "I cannot take my eyes off of you, my dear. You are so very lovely. Besides, if I look away you might disappear again, leaving me to wonder if I was only dreaming."

Embarrassed by his endearing expression of admiration and not knowing what to say, she just smiled. Then, as she looked into his eyes, he patted her hand and said, "I do not think I have ever seen you look more beautiful than you do this evening. I have missed you so much, and I am so sorry about our quarrel. I can hardly wait to be married to the most wonderful lady in the world...that is, if you will still have me?"

"Oh, Adam...I do love you, and you know that I could never marry another. I am sorry, too." Then she rose up on her tiptoes and kissed his cheek. "Of course, I will still marry you!"

"Great! Did you hear that? It is the famous gong they sound at the Willard to announce the early dining hour. At first, I thought it was the rejoicing of my heart! I hope you do not mind that I made our reservation so early...I simply could not wait to see you."

They were promptly seated in the luxurious dining room and given their "Bill of Fare".

"Well, I don't mean to sound like a simple country girl, especially after that quarrel we had, but I would sure like an explanation of some of these dishes. What in the world is 'Hog's Head Cheese in form'...and who would eat 'Calf's Head and Feet smothered aux. Fine Herbs, Country Style' or any other style for that matter?"

Adam laughed aloud and said, "Oh, how I do love you!" Then, with a twinkle in his eye, he said, "Since I know that you aspire to display the epitome of pompous society etiquette, I had planned to order one of those grand dishes for you...unless, that is, if you would like to remain the loveliest, most gregarious simple country girl I know."

They laughed together, as she flipped her napkin at him under the table and said, "I think I will just remain a simple country girl, if it is all the same to you. I would rather eat food that is fit for human consumption!"

After catching up on the small things happening in both of their lives, Adam took Sara Ella's hands in his, looked her in her eyes, and with a very serious tone in his voice, said, "After a lot of soul searching, I have come to realize that I have always had my priorities in the wrong order. For some reason, I assumed that my first priority was myself, so I have lived my life accordingly. But, after talking with Chaplain Gray and reading scripture..."

Sara Ella looked at him with a questioning look, but he continued, "...that's right, dear, I have been reading my Bible. Chaplain Gray directed me to some scripture to help me understand about the priorities a Christian should have. I know now that, Jesus is supposed to be my first priority, then my family, my church, my nation. I am actually way down the list."

Then Adam sat back in his chair and spilled out all that was in his heart, like he had never done before with her. She sat spellbound as he talked on and on. "I do not think life has to be as difficult as I have been making it. Somehow, I never understood that true faith is learning to depend on Christ completely...totally...for everything.

"I always thought that God blessed people only when they are obedient to Him, so I tried my best to please Him. But the truth is, I fail more often than not. Oh, I can look okay on the outside, but my heart is full of all the wrong things. I have come to realize that, left to only my own resources, it is impossible for me to honor God with my life.

"It is only by His grace and in His power that I can do anything right...the pressure I have been under, trying to live like a Christian, has been unbearably hard. I am still learning, but I know so little...please be patient with me, Sara Ella. I know that the Lord will help me, now that I am learning to trust in Him, instead of just looking to my own strength."

Sara Ella had tears in her eyes, as she saw Adam's enthusiasm. Now that he was sharing his heart with her, she began to understand a lot more about him than ever before, and she was grateful. While it had been difficult, she could see that their time apart was truly a blessing for both of them. She reached out and placed her hand on his, saying, "I love you more than ever now, Adam Layne. I am so anxious for us to be married!"

Sadness came across Adam's face as he swallowed hard and said, "Well, there is some bad news about that, my dear. I have been dreading having to tell you this, but Chaplain Gray told me that the church where we plan to get married was so damaged in the recent storm that it cannot be repaired in time for our wedding. I know our wedding date is only a week away, so what should we do? I do not want to postpone it any longer, do you?"

Much to Adam's surprise and relief, Sara Ella laughed and said, "Absolutely nothing will be allowed to postpone our wedding date another minute! If you would be satisfied to have our wedding outside in the church yard, then leave it to Marie and me. We will make it work!"

"Right now," Adam responded, "I would be elated to be married in the street, on a roof top, in a barn or anywhere else, my dear. I love you, and cannot wait to make you my bride!"

"Well, okay then! That is what we will do! I am so excited! It will be perfect, you will see. Who says we have to be married in a church building? Not me!"

Adam was so relieved with Sara Ella's response that he completely relaxed, basking in her beauty and remembering all of the reasons that he had fallen in love with this exceptional lady. They hardly tasted their meal when it arrived, because they were busy discussing wedding plans.

After supper, as they were eating dessert, Adam changed the subject when he asked, "Do you remember that I took Benjamin and Walter to a meeting at the Capitol with the Freedman's Bureau?"

"Oh yes, I certainly do remember. Well, Benjamin will never be the same after that meeting. After encountering them personally, he had great admiration for Frederick Douglas and Professor Vashon. I think he saw a vision for his own life after that day," Sara Ella responded.

"I have seen the same thing in Benjamin. At that meeting, we also met the Commissioner of the Freedman's Bureau, General Oliver Howard, a very fine man. He has divided the Bureau into four divisions: Government-Controlled Lands, Records, Financial Affairs, and Medical Affairs.

"When I talked with him after the meeting, he told me that Education currently falls under the Records Division. However, he personally thinks that it is the most important part of the Freedman's Bureau, because without an education the freed slaves will be severely limited. I mentioned to him that you are a teacher and that you taught primary school in the South. He is interested in discussing the matter with you to see what ideas that you might have, as to the best approach for providing an education to all of these people."

"Oh, Adam, I do not know. I had not given it much thought, beyond wanting to teach the children at Oaklayne when we get back home."

"Would you be willing to meet with him? He has some ideas about higher education, but does not know a lot about primary schools. He really would like to speak with you and tap into your experience with younger children."

"I would be glad to meet with him, if you think that I could be of any service to him," Sara Ella said, sounding doubtful.

"Thank you, dear. He will be delighted, I am sure. I will get in touch with him right away to make the arrangements." Then he shifted in his seat and continued, "There is one more thing we should discuss. Remember when I showed you the second telegram that Lisa sent? Not the one about Randy being happy at school...I am talking about the second one that just said, 'delayed because of family issues', do you remember it?"

"Yes I do, because we were both unaware that she had any family up that way," she said, wondering what might be going on.

"Well, what do you think of this one?" Adam handed a new telegram to her, and waited for her to read it. It said, simply, "I will arrive at the train station Wednesday at 6:00 pm with son, Samuel. Lisa."

Sara Ella stared at the telegram in amazement.

Adam broke the silence when he said, "Well, what do you think? First it was Angela, now this? What does she mean by 'with son'?"

"Adam, I surely do not understand. I thought she was doing much better when she left to escort Randy to school. I am not sure what to think about her claim that Angela is still alive and living with a black family...but I am certain she does not have a son named Samuel."

"Would you please go with me tomorrow to pick her up at the train station? She may not be well, and I would sure like to have someone with me."

"Certainly, I will go with you. How could I not, now that my curiosity has piqued. I would have wanted to go with you to greet Lisa anyway, even before she sent this strange telegram."

The rumbling noise of the train softened as it slowed, then Lisa and Samuel heard the screech of the brakes on the massive wheels of the big steam engine, as they struggled to bring the train to a stop. The loud whistle was sounded twice to announce their arrival at the station.

Adam and Sara Ella had to stand back as dozens of people began to disembark. The acrid smell of smoke filled their nostrils, as they searched the faces in the crowd, looking for Lisa.

"Over there, Adam! Could that be Lisa?" Sara Ella said as she pointed all the way up to the front of the train toward the big engine.

What they observed was quite surprising! Climbing down with some difficulty, because of the fullness of her skirt, they saw Lisa descending from the Engineer's cab of the steam engine, with some assistance from the Conductor. Following behind her was the Engineer, holding the hand of a boy who was talking excitedly. When she was settled on the ground, the Conductor reached up and the young lad almost jumped into his outstretched arms.

Adam and Sara Ella rushed toward them. They arrived at the engine just as the boy turned from shaking the Engineer's hand to hug Lisa around the waist. "Thank you so much, Mother! That was fun!" they heard him say, as they looked at each other with confused expressions, then back at Lisa.

"Oh look, Samuel! This is your Uncle Adam, and this lovely lady will soon be your Aunt Sara Ella. They are going to be married, you know." Lisa took Samuel by the shoulders and turned him to face them. Little Samuel extended his hand to Adam immediately and said, "Pleased to meet you, sir. My name is Samuel Layne." Then he turned to Sara Ella and bowed, as he took off his hat and swung it down low, saying with a smile, "Ma'am."

Adam looked nervously at Sara Ella, then at Lisa, and finally said to the boy, "The pleasure is all mine I am sure, young man." Sara Ella just smiled. Then he turned to Lisa and said, "I assume you will be offering an explanation soon as to what is going on?"

"Of course, Adam. I will fill you in at a more opportune time, if that is okay." Lisa looked at Samuel, then back at Adam, smiling but obviously somewhat tense.

All the way home in the carriage, Samuel talked incessantly about his ride in the train engine with the Engineer. "He told me how big the engine is, how they have to shovel coal in it, how fast it is, and most important of all, I got to pull the whistle twice when we stopped at the station." He repeated it all again to the Bryan family when they arrived at their home.

After dinner, Lisa and Marie put Samuel and the three Bryan children to bed.

"Thank you, Marie, for taking Samuel and I into your lovely home. It does make more sense for us to be here, instead of with Adam, since Sara Ella is staying here until after the wedding. I love the way you read a story from the Bible to the boys in the evening. They sure enjoy it!" Lisa stopped talking as they entered the parlor, where Adam, Sara Ella and Scott were anxiously awaiting an explanation from her about the boy, Samuel.

"Lisa, please sit down and explain what is going on. Who is that boy? And, why does he call himself Samuel Layne? What on earth?" Adam had lots of questions, and Lisa knew she needed to explain.

"He is wonderful, is he not?" Lisa said with a joyful laugh, adding, "I understand completely that it looks like I have completely lost my marbles, but I assure you that Samuel is truly my son. The explanation in a nutshell...I adopted him."

"Just like that?" Adam said.

Lisa smiled and told them about seeing Samuel on the orphan train, and how he was obviously very sick. She told them about the authorities deciding to break the rules of requiring her to have a husband and let her adopt him. They knew he needed to go to the hospital for treatment and ongoing care to nurse him back to health.

"He was terribly ill, and still tires very easily. They told me at the hospital that he had pneumonia, and it was a good thing I brought him to them when I did. Otherwise, he might have died. With treatment, he has recovered nicely, except for an occasional cough and tiring out. He has medicine that I must administer for a while, but he is not contagious, so do not worry.

"He is obviously a tough lad, to pull through as quickly as he did. He has been fighting to survive on the streets of New York City with several other children for some time now. He has led a very hard life, and I intend to do my best to change all that from now on. I am sure it will be difficult at times. But he is a good boy, and I have found it easy to love him."

Sara Ella jumped up, put her arms around Lisa and said, "I am so happy for you both. I am sure you will face some challenges ahead, but you will be able to deal with it."

"I know," Lisa said, "I have already experienced a few of those. On the train I caught him stealing bread from someone who had turned their back. And he lied to the waiter about not getting a sweet roll with his breakfast. Both times, he did it knowing I was watching, as if I would approve. We have had some long talks about stealing food. But, it is hard for him to understand that there will always be food for him to eat. He seems determined to always put some food aside, so he will have it later for another meal."

"It is hard to comprehend how difficult it would be for a child so young to make it on his own on the streets of a big city," mused Sara Ella.

"I am telling you all of this, so you will know to watch for anything missing. Please be sure to hide anything of value for a while. I do not know Samuel well enough to know what to expect, yet. If you suspect anything, please be sure to question him or tell me about it so I can do so. I do not want him to get away with anything, so I can hopefully get this behavior corrected as soon as possible. Scott and Marie, under the circumstances, I understand completely if you are not comfortable having us here in your home."

Scott spoke up and said, "We are so happy for Samuel that he has you to love him through this huge transition in his life, Lisa. And, we are more than happy to help you with him in any way we can. Do not be afraid to be tough on the principles that matter most, because he will test you. Boys do that, don't they, dear..." he said, looking over at Marie. She laughed and rolled her eyes.

Adam was pleased to see the joy on Lisa's face, as she talked about the boy who would most certainly bring her both heartache and happiness. He could see that having someone who needed her so much, gave her a reason and permission to enjoy life, in spite of her losses. He could not bring himself to offer any words of caution, though he was concerned. So, he just embraced Lisa, smiled and kissed her on the forehead.

To avoid the tears she could feel coming to the surface, Lisa asked, "So, are we ready for a wedding?"

Adam pulled Sara Ella close, and they both said, "More than ever!"

Chapter 30

It was a beautiful star filled night. The stars twinkled more brightly than usual, because there was no moon. Small creatures and insects of the night rustled the leaves on the ground as they scurried around in the dark. The occasional hoot of an owl reminded Norman of his love for nature. As he looked up in wonder from his seat on the porch of the bunk house, his eye caught the glorious sight of a shooting star just above the saw mill.

That's when he saw it—flames coming from the far end of the saw mill! He immediately jumped to his feet and frantically began ringing the bell that Emma Lou always rang to call everyone to supper. Suddenly, men came pouring out the doors of the buildings in a panic, like so many ants scramble out of their hill when it floods. Over and over, Norman yelled, "Fire! Fire! Fire at the sawmill!"

"Steven!" Oscar yelled, "You and Ross go get a horse and rigging for the buckboard! Darrell and Michael, go with them and throw all of the buckets you can find in the stable into the buckboard, then come back here to get every container you can find from the kitchen! Hurry down to the river and fill up everything to the brim! Brandon, go with them to help! Bring the water to the saw mill as fast as you can! Keep filling the containers as quickly as you can, as we empty them on the fire! Keep them coming! The rest of you men bring all of the blankets you can find and run for the saw mill to see what you can do!"

When they reached the sawmill area, Oscar was relieved to find that the fire had not yet reached the equipment they used to cut the trees. But, the whole west end of the building was now an inferno.

"Roy and Joseph, go get axes from the timber wagon, as many as you can carry! Nathaniel and Vernon, do what you can to snuff out the fire with those blankets. You men who are timber cutters, get up on the roof in that smoke and cut off the west end of the roof as fast as you can! Odell and Mathias, grab an ax and help me chop off the end of this building the best we can! Hurry! We just might be able to save most of it!"

The bucket brigade arrived just as a big section of the end of the building fell and caught the grass on fire. Nathaniel and Vernon used wet blankets and quickly put out the subsequent grass fire. The bucket brigade emptied the buckets of water on the fire and threw them back into the wagon as fast as they could. Steven held the bridle of the frightened horse and covered its head with a blanket to keep it from bolting. Then, when the men were ready for more water, he carefully turned the horse and headed it back down toward the river for refills. They had to run to catch up with him, so they could help him fill the buckets again.

After over an hour of intense and frantic activity, at last someone yelled, "We did it! We did it! We saved the saw mill!" Panting, whooping and hollering and marching around in circles like a bunch of drunken Indians, the men celebrated their hard fought victory. Then, as the adrenaline began to subside, they quaked with exhaustion and fell to the ground. About that time, Emma Lou, Elsie, Beverly Jean and Jessica arrived on the scene with towels and fresh water in bowls and pitchers from their cabin. As they handed each man a cool wet towel and a dipper of fresh water, they congratulated them on handily winning their fierce struggle to save the saw mill.

Early the next morning, Oscar sat at the kitchen table having coffee, which had become his customary routine. He still could not admit to himself that he liked to be near Elsie. In the mornings he could always count on her to get up earlier than everyone else and start working, organizing everything for breakfast. He convinced himself that he needed to make sure that the ladies working at Oaklayne found him approachable, just in case they had a problem of some sort, and might need some help.

This particular morning, he was pondering what they might find at dawn when they would be able to investigate what caused that fire the night before.

"Do you realize how hard it is going to be to cook your breakfast with no pots and pans?" Elsie said, interrupting Oscar's thoughts, as she banged things around looking for some way to cook a meal for the crew that she knew would soon be arriving with a tremendous appetite.

When Oscar did not reply she looked at him and saw that he was clearly in another world. "Hello?" she said sarcastically, while waving her hand in front of his face.

"What? What is it?" Oscar said with a scowl. Then, realizing he was reacting rudely to being distracted from his thoughts, he said, "I am sorry, Elsie. It is just that I am puzzled about how that fire could have started spontaneously, in the middle of the night like it did. I hope we can figure something out when we go up there and look around in the daylight."

"Well, I need somebody to go on up there right now and retrieve some pots and pans if we are gonna' fix breakfast 'round here," Elsie said, grinning with her hands firmly planted on her hips. Though she understood Oscar's concern, she was trying to keep the mood as light as possible.

"I am sure the men will be quite co-operative when you tell them you will need those things brought to the kitchen if they are going to start the day's work with a full stomach!"

The night was short, and the men slept fitfully after they finally went to bed. But even so, they were outside early, anxious to see the saw mill in daylight and hopefully figure out what had caused the fire. As soon as it was light, they climbed the hill and saw that Nathaniel was already picking through the ashes and charred timbers.

In his usual drawl, Nathaniel expressed confusion, explaining that nothing combustible, such as the oil used to lubricate the big saw, was stored in the end of the mill that burned. But, there was clearly oil soaked into the ground on that end of the building. Nathaniel sat down on a stack of lumber that had been spared and scratched his head, "How did that oil get there?"

"Norman, I am amazed that you happened to notice this fire when you did. Thank you for being so alert when you were on watch." Oscar congratulated.

"Guess watchin' for them Johnny Rebs for as long as I have will do that to ya', Colonel."

"I know this is quite a distance from the house, but did you hear any noise up this way at all last night?"

"No sir, I shore didn't." Norman replied.

"Hey, look here," Brandon said. "Did any of you walk around behind the mill last night, or any time recently?"

"No, there's too many tall weeds growin' back there! Why, a man could get lost forever in that jungle! I never saw no need to go back there fer nothin'," Darrell replied. Everyone agreed with him, except Oscar, who reported that he had gone behind the mill the night before when he was working with an ax to chop off that end of the building to keep the flames from spreading.

"That is what I thought, Oscar. But the grass is really packed down back here, where it appears someone has been going back and forth, a lot." Brandon pointed out.

The men all made their way around behind the sawmill to see for themselves what Brandon described. That's when someone noticed something that looked suspicious about four feet out into the tall grass.

Ross investigated and found it to be one of their oil barrels. It was empty and appeared to have been hurriedly thrown out there to conceal it in the natural cover of the weeds.

"Well, someone set this fire, that's for sure!" Norman interjected. "This barrel explains why I didn't see anybody last night. I couldn't have seen them if they were behind the building when they set the fire."

Oscar spoke up and said, "Gentlemen, this appears to confirm arson, unless we find out something more about this fire that we are not privy to at this point. Do any of you have any idea who could be behind this?"

Nathaniel raised his voice and suggested it was probably Burt and the men he hangs around with all the time, since they had previously been behind a lot of the trouble at Oaklayne. "Ah'm jes' glad yo' decided ta' post a watchman, Sah'. That sawmill be gone fo' sho', if'n Norman hadn't seen that fire when he did!"

"Thank you, Nathaniel," Oscar replied. "You are probably right about Burt and his cronies. We will need to look into that possibility. Anyway, I say let's continue this conversation after breakfast. We will need to organize a team of men right away to repair the burned out end of the saw mill. Oh, do not forget to pick up all of the buckets for feeding and watering the horses, and of course, the pots and pans the ladies need for the kitchen. The horses will be hungry, I am sure...," he said with a smile, "but, not as hungry as we will be if we do not take the pots and pans to the women pretty soon!"

Chapter 31

Tiny rays of sunlight came peeking through the leaves of the trees outside Sara Ella's window, winking lightly on the side of her face, as if tickling her awake with a feather.

"Oh!" she said aloud, as she suddenly sat upright in bed and stretched. "It is my wedding day!" With a giggle in her voice, she said, "Thank you Lord, for the lovely wake up call."

In another house nearby, Adam was already walking the floor. He was firing readiness questions at Tom, like the military man that Tom expected Adam would always be, at least to some extent.

"Have my shoes been shined? Do you know where we are supposed to pick up the flowers? Do you think I should get my hair trimmed? I guess there is not time now...or is there? Has the carriage been cleaned and polished?" On and on he went, as he paced back and forth while wringing his hands.

Tom smiled and very patiently confirmed that he had completed each task as directed. As was his custom, he had Adam's clothes all laid out in the order of how Adam put each piece on. Everything was appropriately and perfectly cleaned, pressed or shined. On this particular morning, however, Tom had added a cluster of orange blossoms, the traditional Victorian symbol of fertility, on top of the wedding invitation, for a special touch. And, next to Adam's black dress coat, which would be the last garment for him to put on, Tom had wrapped the wedding gift that Adam had purchased for Sara Ella. It was a beautiful gold locket, engraved on the back with "June 24, 1865, Christ First."

Very early that morning, Randy sent a telegram to Adam from the train station in Boston, announcing that he would unexpectedly be able to attend the wedding. He wanted Adam to know that he would be arriving at the B&O Station at 1:00 pm and would need someone to pick him up there. Randy was traveling on a train from the Perkins Institute for the Blind in Watertown, Massachusetts with the Director of the school, Samuel Howe, and his new music teacher, Francis Campbell, who was also blind. Both men were on their way to Washington City to request financial aid for the school.

Later, Randy explained that outside his music class one day, he overheard Director Howe and Mr. Campbell talking about their trip to Washington City on June 24, so his ears perked up. After class he approached Mr. Campbell and asked, "I apologize for overhearing your conversation with Director Howe. I was not eavesdropping, I just happened to pick up on two details of your conversation, Washington City and June 24th. I was just wondering, sir, is there any way that I could accompany you on that trip?"

"My goodness, Randy, are you already getting homesick? You have only been here a short time," Mr. Campbell said, walking toward Randy.

"Oh, no sir! I am not homesick at all. I have already been so encouraged at this school, especially with all that you have shown me regarding music and the importance of the rhythm and background I can provide with my drum to almost any kind of music," Randy assured him.

"Well, I have been impressed with your natural feel for the rhythm of music, Randy. And with some training, I think you will be a great asset to our music department here at the school," Mr Campbell responded. "But, what is this about you wanting to go home already?"

"Well, sir," Randy explained, "my father is getting married on the 24th to a very special lady, and I would sure like to surprise them and show up for the wedding unexpectedly. You see, my father, General Adam Layne, was very uneasy about my coming here alone. I think he would be comforted that I can manage to live a productive life without him watching over me all the time. If I could show up for the wedding, having made my own arrangements to travel that far safely, it would go a long way toward helping him to see that he need not be worried about me and my future."

Now, Randy was on the train, enjoying lively conversation with Director Lowe and Mr. Campbell, only hours away from joining with his family in celebration of the long awaited marriage of his father and Sara Ella Gary. He was giddy with excitement.

Lisa was sound asleep when suddenly she was awakened abruptly, as Samuel landed right in the middle of her, announcing, "Good morning Mother! Look what I have for you!"

"Ohhhh, ughhh," Lisa groaned, "you are heavy Samuel! Oh, my goodness! What is all of this dirt? Look at you! Where have....?"

Just then, he thrust out from behind his back a big bouquet of beautiful garden flowers, exclaiming, "Look what I brought for you Mother! Ain't they purdy?"

"Yes! Yes, they are beautiful Samuel! You brought these for me? I love you, Son. Thank you so much!" She said this, as she studied the earth laden roots of the flowers, wishing she did not have to ask where they had come from.

"I know that today is Aunt Sara Ella's special day, and I did not want you to feel left out. Uncle Adam loves her, you know. And, I want you to know that you have a man that loves you, too...me!" Samuel said with pride, as he puffed out his chest and smiled his best smile.

"Samuel, you are such a blessing to me, and I love you too," Lisa said as she pulled him close and gave him a big hug. But, when she started to kiss him, he pulled away and said, "Awe, we don't need to go and get mushy 'bout it, do we?"

Lisa understood the demonstrative limitations of the affections of a boy his age and how delicate his feelings would be if she was not careful how she questioned him about where the flowers came from. So, she very cautiously asked, "Would you mind telling me where you found these lovely flowers, Son?"

"It was easy! Just a couple of doors down from here, this big house has whole bunches of flowers all along their fence. There's lots more flowers than they'll ever need. Don't worry, I got them early this morning, before the sun come up, so I'm sure nobody saw me."

Lisa was horrified, but did not let on. She just quickly stuck her nose into the beautiful bouquet in her hand. "I tell you what, Son, you go get all of that dirt washed off of you, while I get dressed. Then we will go for a little walk, okay?"

"Sure!" Samuel answered as he bounded off the bed and ran off, leaving a trail of black dirt behind.

Since it was Saturday, Scott Bryan did not have to work at the newspaper office. He was busy preparing breakfast for his boys who had promised to subsequently help him clean up the courtyard. With her family otherwise occupied, Marie had the freedom she needed to decorate Adam and Sara Ella's wedding cake. She had already baked the many layers early that morning, and she hoped the final product would be a masterpiece that would honor two of her favorite people in the world, Mr. and Mrs. Adam Layne.

After finishing his breakfast, Adam continued walking the floor in the dining room. Tom had long since given up trying to get him to relax, when there was a knock at the front door. Adam overheard Tom say to the person at the door, "Yes, this is General Layne's residence. How may I be of service to you?"

Then he heard someone say, "Please inform General Layne that Mrs. Chadna Gary, her son, Wesley, and his wife, Cora, are here, concerning his wedding with Miss Sara Ella Gary."

Adam immediately burst from the dining room calling, "Tom, please invite them right in! Mrs. Gary! Wesley! It is so good to have you here! Sara Ella does not know you are here, does she?"

"No, we wanted to surprise Sara Ella, so we did not tell her we had decided to come," Wesley said. "Actually, we intended to arrive several days ago, but the roads were awful. I do hope that we are not going to be an inconvenience to you and Sara Ella."

"Of course not! She will be thrilled to see you both, as I am. Please have a seat, and tell me all about your trip. You must be exhausted."

"Thank you, Adam," Mrs. Gary said as she lowered herself into the wing back chair that was always a favorite of Elizabeth Layne, Adam's late mother. "We certainly were spent last night when we finally arrived in Washington City, and it was much too late to come here. So, Wesley found us a nice place to stay. Actually, I feel quite refreshed this morning, after a good night's sleep in a comfortable bed."

Tom realized immediately that the unexpected arrival of Sara Ella's family left Adam a little off balance. Knowing he had been already frazzled, even before this change in plans, Tom spoke up and asked, "Adam, is this a good time for me to rig the carriage to escort the Gary family over to Mr. Bryan's home to see Sara Ella, or shall I wait a little while?"

Relieved that Tom saved his skin again, as usual, Adam cleared his throat and replied, "Tom, thank you for asking. I expect our guests will want to rest a bit, but it would be good to have the carriage out front for when we are ready for it."

"Yes, sir. I'll get right to it," Tom said, as he turned to go to the carriage house.

"Thank you General Layne," Mrs. Gary said. "As you might imagine, we are quite anxious to see my daughter."

"Please, Mrs. Gary, call me Adam. I am so pleased you are here, and I am looking forward to knowing you better. After all, you raised the most wonderful lady in the world!"

"I would be pleased to call you Adam, and would like for you to call me Chadna...at least, until it is appropriate for you to call me Mother that is," she said with a demure smile.

"After I have had a chance to greet Sara Ella, would it be too much of an inconvenience for me to come back here with you, Adam?"

Wesley asked. "I expect I will be out of place with all the wedding preparations of the ladies going on."

"Of course," Adam answered. "Perhaps you can help me calm my wedding jitters. I do not know why I am so anxious...I have been very ready for this for such a long time."

Lisa had her arm gently placed around Samuel's shoulders as they strolled down the street together. She was very cautiously trying to explain to him again that it is never right to take things that do not belong to you. For this boy who grew up on the streets of New York, surviving on only what he could find, getting her point across had proven to be a daunting task. "We have talked about this before, Son."

"But I thought flowers belong to God, Mama. I mean, you said that God made 'em, right? So, why can't anybody have 'em that wants 'em?"

"If that's what you think, Son, then why did you make a point to take them when nobody could see you?"

"Because they might get mad at me, that's why..."

"Why would they get mad at you if it is alright for you to have them?"

"Because, they don't know that everybody should share what belongs to God. I think flowers are different than the other things you told me not to take."

"Well, here we are Samuel. This is the place where you said my beautiful flowers came from, right?"

"...uh-huh...I mean, yes, ma'am."

Lisa turned Samuel toward her, swallowed hard and put one hand on each of his shoulders. Then, choking back tears, she leaned over, looked him square in the eye and said, "Son, you know that I love you more than life itself...and I have never received a more wonderful gift from anyone than the flowers you brought me this morning. But, it is important that you learn that you must not take things that belong to others. So now, we are going to knock on these people's door and apologize to them for having taken their flowers without asking. Do you understand?"

"Well, I don't see why you said 'we' are going to apologize...you ain't... I mean you aren't the one that took 'em, so why do you need to apologize?"

"Because I am your mother, and whatever you do reflects on your mother's training."

Samuel looked down and began nervously fidgeting with his hands. He clearly did not understand, but she knew that apologizing might help her get through to him somehow.

"Please knock on the door, Son."

"Yes, ma'am."

A middle-aged, full figured woman was drying her hands on her apron when she answered the door with a quizzical look on her face.

"Yes, may I help you with something?"

Samuel did not hesitate when she opened the door. He held the dirt and root laden flowers out to her, spoke up clearly and said, "I'm sorry, I took your flowers Ma'am. I promise I won't do it again."

"What on earth!" the lady said startled. "What is the meaning of this?"

Samuel pointed to Lisa and said, "Them flowers was so beautiful, I pulled 'em up from your yard, out by the fence, for my Mother early this morning. But, she told me I shouldn't a done it."

Lisa stepped forward and said, "I am so sorry, ma'am. I see from your mailbox that you are Mrs. Wilson, right?"

"Yes my name is Mrs. Wilson."

"We are pleased to meet you, though I must admit that these circumstances are somewhat embarrassing. My name is Lisa Layne, and this is my son, Samuel. He is not aware of the time and effort it takes to grow such a beautiful garden. If possible, we want to make this right for you. Do you have any suggestions, as to how we might do that?" Lisa said as she looked out at the flower garden and back at Mrs. Wilson.

"I see. I think I understand the situation we have here," Mrs. Wilson said, continuing to wipe her hands on her apron. "Young man, will you come out here with me please?"

Samuel followed Mrs. Wilson around her garden, as she proudly showed him all of the different kinds of flowers. She explained the planting and growing process and the many hours that she had put into nurturing all of them. To Lisa's surprise, he was impressed with what Mrs. Wilson had accomplished and asked many questions along the tour.

"I guess, I always thought flowers just come up wherever God wants 'em to. Now I see it differently."

Mrs. Wilson laughed, and then said, "Now, about making this thing you have done right. If it is okay with your mother, I would like for you to plant those flowers right back in the ground where they came from. Then I would like for you to come by every day for the next week, or so, to water and tend to them, so that hopefully, they will not die. Do you think that might be fair?"

Samuel scratched his head in obvious thought, and then said, "Well, with what I know now, that sounds like a lot of work."

"It's not any more work for you than it was for me, before you dug them up, don't you agree?"

"Yes, ma'am. I see your point. I do believe that would be fair. I'll start right now if that's okay."

Lisa looked up at Mrs. Wilson with a smile and said, "If you do not mind, I will help him, since I am his mother and therefore ultimately hold responsibility in this affair."

"It is refreshing to hear you say that, Mrs. Layne. Some parents do not understand or accept responsibility for the actions of their children."

"Thank you for being so understanding. Please give Mr. Wilson our apologies as well."

Mrs. Wilson's smile turned to sadness as she said, "I find myself a widow these days, dear. So, I have very much enjoyed your company, Lisa and Samuel. Come and visit me any time you would like."

As Lisa and Samuel were coming back to the Bryan's home, they saw Adam's carriage arrive. A gentleman and two ladies were getting out, and Tom was helping the older of the two ladies to the ground.

"Good morning, Tom! Who might you be escorting this fine morning?"

"Hello, Ms. Lisa," said Tom. "This is Miss Sara Ella's family, here for the wedding."

"My name is Cora," said the young woman who was closest to her. "I am the wife of Sara Ella's brother, Wesley," and she gestured to Wesley, who was helping her down from the carriage. Then turning around she continued, "This is Sara Ella's Mother, Chadna Gary." Then smiling and putting her right index finger on her mouth to indicate the need for silence, she lowered her voice and said, "Sara Ella does not know that we are here yet."

Lisa clapped her hands in delight and said, "What a wonderful surprise for her on her wedding day! Please come on in. I cannot wait for her to see that you are here!"

As they came into the house, Marie was starting up the stairs with Sara Ella's wedding gown over her arm. Hearing the commotion, she turned to see who was coming through the front door. Lisa made all the proper introductions, then turned to Marie and suggested that Mrs. Gary accompany her upstairs to see Sara Ella.

Marie gladly handed Sara Ella's wedding gown to her mother, saying, "Oh, that would be so grand! She will be so pleased that you are here. Why don't you take her gown up to her...please!"

As she started to ascend the stairs with the gown over her arm, Chadna smiled gratefully, and answered, "Thank you ladies, for letting me surprise her this way. You will never know how much it means to me!"

"Come on in...," Sara Ella said casually, upon hearing a soft rap on the door. She was standing in front of the mirror, trying to decide if she should change her mind about how she had planned to wear her hair today.

"Here is your gown, dear," her mother said softly as she entered the room.

Sara Ella whirled around, dropped her hair brush and squealed, "Mother! Oh, Mother, you are here!" She ran to her mother's side and embraced her joyfully. "Only moments ago, I was wishing you were here to fix my hair, like you always did for special occasions. And now you are here! I cannot believe it! You are here..." she said again and again, while holding her mother in her arms. "Now it is perfect...my wedding day is perfect!"

Adam had been distracted all morning, trying to remember every detail of his responsibility for the wedding preparations. He was also feeling a little melancholy over his family members who would not be present to celebrate his wedding with him. His parents, his brother Goddard, and sister Laura...all gone. The war had cost him dearly. He surely missed Randy and Benjamin every day, not just today. But, he understood why they felt that they needed to be out in the world on their own. Pulling himself together, he knew it was time for him to stop dwelling in the past, and focus on Sara Ella and all the joy she had brought into his life.

Already dressed for the wedding ceremony in black trousers and dress coat, with a white waistcoat and white cravat, Adam walked into the parlor, where he found Tom and Wesley enjoying some light conversation.

"Thank you, gentlemen, for helping me make it through this morning. I am finally dressed in my ceremonial garb, and I think I am as ready as I will ever be for my wedding day, what do you think?" He bowed exaggeratedly low, with his black top hat in his hand, acting silly to lighten the mood as much as possible.

"You look great...well, except for those bare feet. Somebody might notice that, Adam!" Tom said with a straight face, winking at Wesley who was sitting across the room smiling and watching Adam's performance.

Instinctively, Adam looked down at his feet. His face immediately flushed with embarrassment. Then, though it was completely out of character and entirely undignified, Adam grinned and started chasing Tom around the room the same way he did when Tom teased him as a child. The three men laughed hilariously.

Just then, they heard a loud knock at the front door. Relieved to escape imminent danger, Tom laughed, regained his composure and excused himself to go answer it.

"This is General Layne's residence. May I help you?" Tom said as he opened the door.

"I have a telegram here for General Layne. I am so sorry it has taken us so long to deliver it. It arrived in our office earlier today, but was inadvertently misplaced. Please offer our profound apologies to General Layne, and tell him that we hope our delay has not caused him any inconvenience."

"Thank you," Tom said and turned to take the telegram to Adam.

As Adam quickly read the telegram, his jaw dropped and he gasped in amazement. "Oh, my goodness! Listen to this, Tom! It is from Randy. He says, 'Surprise! Arriving B&O Station at 1:00 pm today.'"

Adam's shocked expression, combined with awareness that telegrams are uncommon and often did not bring good tidings, Wesley asked, "Is everything alright, Adam?"

As the unexpected news sunk in, Adam was clearly excited. "Oh yes, everything is wonderful, Wesley! My son, Randy, is going to be here for the wedding! Nothing could be more wonderful! I expect I feel about the same way Sara Ella did this morning when she saw you and your mother."

Relieved, Wesley sat down.

"Oh, no!" Adam exclaimed, as Wesley jumped back up.

"What's wrong?" Wesley asked.

"He will be here at 1:00! Tom! Randy is to arrive at the train station at 1:00. It is almost 1:00 now! I have to leave right away!" Adam exclaimed, as he circled the floor in confusion. Then, grabbing his coat, he ran out the door and down the stairs.

"Adam..." Tom said calmly, as he stood fixed at the top of the stairs.

"What is it, Tom? Come on! We have to leave right now! Get a move on, man! We have to hurry!"

"Well sir," said Tom, "I still think you should wear shoes to your wedding...I will get the carriage ready while you put your shoes on."

Adam looked down at his feet, then ran up the stairs two at a time, while Tom and Wesley had a good laugh at his expense.

The three men, all properly clad in shoes, made a fast dash for the train station in the carriage. On the way there, Adam said, "Tom, after you drop me off at the train station, go directly to Bryan Scott's house and start taking everyone there to the church grounds. I do not know how many trips you will need to make. Oh, and tell Sara Ella that I will bring a surprise with me, but do not tell her that Randy is coming!"

Tom rolled his eyes at Wesley and said, "Adam, we have already been over this at least four times. You know I will take care of it. Everything is under control, so you can relax."

"Oh, and do not forget to come and get me and Randy. I guess we should probably be there for the wedding, do you think?" Adam said with a grin.

"Yes sir," Tom said with a smile. "I promise I will not forget that either."

Sara Ella looked radiant in her lovely wedding gown that was made of imported white silk. In keeping with her personality and her tall, slender frame, she had chosen a tastefully modest, perfectly plain bodice with ornamental pearl buttons and a wide satin waist ribbon. The mousquetaire sleeves were cuffed with a simple ruching, while her delicate under sleeves were adorned with a frill of lace and satin at the wrist. The cartridge pleated, three tiered flounce skirt was supported by a petticoat and crinoline that were elaborately enhanced along the hemline with trim to match the satin and lace of her under sleeves. This fancy petticoat would occasionally peek out from under her skirt as she glided across the floor. She wore a plain illusion veil with a silk cord at the top of the lower hem. Her mother had carefully pinned up her beautiful long brown hair into a traditional style that enhanced the clusters of orange blossoms that formed a wreath around her head.

So that she would be free to help Sara Ella dress, Lisa had finished dressing earlier in the Maid of Honor gown that Sara Ella had chosen for her to wear. The style of her peach colored satin dress was similar to the bride's dress, except that there were no lacy under sleeves and her skirt was plain, instead of flounced. The bride's mother was wearing an elegant green satin gown that she made for herself at home before she came, knowing that, regardless of the colors her daughter may have chosen for her wedding party, green would coordinate nicely with the flowers.

Waiting for the festivities to start and wishing her father was there to give her away, Sara Ella held her mother's hand tightly, as if she were a little girl, afraid to cross the street alone. Looking out the window where she was waiting in the Bride's Room of the church, she noticed as Secretary Stanton arrived.

Pointing Stanton out to her mother, she said, "Oh Mother, look! There is Secretary Stanton, and that is Chaplain Gray walking along beside him. Remember, I was telling you about Chaplain Gray meeting with Adam and helping him so much. And, that is Congressman Ben Wade and his wife on the other side of Secretary Stanton. Everything looks so beautiful. Marie did such a good job decorating the church grounds, did she not? What a blessing she has been to me."

"Have you seen the groom yet, dear?" Chadna asked.

"Oh, no Mother! I am not supposed to see him until I walk down the aisle," Sara Ella protested with a smile.

Turning back to the window, Sara Ella continued to announce the wedding guests to her mother, as they arrived. "Look, Mother, there is Congressman Thaddeus Stevens. He and his wife just sat down on the other side of Chaplain Gray and the others. Oh, there are so many important people here that I have never even met, all friends and associates of Adam. I sure hope he will be pleased with the arrangements Marie and I put together. I do not want him to be embarrassed."

"From my brief encounter with him, my dear, I would say it is pretty obvious that as long as you are here, nothing else would matter to him. I am afraid he is quite smitten with you, which is perfectly understandable!"

Just then there was a tap on the door. Lisa said, "Let me get the door for you, dear, so no one will see you until the time is right."

There were soft voices at the door, then Sara Ella heard Lisa say, "Yes, I think she would want to see you, young man. Please come right on in."

Sara Ella turned around from the window, and there in front of her was Benjamin, smiling from ear to ear! He was dressed impeccably, as if he were going to his own wedding.

"Benjamin! You are here! I did not know...does Adam know you are here?" she said as she embraced him warmly.

"I would not have missed this for anything Miss Sara Ella. You look really beautiful. No, Adam does not know I am here. I thought I would surprise you both. But, I found you first. I could not find him, or anyone who knows where he might be."

"What do you mean? Isn't Tom out there? Adam will not be far from Tom," Sara Ella mused.

"No, ma'am. I could not find Tom, either. Nobody seems to know where Adam or Tom could be."

"That is strange. Please keep an eye out, Benjamin, and send word to me when you find him. It is strange that neither of them is here. I would sure like to know about it when they show up," Sara Ella said with a puzzled look on her face.

"Yes, ma'am. I would be happy to do just that. You will be the first to know when I find them."

Meanwhile, at the train station, Adam was restless and impatient. Randy's train was not there yet, and it was getting close to time for the wedding ceremony to begin. Tom had finished delivering everyone from the Scott residence to the church, and had come to the train station to pick up Adam and Randy. But, Randy's train was late.

Wringing his hands with anxiety, Adam said to Tom, "Please, go back to the Depot office again to see if they know anything, yet. I am afraid to leave here to go to the church in case something has happened to Randy. He is blind, you know...I need to be here for him if something has gone wrong..."

"I just came from there the fourth time, Adam. They told me that the train is not late enough for concern, and they do not expect to hear anything until it arrives," Tom answered.

Adam was desperately combing his hands through his hair and pacing the floor. "I cannot send you to the church with the carriage to tell them where I am, because then I will not have a way to the wedding once Randy arrives. I sure wish that train would get here!"

"Well, sir," Tom said as calmly as possible, "Would it work for me to go ahead to the church and tell the preacher what is happening. I am sure they will hold the ceremony until you get there, under the circumstances."

"But, then how would Randy and I get there?" Adam groaned.

"Adam! Relax so you can think! When Randy gets off that train, and I am sure he will very soon, you can hail a cab to carry you both to the church!"

"Of course, Tom! Why did I not think of that? I am so accustomed to you always being there to transport me anywhere I need to go that I completely forgot about cabs. You do that right now, just like you said. Go to the church, and tell the pastor that I will be there just as quickly as I can. Surely the train will come right away."

There was another tap on Sara Ella's door, and Marie entered, a little out of breath. "I know the wedding was supposed to have started a few minutes ago, but we have a couple of hitches about which you need to be made aware.

First, I think Benjamin already told you that we have not seen Adam all morning. Tom has not been seen since he brought everyone here from my house earlier. Wesley said that Tom and Adam are at the train station, but that does not make any sense. Even more disturbing is the news that Pastor Kilgore was rushed to the hospital a little while ago. Apparently, it is not serious, but he is unable to be here for the ceremony."

"How can this be happening? Another delay! Will Adam and I ever be married?" Sara Ella fought back tears, as her mother rushed to her side.

"Honey, you know you can depend on the Lord to make this work out for the best."

"I am so glad that you're here, Mother. Thank you for helping me trust Him."

"Do not worry, Sara Ella," Marie said. "I have an idea that I think will work. I will see if I can find someone to entertain this crowd, while I make some preparations. I will let you know when things are on track. Do any of you ladies have any ideas about some impromptu entertainment?"

Sara Ella looked down at the floor and then back up at Marie, "Did you say that Benjamin has a friend with him?"

"Yes, he does," Marie answered as she headed toward the door.

"Is the friend's name Walter?" Sara Ella asked.

"That sounds right. Yes, I think his name is Walter," Marie answered.

"Go and check right now. If it is Walter, I assure you that he will help you with some beautiful music. Walter is a black man, so some people may object. But, if their hearts are open, his music will surely not disappoint," Sara Ella told her, with confidence in her voice.

"Walter it is, then!" Marie said with a smile. "Just leave this to me, and I will have the wheels of progress going again shortly!"

Chaplain Gray agreed to fill in for Reverend Kilgore, with Marie coaching him on names and particulars for the ceremony. The inspiring special music Walter provided was well received by almost everyone.

Even after about three quarters of an hour of waiting, for the most part, everyone seemed to understand the delay after the announcement was made about having to arrange for someone to fill in for Reverend Kilgore who had suddenly taken ill.

Sara Ella was watching out her window when she saw Tom arrive in the carriage alone. "Oh, Mother, what could that mean?"

"I am sure that we will know something soon, dear. As you can see, he is walking this way, and Marie is hurrying out to meet him."

"Come on in, Tom," Marie said, as she ushered Tom into the bride's room. "I am sure she will want to hear directly from you."

Tom was smiling which put Sara Ella at ease now. "Miss Sara Ella, Adam asked me to reassure you that he will be here just as soon as possible. You see, he received a telegram this morning from Randy that he was coming in on the train. But, the train is late, and he is afraid to leave in case something is wrong. He said that as soon as Randy gets here, he will get a cab and bring Randy right over. He is so sorry for the delay. Hopefully, they will be here right away."

"Oh, I am so relieved! Thank you so much for the news, Tom. I was getting so worried that something terrible might have happened to him," Sara Ella sighed.

"Well, ma'am," Tom laughed, "...something surely has happened to him today! I have never seen him so nervous! Not in the war or anywhere, ever! He's...well he is just smitten...just plain incurable until you get this wedding over with!" Everyone in the room laughed with him, and then he turned to leave.

Sara Ella took a deep breath and said, "Marie, could you please make another announcement, this one about an unavoidable delay by the groom. I know that some people have already gotten impatient and gone home. But, please invite those remaining to help themselves to all refreshments except our beautiful wedding cake. Please assure them that we understand if they need to leave, and thank them for coming. Remind them to sign the guest register if they haven't already."

After another half hour had passed, most of the guests had enjoyed the refreshments and reluctantly began to leave. Sara Ella set her jaw and announced to her mother, Lisa and Marie, "I think it is time for us to go to the train station! Marie, please go out and invite anyone who would like to go with us to feel free to join our parade!"

Randy and another blind man right behind him were disembarking the train with the help of the porter, when Adam began pushing his way through the crowd calling, "Randy, I am coming Randy!"

"Father!" Randy responded, as Adam reached him and embraced him. "Father, it is wonderful that you are here, but I expected Tom to be picking me up, since we are so late."

"Well, I sent Tom back to the church to tell everyone I would be late, because I was here waiting here for you. What happened?"

"Apparently a train ahead of us had a problem, and it was difficult to clear the tracks for us to pass. I am so sorry I delayed your wedding." Then turning to the men with him, Randy said, "Please meet my friends, Father. This man next to me is my music teacher Mr. Francis Campbell. Can you believe that he was appointed Music Master at the Tennessee School for the Blind when he was only 16 year old! Then he was Musical Director at the Wisconsin School for the Blind, before he came to Perkins Institute. He is teaching me to play drums with an orchestra, Father!" Randy said with excitement and pride. "It is fantastic! I have already learned so much."

Adam reached out his hand and grasped Mr. Campbell's hand as he said, "I have not seen Randy this encouraged for a very long time! I owe you a great deal of gratitude, sir."

"Oh, and Father this is Samuel Howe, the director of Perkins Institute. He and Mr. Campbell are here to talk to Congress about more funding for the school. That is how I was able to come to the wedding. They allowed me to travel here with them!"

Both men laughed and said, "You have a very persistent and determined son, sir. He kept after us....," Director Howe started to say, when he noticed some commotion over Adam's shoulder. "What on earth is going on?" he then exclaimed.

Adam turned around and saw a beautiful woman wearing a wedding dress, running their way, with a whole crowd of people chasing after her! Puzzled at first, then in astonishment he shouted, "Sara Ella! Over here, Sara Ella!" He ran, with his arms open wide and upon reaching her, picked her up and swung her around, unashamed as tears rolled down his cheeks. I am so sorry for ruining our wedding day, Darling. I love you so much! I am finding myself totally incomplete without you by my side. How can I make up to you what I have done today? Please forgive me..."

Sara Ella said, "I will forgive you on one condition..."

Adam with great concern on his face, said, "Anything, my love, anything you want."

"Okay, I will forgive you if you will marry me right here, right now. No more delay's..." she said with a twinkle in her eye.

Adam, a little startled and struggling to figure out how that could be accomplished, was relieved when Chaplain Gray stepped forward out of the crowd that was gathered behind Sara Ella.

The Reverend said, "Adam...have I not been telling you that all things are possible with our Lord Jesus Christ?"

"Well, yes...," and then with a big smile Adam asked, "Please, Chaplain Gray, will you marry us right here, right now? Before any more delays can get in the way of our being joined together?" At that moment, the loud whistle of a train coming into the station obliterated the sound of his agreement.

Adam took Sara Ella's hand and led her to a bench in the center of the Depot. Then, lifting her up onto the make believe alter, making sure that she was steady, he climbed up beside her. Chaplain Gray took his place in front of them, while the wedding party crowded around. Before long, others in the station began crowding around to join the wedding party.

After exchanging vows, Adam jumped down and whispered something in Chaplain Gray's ear, then jumped back up beside Sara Ella, smiling.

The Reverend very dramatically turned to Adam and said, "You may now put the ring on her finger."

When Sara Ella saw the long-lost ruby ring that Adam had given her before the war, tears came to her eyes. "How on earth...you said my ring was left at the mansion before the war! I did not think I would ever see it again..." She choked out the words as best she could, considering the extent of her emotion.

"This ring was resurrected from the destruction and ashes of Oaklayne, my dear, as were we," Adam exclaimed.

Chaplain Gray pronounced, "With this ring I thee wed. You may kiss the bride."

With that, Adam kissed Sara Ella tenderly. He did not want to let go of her...ever.

The crowd cheered so loudly that they drowned out the sound of the next train coming in to the station!

Chapter 32

"Now this is ridin' in style!" Richard called out from inside the covered buckboard. "I could sleep like a baby in here, even on the roughest of roads."

"You may change your mind when you realize there is not much left of roads. Sherman and his men really did wipe things out," Ralph responded from the seat out front.

Richard replied, "Nothing could dampen my spirits right now."

"I was pleased that Dr. Combs agreed to let you come with us when I told him of my credentials and ability to care for you on this journey," Ralph said over his shoulder.

"You have no idea how much I appreciate your willingness to push through and convince him to release me. I am afraid I would have had to insist, if he had continued to refuse to let me out of there. He is a great doctor, but I am excited to be headed north. I want to get as far away as possible from Andersonville Prison!" Richard said emphatically.

"Dr. Combs seemed grateful that the war was over also," Ralph sighed. "He said that out of the twenty three companies of soldiers Macon furnished the Confederacy, only enough men to fill five companies had survived to be fit for duty by the end of the war. He said it seemed like a slaughter to him, and I am sure it did to the residence in Macon, also."

"No one on either side of this awful war came out ahead, if you consider the horrendous loss of life. I know at Andersonville Prison, or "Camp Sumter", as it is called by some, it was not at all uncommon for one hundred men to die in a single day. Though it only operated for 14 months, almost thirteen thousand men died there from hunger, exposure, disease, or sometimes all of those combined. It is only twenty six acres of land, but at one point there were thirty three thousand men imprisoned together there. They brought in four hundred prisoners a day, sometimes. One day, because of the heat, a hundred seventy five of us died. We were so feeble that we looked like skeletons, so it did not take much to kill us," Richard explained.

"Did they not have any medical care available?" Ralph asked.

"Very little. The situation was so overwhelming that it is unlikely that medical help could have made much of a difference, anyway. We were crammed in so tightly that it was hard to stay off of the 'deadline'."

"The deadline?"

"Yes, that was the demarcation line that kept prisoners away from the stockade wall. If we crossed the 'deadline' or even touched it, we were shot by the guards who were posted in the 'pigeon roosts', about thirty yards apart all around the wall. Some men would become so desperate that they crossed it purposely, knowing they would be shot. We called it 'paroled', when that happened."

"I'm so thankful we found you alive, Richard. There are those who were a little skeptical that you could have survived that place." Then raising his voice, Ralph said, "Look, here comes August!"

Returning from scouting up ahead, August brought Thunder to a halt beside the wagon in a cloud of dust. The way he rode up in such a hurry, Ralph could tell something was urgent.

Panting and talking fast, August said, "There is a black family up ahead with a little girl who is hurt, Doc. Take Thunder and go help her. I will bring Richard and the wagon behind you."

"Is it a serious injury, or did she just skin her knee?" Ralph questioned impatiently, knowing that August had a propensity to get them involved in things that were often precarious and none of their business.

"I don't know how bad it is, Doc. She fell and hit her head, and she was not moving when I left. I told them I would bring a doctor right back." August was obviously concerned. "I think they tried to hide when they saw me coming. That is when the little girl fell and hit her head."

Ralph retrieved his medical bag from the wagon, mounted Thunder and rode off in the direction from which August had come.

When August and Richard arrived with the wagon, Doc was bending over the little girl, cleaning the wound and watching for her to come around. Holding a very large mule by the reigns, a huge black man was consoling the little girl's mother and brother, assuring them that the doctor would know what to do.

As the little girl regained consciousness and opened her big black eyes, Ralph said, "Well, hello, little one." He gently cradled her in his arms, while he put some ointment on her head wound and wrapped it with a bandage.

She smiled weakly and rubbed her head. "It hurts," she said.

Ralph smiled and said, "I know it hurts, Darlin'. Do you think you could get up for me?"

Looking at the little girl's weeping mother, Ralph continued, "I need to see if she can stand and walk to determine whether she is dizzy or faint. Could you please help her stand up, ma'am?"

The mother took her daughter's hands in hers and steadied her, as she got to her feet. But, the girl lost her balance and started to fall, when her mother let go of her.

Doctor Fowler kept her from falling, embraced her warmly and announced, "The little one's injury does not appear to be serious, ma'am. But, she will need some time to rest until that dizziness goes away."

Laying the girl safely back down on the ground, Ralph stood up, extended his hand to the mother and said, "My name is Doctor Fowler, and this young man with me is August. If it is okay with you, we will put your daughter in our wagon and help you take her home safely. Please, feel free to ride in the wagon with her."

Lifting the little girl into his arms, Ralph looked into her beautiful eyes and said, "We have an injured man in the wagon., too His name is Richard. He is a very nice man, so I am sure you will become friends right away."

As Ralph started toward the back of the wagon, carrying the girl, August approached and said, "Doc, the big man is the little girl's father. He says they do not have a home. All they have is that big mule, loaded down with their meager belongings. They take turns riding it. They have been working their way north, trying to stay out of sight. The big man's name is Ezra, his wife is Rachel, and the children are Zeke and Dorothy.

"I feel responsible, Doc. It is my fault that the little girl is hurt...Thunder and I startled them."

Ralph looked at Ezra, who was standing beside the mule with his son, obviously concerned for his little family. "Where did they get the mule, August?"

"Ezra said it belonged to the owner of the plantation where they lived for many years. The plantation owner had Ezra hide the mule from the raiding soldiers, as they came through the area. That plantation is now destroyed and completely deserted."

"Will that plantation owner not come looking for the mule?" Ralph questioned with concern.

"Well, Ezra said he has been feeding and taking care of the mule for well over a month now. They could not stay any longer in the ruins of their former home, and he knew the mule would die of neglect if they did not bring it with them."

"What on earth have you gotten us into now, August!" said Ralph, amazed and somewhat perturbed. "Tell me, young man...exactly how is it that you have managed to live to such a ripe old age?"

"Me? What did you want me to do, leave that little girl to die, or worse? Doc, you know these folks will never survive on a trip like that alone. But, they won't survive if they stay here either. That little girl cannot walk, and she cannot ride that big mule either. We cannot just leave them here, can we?"

August did not seem to understand that Ralph was anxious to get home to his wife, Joy. That is why he was not particularly pleased with August's plans to bring these "stray kittens" along on their trip north.

"Well, Richard, what do you think we should do?"

"Ahem...well, I have been thinking how much better my time alone in the back of this wagon would go if I had some company for a while."

"I already know your answer, August," said Ralph, sighing. "Okay, your friends are welcome to join us on the trail north." He did not finish his sentence, before August let out a holler. "But, I want to make it clear that it will be a hard trip. Everyone will need to stay close to the wagon at all times. Looking at Ezra, Ralph said, "Understood?"

"Yes, sah!. Lo'd knows Ah don' wanna' bring no trouble yo' way," Ezra answered.

After loading Dorothy and Rachel into the back with Richard, Ralph climbed up, sat down on the wagon seat and grabbed the reigns. August threw a thick saddle blanket over Ralph's mare's back, as she was tied behind the buckboard. Then he gave Zeke a leg up, where he held onto her mane for stability.

"Git up Goliath!" Ezra prodded, as he thumped the mule's sides with his bare feet. And with that, all seven of them were off together on the trail north.

Chapter 33

"Good morning Elsie," Oscar said, as he reached for a coffee cup.

"Why are you so cheerful this morning?" she responded, as she picked up the coffee pot and filled his cup.

Expecting it to be very hot, Oscar took a cautious sip of the steaming brew and said, "Well, I was just thinking about Adam and Sara Ella, realizing that they are married now if all went according to plan. They should be arriving back here at Oaklayne in less than two weeks, and I am really looking forward to seeing them. They deserve to be happy, after everything they have been through together. I sure hope Adam will be pleased with all the progress we have made in his absence."

Elsie responded, "I expect he will be amazed that you were able to repair the saw mill so quickly after that awful fire."

Oscar stretched his long legs out in front of him, his countenance revealing his pride in the remarkable accomplishments of his team.

"Did you ever figure out who set that fire?" Elsie questioned, not allowing their conversation to slow her pace, as she continued to organize the kitchen for the cooking of breakfast.

Oscar sighed, "No, but I have my suspicions. I cannot imagine what would motivate someone to do that. It is true, Burt was unhappy when he left here, but arson and threatening the work crew is kind of extreme, I think."

"Yes, I agree. But, I guess bitterness can cause people to do some very ugly things that don't make sense to anyone but them. Some folks cannot abide humiliation, and Burt was clearly humiliated in front of the other men. Of course, we know that he brought it on himself, but he probably wouldn't agree. I wish people could just forgive when they get their feelings hurt, instead of holding a grudge. Grudges ultimately turn into bitterness, with consequences that are never good."

Elsie's words shook Oscar to his core, because her thoughts struck a very tender nerve. He could not help but think of his own reaction to the humiliation of being rejected by Sally May after he returned home from the war. Therefore, he immediately over reacted to her evaluation of the situation, and said with his voice raised inappropriately, "That is kind of harsh and judgment, isn't it?"

"Excuse me? What is wrong with you? Are we talking about the same thing here?" Elsie said, as she rose up under a cabinet door and bumped her head, subsequently dropping a pan on the floor with a loud clatter. Rubbing the top of her head with her hand, she bent over to retrieve the stray pan and spouted, "What did I say that upset you? You are impossible, Oscar Baynes!"

"I'm not upset!" Oscar said, slamming down his cup on the table, spilling coffee on his hand. Shaking the hot liquid that was burning his flesh, he stomped out the door, growling, "Never mind!"

Frustrated and feeling like a cornered injured animal, he paced around the yard in the predawn darkness, running his scorched fingers through his curly brown hair. Finally, he plopped down under a tree, put his head in his hands and wept.

What is wrong with me? Why are the tears coming now? I have never broken down over what Sally May did to me. Facing his hurt full on, Oscar could not stop the flow of tears that ran down his sun darkened cheeks. Why does it still hurt so much? Until now, I have stayed strong. Is that not what men are supposed to do? Why did she not wait for me, while I was gone to war?

Just then, a door slammed at the bunk house. Oscar knew that men were beginning to stir, getting ready for another busy day. He watched as one man headed to the barn to feed and water the horses. There was a faint glow on the horizon, announcing that the sun would soon begin to shed light and warmth on the day.

Elsie is right...I need to put this behind me and move on with my life. If I truly loved Sally May, then I would be happy that she has found a man she loves more than I thought she loved me. I cannot change that, and it is not good for me to keep dwelling on what might have been.

Oscar jumped up from under the tree with a new resolve to stop living in the past. Just because things with Sally May did not work out the way he thought they should, did not mean that he could not still have a good life.

After breakfast, Oscar watched the ladies working together efficiently to clean up the kitchen, already beginning preparations for the other meals of the day. He went out of his way to be kind to Elsie, hoping she would forget about his earlier emotional outburst. She seemed to be willing to put the incident behind her. Not wanting to interrupt progress, he asked Emma Lou if it would be possible for him to talk with all of them before he started his days' work. She agreed to call them together right away, curious about what he wanted to say.

"Ladies, I need your help. We have been working on Adam and Sara Ella's cabin, but we need your feminine touch for the finer details. We have added wood flooring and replaced the windows. We sanded and refinished the whole interior of their cabin, adding a thin layer of cedar to the walls to control insects and make everything smell sweet and new. Nathaniel finished a beautiful piece of walnut for their fireplace mantel. Steven added some fancy decorative wood carvings to make it look less rustic. We enclosed the big back porch that overlooks the river, which provides some security and privacy. I have already purchased a nice new bed for them that should be delivered next week. But, we men are at a loss about what to do to make it look more like a home. Could you help us with that, please?"

Emma Lou was the first to speak up, "Well, Ah'm a thinkin' it'd be nice if they had some curtains fo' the winda's, an' maybe a rug on the flo', too." Then, turning to the other ladies she asked, "Ah' done a little sewin' in my day. Do any of y'all know how ta' help make a rug an' sew winda' curtains?"

Jumping to her feet immediately, Beverly Jean responded with a shy smile, "Yes, Ma'am. Ah sho'ly does! Ah done all the sewin' at the Sheldon Plantation 'fore the war. Guess yo' could call it my specialty, an' Ah sho' loves doin' it!"

Oscar was excited to hear about that, telling her, "That is great news, Beverly Jean! We will need to use your skills in the big house, too, after it is finished. This is your chance to show us what you can do."

Emma Lou added, "We'll need ta' buy some textiles fo' doin' this, Sah. Ah knows Miss Sara Ella's fav'rite colors 'r soft gold an' red. So, if'n we have time, it'd be nice if we could make a purdy red an' gold bed coverin' fo' their new bed an' curtains ta' match. We don' have no good quilts 'round here no mo', so maybe we should see if'n we kin buy new quilts fer the bed? Wish they was time to make new quilts..."

"I expect they will need a little more furniture to go with the new bed you ordered for them," Elsie added. "It will be great for the newlyweds to have that new bed and new bedding on the mattress. That was very thoughtful, Oscar. They will also need a small eating table with a couple of chairs. We could put a nice tablecloth on the little table and padded cushions on the chairs. I think it would be cozy to put two matching chairs for relaxing on either side of the fireplace. And, how 'bout getting a night table to put next to the bed, with a beautiful kerosene lamp, and another lamp on the eating table?"

Jessica added, "Dominique showed me them rockers that he, Nathaniel and Steven are 'bout finished wit' fo' the back porch. Can Ah makes some cushions fer them chairs, too?"

"Wow! I'm impressed with all of your thoughtful input, Ladies. It is clear that you are the right people to turn this responsibility over to! I tell you what. Make me a list of everything you described and I will head out to Richmond early in the morning to pick up what you need. Rest assured, there will be a nice bonus for all of you for your extra work on this."

Emma Lou, Beverly Jean and Jessica sounded like an active hive of busy bees, as they made their way back to the kitchen. But, Oscar asked Elsie to remain behind.

"Elsie," Oscar said, "I wanted to apologize for my behavior this morning. I was rude, and I am sorry that you felt the brunt of my selfishness. Will you please forgive me? I will do my best to make sure it never happens again."

"Well, I appreciate that. But, I do not understand what I said or did to upset you?"

"Actually, you said exactly what I needed to hear at the time. Thank you for speaking your thoughts. You were very helpful to me, Elsie. Perhaps someday I will be able to explain more, but for now my apology will have to be enough." Oscar said as he got up to leave. "By the way, would you consider accompanying me into Richmond tomorrow to purchase the things you ladies want me to buy? All of the ideas sound really great, but I don't feel confident that I will be able to handle it on my own. I'd really appreciate some help."

Elsie laughed and said, "Sure, I'd be happy to go along. I confess, I had my own reservations about how well your domestic skills would serve you in this situation."

"Now wait a minute. Are you insinuating that I do not have a soft side?"

"Oh, no! I'm very aware that you have a soft side, Oscar. It just does not happen to have any feminine overtones!" She giggled and ran quickly for the house with Oscar on her heels. When she reached the door, she whirled around and said, "I would love to accompany you into Richmond in the morning, that is, if Emma Lou will let me off of kitchen duty."

"Dominique eagerly volunteered to help the kitchen crew out in the morning." Oscar said, rolling his eyes. "He's even going to stay here in the bunkhouse tonight, so he can start early in the morning like you do." Elsie's head of soft dark brown curls bounced gently, as she laughed, opened the door and disappeared inside.

Oscar walked outside for some air, as Elsie continued to examine bolt after bolt of fabric at the Mercantile. They had already pick out some finished goods that she seemed very pleased with, but was having trouble settling on just the right thing for the curtains and bed coverings. Oscar did not think such things mattered much, but it seemed to be very important to Elsie that everything be perfect for Sara Ella. Finally, she decided on some different prints and solids that were all coordinated colors and textures, and Oscar paid for everything.

Next, they made their way to the store where they sold ready-made furniture. Oscar was grateful that it did not take Elsie very long to pick out the furniture she thought would be just right for the little cabin. He signed for everything, as the buckboard was being loaded with the new furniture.

Elsie was in the General Store shopping for some fancy smelling soap and candles, so Oscar left the buckboard with her and went walking down the street, hoping he might find Sergeant Clifford O'Reily.

He had not gone far before a big hand caught him on the shoulder and a gruff voice said, "What do think you're doin' here, stranger?"

Oscar instinctively broke the man's grip, as he spun around like a cat ready to pounce. But, he was relieved when he found himself face to face with Sergeant O'Reily's smiling face.

"Are you trying to get yourself killed, man?" Oscar said as he caught his breath.

"Naw, I just thought you might be lookin' for my handsome face, and that was the only way I could get you to turn around!" Sergeant O'Reily boasted, as he slapped Oscar on the back. "Come with me to the office and fill me in on how things are going with the reconstruction project you're workin' on."

"As a matter of fact, there is something that I am hoping you might be able to help me with." Oscar sat down across from O'Reily's desk and began telling him about the problems they were having at the plantation. He filled him in on the strange visit by James Hatfield, the neighboring plantation owner, and the harassment and threats that his men continue to get, going to and from work. He also told him about the sawmill fire, and the evidence they found to indicate that it was arson.

Clifford scratched his chin, as he studied on what Oscar had shared with him. "Somethin' don't make sense here. Why would anyone care what your doin' to rebuild that plantation, if it doesn't affect them? And, if it does affect them in some way, then you need to know how.

That's the only way you'll get to the bottom of this. What did you say that plantation owner's name is?"

"He calls himself Colonel James Hatfield. I have no idea if he was ever in the military. He sure does not act like a military man. He acts like a blithering idiot, if you ask me! He says that he is a plantation owner. Have you ever heard of him?"

Clifford sat back in his chair and whistled between his teeth. "Oh, my! I'm afraid you've tangled with a fat peacock! That man prances 'round here with that big nose of his up in the air, like he's a king or something, orderin' people around. I'm not sure what he does, but he's got something goin' with government grants I think. I do know that he's been buyin' up a lot of property in the area. In fact, now that I think about it, just recently there was some kind of tussle he was involved in with another big plantation owner out your way. Those folks insisted that "Colonel Peacock"...I mean Hatfield forced them out. I don't know any of the particulars, mind you...that's just what people are sayin'."

"Interesting...," said Oscar. "Wonder if there is any connection to Oaklayne in this? Would you mind keeping watch for me about this character? I do not know if he is a problem or just a nuisance. I would like to keep my eye on him until I know for sure what is going on."

Clifford grinned and said, "Sure thing! I don't trust that Peacock feller one bit, myself. So, it will be a pleasure for me to watch him like a hawk. I'll keep you posted if I learn anything." Then, changing the subject to lighten the mood, he said, "Hey, do you have time to come by my place and see Patricia? I'm sure she'd love to see you...well, maybe not 'love'...her love is reserved for only my handsome face, you know."

Oscar laughed and responded, "Thanks Clifford, but I am on a tight schedule, picking up some things here in town for Adam Layne and his new bride, who will be coming home soon. Perhaps, next time?" Oscar rose from his seat and offered his hand to his friend, before heading back up the street to get Elsie and the loaded buckboard.

On the way back to the plantation, Elsie talked on and on with excitement over all the beautiful things they had purchased for Adam and Sara Ella's cabin. "It's going to be perfect, Oscar! Their little honeymoon cabin is going to be so sweet, maybe they won't even care about finishing the big house!"

Oscar was thoroughly enjoying the sound of her voice when suddenly there was a loud cracking noise and a small tree fell across the road right in front of the horses! Oscar was caught off guard and had his hands full, trying to get the spooked horses under control. Then without warning, three men rushed out from behind the trees just off of the road. Two of them grabbed the screaming Elsie, pulling her off of the buckboard seat and onto the ground. The other man had a rifle pointed at Oscar, who demanded in his most authoritative voice, "What is the meaning of this?"

Sarcastically, one of the men said, "Well, we jus' thought we might have some fun with this here purdy little lady. Would you like to come and watch? Or, would you pre'fer ta' mosey on back to that plantation where you's the big Boss man? Don't make no neva' mind to us. We jus' want you to 'member from now on that folks from your plantation jus' ain't welcome on this here road. I 'spect you might jes' recall that fact, when you're missin' this little gal's purdy face. Now, come on darlin', we's gonna' have us a real good time." Then, the two men holding Elsie tightly, as she squirmed and yelled at the top of her lungs, began walking backwards toward the woods while the third man kept the gun on Oscar.

Oscar was filled with horror at what these men were planning. Yet, he knew he had to keep his wits about him to keep from endangering her further. He simply had to get control of the situation if he was going to protect Elsie's life and honor.

Keeping his voice calm, he said, "I have idea gentlemen. Why do you not let her get back up here and go on to the plantation, and take me instead. After all, I am the one who is messing up your interest in this road, now is that not right? If you do away with me, you will have what you are really after. Now, is that not the smartest thing to do?"

The three ruffians were obviously not accustomed to doing much thinking, so did not quite know what to do when someone suggested an alternative perspective on their goal of controlling access to the road. Sensing a change in the dynamic of the situation, Elsie stopped struggling and felt the two men holding her loosen their grip somewhat. Then the third man turned to see why she stopped screaming, just as she put all of her weight on the arms of her two captors, lifted herself off the ground and kicked the man with the rifle in the groin so hard that the gun flew out of his hands and landed a good distance away, not far from the wagon.

Oscar reacted so quickly that later he could not even remember how he ended up with the rifle in his hands. Nevertheless, the three scoundrels left Elsie behind, as they escaped for their lives into the woods.

Oscar cradled Elsie in his strong arms as if she was a treasured child...but what he was feeling was anything but childish. She relaxed in his embrace and cried softly, and he assured her that she was safe from harm. He was so proud of her courage and presence of mind in the face of such danger, and he told her so.

Chapter 34

The next morning, Sara Ella felt like the princess in a magical fairytale. As she laid her head on Adam's shoulder, they snuggled together on silk sheets in the most elegant mahogany four-poster bed she had ever seen. The Bridal Suite at the Willard Hotel was so luxuriously decorated it was clearly fit for a queen. Who would have ever guessed that she, Sara Ella Gary, would ever be allowed to even see such opulence in her lifetime, much less stay there on her honeymoon!

Then, looking at her long lost ruby ring on her left hand, it occurred to her...she is no longer Sara Ella Gary, but Sara Ella Layne! And this room was definitely appropriate for Mrs. Adam Layne! She giggled, and poked Adam in the side with her elbow in good humor.

"Hey!" Adam complained. "If you are going to sleep in my bed, you will have to learn some manners, Mrs. Layne!"

"Oh, Adam...I could not be happier! I love you so much, Sweetheart."

"My dear, this is just the beginning of a much bigger love affair than we could have ever imagined when we fell in love years ago. You have filled my heart so fully that I can hardly contain myself. Just think, you and I will be together always. Even death cannot separate us, because you and I will have eternity together with Jesus. I love you so much," Adam said, as he tenderly kissed her and pulled her close again.

After an elaborate breakfast in their suite, Mr. and Mrs. Adam Layne decided it was time to get on about their first day together. As they discussed over the breakfast table what to do next, Sara Ella said, "You know, Adam. I feel like a queen, here in this beautiful place. But, the truth is, I am anxious to get back to Oaklayne and begin the adventure of the rest of our lives."

"I had a feeling you'd be restless, living in all this luxury with all these people waiting on us. So, I'm not at all surprised that you are ready to go home."

Sara Ella was obviously preoccupied when she appeared to ignore Adam and said, "When I had that meeting with General Howard about the Freedman's Bureau, he gave me some ideas about starting schools that I am anxious to implement when we get back home to Oaklayne. That sounds wonderful, 'home to Oaklayne', doesn't it, dear?"

"You have no idea how good it sounds," Adam replied. "I am so grateful that you feel the same way, especially since we will have to rough it in that little slave cabin for a while. You will be missing this place in short order! I did ask Oscar to make some needed repairs, but we will definitely be roughing it!"

"Oh, fiddlesticks! You know I will be happy anywhere you are, Adam. You are all I need."

Tom pulled up to the front of the Layne townhouse and jumped down to help Sara Ella down.

"Tom, thank you so much. You certainly are a much appreciated pillar of this family. Adam told me how you helped him keep his sanity in the weeks and days before the wedding. There is no telling what kind of trouble he might have gotten himself into if you had not been there to keep him pointed in the right direction!" They both laughed, and Adam joined in cheerfully.

"My pleasure, Mrs. Layne," Tom said, bowing low in a gesture of respect. "It is good to have you home, ma'am."

"Mrs. Layne...I do like the sound of that," Adam said, as he escorted Sara Ella up the stairs.

Opening the door to let Sara Ella inside, Adam was immediately astonished, when Samuel came running past him squealing in laughter, with Lisa chasing closely after him.

"Oh, my!" Lisa said, as she came to an abrupt halt. She lost her balance and almost knocked Adam down. Then there was a loud crash in the parlor, and her eyes widened as she turned and ran in that direction.

"Sweetheart," Adam said to Sara Ella, "Perhaps, the honeymoon is over..."

"Oh, it is alright. The boy just needs all of the room at Oaklayne to run and use up some of that energy!" Sara Ella giggled.

JULY 4, 1865

The Independence Day celebration was a tremendously spectacular event. This was the first national Fourth of July celebration by African-Americans in the United States, with parades representing the National Colored Monument Association and other groups. It was held in memory of Abraham Lincoln on the grounds of the Treasury Department to raise funds to establish an educational institution for African Americans. John F. Cook, Chairman of the Association, led the event. Letters of tribute were read from a host of notables, including Governor John A. Andrew of Massachusetts, Horace Greeley and Frederick Douglass. Senator Henry Wilson of Massachusetts was orator of the day. Both he and the event drew national attention.

The streets were crowded to overflowing. Sara Ella and Lisa were dressed in finery with matching bonnets, while Samuel ran around in circles talking incessantly with Adam and Tom. They packed a picnic that they took to the park down by the Potomac River, where they were able to hear all of the speeches and listen to the patriotic music. It was also the perfect spot from which to see the fireworks display. After so many years of war and division, Adam thought it was good to see Americans enjoying such a festive occasion.

There was a flurry of activity at the Layne townhouse the morning of July 7, 1865, as they packed and loaded the last of their belongings. Later that day, they would all board the train headed for Richmond on their way to Oaklayne. Tom would stay behind for a few days to see to it that the townhouse was thoroughly cleaned and properly prepared to be vacant again for a while, until Adam came back to Washington City the next time.

Sara Ella pleaded with Adam, as he finished dressing in his military uniform, "Isn't there someone else who can go?"

"No, I am sorry. Stanton wants me to go and then report back to him. I am dreading it, but it has to be done. The only bright side of this day is that we will finally be at Oaklayne tonight!" he said, as he straightened his scabbard and walked toward the door.

"I will be praying for you, as you witness such a horrible sight. I know you have seen terrible things in the war, but it still will be a heavy burden to see something like that," she said.

"I will just focus on your beautiful face, and that will help shield my heart from the ugliness of it all," Adam responded as he held her face in his hands and then kissed her goodbye.

Sara Ella was deep in thought as she closed the front door and turned around. Lisa approached and asked, "Have you seen Samuel? He is not in his bed, and I cannot find him anywhere."

"No, I am sorry I have not. But frankly, my mind was on Adam, so I may not have noticed him," Sara Ella said absentmindedly.

"Thanks...that boy, what is he up to now?" Lisa said as she rolled her eyes in exasperation. "I need him to get all of his things in his trunk, so Tom can take it to the station with everything else."

Sara Ella was busy packing the last of her belongings, along with some things she had purchased for Emma Lou and gifts for the other ladies at the plantation, when Lisa suddenly came rushing into her room.

Obviously frantic, Lisa said, "I still cannot find Samuel, Sara Ella! Where could he be? He knows all about our trip, and that we will be leaving soon. Something terrible must have happened to him! Sara Ella, please help me find him! What will I do without him?"

Sara Ella rushed to Lisa's side and tried to calm her down. Speaking softly she said, "I am sure he is okay, Lisa. Let's just slow down and go through this step by step. Are you certain that he is not anywhere in the house?" Sara Ella asked.

"Yes, yes...I have checked every nook and cranny he could fit into...you know, in case he is hiding or something...he loves to play, you know," Lisa cried.

"Okay, then. Where outside have you checked?" Sara Ella asked as she started for the door.

"I have been all the way around this block, and then all the way around all of the blocks that surround this one. He knows that he is not to go any further than this block though, and he has always obeyed that rule in the past, at least, as far as I know."

"Have you been calling out his name?"

"Yes, of course." Lisa responded as they were walking and calling, "Samuel! Samuel!"

Secretary Stanton reached toward a stack of papers on his desk as he gestured to a chair, indicating that he wanted Adam to sit down. "Oppressive business this is, Adam. But it has to be done right away to appease a nation that wants this war put behind them." Without looking up, Stanton said, "I have a report here from the Military Commission. As you know, by June 30, after several hearings and deliberating for seven weeks, the surviving conspirators involved in Lincoln's assassination have been tried and convicted."

"Yes sir. I think everyone knows that by now, since it is in all of the papers," Adam responded.

"I am sorry to put such a morbid duty on you, but I need a firsthand account of the hangings of the four that are to be executed today. They are Lewis Powell, George Atzerodt, David Herold and

Mary Surratt. Four of the other five are sentenced to life terms, while one will get 6 years in prison. It will not be long now until the worst of this will finally be over."

With a heavy heart Adam said, as he rose to go to the Old Arsenal Building where the executions were to be held, "I just hope this will bring some healing to our country. But, it is still a difficult duty, regardless. I will report back to you promptly, sir," were his last words, as he closed the door behind him.

As Adam neared the Arsenal, he saw armed soldiers standing guard and a crowd gathering outside. Showing his credentials, he was admitted through the tall courtyard doors into the courtyard, where he saw the scaffolding. Ropes were hanging over near one corner of the scaffolding, and men were busy getting ready for the executions to take place. Not long after Adam settled into his seat, the convicted conspirators were escorted up the steps. Men gathered around each of them to prepare them individually for hanging.

Adam noticed that it was just a little after 1:30 in the afternoon when he heard George Atzerodt's last words, "May we meet in another world," as the gallows door was sprung, and all four were hanged simultaneously.

Sara Ella and Lisa ran door to door, asking all of the neighbors if they had seen Samuel, but he was nowhere to be found. "Did he seem distraught about anything last night?" Sara Ella asked, as they headed back to the townhouse again.

With tears in her eyes, Lisa said, "No, I do not think so. I have been going over and over in my mind the events of last night. I remember telling him how wonderful the plantation is, and how he would have so much room to play in the trees and go fishing in the river. He just looked at me and listened, until we had our bedtime prayer and he turned over to go to sleep."

"Look!" Sara Ella said. "There are some people on our stairs. Maybe they will know something." Sara Ella was worried now too, but she did not want to let Lisa know.

Lisa gasped, "I hope that nothing has happened to him. Who could it be?"

An older woman stood up and looked their way. Lisa recognized Mrs. Wilson, the lady with the flower garden. As they approached, she could see that the other person up on the steps was Samuel.

In enormous relief, Lisa ran headlong to her son and pulled him into her arms. "Samuel! I have been worried out of my mind! Where have you been, Son? How could you do this to me?"

Samuel looked dumbfounded at Lisa. He was completely unaware that she would be so distraught when he left. "I am sorry, Mother. I did not mean to cause any trouble. I just thought that you would go on to Oaklayne without me if I was not here."

Confused but relieved, Lisa looked at Mrs. Wilson and said, "Thank you so much for bringing him home to me. Where did you find him? Earlier, when we came to your door, you said you had not seen him."

Mrs. Wilson smiled and said, "Well, a little bit ago, I was in the back of my house having a bite to eat, when I heard the faintest noise. It sounded a little like the whimper of a puppy, so I went out on the stoop to see what it was. That is when I found little Samuel. He was curled up in a little ball up in the garden, up against the house. I did not want to frighten him, so I sat down beside him. I asked if he would like a little something to eat, and he agreed to come in the house with me.

"That is when he told me that you are moving to the country. He shared with me that he had never been to the country before, and was afraid he would not be able to take care of himself in that environment if he were left alone again. My, oh my! What remarkable stories he told me of the detestable places he found food and the things he needed to survive. It is a wonder that boy is still alive. I told him that anyone could see how much you love him and that you would always be there to take care of him. He is a good lad, just scared of the unknown."

"Thank you so much, Mrs. Wilson." Lisa hugged her warmly and said, "You have been such a good friend to both of us. I am glad that you found Samuel...and that he found you."

Adam was pleasantly surprised when Oscar greeted them at the train station with what seemed to Adam like an army of men. They brought with them the carriage, wagons and extra horses. Slapping Oscar on the back, Adam said, "What is all this?"

"Well," Oscar said, "I guess we just could not wait to see you!" Oscar was anxious to get Adam alone, so he could fill him in about the disconcerting events of late at Oaklayne. He thought it best to not involve the ladies until Adam was ready to tell them, so they would not be worried needlessly.

Chapter 35

"Ezra, I talked to Richard and August, and we have decided it would probably be best if August and I go into Tennille alone to scope things out quietly, before the rest of you arrive. We will leave the wagon here by this creek, so y'all can just relax for the rest of the day. We will come back later this evening with further plans," Ralph explained.

"That'd be a mighty fine plan, yes Sah," Ezra responded respectfully. "We be pleased to rest a spell."

Little four year old Dorothy who had often ridden on the buckboard seat with Ralph, ran up to him, threw her arms around his legs and cried, "Ah'll miss yo' Doc, pwease huwy backs."

Reaching down to pick her up, Ralph gave her a squeeze and a kiss on the cheek, then responded, "I sure will little one."

To her brother, who was almost ten and standing nearby, Ralph said, "Zeke, would you please keep an eye on Richard for me, the way I have shown you. Mostly watch to see if his temperature goes up. You can report to me about how he is doing when I get back, okay?"

"Yes, sah!" Zeke said with his chest all puffed out. "Ah'll surly be a checkin' on 'im. He be jes' fine whiles Ah's in charge of 'im. Don' yo' worry none."

Richard looked out the back of the wagon, grinned at Ralph and rolled his eyes. He knew he would not be getting any rest while under Zeke's diligent medical care.

After mounting Thunder, August tipped his hat to Rachel, forgetting how much trouble he would have getting his unruly hair back under control. Riding off with Ralph, he said under his breath, "I sure hope I can get a haircut while we are in town."

When they arrived in town they could not help but notice Union soldiers patrolling the streets. "Did you see that Ralph, at least two of them I saw were black? Does that seem odd to you?"

"Actually, I'm just a little surprised that they're still alive," was Ralph's response.

Joy was sweeping off the front porch of her husband's Doctor's Office when she saw the two men riding up the street. She would know Ralph and his horse, Maggie, anywhere! She dropped her broom and ran out into the street, as Ralph simultaneously saw her and dismounted, taking her into his arms in a long awaited embrace. He picked her up off of the ground and kissed her passionately, knowing he had already compromised the quiet entry into town they had planned. People began coming out of their shops yelling, "Hey, Y'all! Look, Doc's back!"

"August," Joy said, realizing he was being ignored as everyone greeted Ralph, "Thank you so much for bringing him home safely. Come on down here where I can give you a big hug."

August answered, "If it were not for Doc here, I doubt if I would ever have made it to Macon. He is a very wise man, Joy. He kept me out of trouble, time and time again. Thank you for allowing him to escort me."

The crowd cheered and asked, "Did the Andersonville Prison man you went to get make it, or had he died in prison?"

"We're happy to report that he did make it," Ralph said, "and, we would like to tell you all about it. But right now, could you please give us some time to get something to eat and clean up? Then we can meet any of you who are interested at the church down the street later today?"

There was a cheerful rumble in the crowd, when one man spoke up and said, "That's a great idea, Doc. I know that my Ida will want to come. I think she and the other ladies will want to bring some food, so we can celebrate together. What do y'all think?"

Everyone was clearly in agreement, and the women began discussing plans for what to bring.

Another man shouted out, "Doc, we want to tell you what's happenin' with the work on our bridge, too."

"That's right," said someone else, "the men will be back from there by then and can give y'all an up to date account. We'll let them know that you're here and when to be at the church." Others were talking joyfully all at once as they began to walk away.

Ralph was glad to see the town's people leaving, because he was anxious to get alone with Joy. She had never looked lovelier to him, probably because he had never been away from her for such a long time before.

"Joy, I've missed you so much. It is so good to be home."

Joy smiled and hugged him again saying, "I will fix you both some ham and biscuits to eat while I am heating the water for your baths."

"Thank you, ma'am, I would really enjoy the ham and biscuits. But, I think I will head over to the barber shop for a bath and a haircut," said August. He knew it would be good to leave Ralph and Joy alone for a while, and he was anxious to see if he could find his brother, Trevor.

Walking down the street toward the Barber Shop, he noticed the mercantile store, so he stopped in and got some new clothes.

August asked everyone he passed on the street if they knew where he could find Trevor, and everyone smiled and said Trevor would be at the bridge construction site. He figured Trevor's wounds must have healed alright, since he was working and people seemed friendly enough at the mention of his name.

"There!" August said, as he tapped the top of his hat down easily over his neatly trimmed locks. "That is the way a hat should fit!"

"I agree!" Trevor said, as he came in and closed the door behind him.

Spinning around on his heel, August was so excited to see his brother that he impulsively reached out and gave him a big bear hug. Then, embarrassed to have lost control in front of the barber, he backed away and shook Trevor's hand. He could not help but notice that his brother's hair was uncharacteristically long and his beard was unkempt. Trevor had always been meticulous about keeping his hair short and his beard trimmed neatly. August, on the other hand, liked a clean shaven face, with longer hair. That is how, through the years, they had found it easy enough to conceal the fact that they are not only brothers, but twins.

"Gentlemen," the barber said, "you may be able to cover the fact that you are twins with most folks. But, do not forget...I have seen both of those faces up real close! I do not know why you prefer for everyone to think you are merely acquaintances. That is your business. Just know that your secret is safe with me. Now, Trevor, get in this chair, so I can finally do something with that head of hair."

"But, I have been enjoying this mountain man look! What do you think, August? This man has been pestering me to come here again for weeks. Do I need a haircut?"

"Well, you are really starting to look like me, Trevor. You do not want that, now do you?" August said, slapping Trevor on the back and pointing the way to the barber chair.

Trevor tried to answer all of August's questions, as they walked toward the church for the meeting.

"August I really hate to leave the men right now. We are making good progress, but we are actually just started. They appear to be enjoying learning how to use the available materials, together with engineering principles, to make that bridge strong. This experience is giving them the hope they need to see that eventually they can rebuild this city. Sherman did not leave much to work with, but it can be done if they will persevere."

"But Trevor," August implored, "this work could take a lifetime to complete! At some point you have to let these people do it themselves."

"I completely agree with you, August. It is just that I am not sure they are ready to be left alone, yet."

"Are you sure the problem is not that you just don't want to leave, because you are enjoying the experience of helping them? Are you truly concerned for them or for yourself?" August sincerely questioned.

"That is a good question, and I am not sure I have an answer. You might be right. Please come out to the bridge with us tomorrow. Perhaps, together we can make that determination." Trevor willingly surrendered to August's concerns, and knew that he would be better able to be objective.

August remarked, "It is hard to believe that the same folks we came upon making such a mess trying to build a bridge awhile back...the ones that nearly killed both of us...you have actually got them building a workable bridge?"

"You will see for yourself when you check it out tomorrow," Trevor said with pride.

As they approached the church they could hear lots of people talking and laughing. Then, as they walked through the door they heard someone say, "Look! There they are now!" and everyone suddenly became quiet.

As Trevor and August slowly worked their way down the aisle, looking for a seat in the packed church, people started to clap and then broke into full and vigorous applause. Standing to their feet and turning toward the young men entering the church, some in the crowd even began hooting and hollering.

Confused and bewildered, August and Trevor both simultaneously turned to see who was behind them to bring about such a celebration, which produced a roar of laughter from the crowd.

Billy Joe, who had not had a drop of alcohol to drink since he had started working for Trevor on the bridge, ran up to the front of the church and shouted, "Quiet please, everyone! Since I was the first man to attack these two kind gentlemen, I think I should be the first to apologize for my rudeness. Trevor and August, it is because of you that I have my family back. And when this bridge is finished I plan to rebuild my construction company and offer jobs and services for all of the people in this town. I regret that I was so bitter because of the war. I saw no way that this town could ever recover from our loss. You men have given all of us hope that we can work together to bring this city back. I'm so sorry for misjudging you both. I am in your debt. Thank you for your willingness to help this helpless man and this hurting city."

Thunderous applause broke out, as Trevor and August stood there, looking at each other in bewilderment.

Matthew, Jimmy, Tom and Martin shared their feelings of regret for having nearly hung the young men who they now understood were only trying to help. Then some of the wives talked about how their husbands had changed after realizing the awful abuse they had done to August and Trevor. They felt badly about the boys having to change their plans in order to help heal a bitter town.

On their way back from the church August said to Trevor, "Man, I hardly recognized Billy Joe. It is hard to believe he is the same man who led that drunken crowd against us that day. I thought we were both goners, didn't you?" Just then, they saw two black Union soldiers approaching them.

"Yo' be new here?" one black man demanded of August.

"Yes, I just got here this afternoon," August answered.

"They's a curfew 'roun here, an' yo' betta' be inside by 10:00," the soldier said roughly, as if wanting to start a confrontation.

"Yes sir, no problem," August said a little unsure of the circumstances.

"Yo' jus' sees to it," the soldier grunted.

Trevor said nothing until they walked away and August asked, "What was that all about?"

"Our federal government decided that all southern cities need guards posted to keep the peace, so he was just doing his job."

"Well, that would have certainly helped when we first came here," was August's immediate response.

"That was my first thought, then I saw how the people here gradually changed, after what they did to us. I know that will not be the outcome everywhere in the South, but I am glad these folks have had a change of heart. You know, we could have been hanged."

"You are right about that."

"The bad side of these troops being here is that some of these black soldiers were once slaves on the surrounding plantations. Those owners are deeply embittered and many of them have completely lost their plantations because they cannot operate without slave labor. I do not see healing coming for a very long time, if ever. Those former slaves wearing military uniforms and ordering people around do not sit well with those folks."

Ralph asked Joy to accompany him out to the campsite to meet Richard and Ezra's family, just as August and Trevor arrived. He explained the situation to her and asked her advice about them coming into town.

"I would love to go with you Ralph. Just give me a minute to get a wrap."

Ralph turned to August and Trevor and continued, "I spoke to some of the men here in town about us bringing Ezra and his family into town. They are concerned, as I am, that it could be a challenge to delicate feelings on both sides of the fence. We have both black soldiers and bitter plantation owners, two drastically different points of view to consider. I think we need to explain things to Ezra and see what he thinks. What are your thoughts?"

"What about Richard?" August asked.

"Well, I need to get him in here to clean him up and let him get a good night's sleep in a real bed. I thought perhaps Joy and I should take our buckboard with us out there to bring him back here. Then Ezra and his family can use the other one until we are ready to go."

When August, Trevor, Doc and Joy arrived, Dorothy jumped from the wagon and ran to Ralph in her night dress. "Ah' tol' mommy that yo'd kiss me g'night, Doc," the little girl cheered.

Once Dorothy had been put to bed and Zeke had given a lengthy dissertation of his doctoring skills while taking care of Richard, Ralph turned and addressed everyone. "The city of Tennille is undergoing a lot of healing, but there is still a lot of uncertainty. Ezra, you and your family will need to understand the situation there, so you can make a decision about whether to stay here or go into town. Richard will be going with me in to town for medical treatment. But, you can stay here if you prefer and not take a chance on how you might be received by the town's people in Tennille and anyone else we might encounter along the way going further north."

"Doc, Ah' knows that we's in a heap o' trouble, one way or t'other, any wheres we's go," Ezra remarked. "Ah's willin' ta' do what yo's thinks is bes' fo' us."

"We want you to know that we welcome all of you, but cannot say how you will be received by others. This must be your decision. As August said, you are welcome to go along with us as we take Richard on up north. There are black Union soldiers guarding the cities, some of which are former slaves of the nearby plantation owners. Perhaps, they can help you make a life here? You could find yourself in the middle of the tension between the black soldiers and the plantation owners. People of your race have been treated badly everywhere, even murdered. I am sorry that circumstances are so difficult, Ezra. The guilty parties are not being held accountable for their unspeakable actions so far, so this could be a hindrance for a very long time, yet. I do not know, I expect you will want to talk it over with Rachel before making a decision. There are simply no easy answers to your dilemma."

Ezra and Rachel expressed their appreciation for the wise counsel. After discussing the situation, they decided to stay with the wagon and wait to meet back up with them when it was time to take Richard further north.

"I just wish I had better news," Ralph said. "Both August and Trevor brought their bed roles to stay out here with you tonight. Trevor offered Richard his room in the boarding house, so he will have a place to stay in town until he is ready to travel on."

"We'd be mos' grateful if'n yo' boys 'll keep us safe," Rachel said, as she got up and walked over to take Ralph's hand. "Do'thy will mos' sho'ly miss yo' Doc, and so will Zeke. He want's ta' learn ta' he'p sick folks like yo' do, Sah'."

Arriving at the bridge the next morning, August asked, "Trevor, how did you get all of these people to work together on the bridge like this?"

"Well, it was the strangest thing. After a few days of healing from the beating they gave me, people started begging me to show them the plans I had been working on for fixing that bridge. So, even before I could get out of bed, I started sending people out to measure things for me. Then I ask them to give me descriptions of everything else in the surrounding area. As you know, there was a railroad bridge that had also been destroyed. The usable materials from that bridge were much larger and stronger than what we needed for our bridge, so I assigned some of the men to confiscate those materials and move them."

"I remember talking with you about that railroad bridge when we first saw what they were doing," August said.

"I know, it is hard to believe they did not think of using those materials. Anyway, when I started showing them what I had planned, it seemed like everybody in town wanted to help. I also showed them that a lot of the unused materials from that railroad bridge could be used to rough in many of the buildings in town. They seemed very encouraged that as soon as the bridge is finished they could get started rebuilding or repairing their stores and homes," Trevor said.

"I am impressed, Trevor! This is absolutely amazing. That man is fitting that joint like he was building the White House! It is perfect," August remarked.

"Yes, it is quite remarkable the pride they are putting into this project. I am sure you have noticed the way they keep asking me to approve what they are doing?" Trevor said with obvious pride.

"How could I miss it. We are interrupted every few minutes. I have also noticed that they seem more concerned about pleasing you than to actually get instruction. They really seem to know what they are doing and even understand the big picture of how to finish it," August added.

"Well, now that you mention it, I realized last night, when I should have been sleeping, that they are ready to finish this project without me. I had to admit to myself that you were right to suggest that I was enjoying the attention," Trevor admitted, looking down at his shoes. "It is time for me to get my head around taking Richard back to Virginia, as planned."

"You certainly have accomplished what I thought was impossible, considering the people I met before I left you here to go find Richard Moreland. To be honest, I was thrilled to find you were still alive when we got here. But, now this...well this is...it is unbelievable that you accomplished so much," August said shaking his head in amazement.

"Hey, I cannot take the credit. Truth be known, it was these people, not me. They did this. Once they saw the vision of what they could do, there was no holding them back." Turning aside, Trevor called out, "That is great Martin. You finished another one perfectly!" Then turning back to August, he said, "You can see the joy on their faces, as they do the work. I am really quite proud of them all."

Back in town, Doc was busy again this morning cleaning the stump, where Richard had lost his leg.

Looking Richard in the eye, Doc said, "With some suggestions from August, our engineer friend, I made some adjustments to this crutch the hospital provided for you. I think it will be much easier for you to use now," Ralph said, examining the stump more closely. "We will get started practicing with it in a minute."

Richard shifted his weight, leaned back on his hands and said, "Doc, what is going to happen to me? It does not look like I will ever be able to ride a horse again. Before I joined the Army, I worked as a lumber jack. I surely cannot do that again."

Doc sighed, "I won't lie to you, Richard. Life will not be easy. Getting accustomed to living your life without your leg will be much like me getting used to living without my son," Ralph said, without looking up. "We both need to focus on what we still have and make the most of it. Life is not over, now that we have sustained such great losses. It will just be different than we expected. I see no reason why you cannot do whatever you determine to do, Richard. You still have much to offer, even without your leg."

"Thank you Doc for all of your help and encouragement," Richard responded. "You have helped more than just my leg. There were so many people with problems even more serious than mine in that hospital that it was hard for the doctors to spend much time with my leg. It is already doing so much better with all this attention. I really do appreciate it."

After working with Richard and his modified crutch in the office for a while, Doc took him outside and told him to continue practicing with it on more difficult terrain. Then he went to find Joy.

"Richard really needs prosthesis, Joy. But, I do not have all of the materials here to make one for him. Richmond would have much better parts for me to work with to fit it properly. Hopefully, his stump will be healed by the time he gets there, and I could make a perfect fit for him. He is a good man, Sweetheart, and I would like to see him through this," Ralph explained imploring her with his eyes.

"Oh, no you don't, Ralph Fowler! I am not staying here, wondering about you. If you must go and do this, then I am going with you!" she said firmly.

Ralph drew her close and said, "I know, dear, I do not want to be apart any more, either. But Joy, you do not understand how hard that trip will be. The roads are mostly gone, and it is a very rugged ride. Our buckboard is not covered, so you would have to be exposed to the elements constantly, and even sleep outside," Ralph cautioned her.

"Hello," Richard said, as he struggled to open the office door. "Just look at how smartly I can get around. This remodeled crutch is fantastic, Doc! Oh, hello, Mrs. Fowler. Your husband is a miracle worker. This thing was hardly usable at all before, but now I am hobbling right along," the young man said with a big smile.

After Richard left the office, Joy understood. "That young man reminds you of our Jamie, doesn't he? I see now why you have fallen in love with him and want to help him as much as you possibly can."

"You see it too? I'm sorry, Joy. I just could not help myself. You have seen his smile and his mannerisms. How could it be that he has come all the way here from Michigan to comfort us in our loss?"

Chapter 36

Excited about finally being back at Oaklayne, Adam woke before dawn and dressed quietly, so as to not wake Sara Ella. It was still dark as he stepped outside and noticed a man sitting on the porch of the temporary house with a rifle across his lap.

"Good morning," Adam said as he approached the area.

"Good morning, sir. I hope you and Mrs. Layne slept well," Brandon said.

"Yes, we slept very well indeed! The new bed in our wonderful little honeymoon cabin could not have been better," Adam responded. "What brings you out so early this morning, Brandon?"

"Oh, it's just my turn to keep watch," Brandon said.

"To keep watch?" Adam questioned. "What are you watching for?"

"Well sir, we have been having some trouble here," Brandon explained. "I am sure Colonel Baynes will fill you in on the details. I know he will be here in a few minutes, because I see Elsie coming. He always arrives in the kitchen about the time she has coffee made. He will probably come out here, since there are ladies sleeping inside."

"Good morning Elsie," Adam acknowledged as she approached.

"And a very good morning to you, Mr. Layne," Elsie responded. I hope that you and Mrs. Layne enjoyed your cabin."

"Next to the restored plantation house, I could not have been more proud than to present such a lovely home to my new bride. I was told of all the work you ladies did to make it cozy and beautiful. Thank you for all of the loveliness and creativity that you put into it for us."

Blushing as smoothing the wrinkles from her apron, Elsie said with smile, "Oh, we really enjoyed working on it for you both. I am so glad that you approve. I would invite you in to the kitchen, but we should probably keep the commotion under control as much as possible so we don't wake Mrs. Gary and Lisa. I will bring you and Brandon a cup of fresh coffee when it is finished brewing."

"Thanks Elsie, I'm sure ready for it after sitting here all night," Brandon answered as he stood up and stretched.

"Elsie did you happen to notice how Mrs. Gary was feeling last night, when you were helping the ladies get settled in?" Adam asked with concern. "That was a long trip for her."

"Yes sir, I did," Elsie responded with a frown. "She looked quite flush to me. I asked Lisa about her, and she told me that Mrs. Gary was still feverish. When I left for my cabin, Lisa was attempting to bring down her fever with cool, wet cloths on her forehead. I do hope that she will be much better today. I am so glad that Lisa was with her all night and knows what to do for her," she said, as she reached the door and went inside.

Moments later, the door squeaked as Oscar tiptoed out as quietly as possible to join the men on the porch. Closing the door gently behind him, he smiled and said, "Good morning gentlemen. I hope that you slept well, Adam, and that you did not sleep well, Brandon."

Adam and Brandon looked at each other and then replied in unison, "Yes, I did, thank you."

Soon, they were joined by Nathaniel and Tom and decided to move their discussion to under the pavilion roof, fearing that they might disturb Mrs. Gary and Lisa who were still asleep after a long and difficult night. Oscar and the others told Adam all about the threatening attacks on Oaklayne and the construction workers, as well as the measures they had taken to diminish the threat. They included the strange visit to Oaklayne by Colonel Herbert Hatfield, the fire at the saw mill and the recent attack on Oscar and Elsie along the road.

"Have you been able to pinpoint any motive behind all of this?" Adam asked.

Oscar replied, "Well, at first we thought it was retribution from a man I refused to hire because he objected to working for Nathaniel, due to his being black. We do think he is involved somehow, but do not see him as capable of any kind of leadership role in this. He simply is not a man that others would follow. This kind of trouble would require that several men be under someone's direction."

"Interesting...," Adam said, as Emma Lou came from the ladies cabin, followed by Beverly Jean and Jessica.

"Mo'nin', Massa Adam," Emma Lou said, with a big smile on her face and her arms outstretched. Adam rose to his feet, returned her smile and enjoyed her warm embrace. "Ah thanks yo' fo' fetchin' mah Benjy home fo' a spell. It sho' be mighty fine to see hows he's comin' to be a great man."

"I agree, Emma Lou. Benjamin is finding his way in this world in a most respectable manner. It does feel good to have those two boys of ours home," said Adam, as he saw Sara Ella coming toward him from their cabin.

"Why, Adam Layne! We have only been married a few days, and you are already hugging other beautiful women! What is the meaning of this?" Sara Ella said in the sternest voice she could muster without breaking out into laughter.

Adam playfully reached out and grabbed her as he responded, "My dear bride, I have been in love with this lady many long years before I even met you! So, I guess you will just have to get used to it."

"Well, I never! And with all of these people watching! And my mother is even here!" She started to laugh, then her face turned concerned as she asked Adam, "Have you heard how mother's doing this morning?"

"No, dear. I have not. All I know is that Elsie said she seemed to still have a fever last night. But, Lisa is tending to her."

"I think I will go right now and check on her," Sara Ella said, as she headed inside. I will relieve Lisa, so she can get some rest.

The atmosphere was spirited over breakfast, as all of the men were excited about sharing with Adam what had been accomplished thus far at Oaklayne. Caught up in their enthusiasm, Adam was anxious to tour the plantation and see the progress for himself.

"Lisa, what do you think is wrong with Mother? Wesley and Cora will be here any day now with the wagon to take her back to Macon. But, she cannot go like this. That is a long and stressful trip. I am surprised that she came all of this way at her age to attend the wedding. I know how bad the roads were between there and here, when Adam and I came north from Andersonville together, not so very long ago. It is amazing she has survived."

"Mrs. Gary is a very brave and strong lady. And you are correct, the trip up here was rough on her. But, she told me that wild horses could not have kept her from being with you on your wedding day, " Lisa said. "I am suspicions that she has an infection of some kind. If so, she will need a lot of care and rest, which will be difficult in this busy environment. It is perfectly understandable that people need to constantly come in and out through the relaxing room. But, since your mother is too weak to use stairs and she sternly refused to use your cabin, we have nowhere else here at Oaklayne more suitable for her recovery."

"Do we need to take her to the hospital in Richmond?"

"No, I would not recommend doing that. There are so many soldiers being cared for there that she would not get the attention that she needs. I thought this through last night, and I think that I might have a solution that would be best for her."

"We will do whatever you think is best, Lisa. I trust you completely with anything relating to medical needs. Your experience is far beyond most doctors, considering the work you did with Goddard during the war. Whatever you think is best for my mother is what I want to do," was Sara Ella's response.

"Well, Sara Ella, do you remember Warren Callahan who brought me here to Oaklayne after the war?" Lisa asked.

"Yes, the tall silver haired gentleman who brought you here in his carriage. Yes, I remember him. Adam knows him, and said he is a very kind and generous man."

"Right, that is a good description of him. Mr. Callahan told me when I left that I was welcome to come back to his home anytime, for any reason. He has plenty of unused rooms in his plantation home. I had already decided that Samuel and I should go there, since there really is not room enough for us here. If he is agreeable, and I expect he will be, I am thinking it would be best for Mrs. Gary to stay there with me for a while, so I can tend to her in his quiet home. What do you think?" Lisa asked.

"Well, it is hard for me to let her out of my sight right now. Why don't we go ahead and move her into our honeymoon cabin, even if it is against her wishes? It would be for her own good. Adam and I would not mind sleeping here in the temporary house."

"I thought of that, but something tells me she would not rest very well, knowing she displaced you newlyweds into a place that is not even private. I am afraid she would try to rush her healing. Besides, it would not be easy for her to manage the few narrow stairs out in front of your cabin. She will have to have someone along-side her on any stairs for some time to come."

Sara Ella sat down and folded her hands in her lap as she admitted, "I see what you are saying, Lisa. You are right. Most likely she will not hear of moving into our cabin, and if she did she would stew about it and not rest. You are right, that is not an answer. You know I would do anything for my mother, and if having her go with you to Mr. Callahan's is the best thing, then that is what we need to do. I will ask her again about moving to our cabin, even though I do not expect she will agree. Then I will see how she feels about going with you. I think I will go find Adam and see what he says first, though."

Lisa reached over, patted Sara Ella on the shoulder and said, "If everyone is in agreement, I would suggest that you stay with your mother for a bit, while Tom takes me and Samuel to Warren Callahan's right away. When I am there, I can discuss the situation with him and hopefully get his approval to stay there with Samuel and your mother for a while. I would like to move Mrs. Gary later today when I get back, if possible. She certainly cannot get much rest here with all this work going on, but there she can rest easy and be tended to properly."

Adam was impressed with the obvious diligence going into the completion of the work on the plantation house. He was amazed at the tight fittings of the tongue-and-groove hewn 12x12 base plate and the joists, as well as the flooring and stud walls, which already had some lathing on them. Steven showed Adam some of the intricate carving he was working on for the fireplace trim and capitals for the inside columns.

As Oscar and Adam were starting toward the saw mill, they heard Sara Ella call out. After hearing about Lisa's suggestion, Adam agreed with the plans for Mrs. Gary's recovery at Warren Callahan's. He suggested that Tom and Lisa stop in Richmond and pick up whatever may be needed in the way of supplies to take with them.

Oscar interrupted to advise Adam that an escort of men for protection would be needed, and he would take care of arranging that escort for Lisa's trip alone and again with Mrs. Gary later in the day. Adam went back to the Temporary House with Sara Ella to help look after Mrs. Gary until Lisa's return, and then to be available to assist in loading her into the carriage for the ride to Mr. Callahan's house.

"Adam I would like to ride along with Lisa when she gets back, so I can introduce mother to Mr. Callahan. I want her to be as comfortable as possible with this arrangement," Sara Ella explained. "From what Lisa said, it is not far. So, I should be back in time to help get supper on the table."

"I understand completely. Just be careful on the road. From what Oscar has told me, it can be dangerous out there. So, be sure that the men are escorting you at all times. I will explain more about that tonight when you get back."

Later that day, Adam watched Tom turn the carriage around and pull away toward Warren Callahan's with Lisa, Samuel, Sara Ella and Mrs. Gary inside and the escort of protection following. He was pleased to know that this seemed to be a good answer to several problems.

Just then he noticed Randy and Benjamin talking excitedly under the pavilion. "Hey, what is so interesting?" he called out to them as he approached.

"Father! We're excited, because we just discovered that in this short time apart at two different schools, we each have the same plans for a career! Can you believe it? We have the same interests and even the same motivation!" Randy said, beaming with excitement.

Adam took a seat at one of the tables and said, "Well, it does not surprise me at all that you have the same interests, there is nothing new about that. But, that you both have the same career plans already in such a short time, while spending time apart is curious, I have to agree."

"Father, you remember Mr. Campbell, the teacher I introduced you to when you picked me up at the train? Well, he told me that blindness does not have to be a handicap. It can actually be an opportunity. He told me about a time he was teaching in Wisconsin, and it became publicly known that he had strong anti-slavery views. He was issued an ultimatum that if he did not renounce his view within 24 hours, they would hang him. When he refused, it was his blindness that caused public sympathy and kept him from being hanged."

Adam warned, "Yes, but he might also have been hanged. Do not get your hopes built up so high that you will be disappointed or wind up fighting for some cause that gets you hurt or killed, Son." Adam was not sure where Randy was going with this line of thinking, but he did not like imagining his son putting himself in a dangerous predicament, at all.

"Just hear me out, Father. Mr. Campbell told me about a man in England whose name is Henry Fawcett. This man was blinded when he was 25 years old, but continued his studies at Cambridge. Father, he eventually became a professor at Cambridge, and this year was elected to hold a seat as Member of Parliament for Brighton. He also campaigns openly for women's suffrage."

"Okay, but what does that have to do with you? Do you want to move to England and go to Cambridge?" Adam was completely confused.

"No, Father. But, I fought for the Union in the war, where I was blinded in battle. This is my opportunity to continue to fight for equal rights for all people. There is so much that still has to be worked out, now that the war is over." Randy said with authority.

"What do you mean fight?" Adam said, squirming and bracing for a conflict with his son.

"Father I want to be a lawyer for civil rights, and so does Benjamin."

Adam was so astonished that he could not find words to say. That is when Benjamin spoke up and said, "Is it not exciting, Mr. Adam? Randy and I can both be studying and preparing to support one another in the same work after we finish our schooling."

Adam, not wanting to dash their enthusiasm with a dose of reality said, "I tell you what, let's continue this conversation later. I need to join Oscar now to finish my tour of the work being done on the plantation."

When Adam stood, he noticed a buggy coming down the lane toward them, a dust cloud following. "Now, who could that be?" he said absentmindedly. Walking toward it, Adam noticed that the rotund man struggling to remove himself from the buggy met the description Oscar had given him of Colonel Hatfield.

"May I help you?" Adam asked politely.

In a gruff, unfriendly manner, the man answered, "Yes, you can help me, Adam Layne. You have not changed much since the last time I saw you. You were about 15 years old then, and rather scrawny, I might say. Nevertheless, it has been so long ago that I might not have recognized you, if you did not remind me of Mason Layne."

"I am at a disadvantage sir, who might you be?"

Scowling with his eyebrows raised, the paunchy man announced himself, "I am Colonel Herbert Wade Hatfield of Royal Hatfield Plantation." His chest was swelled out almost as far as his belly, indicating that he thought everyone should recognize a person as important as himself.

"Well, then...Colonel Herbert Wade Hatfield, I ask again, may I help you?" Adam asked, not offering the man a place to sit down, though he had noticed the large man looking over his shoulder at the table and chairs in the shade of the pavilion. Normally, Adam would have been more hospitable, but Oscar had warned him about this man whose demeanor was so pompous.

Wiping his sweaty face with a handkerchief, Colonel Hatfield cleared his voice and said, "You will be pleased to know that I have a lucrative proposal for you that I am sure you will find extremely generous. In fact, my offer is probably too high, but my family has always had the resources to buy anything they were interested in."

"Is that so? Then your family was not affected by the war like nearly everyone else?"

"Well, let's just say that smart investments and knowing which side to support at any given time has paid off," he said smugly, assuming that Adam conducted business according to the same self-indulgent principles to which he held. "I have been doing a little research and found that the value of property all over the south has diminished greatly. I have also learned that you are working in Washington City and living comfortably there in your father's townhouse. It has also been brought to my attention that there have been a lot of reports of violence and crime this area lately, making it a dangerous place to live. Personally, I do not understand why those rascals would want to cause so much trouble around here. But, I realize you have been gone, and may not be aware of all of the ruffians on the roads 'round here."

"Colonel Hatfield...I ask again, may I help you?"

"Well, yes. I was just giving you a little history lesson. You see, now that you are comfortable living in Washington City, and knowing the problems out here where property values are so low, I thought you might be relieved to know that you do not have to spend so much of your military wages trying to put this place back together."

Adam grabbed Colonel Hatfield firmly by his arm and escorted him immediately toward his waiting buggy, saying, "Colonel, you need not worry yourself further about my affairs and my priorities. While I appreciate your concern, I have no desire whatsoever to sell Oaklayne Plantation to you or anyone else, ever! Now, I have a great deal to get accomplished today in the rebuilding of Oaklayne Plantation, so you must be on your way. DO NOT come back here. Do I make myself clear, sir?"

"No...you don't understand...." grumbled Colonel Hatfield. "I have come to help you."

"Oh, I do not see that you are helping me at all," Adam said unwaveringly.

Obviously shaken and perspiring profusely, Colonel Hatfield said, "You are obviously not the business man your father was, Adam Layne. I have explained to you how this property is no longer in a desirable area. You can check in Richmond if you do not believe me. They will tell you about others moving away from here because of the rabble rousers around here...and you know how the property values had already dropped substantially. Then, of course, it is obviously not convenient for you to live here, since your employment is in Washington City. It is clear to anyone that this property is not suitable for you at all."

"My goodness, Colonel Hatfield. How many times do you need to reprimand me for being such a poor money manager?"

"Well, Adam, I am certainly glad that you finally understand that now. You see, I am willing to offer you a substantial sum of money for this property, in spite of the fact that it has declined in value dramatically, due to unfortunate and unavoidable circumstances..."

Adam interrupted the Colonel with, "Regardless of the wisdom in doing so, this is my decision to make, sir. And I have decided to rebuild my home. Therefore, I will not be considering any offers today or any other day. Now, be on your way. Oaklayne Plantation is NOT for sale."

"But, you have not even heard my offer. I am sure that..."

"Good day, Colonel Herbert Wade Hatfield. There is no amount of money you could offer me that would interest me in the slightest. You are wasting both our time discussing this further."

"But, you don't understand..." he said, as Adam forcefully helped him up into his buggy.

"Oh, but I think I understand perfectly, sir. You want to buy Oaklayne, but it is NOT for sale. Do I make myself clear?"

"You will regret this decision, Adam Layne. When you see how dangerous it is to live in this area, you will come running to my door begging me to buy you out. But, know this young man, my offer will not be so good then as it is today!" Then the red faced Colonel stuck his nose in the air, whacked his horse with the buggy whip and took off back down the road from whence he had come.

As Adam turned to go back to the house, he saw Oscar coming toward him. "I see you met his highness, the Colonel. He is quite the specimen of haughtiness, is he not? When we saw him coming down the road to talk to you, a couple of the men stood with me behind the house, in case you had any trouble with him."

Adam rolled his eyes and said, "That is undoubtedly the most arrogant man I have ever encountered in my lifetime! I wonder why he is so interested in Oaklayne."

Chapter 37

"Trevor, I sure do not like the way those men looked Ezra over, sitting on his mule like that," August said in almost a whisper, leaning close so he could be heard only by his brother. He did not want to alarm Rachel and the children, riding in the back of the wagon with Richard. It had been raining all morning, and the wagon offered some shelter for the women and children.

"I know what you mean," Trevor agreed. "I sure wish Ralph could have come with us. That Southern drawl could sure come in handy about now. I wish he was driving this wagon, too. I would much rather be riding Lightnin'."

August chuckled as he looked back at the horse tethered to the back of the wagon. "Yep, he is obviously feeling the same way. He is hanging his head like a scolded puppy."

"It sure felt safer when we were taking those back roads like Doc suggested. But, the wagon was just too hard to handle, especially after it got so muddy. I am not surprised that Richard could not manage the wagon in that mud. It was all I could do to keep it on the road when I took over for him. He is getting stronger, but that was brutal."

"I told Ezra to keep his hat low on his face, but you cannot mistake those big black feet of his," August said, as he pulled his hat down lower over his face for more protection from the rain. "I am glad Rachel and children agreed to ride inside out of the rain. Those men might have stopped us for sure, if they had seen them with us, too."

"You are right. Too bad there is no room for Ezra in the wagon with them. This rain makes for some difficult travel, but it also provides us some cover," said Trevor.

August smiled and said, "Though it is harder for us without him, I am glad Doc listened to reason and decided to stay behind with Joy to help the town's people, instead of coming with us. Richard can look for someone in Michigan to build him prosthesis, after he gets there. His remodeled crutch seems to be serving him well."

Later that afternoon the rain was falling in torrents. Even on the main road, conditions were bogging down the wagon. As they continued to press the horses to keep up the pace, they hoped to find a place to pull off and rest where no one would notice them. They knew that the Savannah River was not far ahead and hoped to catch the ferry there early the next morning. If they were the first ones there, maybe they could get across before others arrived. At least, that was the plan.

August rode on ahead to look for a good place on higher ground to pull off the road for the night. Ezra followed along behind the wagon, looking somewhat like a giant gorilla riding on a very large mule. But, he was trying to be as inconspicuous as possible, under the circumstances.

Just then the right front wagon wheel fell heavily into a mud hole, and the horses stopped abruptly. Trevor tried to coax them on, but to no avail.

Ezra handed the hackamore reins of Goliath to Trevor and jumped down into the mud saying, "Let's me see if'n Ah can he'p dem ho'ses a bit."

August watched in disbelief while Ezra spread his tree-trunk size legs apart, squatted slightly and gripped the wagon wheel with both hands. With a great groan, his wet, bulging muscles glistening in the rain, Ezra lifted the wheel, allowing the horses to pull the wagon free. Trevor quickly turned the wagon team so the back wheel would clear the hole. Ezra wiped his muddy hands on his pants and very matter-of-factually walked back to Goliath. Both August and Trevor stared at one another in awe.

When they finally found a good location for a campsite, the children were elated to be out of the wagon, even in the rain.

"That is very tight quarters for four people to spend such a hot muggy day together," Richard said to Ezra. He was the last one to emerge from the safety of the wagon's womb that had been their sanctuary for the day. Ezra helped him down and handed him his crutch as he reached the ground.

Trevor and August laughed, as they kidded Richard about having everyone sleeping in the wagon with him for the night. While Rachel began working to start fixing something for them to eat, Ezra unhitched the team and tethered them with the other horses. The other two men attached a canvas tarp to the side of the wagon for a little shelter from the unrelenting rain.

Having completed his work, Ezra excused himself and hurried off back toward the main road and into the woods to relieve himself. On his way back to camp, two men suddenly grabbed him from behind, and two others appeared in front of him with a menacing countenance. They were well dressed like gentlemen, but clearly not gentlemen at all.

"Now, isn't it quite obliging of this darkie here to save us all the trouble of taking him from those two cowboys," whispered one of them who had a gun pointed at Ezra's head, while the others pulled him quickly toward the main road. "Keep your mouth shut, Darkie, or we'll shoot you right here."

Ezra knew he could get away from these men without too much difficulty, but he could not risk them learning about his wife and children back at the camp. So, he went along quietly.

The youngest looking of the men spoke up now and said, "We have a party planned for you, boy. This road to the ferry has been very productive for us in finding black runaways, like yourself."

When they reached the road Ezra could see that there were two additional men with guns on horseback. With them were two black men with their hands tied behind their backs and ropes around their necks. "How did you get him so quickly? He's that big buck I told y'all about. Somebody's hurting bad, not having him workin' in their fields."

"Keep your voices down and let's get out of here before somebody back there misses him. We can have this party down the road a little way and then get out before they find us," another man said, as someone put a rope around Ezra's neck.

Ezra was noticeably missing when Rachel announced that supper was finally ready, back at the campsite. She was grateful that they had packed some dry kindling in the wagon, enabling them to have a fire to warm their food.

"Where is Ezra?" Rachel asked, as she scooped beans into a bowl.

"I don't know, I have not seen him for a long time. Trevor and I have been busy trying to clean the caked mud from the wagon axles, so I did not notice whether or not he came back," August answered. "Richard have you seen Ezra?"

Richard looked away from playing with little Dorothy, laughed and said, "I guess you can see that I have had my hands full! How would I know where Ezra is? Zeke's been inspecting my leg like a surgeon, while this little rascal keeps tickling me!"

Rachel quickly jumped to her feet with a worried look on her face and said, "He should be back by now."

"I think I will head back toward the road in the direction he went earlier," August said as nonchalantly as possible in an attempt to not upset Rachel any further. Trevor strapping on his pistol and followed right behind him.

Since the rain had stopped, they did not have to go far until they found lots of footprints in the soft mud. Ezra's large barefoot prints mixed in among the others were easy to make out. August looked at Trevor with an expression of concern, and they both took off together in a sprint toward the road. There they found the hoof prints of at least six horses mingled with human footprints.

"We had better get our horses and rifles."

"Yeah, and be sure Richard is armed in case someone tries to attack the camp while we are gone."

The rain returned, but not so heavy that they could not still make out fresh tracks in the road. On horseback with rifles ready, August and Trevor did not speak so they could hear but not be heard. Occasionally, one of them would dismount to examine the muddy tracks more closely, but they were sure they were following whoever was holding Ezra captive.

Ezra fell twice in the slippery mud, as he was being pulled along with the other two black men, each with a rope around his neck.

"Hey Darkie, it don't matter to me if you hang yourself here on the road or wait for us to hang you in a tree," said the man who was dragging him. His voice sounded so cold. Ezra wondered what had caused him to be so angry and cruel.

"Awe, come on now. We don't want to spoil the party we have planned for tonight's catch, do we?" said one of the other men. "It seems like we should be about there. It sure is hard to see that crooked tree in this darkness."

Just then, a bright flash of lightning lit up the sky and the road in front of them.

"There! Up there," one man called out. "I saw it. It's not far ahead."

The next time he got down from his horse, August said, "Whoever they are, they have sure made a mess of this road. At least, they are easy to follow. Still wish we had some moonlight, though."

"But, if we had moonlight they might see us following them. Now, quit talking," Trevor reprimanded.

Ezra racked his brain, but could think of no way out of his predicament. If he broke free of these men and ran away, they would go back to the camp looking for him and find his wife and children. No matter what they did to him, he simply could not allow that to happen. Though it sickened him, Ezra knew full well that white men are legally allowed to sexually abuse black women, without it being considered rape at all. His beautiful Rachel and little Dorothy were counting on him to keep them safe, and he would do just that, at all cost.

Too much to drink making him slur his words, one of the men on horseback said, "Hey, big man. Did you really think you'd be able to get away with running? Well, you're gonna be another example of what happens to darkies like you who try to get free. They'll find you hangin' here in the morning and learn a lesson from it!"

The man who was trying to pull one of the other black men up into the big tree by the rope around his neck, dropped his whiskey bottle. It made quite a racket when it crashed on a big rock at the base of the tree.

"Did you hear that?" Trevor asked in a whisper.

"Yeah. Let's tie these animals here," said August.

The mob of men up ahead was rowdy and distracted enough that August and Trevor did not actually have to work very hard at being quiet, but they did anyway. As they made their way closer, they could see that three black men were sitting astride horses. Two of them already had ropes around their necks that were tied to the tree. Someone was busy working with Ezra's rope, while another man held the horse steady. Was Ezra hurt or something? Why was he not breaking free of these men?

"Hurry up! That stallion of mine is straining under the weight of that big man. Can you not see, his feet nearly dragging the ground! I do not want to mess up a perfectly good horse trying to dispose of that filth. Get on with it!"

August and Trevor walked boldly into the middle of their lynching party, being careful not to spook the horses that were still keeping Ezra and the other two black men alive for the moment. They each had a rifle in one hand and a pistol in the other.

"Now, gentlemen," Trevor said with an intentional chill in his tone of voice, "...if I were you, I'd hold the reins of those horses real tight. My companion and I would sure not want to needlessly spill any blood here tonight."

When he set eyes on August and Trevor, Ezra easily ripped the bonds loose from around his wrists and quickly removed the noose from around his neck. Then, without saying a word, he immediately dismounted and began setting the other two black men free.

"I would drop those pistols you are getting ready to reach for, before you get hurt," August warned the two men who were still on horseback, as he walked up behind them. "My brother is a really good shot, but I was always quicker than him. Between the two of us, you do not stand a chance of getting out of here alive if you persist. I really do not feel like digging a bunch of graves in all this mud. So it would be better for everyone if you would just stand down."

"Now, Ezra, I'm sure that each of your two new friends would appreciate having one of these horses to take them as far away from here as possible tonight, while it is still nice and dark. You are really good with animals, so make sure you pick out the two best and potentially fastest horses for them. We brought Goliath with us for you to ride, so do not be concerned about a horse for yourself. Then, please tie up all the rest of the horses back there in the woods, so they will not alert anyone by running home right away. And, tell me, what do you think we should do with these men who were about to murder you and these other men? Any ideas?"

Ezra did not hesitate for a moment before he said, "Well, Massa August, how 'bout we hangs em?" Then he added, "Ah'd like 'em to know what it feel like ta' have a rope 'round they neck."

"That sounds fair to me," said August. "Trevor, what do you think?"

"Now wait a minute!" interrupted one of the men still on horseback. Earlier he had been the meanest of the bullies, but now he was clearly frightened and did not know how to handle this turn of events. "You men are obviously from the North and do not understand our culture here in the South. These men are breaking the law. We have been hired to patrol these roads and be sure that they do not get away. You will be breaking the law if you interfere with our duty to uphold the law."

August did not take his eyes off the man when he said, "Trevor, does something about that sound familiar to you? I was thinking we just fought in a war about that very thing. And we won that war, did we not? Do you remember something about that? No, I do not buy your explanation. This is a clear case of attempted murder, and you WILL get down from those horses immediately, gentlemen."

"We only have nooses enough to hang three men," said Trevor. "So, we will need more rope from the horses before you take them away, Ezra. And, we should probably tie their hands behind their backs, too. That is what they did to you, and we want them to have the same experience."

August asked the other two black men to remove all of the weapons from each of the six members of the lynch mob and dispose of them in the woods in every direction.

The rain had subsided when Trevor, August and Ezra arrived back at camp in the early morning. Rachel and Richard had not slept all night, because they were so concerned for Ezra. The children had finally fallen asleep, but rushed to hug their daddy when they heard his voice.

"What happened?" Richard was the first to ask. Then the others chimed in, all asking questions at once.

"Ezra, why don't you tell them," Trevor said stoically.

"Well, them men was fixin' to hang me and two other men. But, we hanged them instead," he said.

"What? Why was they hangin' yo'?" Rachel squealed, and then in shock said, "What do yo' means, yo' hangs them?"

August could not stand it anymore and let out a whoop. "You should have heard them crying, then pleading! Then they got real angry. They were a mess!"

Richard was dumbfounded. He had no idea these boys could be so hardhearted! August seemed almost jubilant about having hanged some men. Ezra had always seemed so gentle. Richard did not know what to think.

Zeke's eyes were wide, as he looked at his father in astonishment, so Ezra knew he had to tell everyone the rest of the story. "Well, you see son, they be mo' than one ways to hangs a man."

Once again, August could not contain himself. "They kind of looked like Christmas tree ornaments, hanging under those big live oak trees like that!"

"Ezra! Hows could yo' do such a thing?" Rachel cried.

"That is enough, guys" Trevor said, trying to hold his composure. "You see, what actually happened is that we tied their hands behind their backs. But, instead of putting a noose around their necks, we put it around their chest, under their arms. Then we hung them from the big oak tree branches with their feet just barely touching the ground. They are a little uncomfortable, I am sure, but they will live."

"Yeah, they are close enough to the road that eventually someone will hear their bellerin' and let them go. So, that is why we need to pack up and get out of here right away."

Richard laughed, "You boys sure had me going for a while! But, I agree that we need to get moving."

It did not take them long to load up and hurry down to the Savannah River. But, even before the sun was completely up, they could tell that the river was swollen and raging from the heavy rain. The Ferry Master had arrived for the day and was busy making arrangements for taking on passengers.

Chapter 38

Chadna Gary was exhausted by the ride to Mr Callahan's home, but now she was resting comfortably. The room to which she was immediately taken was very lovely, and the comfortable bed allowed her to rest easy. Lisa told her that she had been taken to the same room when she was suffering from exhaustion, after learning at Chimborazo Hospital that her husband Goddard had been killed.

Sara Ella was glad that her mother seemed pleased with the arrangements. "Mother you will be so much more comfortable here than at Oaklayne, with all the work that is going on there. This is a beautiful place and these people are more than accommodating. Most of all, there is no one I would trust to care for you more than Lisa."

Mrs. Gary smiled demurely and patted her daughter on the hand saying, "I know you want what is best for me, dear. I am sorry for causing such an inconvenience for so many people. I will do exactly what Lisa tells me, hoping that I will soon be well enough to return to my own home with Wesley and Cora.

"But, I am not sorry that I came, mind you. I would not have missed your wedding for anything! If someone tried to explain to me what happened, all of the mix-ups and drama involved, I would never have been able to believe it. What joy it brought me to be there to comfort you and share in the wonderful memories you created on that day."

"Oh yes, Mother! It would have been so hard if you had not been there with me. But, I am concerned that this trip has been so difficult for you. What a sacrifice you made for me. I will never forget it. I love you so very much."

Just then, Lisa opened the door quietly and moved gracefully across the room carrying a bowl of warm broth for Mrs. Gary. "Mr. Callahan is walking the floor downstairs, quite put out that you insist on providing monetary assistance for your mother's food and accommodations, as well as mine and Samuel's," she said to Sara Ella. Then she giggled and said, "He does not seem to grasp that he is penniless. The reality is that Moses and Martha grow vegetables here on the plantation and Moses brings down wild game with his rifle, but they do not have access to anything else for food. They depends on their friends and neighbors to provide grain, eggs and milk in trade for vegetables and work that Moses and Martha do for others in the area.

"So you see, you are actually a godsend for the Callahan Plantation at this time. Thank you for providing for me and Samuel, as well. I do not have any money until I can find a nursing job to provide for myself and my son."

"Nonsense, you are working for me, nursing my mother back to health. I intend to pay you a fair wage for your services, as well as providing for your room and board while you are staying here," said Sara Ella. "Besides, you are a Layne by marriage, making you an heir to the Layne family heritage. I accept that you have your reasons for wanting to make your own way with as little help as possible. But, please be aware that it brings Adam and me both a lot of pleasure to be able to help you whenever we can."

Sara Ella continued, "Mr. Callahan seems like a fine man. Do you have any idea how he is going to be able to continue to support Moses and his family? They do so much to keep this place running and take care of their benefactor, as well."

"Moses and Martha are so grateful that he provides them a safe place to live that they will not take any pay for what they do here. I know they have expenses for those little girls who are growing like weeds. But, with the help of friends and neighbors, they all seem to scrape by somehow," Lisa said, shaking her head. "Mr. Callahan is always so full of peace and joy, that you would never know how destitute he is, just by being around him. I have never known anyone like him, or like Moses and Martha, for that matter."

"So, he has never shared with you his plans for the future?" Mrs. Gary asked.

"Well, mostly he just says he knows the Lord will provide for him and those who depend on him. When I was here before, I heard him mention to some men at his church that he would like to find some sharecroppers or tenant farmers to work this land. That could bring in a pretty good income, because he has quite a lot of land."

"What does that mean, sharecroppers and tenant farmers?" Sara Ella asked. "I have so much to learn about plantation life."

Lisa smiled and said, "I did not know what it was either, until I asked him about it later. He explained that since the war, landowners have to come up with new ways to run their plantations. Sharecroppers are farmers he would contract with to grow crops on a portion of his land. Then, when the crops are sold at the end of the year, he would get a portion of the proceeds, and so would they. Thus, the name 'sharecropper'."

"How clever! That way he does not have to invest any cash to make a profit from his land. What a great idea..." Sara Ella mused, pleased that she understood. Then she turned and asked, "And what about tenant farmers? How does that work?"

"Well, it is a little different from sharecropping. A tenant farmer rents a portion of land for a fixed amount of money. Then he can grow whatever he wants on that land and keep all the profits for himself, rather than sharing it with the landowner. Mr. Callahan says that tenant farmers are considered to be of a higher social status in the community than sharecroppers, and thus, are more desirable." Lisa was pleased that she was able to answer their questions with confidence.

Looking over at Mrs. Gary, Lisa smiled, realizing that the older woman had fallen asleep with the empty soup bowl beside her on the bed. Sara Ella followed Lisa's gaze, and was pleased to see her mother resting so well. Both ladies quietly gathered up their skirts and tiptoed from the room, Lisa carrying the soup bowl and spoon.

At the bottom of the stairs, Lisa nearly dropped the soup bowl, as Samuel ran right into her, almost knocking her down.

"Whoa, young man! How many times do you need to be told to not run in the house?" As she was scolding him, she was surprised to see him respond with a grin, looking behind her instead of respectfully giving her his attention. Twirling around, she found herself face to face with Warren Callahan, moving his right index finger away from his lips in what had obviously been a signal for Samuel to keep quiet.

"What is the meaning of this? Are you promoting bad behavior in my son?"

Warren playfully hung his head and responded rather shyly, "Oh, I am afraid it is worse than that, my dear. I must confess that the bad behavior is all mine. Young Samuel here was only following my instruction. You see, we are playing this silly game, where I continually lose things and he goes and finds them for me. I describe what I have lost, and then time him while he searches and brings me what he found. It works out rather well, actually. But, we both find ourselves in some rather strange predicaments, it seems."

Lisa rolled her eyes in mock disdain and said, "I do not know which of you to reprimand first!"

Samuel held up the spectacles he had retrieved to prove his innocence. "Not me! I was just returning these, and I had to hurry, 'cause I was almost out of time!"

Sara Ella laughed and said, "Looks like you are going to have your hands full with these two, my sister! ...Oh, I like how that sounds...now I have another sister, you and Ila May!"

Then, walking toward the front door Sara Ella's countenance dropped a little as she continued, "I wish Laura was here too, Lisa. I know she was your best friend, and she is Adam's sister. I wonder whatever became of her."

Lisa took Sara Ella's hand, and with a tear in her eye said, "You have no idea how often I think of Laura. She was my closest friend ever."

"Well, I should not keep Tom and the other men waiting any longer. I need to get back to Oaklayne in time to help as much as possible with supper. That is a lot of men to feed, and I should do my part. Please tell Mother that I will come to see her as often as I can. Thank you so very much for tending to her. You were right about this being the best place for her to recover."

"Do not worry, dear. I will regularly send word to Oaklayne about how Mrs. Gary is feeling. I have to confess that she has become like a mother to me also, so it will be a pleasure to care for her. What a joy she is."

The trip back to Oaklayne was without incident. Sara Ella noticed some clouds building in the south. She felt over protected, with all of these men escorting her, and decided to have a talk with Adam about it. She had always been able to take care of herself, and did not feel a need to be fussed over like this. Those men could have been doing a lot more productive things with their time.

After the evening meal, while the men were still sipping coffee and relaxing, Adam asked Sara Ella about her trip to take Mrs. Gary to Mr. Callahan's house.

"Please do not ever send an army along with me like that again, Adam," she said, as Oscar choked on his coffee and Brandon began slapping him on the back. "I was embarrassed having such an entourage with me! People looked at me like I think I am some kind of queen or something. And another thing, having to cut my time short so they can all get back to work is completely unacceptable. I need more flexibility than that."

Adam was startled by her outburst and did not know what to say. "I am sorry, my dear, but...."

Oscar interrupted to say, "I am sorry, ma'am. It was my fault that those men went with you. I do not want you to be frightened, but there have recently been some incidents on the road between here and Richmond and here at Oaklayne as well. Perhaps it would be a good idea for you to talk with Elsie. She was with me one day when we were accosted by some men on that road you took today. We were lucky to get away with our lives," he said looking at Sara Ella, then at Adam. "I am sorry sir, for interfering in your business. I probably should have explained the situation up front, instead of trying to protect you from the frightening truth. I wrongfully assumed it would be better if you did not know the whole story. Please accept my apology. But also, please reconsider using the escort when you travel. I really think it is necessary."

With Oscar's explanation, Sara Ella's annoyance over the situation subsided and she calmly went back to her duties, helping with the dishes. Adam followed her and asked how her mother was feeling when she left her at the Callahan Plantation.

"Oh, Adam, she is in a wonderfully appointed room in a quiet atmosphere. Lisa is doing a beautiful job taking care of her, and it is clear that she likes Lisa very much. I know she is in the best possible place."

"What is the condition of the plantation?" Adam asked.

"Well, it is strange...when you pull up out front, you cannot help but notice that half of the plantation home is missing. However, it is not noticeable once you are inside, because the entry is intact. There is a large drawing room and a huge dining room, with a good sized set up room beyond, on the unaffected side, and 5 bedrooms remaining upstairs. Actually, the only room that is missing is the grand ballroom. It was destroyed the same day that Mrs. Callahan was killed by mortar shelling. Lisa told me he lost everything, his wife, his money that he had invested in crops that were destroyed, and all of his field hands, of course. One family that had previously been his most valued slaves are living there now and helping him."

"How does he plan to keep his plantation? Necessities and upkeep will eventually be required to maintain the place."

Proud to be able to explain about sharecropping and tenant farming to Adam, Sara Ella sounded like an expert. A few of the men overheard and asked her some questions about it, Steven and Brandon in particular.

"What about Mr. Callahan? Did you feel comfortable leaving your mother in his home?"

"Oh Adam he is such a kind man. It was hard for him to accept my offer to pay for her room and board, as well as for Lisa and Samuel. But, I insisted, so he finally agreed to it," she said, as Adam lifted an eyebrow.

"Should I be jealous of this perfect man?"

"No dear, there is no one as perfect as you," she said, leaning toward him. Then, when she was almost close enough to kiss him, she said, "Even if you do treat me like a helpless waif of a girl!"

Then she flicked her dish towel against his leg, to which he grabbed her and pulled her into his lap. She put her arms around his neck and kissed him sweetly on the cheek. That is when the men around the table started shuffling their way out into the rain.

Chapter 39

Everyone had to yell to be heard the next morning along the bank of the Savannah River. The wind was strong and the rain was pouring down in heavy torrents. The river roared, as angry currents of flood waters churned.

"What did you say?" August yelled to the ferry boat Driver. "I cannot hear you."

Trevor looked back over his shoulder, hoping the rain would keep the thwarted lynch mob hanging in that big oak tree all day long.

"I said that I have never seen the river this high, and I am afraid it is going to get worse. That is why I arrived early this morning to try and save this ferry."

"Can we help you?" August yelled back.

"Maybe," he yelled back. "It is risky to take her there, but the ferry would be safer if she was on the other bank of the river."

"How risky?" Trevor called out, as he came closer.

"Water's going too fast to let me hit my usual port on the other side. I would have to let 'er float on down to the next inlet. But, that would put her a lot farther downstream when the storm is over. I would have to bring her all the way back up here, which would be expensive. It is dangerous, but safer for the ferry than leaving her here. She cannot take much more of this pounding."

"Would it be to your advantage if we were willing to take a chance on making it across with you?" Trevor yelled. "We can pay you enough to get her brought back up here when the storm is over."

"Sure! But, it will be a ride you will never forget! I am confident the ferry will make it, but I cannot vouch for anything on it," the ferry master yelled back. "You would be taking a big chance if you get aboard!"

"I will talk to the others, be right back," said August.

After weighing the odds of the river against those men who were hopefully still hanging in that tree, they decided to challenge the river.

"Like I said, it is going to be a mighty rough ride. I would like to be paid up front, if you don't mind, just in case you don't make it to the other side. Either way, I will need that money to cover my expenses to bring her back up the river."

When the money had been paid, the weathered old ferry master said, "Thanks. Now, if I was you I would tie them little 'uns and that gal fast to the ferry," he motioned to Rachel and the children, who had just climbed out of the wagon.

"Thanks for the advice. We will take it."

"That ain't all," he yelled, "Get aboard as fast as you can. This here river will be getting worse by the minute. Tie down that wagon in every possible place. It will give you a place to tie up the horses, with the rigging left on the work horses. Keep the ropes short on all the horses. They will be hysterical in short order, and we do not want them to be able to buck. Cover their heads if you have time. When I yell, 'We're off,' grab something, anything and hold on fer yer life! If you have time, tie yourself to something. Whatever you do, do not let go until I tell you it is safe. This river will try to trick you. You will think it is safe before it is."

The old man had not exaggerated. Trevor mistakenly figured riding the river would be easier than riding some of the wild horses he had broken in the past. The pitching and turning of the ferry boat was much worse. Rachel and the children were tied tightly to the side rail of the ferry, getting soaked by the river and the rain, but being brave. Ezra was on one side of the front, hanging on for dear life. Trevor and August were on the other side near the back, trying to balance out Ezra's weight.

When they were near the center of the river, Trevor motioned for August to look back at the shore behind them. They could see six men with only four horses. The men were jumping up and down, shaking their fists and obviously yelling unmentionables. It was the same men they had tied up and left hanging in the woods when they rescued Ezra. Thankfully, as they floated on down the river and out of sight they could no longer make out what the men were saying.

Lightning flashed across the sky, then the thunder crashed, throwing Trevor's horse, Lightnin', into a frenzy. Instinctively and without thinking, Trevor let go and ran to him, just as the boat pitched down in the front. That threw Trevor forward, sliding off of the open front of the ferry. August yelled in anguish, seeing Trevor lose his balance and go overboard.

It seemed like an eternity as he searched the water for Trevor to emerge. He could not imagine life without his twin. They had always been together. He remembered when Trevor was raising that horse from a little colt. When he could not break him from being afraid of storms, he decided to just call him Lightnin' from then on.

Not knowing what else to do, August ran to the back of the boat with a rope, knowing that Trevor would most likely emerge behind them. He hoped his aim would be good enough in this violently pitching boat to be able to throw the rope to him in time to save his life.

Hanging on to the back of the boat, while searching every wave of the water for his brother, August was soon devastated when Trevor never floated by in the water.

Realizing that Trevor must have been struck by the thrashing ferry as it went over him, August cried out, "No, God! Please do not take my brother, Lord. Tell me what to do! I cannot live without him..." Then, August fell to the deck, not caring if he was washed overboard, as the boat continued to buck and pitch back and forth.

Up and down, back and forth they pitched. Then finally the current smoothed out as the ferry was being steered close into shore around the leeward side of a knoll.

"Grab that pylon up front and throw that line around her. The current will bring her around, then we can move her forward to unload." The ferry master yelled to the front, but August did not respond, completely unaware of what was going on.

Slowly the boat moved forward, as men brought horses with lines to drag it up to the pier in front. They fastened her down tightly and yelled to the old ferry master, "What are ye doing out here in this weather old man? Have ye lost your mind? There's a flood out here, in case you hadn't noticed!"

The men from shore started helping with the horses, and soon the wagon started moving. But, August was still sitting in the back of the ferry, staring down at the deck. *How can I get all of these people up to Virginia by myself? Trevor is the one who always did the thinking for us...how could he be..."*

He felt a hand on his shoulder and he knew he had to get up. Then he heard a familiar voice say, "Are you hurt?"

It seemed to come from a tunnel somewhere, almost like it was Trevor talking to him.

Then he felt a push and again he heard, "You hurt? Or sick, or maybe just plain lazy?"

Well it definitely sounded like Trevor's voice, or someone who sounded just like him. Then August lifted his face and looked right into the face of his brother...or at least he thought it was his brother. Maybe they had both died? He still could not speak, but the thought occurred to him that perhaps he was in shock or having some kind of nightmare.

Had he not seen Trevor go overboard? Had he not looked for him in the current? How could....

Now he was being shaken violently. "What on earth is wrong with you, August?"

Stuttering in disbelief, August said, "Trevor? Are you...is it you? How can it be? I saw you go overboard and you did not come back up. I thought you were dead..."

"Oh that. I did not follow orders very well did I? I know, I am usually the one telling you to do what you are told. Sorry for being so sentimental...I just thought I should help Lightnin' not be so afraid."

"Well yeah, but I saw you go overboard." August was still not sure what to think.

"Well, I am still a little stunned by that too. You see, just as I slid off the deck, Ezra's powerful hand grabbed my arm and flung me up on the deck behind him. Then he put my hands on that side rail, patting them like I was a little kid, telling me to not let go. I did not know if you had seen what happened, but I certainly was not going to let go to come and tell you about it until after we docked."

August was still in a daze, as Trevor led him off of the ferry, telling the story over and over, adding more dramatic detail with each telling. "He saved my life, August. I tell you, Ezra saved my life. I do not have any idea how he kept from falling into the river himself. But, he saved my life, and I am grateful."

Chapter 40

Adam was eager to start building Oakville, the cabins for the families who had been slaves at Oaklayne before the war. He was most anxious for Tom to have a cabin of his own. Tom was still a bachelor, but hopefully he would soon find a wife and want a home of his own to provide for his family. He also looked forward to Nathaniel having his own place. His wife had died before the end of the war, but Nathaniel certainly deserved to live out his days in a home of his own. Adam wanted Oakville to be a happy village, families living comfortably with little children playing together in their own yards.

Sara Ella was pressuring him to build the Oakville school house first. As soon as possible, she wanted to begin teaching the black children the same lessons the white children were learning in their schools. The last time she went to Warren Callahan's to see her mother, she talked to Martha about being a school teacher, and Martha was excited about helping.

Adam had the village laid out around a town square that would house both the school building and a small church. He hoped he might be able to get one of the merchants in town to set up a small market in the square. That way, if the women needed something for the kitchen, they would not have to go all the way to town, but could buy it in their own village. He definitely wanted a large area dedicated to the children for a community playground. He envisioned a square with seven plots on each side, and three at each end.

Each cabin would have a living room, a kitchen, and at least three bedrooms. Adam could think of nothing nicer to do for the people who had served his family so well for so many years. Their property at Oakville would be deeded to them, even if they chose to work for someone else instead of continuing to work at Oaklayne. He also planned to give each worker a fair wage for all the time they had previously worked for Oaklayne. They could use that money to buy what they would need to make their house a home and begin to work their land.

The next step would be to locate his former slaves and tell them of his plans. He would offer them each one of the 25 acre plots with the cabin, in appreciation for their years of service to Oaklayne. He had no doubt they would be pleased with his offer, if he could just find them.

After breakfast Adam was pondering over his plans in his mind, when Tom came and sat down at the table with him. They were both sipping their coffee when Adam leaned back in his chair and asked, "Tom, have you ever thought about having a place of your own?"

Tom's expression was quizzical. "No, I have never thought about it, Adam. It has never crossed my mind, because it has never been possible. Some things are foolish to consider. Just like it would be a waste of time for me to consider whether I would like to be the King of England. No, I have never considered what it would be like to have a home of my own. I am wondering, why do you ask?"

"Oh, I was just thinking. I would like to pay you a fair wage for all the years you have worked for me, and give you 25 acres of Oaklayne to call your own. We can build you a cabin on your land as well, that is, if you would like that. Actually, I would like to do that for all of the people who were faithful, hardworking slaves of Oaklayne before the war. We can section off an area of the plantation for each of those families to settle down on their own land that we will call Oakville. The problem is that I do not know how to find those people. Do you know where they are?"

Tom was stunned and was unable to speak. He could not believe his ears! Why would Adam do such a thing?

"I would appreciate it if you would not say anything to the others just yet, at least until I work out some more of the details. Sara Ella wants to build the school first, of course. Then we will need to work on the church, the well and other necessities for the little town of Oakville. Tom, are you listening to me? Tom? What is wrong with you, man?"

"I...I...I don't know what to say, Adam. I have never even dreamed of having a home of my own. I simply cannot get my mind around it."

"Well, you had better get your mind around it, because I am going to need a lot of your help figuring all this out!" Adam grabbed Tom's hand and cradled it in his own two hands. "I could never thank you enough for all you have done for me through the years, Tom. Now, shall we get to work?"

The next afternoon, Adam asked Tom to get the carriage ready to take him into town to see a lawyer. When he mentioned needing to go earlier that day, Randy and Benjamin asked if they could go along. So, it made more sense to take the carriage instead of just riding his horse.

Nathaniel came in from the sawmill while they were waiting for Tom to bring the carriage around. Adam asked, "Nathaniel, do you know where any of the former slaves of Oaklayne are living now? I would like to find them, but I do not know where to start looking."

"No, sah. They's a few fam'lies that still goes to ma' church, but mos' of 'em has lef' here, 'cause they's no work fo' 'em. Why?" asked Nathaniel.

Adam explained his plan to Nathaniel, as he had with Tom. The older man's face began to glow and a smile filled his wrinkled eyes. "Mr. Adam, yo' would do that fo' us? Ah'm so happy ah could cry, sah! The Lo'd, He is good, Sah! Yes, Sah...He is good." Nathaniel had tears in his eyes as Tom arrived with the carriage. "Ah only wish ma' wife was here to 'njoy it wit' me."

"I would appreciate it if you would keep this to yourself for now, Nathaniel. Tom knows about it, but I would rather wait until I have more of the details worked out before we tell the others. Please keep your ear to the ground on where to find others of the former slaves, though. Let me know what you find out."

"Yes Sah, Ah will, Massa Adam. Ah always knowed yo' was a fine man, jus' like yo' daddy," said Nathaniel. "Does yo' min' me askin', Sah...where does yo' plan ta' make this Oakville?"

Adam smiled and answered, "You know that area over on the other side of the mansion, where we have been clearing and taking out trees to build with? That is where Oakville will become a village. I expect you were made aware by my father, Nathaniel, that my great-grandfather was given ten thousand acres of Virginia land by King George III of England? And I am not concerned about giving away part of that land to build Oakville for the hardworking people who helped build Oaklayne into the plantation it will be again. This is not a gift, gentlemen...it is payment for services rendered that is long overdue."

"But, that is some of the best land around here, Adam!" Tom said in amazement.

Adam's eyes sparkled to see how much these two loyal men appreciated being acknowledged for their hard work. Nathaniel's tears brought Adam a lot of joy.

"But, Massa Adam... yo' sho' 'bout this?"

"Yes, Nathaniel, I'm very sure. You and Tom will each have your own acreage, a cabin, a barn for a horse and a milk cow, plenty of room for your women to grow vegetables. You can even plant fruit trees if you want! Of course, Emma Lou will be given her own place, too.

Then, there will be seventeen more plots of land for other former slaves, if we can find that many. The three of you will be given the prime spots, and you will need to help Emma Lou pick out her special place."

Nathaniel wiped the tears from his eyes and shook his head. "I jes' can't believe it, Massa Adam. Yo' don' owe us slaves a thing. The law don' set us free, but yo' don' have ta do this, Sah."

"I want to do it, Nathaniel. Do you think you can help me find some of our former slaves? Remember, this is only for former slaves of Oaklayne that were loyal, hardworking people. When you find them, please just tell them that I want to talk with them as soon as possible. I think it is best if I explain to them what is going on myself. I expect there will be some scoundrels who will try to take advantage of me. So, I will need you to help me know who is truly deserving."

"Yes Sah. Ah'll see if Ah can fin' 'em. Ah'll make sho' they's good people fo' yo'."

Tom sat in a daze, trying to figure out what this turn of events would mean for his future. From when he was a small child, he had always lived wherever Adam lived and was rarely out of Adam's sight. Adam had always provided him with living quarters, but he had never dreamed of having his own home with property around it to do with as he pleased. He knew Adam was trying to make light of his sacrifice, but Tom had never felt more loved in his lifetime.

"Adam, I don't know what to say," said Tom.

"Tom, you are and always have been my dearest friend. If there is anything that you need or desire, I want to provide it for you if I am able."

"But, you already do that for me, Adam. I could never ask for a better friend than you have been to me, since we were little boys. You have never treated me like I was your slave, but more like a brother. I am sure you know that I mean no disrespect when I say that. It is the rest of the world that has treated me like your slave, not you."

"As you are thinking this over, Tom, always remember that if you would rather have a room with Sara Ella and me in the manor house, I would be honored to have you there with me. But, if you would appreciate having a home of your own, please feel free to build it any way you want. I am overjoyed to provide it for you in appreciation of all that you are and all that you have done for me through the years."

"Hey! We're ready," Randy called out, as Adam and Tom stood up and embraced like any two brothers would do after such a tender discussion.

The shingle hanging out in front of the lawyer's office in Richmond was printed in lavish gold script: ***General John D. Imboden, Attorney at Law***. Adam was not looking forward to this encounter. If John Imboden had not been the lawyer for his father, Mason Layne, Adam would never set his foot inside of the man's office. As fate would have it though, this particular lawyer had all of the legal records and deeds pertaining to Oaklayne.

Imboden had been Adam's military counterpart in the Confederate Army during the war. Of all people, why did this man have to be the lawyer in possession of the Oaklayne legal documents? Adam knew that his father had come to appreciate this man when they were both elected to the House of Delegates of the Virginia General Assembly. Imboden had even been elected twice. He had often come to balls and other festivities at Oaklayne as Mason Layne's guest before the war. Even Laura Layne had been impressed with Imboden back then. Adam had to admit that he had found no malice in the man, until that dreadful night at Harper's Ferry. How could this friend of the family be the man who commanded the unit that captured Harper's Ferry? Just remembering back to the fires and exploding arms and ammunition brought tightness to Adam's jaw.

Tom cleared his throat, as Randy asked, "Is the office closed Father?"

Brought abruptly back from the displeasure of his memories, Adam answered, "No, son, the office is not closed."

He opened the door and was greeted by a smartly dressed young man who said, "May I help you?"

"Yes, I am Adam Layne. We are here to see General Imboden about some legal matters."

"Just a moment please," he said as he turned and walked over to a closed door that was not far behind him in the room.

"Tom, I would like for you to pay close attention in this meeting because it's about Oakville. I would like for you to understand all of the legalities of setting up the village. Please feel free to ask questions about anything you do not understand."

Tom nodded in agreement, as the young man returned to show them into General Imboden's office.

"Come right on in, Adam!" said the lawyer. "I have not seen you for such a long time. Please have a seat and accept my condolences in the loss of your parents. You know that I admired your father immensely, and your mother was a jewel."

Yeah, right... Adam thought, *if it we not for you and your cause, they would still be alive.* But, Adam did not express his thoughts. He simply said, "Thank you. Now, without further ado, I would like to get to the business at hand, if you do not mind.

"Because of destruction brought on by Confederate soldiers during the recent war, Oaklayne Plantation was completely destroyed. You may already know that I am in the process of rebuilding. What you do not know is that I would like to build a village on my property with cabins, a school house and a church for former slaves as payment to them for their hard work and loyalty to my family before the war."

"There are a few other plantation owners who are doing the same thing, Adam. They think it is the best way for them to keep their slaves producing the much needed crops on their plantations. They are letting them use a portion of their property to produce crops, then the landowner gets a share of the crops when they are sold at market. It is called "Sharecropping", and it seems to be working pretty well so far.

"No, no...that is not what I have in mind at all." Adam squirmed in his seat like a seven-year-old boy in church, disgusted with the man's lack of understanding. He apparently could not comprehend that Adam was not trying to use his former slaves for his benefit. He did not like having Imboden involved in his business, and had hoped this meeting would take only a few minutes.

"I want to honor my former slaves and their faithful hard work at Oaklayne Plantation through the years by deeding a portion of my land to them as their own. They have earned it, and I owe it to them."

"I am sorry, Adam. But, I must completely understand your purpose before I am able to provide you with the best legal protection."

"Well, perhaps I should go somewhere that I can be understood, then."

"Tell me this, Adam. Do you want these former slaves to continue working on your plantation?"

"Well, I hope they will want to do that."

"Of course, you do," Imboden said, struggling to remain professional in the face of Adam's indignation. "Now, what I need to know is how would this arrangement be any different than the cabins that you provided for them when they were slaves?"

Fuming at this man prying into more information than Adam thought he needed, he responded, "I do not see why it matters to you, but these cabins will be much nicer, bigger and new. Do you think I would not provide nicer cabins than they had when they were slaves?"

"Father," Randy broke in, "I think you may have misinterpreted General Imboden's question."

"I do not think so, son. He asked me how the cabins would be different."

"Forgive me for intruding, but I believe he actually wants to know if you will require the former slaves to work for you as a part of this arrangement."

"Of course not! Did I say that? That would be preposterous, and not accomplish what I want at all."

General Imboden, acutely aware of the tension between himself and Adam, acknowledged the young man's astuteness with a smile. It was clear that the young man was blind, making his clear understanding of the situation compelling.

Looking intently into Randy's face, the attorney said, "Excuse me, Adam. I do not believe I have had the pleasure of meeting this young man who came with you."

"I am sorry, I dispensed with introductions when we came in, because I thought we would just be here for a minute. This young man who has challenged his father is Randall Layne."

"Little Randy, the little boy with the drum?" said Imboden with a chuckle.

Randy laughed, "That would be me, sir. Have we met?"

"Yes, you would remember me as John. I have been in your home many times over the years. I even took a shine to your beautiful sister Laura for a while, but she never took me seriously. I am about your father's age, and I am tall with dark wavy hair, a mustache and blue eyes."

Randy excitedly sat forward in his chair and exclaimed, "Oh yes! How could I forget. You always asked me to play my drum for you when you were there. I will never forget how somber we both were at my Aunt Laura's wedding...I would much rather she had married you instead of Hamilton."

Under the circumstances, John Imboden was obviously pleased to enjoy this camaraderie with Adam's son. "Randy, tell me if you do not mind, what happened to your eyesight?"

Adam, feeling somewhat overly protective, started to protest this encroachment into his son's privacy, when Randy surprised him by saying, "I am glad you asked, John! Most people pretend not to notice that I am blind, then they avoid speaking to me. If they do finally say something to me, they often raise their voices at me, as if I were hard of hearing, also. I wonder why they do that. Anyway, my hearing is becoming quite acute as time goes on, and I am surprised at how much I can see when I listen well."

The lawyer and the young blind man continued their discussion as if they were the only ones in the room, ignoring everyone else. "I am very aware of the audio sight phenomenon you are experiencing, and also understand about people wanting to avoid you."

Once again exasperated, Adam protest, "How can you say...?"

"It's all right, Father. John is telling the truth, and I personally find it very refreshing."

"I expected that you would feel that way, Randy. You see, for several years I taught at the Virginia School for the Deaf and Blind in Stanton, VA. So, I have a pretty good understanding of what you are going through. But, you did not answer my question. How did you become blind?"

"It was in the war, sir. I was shot in the head, and would certainly have died if my friend Benjamin had not carried me to where I could receive immediate medical help." Randy reached out for his friend's hand and said, "John, this is Benjamin. We grew up together at Oaklayne."

John reached out, shook Benjamin's hand and said, "So young man, you sound like a very trustworthy and responsible person. Now that you are a freedman, what are your plans for the future?"

"Thank you, sir. I want to be a civil rights lawyer," said Benjamin.

"Impressive! So, you are also ambitious. What kind of education do you have, Benjamin?"

"I am very grateful that General Layne made sure I attended every class with Randy when we were children growing up. And he has now provided me the opportunity to go to Ashmun Institute in Pennsylvania, where I am currently attending classes. Frederick Douglass has inspired my aspirations."

"Interesting. What about you, Randy? What are the plans for your future, now that you are blind?"

"Well, strangely enough, my plans are much like Benjamin's. I also intend to be a lawyer someday. I've spent some time at the Perkins Institute for the Blind in Massachusetts, where I learned that my blindness can actually be an opportunity rather than a handicap. Did you know that there is a blind British attorney who continued his studies at the University of Cambridge after he was blinded. Then he went on to become a Professor at Cambridge. His name is Henry

Fawcett. He was recently elected a member of Parliament for Brighton. As you can see, his blindness did not hold him back."

"Adam, I am impressed with the hope and excitement for the future you have instilled in these two bright boys. You must be overjoyed with their ambitious plans. It is a rare thing in these struggling times."

Adam found himself squirming again. He knew that he had not been overjoyed at all. In fact, he had been fearful, especially for Randy, but for Benjamin, too. How could their hopes and dreams ever be realized? Their goals were too big for the handicaps they would both have to struggle mightily to overcome. Now this traitor to his country was encouraging them both to march headlong into possible failure.

Looking up at Tom, John Imboden continued his exasperating inquisition into Adam's life. "And who is this other gentleman accompanying you, Adam?"

Wondering what ridiculous ideas John would put in Tom's mind, he sighed and introduced him.

"Yes, Tom. I remember you now. Somehow, without anyone hardly noticing, you' have always had Adam prepared for every situation. His wardrobe, his carriage, his brief case, his hat and even his appointments, are you still there for him, Tom?"

"Yes sir. Adam has made it clear that I am a free man. But, there is no place I would rather be than working for him. General Layne has always treated me with utmost respect. I am here today because he wants to honor me with one of those cabins he is talking about. He asked me to come along to meet with you, because he wants me to understand the legal issues involved."

"Adam, you are a lucky man. You are surrounded by worthy, well educated men, who all seem to love you very much. I envy you."

A bit disarmed by his remarks, Adam said, "Thank you, General. Now, may we get on with our business here?"

"Yes, let's do. As Randy helped us clarify, do I understand correctly that these freedmen who receive a cabin and property from you will not be required to work for you?"

"Yes, that is right. However, I guess I just assumed that they would want to work for me."

John sat back in his chair and said, "As your attorney, Adam, it is important for me to help you realize all potential possibilities and ramifications of your plan. Do you plan to deed this property to each of your former slaves?"

"Yes, that is why I'm here to see you. I want to start the legal process of dividing the lots out, so I can provide deeds to my former slaves."

"Do you expect to ever, for any reason, consider offering one of these cabins to someone who was never a slave?"

"No. I will not give a cabin to anyone who was not a slave."

Adam noticed that John was writing all of his answers down.

"Would you ever, for any reason, refuse to give a cabin to anyone who had been a previous slave?"

"Why are you asking all these questions? Is it important to go into all of this now? All I want to do now is break up the land into lots."

"Yes, Adam. We need to think this through before the first step is taken. We must plan for potential legal suits that could come your way down the road."

"I'm not going to have any lawsuits. That is ridiculous!"

Imboden leaned over his desk, looked hard into Adam's eyes and asked, "Do you recall having any former slaves who may have the potential to cause disharmony in your little village?"

At this question, Tom cleared his throat nervously. Adam turned quickly, looked intently at Tom and asked, "Do you have something to say, Tom?"

"I just thought you might want to give this question some serious thought before you answer. I am sure you remember some of those men that your father had to deal with in the past. I would rather not name names here, but it concerns me."

Adam's eyes widened, as he carefully considered Tom's words. "You are absolutely right, Tom. Thank you."

"Yes, I will want to refuse a property to some former slaves. I have said all along that I want only those former slaves who were faithful, hardworking and loyal to my family through the years."

"Would you be willing to make a list of specific reasons you would refuse someone?"

"Well yes, I would. But, I will need time to discuss it with Tom and Nathaniel. Nathaniel is my foreman at Oaklayne. They can help me come up with that list."

"While you are at it, give some thought to another question, as well. If you are truly rewarding these people for the past and you intend to deed the property to them, have you given any thought to what might happen if any of them decide to sell their property to someone else?"

Adam was clearly shocked at the idea. "Why in the world would they sell it?"

"That is not for me to say, Adam. But, you need to understand that it may happen. If you want to attempt to protect the harmony of your village, you need to consider the possibilities. For example, one of the women may fall in love with one of the men and want to sell her home to someone else and move in with him. There are any number of other scenarios where someone may decide to sell, and for good reason."

"This is so much more complicated than I expected," said Adam. He ran his hand through his hair and gently shook his head.

"I can help simplify the complications, as long as you are honest and thorough in your answers. I will need to know how much control you expect to maintain over this village, as compared to letting go and to let these freedmen be truly free with their property."

"You are right, John. I do need to spend some time pondering over your questions. I will also need to seek advice from some of the people who would be affected most by how we go about this."

John Imboden knew he had not given Adam what he came for, but he definitely had given him what he needed. "I can get started down this road with the answers you have given me today, Adam. However, we cannot proceed very far without definite decisions being made concerning the particulars we have discussed. Here is some information you can take with you about the legalities of property deeds. I hope you will find it helpful."

"Thank you, John," Adam said, as he rose from his chair to leave.

"Before you go, I have a couple more questions of a more personal nature. I am curious about Laura. How is she doing?"

"We lost track of her during the war, after we learned that her husband Hamilton had been killed. She was in Charleston at the time of his death. She just disappeared, and we have not heard from her to this day. So many people were lost. We know that my brother, Goddard, was killed in Richmond as Sherman marched through there near the end of the war."

"I am so sorry to hear that, Adam. Laura was always the life of the party, and Dr. Goddard Layne will be sorely missed, I am sure.

"My other question concerns you, Randy. Having worked with blind people in the past, I see an enthusiasm in you that is refreshing. I would sure like to help you realize your dream of becoming a lawyer. If you would consider changing schools to attending the University of Richmond, I will give you a part time job here working on some cases that would give you some on the job training. Of course, you would have to hire someone to read to you. There would certainly be a lot of reading you would need to do."

Randy struggled to keep his composure. He almost let out a squeal that would have made him sound like a 10-year-old boy. "Yes! Oh, yes. That sounds like just the kind of opportunity I am looking for. I will not disappoint you, sir. I will do my very best."

Benjamin cleared his throat rather loudly and said, "Excuse me Randy. Would you consider hiring me to do that reading? Of course, General Layne would need to agree to let me transfer to another school closer to Richmond if I was to do that job."

John saw Randy reach out to Benjamin, then both young men held their breath, as Adam was on the spot.

"Well, it is pretty clear what both of you want. Is it all right with you, Adam?"

Adam was so angry he thought he might explode any minute. John Imboden obviously had no idea what he was doing to two of the most wonderful boys in the world. Adam was clearly in a no-win situation. If he agreed to this idea, he would be participating in the greatest let down of these boys lives. But, if he did not agree to it, they would never forgive him. The only good he could see that would come of it was that both boys would be closer to home and back together again.

"Now, look here...these boys are very impressionable right now. Do not be putting unrealistic expectations in front of them...they both need to be investing their time and energy into more approachable goals."

John smiled and pointed to Randy and Benjamin. "Adam, these two are young men, not boys. They have both been to war and faced much bigger disappointments than they could ever encounter trying to reach their goal to become lawyers. The enthusiasm and drive they have for their future prospects is not only admirable, it is rare. I saw that in you when we were young men, Adam. Do you remember that?"

Adam hung his head in defeat. But, at the same time, he was more proud of his son and young Benjamin that he had ever been before.

John Imboden continued, "Adam, I know that we have not seen eye to eye on very many things in the past. But, I can assure you that we both want the same thing for these remarkable young men. Please let me help both of them. I am equipped like no other, because I know how to help Randy overcome the handicap of his blindness, as well as give him a foot in the door to eventually realizing his dream of becoming a lawyer.

"With my background I may be able to pull some strings to get Benjamin into the University of Richmond, along with Randy. The environment there will be tough for him, that is for sure. But, if he can stand against it, he will get a better education to prepare him for law school. Working here with me will help them both understand the legal process and develop some skills they will need down the road." He looked at Randy and then Benjamin before asking, "So, what do you say?"

Tom had his hand on Benjamin's shoulder when Adam looked over at them. The imploring look on Tom's face was almost as intense as the two boys. Adam knew he had to surrender. The opposition was simply too great for him to continue to oppose the idea.

"Oh, all right then." Suddenly, the celebration in the room was almost deafening. "I can see why they say you are a good lawyer, John. Your arguments are convincing. But, I need you to promise me that you will not coddle these boys..." he cleared his throat and corrected himself, "...I mean young men...and that you will be truthful and honest with them every step of the way."

"I would not have it any other way, Adam. I will also keep you informed if I ever have any doubts, whether either one of them will be unable to reach their goals.

"I will start right away, finding out how to get Benjamin enrolled in the University. I will send the enrollment papers for you to sign as soon as I receive them. You will need to find a place for them to live off of campus, but close to the school and my office. Since Benjamin is black and Randy is blind, they will not be allowed to live in any of the dorms. Fortunately, my office is close to the school, so they should not have any trouble walking here. Before long, I expect Randy will learn how to make his way back and forth alone."

Chapter 41

Emma Lou had already fixed coffee when Elsie arrived in the kitchen to start her days work. She was surprised to see Emma Lou up that early. The two women greeted each other with the unthinking salutations people use without being conscious of the words. It was clear to Elsie that Emma Lou was frustrated when she rose up tall, put both hands on her hips and said, "Chil', where 'bouts did yo' stash ma' bis'kit makin' bowl? Ah's searched ever'wheres, an' I cain't fin' it."

Elsie grinned, suddenly understanding Emma Lou's flustered countenance. She walked over to the cabinet right in front of where Emma Lou always stood to make the biscuits, reached down and pulled back the curtain, then set the biscuit bowl on the counter with a thud. "Here you go, ma'am. I thought it might be easier if it was stored where you use it. So, I moved it some time ago. I did not say anything, because I always get it out for you in the mornings."

"Yo' is sho' spoilin' me, girl! See, Ah cain't even make bis'kits now without yo' hep'n me." Emma Lou chuckled and patted Elsie on the hand in appreciation.

Both women went on cheerfully visiting as they prepared breakfast for the crew that depended on them every day to prepare tasty, hot meals.

As he made his way down the stairs, Oscar was uncomfortable when he realized his disappointment, hearing voices coming from the kitchen. More than he realized, he looked forward to a few moments alone with Elsie every morning, before anyone else showed up to interfere with their trysting time. He suspected that she enjoyed their quiet early mornings as much as he did, but he could not be sure. As he walked into the kitchen, instead of giving Elsie the usual sweet greeting, he just plopped down in the chair.

Elsie's back was turned, so she did not see Oscar come in. She was busy gathering up all the pots and pans they would need to cook a hot breakfast for a multitude of hungry working men. But, Emma Lou heard his footsteps on the wood floor and ask, "What brings yo' down so early dis' mo'nin, Colonel?"

As Elsie turned around, she lost her balance and dropped all of the pots and pans, making a terrible clatter. Then, when she tried to gather them back up again, her hair fell in her face, she bumped her head on the counter and she dropped them all again. The noise was deafening, as Oscar jumped up out of his chair, not knowing whether to offer to help or try to act like nothing happened, so Elsie could save face.

Emma Lou stood there with her hands on her hips, amazed at the clumsiness of this usually meticulous young lady. Then it hit her...Colonel Oscar was usually present when this sort of thing happened to Elsie.

Emma Lou just shook her head and mumbled, "Uh, huh," and went back to her biscuit making duties.

Oscar, not surprised at all by Elsie's behavior, simply asked, "May I please have a cup of coffee? After all that noise, can you still hear me, or do I need to say it a little louder?"

Elsie giggled, then Emma Lou suggested that he get his own coffee, since they were too busy making breakfast to be his waitress. Oscar was disheartened, but slowly trudged over to get his own coffee. Then, Elsie was disappointed when he carried it outside to a table to drink it.

"Good morning, Oscar," Adam said cheerfully. He was surprised to find Oscar outside this morning drinking his coffee at the pavilion table.

"Yea, I guess," Oscar replied, as Adam passed by to get himself a cup of coffee from the kitchen.

"Oscar, what is on your agenda for today?" Adam asked, as he returned with the steaming cup of coffee. Not waiting for an answer, Adam continued, "I would like to spend a little time with you this morning if you can manage that. With the help of the other men and researching the plans from the old house, I have a list of the lumber and materials we cannot get in this area. According to the original plans, there are several things we will need to purchase abroad, before we can finish our work. As you know, I would sure like to follow those old plans down to the smallest detail. I want the mansion to be just as majestic as it was before. Since it will take quite a while for those things to arrive, they should probably be ordered right away, what do you think?"

While Adam was still talking, Nathaniel sat down at the table with them. He broke in to the conversation to remind Adam that he had accompanied his father, Mason Layne, to Charleston during the war when the older man wanted to ship some crops to Europe during the embargo. Doing so, required employing some extraordinary methods.

"Hmmm...I didn't know he did that, Nathaniel. He must have needed the money badly. Do you remember who shipped it for him? He must have been a blockage runner, so he is probably not still alive."

"His name was Wythe, Sah...Cap'n Wythe, an' he was a blockade runner. We met him in Wilmington, but Massa' Mason wrote to 'em in Charleston. Ah'm sho' of it."

"Thank you, Nathaniel. Let me know if you remember anything else about him. We need to try to find him."

"Yes, sah. Ah will."

Adam turned to Oscar, who was being strangely quiet this morning and said, "Oscar, let's go over this list together, then Nathaniel and Sara Ella need to look it over, too. They may think of some things we have overlooked that should be added. I will work on arranging a way to have everything shipped here."

Later that day, Sara Ella took the carriage to the Callahan Plantation to see her mother. She was escorted by Tom, Steven and Brandon. Both Steven and Brandon hoped to ask Mr. Callahan about the tenant farming idea Sara Ella talked about.

"Mr Callahan we heard that you are considering allowing tenant farming on some of your property. Is that true?"

"Yes, it is. I lost my field hands when they were freed, and cannot afford to pay anyone to work my land. So, I need to find another way to produce an income. Would you boys be interested in tenant farming some of this land?"

As negotiator for the pair, Brandon took over and said, "It depends on what it would cost, I guess. We both like this area and would like to settle down here. Both of us would like to have our own property, and of course, we will each need a cabin. Steven is married and quite anxious to bring his wife out here. If we can come to an agreement that we can afford, we would like to take you up on that, sir."

"Wonderful. But, you need to know that all I have to offer is land. I do not have any capital to build cabins or even seed to plant. You boys will need to provide everything you will need to make my land work for you," said Warren.

Steven was discouraged, disappointed that Mr. Callahan had only land to bring to the table. But, Brandon spoke up and said, "Sir, if we built the cabins ourselves on your property, could our rent for the use of the cabins and the land go toward paying off the property? We would buy the seed ourselves, and give you a percentage of the crops we grow, like a sharecropper. That way you would still hold the deed until it is paid off. If for any reason we left before it is paid off, the cabins and the land would be yours. We would benefit by not having to pay interest to a bank to finance owning our own places. With this arrangement, we would both come out ahead. You will have an income, some security and we won't have to pay as much for land of our own. What do you think?"

Warren Callahan knew these men would be good neighbors, because Lisa and Sara Ella had told him about them. But, he had not considered selling his land, only renting it out to tenant farmers.

"Your idea is tempting, gentlemen. But, I will need some time to pray about your proposal. It is very hard for me to give up part of my land. This is my home, and has been for a lifetime. I am sorry, I cannot give you a definitive answer today."

Shaking the dust from his hat as he stood to his feet, Steven said, "Just give it some thought, sir. We both thank you for your time. It has been a pleasure." He reached out to shake Warren's hand and they returned to their horses to wait for Sara Ella.

As Warren walked back into the house, Lisa was coming out of the drawing room into the foyer. Suddenly, he felt the urge to ask her opinion on the proposal the young men had suggested.

Warren explained the idea the young men came up with, including how they felt it would benefit all parties involved. "It is a good idea, I have to admit. But, I also have to admit that I am struggling with the idea of signing over any of this property to anyone else. It has been my home for such a long time. You have had to deal with a lot more loss than I have, my dear. I am interested in any thoughts you may have about all this. Of course, I will be asking the Lord about it before I make any decisions."

Lisa looked long and hard into Warren's bright, but gentle blue eyes, smiled and said, "You are right, Mr. Callahan. I did lose everything I cared about. My husband, my children, my home and everything I owned. But, look at what the Lord has given me since that time. The most important thing I have now is the knowledge of His love for me...then there is Samuel. Oh, how I have grown to love that boy. Then, I also have your friendship, my generous and faithful friend. I have to say, I am a very happy girl, despite my loss. I have peace and joy that I have never known before."

Warren reached out for her hand and said, "Lisa...my dear Lisa. You are a jewel. But, if I am such a good friend, then why do you insist on calling me Mr. Callahan? When do I get to be just Warren?"

Lisa dropped her head and said demurely, "It simply would not be proper for me to call you by your first name, Mr. Callahan." Then, choking back the lump in her throat that was guarding her heart, she regained her composure, focused her thoughts and changed the subject asking, "Have you considered that these boys might be of more service to you as cabin builders than as farmers? You could offer more of your land to sharecroppers and tenant farmers for more income if you had cabins on the property for them to live in. That would bring in a lot more income than if those men are just farming a small part of your land. You could pay them for the cabins from the money you make leasing the land."

Taking her by both hands, Warren grinned and said, "How is it that you are always able to lift my spirits, dear. After talking with you about this, I feel so much better about it! Thank you for helping me take the focus off of myself, so I can look forward, instead. I will spend some time in prayer and see what the Lord would have me do."

Lisa did not feel like she had been that helpful, but responded, "I am glad you felt I was helpful, my friend. I have no doubt you will do the right thing. Now, I need to find Samuel, so I can scrape off the top layer of whatever he has been into, before I put him to bed."

They both laughed, hugged each other briefly, then Lisa started out the front door to look for Samuel.

Shortly thereafter, Sara Ella came outside as well, so Tom went to get the carriage for her.

As Steven and Brandon mounted their horses for the return trip home, Warren Callahan came hurrying out the front door onto the porch. "Gentlemen, would you mind coming inside for just a moment? I am sorry, Sara Ella. This should only take a minute."

Brandon looked at Steven, and they immediately dismounted and went inside. The three men sat around a table together, as Mr. Callahan explained a modification to their earlier offer that would involve them building additional cabins as part of their rent to own plan. It would give them long term jobs and additional income when those cabins were rented. They would then be able to own their own land sooner. He suggested that they write everything down, so it is a written, legal agreement, of course.

"What do you think?" Warren asked.

Steven and Brandon looked at each other, then both started laughing. Not a belly laugh, but much more boisterous than either of them thought they were capable of before.

"Mr. Callahan, you have made our dreams come true," said Steven. "We will need to see if Adam Layne will provide the lumber for the job up front, before we can pay for it. But, since he could profit down the road from the work we are doing here, I feel sure he will agree to front us the lumber. With progress on the work to rebuild

Oaklayne, the need for construction lumber is finally slowing down there, so the timing is perfect. We will talk to him as soon as we get back."

Brandon added, "We are both a lot more comfortable building houses than we are farming. We are willing to learn farming, but we can build anything you want. In fact, we were looking at this roughed in wall you have erected to cover where your home was blown apart. We would sure like to give that wall the same splendor as the rest of your home. Steven is very talented in fine carving, sir. You should come by Oaklayne and see some of his work."

"My home is not a priority, and it will be some time before I could pay for any construction work. That wall my neighbors erected for me is serving the purpose nicely, but I appreciate your offer more than I can say, gentlemen. So, do we have a deal? Shall I go to town tomorrow and have the papers drawn up for us to sign?"

"Absolutely," Steven and Brandon said, almost in unison as they jumped up and shook Warren's hand vigorously.

"Excellent! It has been a joy dealing with both of you. I am sure we are just beginning a long and productive relationship that will be mutually beneficial to us all," said Warren as he walked them to the door.

Brandon was so excited, he asked Tom if he could drive the carriage back to Oaklayne. He could not wait to share his plans with someone, and driving the carriage would make Tom and Sara Ella captive listeners all the way home. Besides, everyone knew that Brandon was fascinated by anything with wheels. So, driving the carriage came natural to him. He went on and on, sharing his plans for his cabin and land, then finally asked Tom if he had given any thought as to what to do with his new place.

Tom jerked himself upright, with a concerned look on his face and asked, "How did you know about that, Brandon? Adam asked us not to say anything to anyone just yet."

"Well, Adam cannot keep something that big to himself, when we all work so closely together every day, Tom. The word is getting around amongst the men in the work crew. We don't know the whole story, but we do know that Adam is planning to build you, Nathaniel and Emma Lou each a place of your own. I personally think that is a great thing he is doing."

"Well, thank you, Brandon. I hope you do not think me rude, but I do not feel comfortable talking about it until Adam gives me the okay."

"I understand, but I want you to know that I would love to help you with those plans when the time comes, so you can have everything just the way you want it."

Tom relaxed back against the carriage seat and smiled. "I would appreciate your help very much, Brandon. In all my life, I have never had the opportunity to have my own home, so I do not even know where to start."

Brandon turned to Sara Ella and asked, "You seem to be enjoying running a big plantation with Adam, Sara Ella, but what else do you enjoy doing?"

Sara Ella knew he was probably only asking her as a kindness, to involve her in the conversation. But, she could not resist telling him about her plans for a school for the negro children, and how she wanted them to have the same educational opportunities that white children take for granted. She told him that Martha had already agreed to be a teacher at the school and had so many good ideas to contribute.

"Sounds like you have some ambitious plans! I think it is great that you care about these children and their families, ma'am. Now, tell me...how is your mother doing? Is she feeling better?"

Sara Ella smiled, glad to report that her mother was feeling well enough that she should be able to go home soon.

Chapter 42

With work to clear the land for building Oakville progressing nicely, Adam was focused on the mansion. After consulting with Nathaniel and Sara Ella, Oscar provided a list of supplies and materials that would need to be acquired abroad. For example, only English walnut had a tight enough grain to hold together for some of the hand carving Steven had yet to accomplish. And, the furnishings and fabrics could certainly not be obtained anywhere in America.

Adam knew it was time to hire someone to procure what he would need to finish the work on the mansion. So, during the supper hour, He asked Nathaniel if he had remembered anything more about the blockade runner he met in Charleston during the war. "I am running out of time, so I had better get busy and find him, one way or another."

"Ah knows that his firs' name is Matthew, Sah, Matthew Wythe. When Ah was there with yo' daddy, he lived in a big house on the Battery in Charleston. It should not be hard to fin' him, if'n yo' was to jes' go there an' see fo' yo' se'f. He might still be livin' there, Sah. Ah'd be pleased to go wif yo' if'n yo' kin spare me from my work here."

"What do you think, Sara Ella? I do not know of anyone else to send on this journey to Europe. If this man, Wythe, served my father faithfully during the war, he may not be interested in helping a Yankee. But then again, he has proven himself to be trustworthy, and that is hard to find. I am inclined to make a trip to the Battery in Charleston to see if I can find him. It would not hurt to ask if he will do this for me."

"Well, I do not see how you can afford to take Nathaniel away from running the sawmill to take him with you to Charleston. We are using lumber as fast as they can produce it. I am not sure they can keep up this pace, if he is not here to supervise," warned Sara Ella.

"Oh, I agree wholeheartedly," said Adam. "Nathaniel, I will just have to do the best I can to locate Matthew Wythe on my own. You are much too important to the work at the sawmill for me to take you away at this critical time. But, thank you for offering."

Tom spoke up and asked if he would be accompanying Adam on the trip to Charleston. "I need to know if I am packing for both of us, or just you, Adam."

"No, I really need you to stay here and help Oscar with security. I believe I can get there and back faster alone on horseback."

"I have saved your skin a time or two already, you know," said Tom with a grin. "Are you sure you will not need me with you? It is dangerous on the road alone these days, Adam."

"Well, you are right as usual, Tom. But, I cannot really afford to take you with me either. Both you and Nathaniel are rather indispensable around here. I will just have to do the best I can alone. I will be alright, especially knowing you are here to help watch over things in my absence." He motioned toward Sara Ella while she was not looking, indicating he wanted Tom to take care of her for him. However, he knew she would resist if she knew, so he tried to be discreet.

"I will need for you to serve as Proctor here, while I am away, Tom. Oscar and Nathaniel each have their responsibilities, but as Proctor, you will be in charge of Oaklayne in my place. It is a big job, but I know you will handle it well. There is no one I would trust more. Are you willing?"

Tom swallowed hard, knowing the honor and the load that Adam was bestowing upon him with this appointment. "I certainly shall do my best, Adam. I am always willing to do whatever you need, so if standing in as Proctor in your absence is what you want, then that is what I shall do." He lightened the tension by elbowing Nathaniel in the ribs, then said with a chuckle, "I will be sure to watch Nathaniel especially closely. He can be a slough off sometimes, you know."

Nathaniel returned the favor with a slap to the back of Tom's head, "An' Ah'll report to yo' 'bout the mistakes he makes when yo' gets back, Sah!" Then, they all laughed out loud.

"I am sure you will, Nathaniel," Adam said, as he turned to Sara Ella. "I will leave day after tomorrow, if that is okay with you, dear? Tom, please pack my clothes into my saddle bags when you have time. I will leave Thursday morning and try to find Matthew Wythe in Charleston. I will start by looking for his home on the Battery."

Early that Thursday morning, Adam left the plantation, headed for Charleston on horseback, exactly as planned. As he began his travel, he wondered what he would find when he got there. Had that city suffered from the invasion of Union forces during the war, as much as Richmond?

Chapter 43

It was a beautiful, sunny morning, as Sara Ella watched the road for Moses and Martha to bring her mother to Oaklayne. She had mixed emotions, because she had enjoyed so much having her mother close by. Visits with the sweetest lady in the world from now on would be seldom, because of the distance that now separated their homes. But, she was relieved that her mother was finally recovered enough from her illness to return to her home in Macon, Georgia. Try as she might, she could not help but worry about the hard trip her mother would still need to endure to eventually return to her home safely.

Wesley and Cora were expected to arrive any time with the covered wagon for their long trip back to Macon. They had been staying in Richmond for the past several days, getting everything they could possibly need to keep Chadna Gary as comfortable as possible on the journey.

Waiting impatiently, Sara Ella swatted a mosquito that had mistakenly decided she could provide a warm breakfast for a hungry insect. Suddenly, she caught a glimpse of movement down the lane. Standing on her tiptoes, she could see the Callahan buggy. She ran to greet her mother, as Moses brought the horse and buggy gently to a complete stop.

"Welcome, all of you!" Sara Ella hugged her mother, then Martha and shook Moses hand warmly. The ladies all went inside, but Moses said he would rather stay outside and watch for Wesley and Cora to come with the wagon. "That would be great, Moses. I will bring you some lemonade in a few minutes."

Sara Ella pouring glasses of lemonade for everyone and choking back tears said, "Mother, I am so glad you are feeling so much better. But, I am also very sad that you are leaving. Maybe it will not be long before they have the train service between here and Macon running again. Then I can come and see you as often as possible."

"I would like that, dear. I must admit that I am dreading the long ride home. But, I sure will be glad to see your Father. I have missed him so much, and I know he has been concerned about me. What a joy it has been to visit with you for a while, my child."

"She reached over, patted Martha's hand and said, "Martha has become a dear friend, as she and Lisa took such good care of me when I was ill. I shall miss all of that pampering! Oh, speaking of Lisa, she said to tell you she was disappointed she could not come with us this morning. As you know she is working as a nurse now at Chimborazo Hospital, and had to be there this morning."

"I am so glad she has that job now. She is such a good nurse, and I so much appreciate her helping you recover so well, Mother."

"If you ask me, Lisa is much more than a nurse. She is more capable than any doctor I have ever known. Are you aware that several days a week the people from her little church come by for her to tend their medical needs. She seems overjoyed to help them. Now that she is working at the hospital during the day, she takes care of her neighbors in the evenings after she gets back from Richmond."

"No, I did not know that, but I am not surprised. When I have been over there to see you, while you were sick, I noticed that Martha often came to get her. But, I never gave it much thought."

Martha spoke up and said, "Lisa did not want you to be bothered by it all, ma'am. So, she has kept her work a private matter. You may not know that Lisa has moved out of Mr. Callahan's home, now that your mother has gone. She did not think it proper for her to be living there now. Moses still takes her to the hospital every morning, and brings Samuel to us to be tutored during the day. We see her each day when Moses brings her after work to get Samuel."

"Lisa has changed so much. It is hard to believe she is the same girl I met years ago, when she first came with Laura Layne to Oaklayne for a visit. She has become such a loving and giving woman, with a servant's heart. What a joy she is to know, " said Sara Ella.

The unmistakable sound of a big wagon arriving interrupted the pleasant conversation and brought all the ladies to their feet. As they stepped through the door onto the porch, they could see Wesley helping Cora down.

Sara Ella called out, "Hello, little brother! That is quite a rig you brought with you. Somebody might think you are planning a long journey with precious cargo."

Wesley smiled warmly, as Cora set her feet on the ground, and said, "Yes, that is exactly what we have planned. Mama, Cora has this prairie schooner rigged up for a queen inside. You should be quite comfortable on the trip."

"Please come inside everyone. Emma Lou will have supper ready before long. I am so sorry Adam could not be here to see you and Cora, Wesley. He had to leave town on urgent business. He did make a trip to the Callahan Plantation to say good-bye to Mother before he left. But, he had no choice but to be away when you arrived."

"Well," Wesley said, "If it is okay with you Mama, Cora and I would like to go ahead and begin our journey right away. Cora has already packed us a delicious meal, so what do you say? Is it okay to take advantage of the remainder of today and make some progress toward getting back to Macon?"

Chadna Gary stood to her feet and said, "I am ready as I will ever be, Wesley." Then, reaching out to Sara Ella, she said, "I am going to miss you, Sweetheart. But, it will not be any easier to leave later than it is right now."

Knowing her mother was right, Sara Ella tearfully hugged them all one by one, as they climbed into the big wagon. Then she watched as they pulled out into the lane. She could not stop staring, wondering if she would ever see her mother alive again.

Martha touched her elbow and said, "I am sorry she has to leave, too. We have become great friends, your mother and I. She is a fine lady, and I will miss her very much."

Sara Ella turned to go back inside after Moses and Martha left in the Callahan buggy. But, out of the corner of her eye, she thought she saw the prairie schooner coming back down the lane. Fearful that something had gone wrong already, she hurried toward the road.

Before long, she realized it was not the same wagon at all. Beside the wagon was a young man on horseback, as well as a giant black man on a huge mule. Another young man was driving the wagon, with a black woman sitting in the seat beside him. She wondered who these people could be, and why they might be coming down her lane. Perhaps, they are lost and need some direction?

"Sara Ella, we made it!" said the young man on horseback, as he rode up beside her, bringing with him a cloud of dust. He was close enough now that she could see it was August. He tipped his hat to her, exposing his unruly hair, then began struggling to gain control of it again by hopefully trapping it under his hat. She assumed the young man driving the wagon must be Trevor.

"Oh, August! I'm so glad you're back! It took you so long, we were wondering if you had encountered some trouble along the way. Did you find any sign of Richard Moreland?"

"Yes, we did," August said, as Trevor greeted her from the wagon. "Come and see," he said as he dismounted and led her to the back of the wagon.

All of a sudden, there were people everywhere. Besides August and Trevor, there were two giggly children, a woman and the biggest man she had ever seen. He was even larger than Moses! Then, when she looked into the back of the wagon, there was another young man. The big man handed him a crutch and helped him from the wagon.

"So you are Sara Ella. No wonder Adam was swooning over you when we were in Andersonville together," said Richard Moreland.

Sara Ella's mouth dropped open as she gasped, "Richard?"

"At your service, ma'am."

"Oh, Richard! Adam is going to be so pleased you are here, and you are okay."

"I cannot wait to thank him for sending these men after me," said Richard. "Without their help, I might not have made it. I know for sure I would not be doing as well as I am. I am lucky to have not lost more than my leg."

"I am so sorry, Richard," said Sara Ella. "Adam is not here right now. He had to go to Charleston on urgent business, but he will be back soon. And, I am sure he is going to be very excited to see you!" Turning to August and Trevor, Sara Ella continued, "Now, please introduce me to these people traveling with you."

August reached up, put his hand on Ezra's shoulder and said, "This giant of a man is Ezra, ma'am." Ezra tipped his hat and gave her a warm smile. "And, this lovely lady is his wife, Rachel, and this is their two children, Zeke and Dorothy.

"Welcome! Welcome all of you," said Sara Ella. "Trevor, if you and Ezra want to unhitch the horses from that wagon and see to their care in the barn, we will have something ready for all of you to eat in the pavilion before long. Rachel, I will show you to a place where you can freshen up if you like. August, you can show Richard to a comfortable spot in the pavilion where he can rest a spell. I am sure you would all enjoy a refreshing glass of lemonade, so I will have some brought to you right away. I cannot wait to tell Oscar you are back, boys! He was starting to get worried about you."

Sara Ella did not finish getting the words out of her mouth before Oscar took off running toward the pavilion to greet his men. By that time, Trevor and Ezra were finished tending to the horses, so he found both Trevor and August together, drinking lemonade with Richard. They were obviously pleased to see each other again, shaking hands vigorously and slapping each other on the back, as men often do as a masculine show of affection.

Then Oscar sat down next to Richard and said, "Adam is going to be so pleased to see you, Richard. He insisted on finding you himself after the war was over, but he was called to Washington City on a matter of national security. So, he agreed to let me send these two no-account kids to look for you, since they were not much use for anything else," he said sarcastically, grinning at August and Trevor. "I knew if you could be found, these two would find you. And once found, they would be devoted to getting you back here safe and sound. Looks like they did not disappoint me."

"Thank you for sending them, sir. They went through a lot to bring me here, when they did not even know me. I will be indebted to them always." Then he turned to Ezra and said, "Oscar, I want you to meet Ezra. He must not be overlooked, as he had a lot to do with my rescue as well."

Oscar shook Ezra's hand warmly and asked him if he was looking for a job or planning to travel on. Ezra told him he wanted a job more than anything in the world, and it did not matter where, as long as it was legal and would help him take care of his family.

"Well, we could certainly use you here at Oaklayne. In fact, I know of something I could use your help with in the big house right now, before Nathaniel steals you from me to work in the sawmill. We have run out of space around here to house any more people, so accommodations for your family could pose a problem just now. But, if you can make do living in your wagon for a short time, you should be able to find a place to live with the salary you will be receiving from working here. I will check with Emma Lou to see if she has work your wife can do, as well, if you are interested."

Of course, Ezra and his family were beside themselves with excitement. Living in the wagon for a while was no problem for them, considering the living conditions they had endured in the past.

After she finished helping clean up after supper, Elsie sat down next to Oscar. He was still sitting at the table where he had eaten his supper. He had a blank look on his face, like he was in a different world. She broke the spell when she asked, "What is on your mind? You look like you are a million miles away."

Oscar smiled and said, "Elsie, you should have seen that big man pick up one end of a 10x12 oak beam and move it like it was nothing. You know, the beams we are using to support the roof joists of that last section of roof we are working on? I tell you, he picked it up like it was a mere 2x4. I have never seen anything like it. I figured we would have to hoist those beams up there using an ox and some tackle. That would have been quite an ordeal, and time consuming. And, he has such a gentle spirit. Just look at him over there, playing with his children. His wife obviously loves him dearly. They look like such a happy family. Yes, Ezra is quite a blessing. I guess I am envious of him. I hope I will have that kind of joy in my life someday."

Elsie put her hand gently over Oscar's hand and spoke tenderly when she said, "It will happen for you Oscar, I am sure of it. Any woman would be crazy if she hesitated to have a man like you for her husband and the father of her children. You deserve to have a happy family, and I know you will someday."

Oscar was shocked by Elsie's response. Does she really mean that? Could she actually care about my happiness? It seems like I always say and do the wrong thing when I am around her. How could she think of me as anything but a bumbling buffoon? She is looking at me...what should I say? I would love to tell her how I feel, but what if...?

Then, despite his reservations, Oscar blurted out, "Do you really mean that? I mean...I mean...I thought you did not like me..."

"Why in the world would you think I do not like you, Oscar Baynes? That is just silly."

"Well...let me see. There was the first time we met, when I made fun of you, and you got angry enough at me to spit nails. Then, there was the time you fell in my lap, causing everyone to question my principles and yours. And, when we were attacked on the road, you thought I was treating you like a child. Also, every time I come near the kitchen you drop things and get angry because I am there. Need I go on, or are you convinced?"

Elsie pulled back in amazement, wondering how this man could so completely misunderstand her, then asked, "Well, if that is what you thought, why did you keep coming back for coffee early every morning? Did you want coffee badly enough to get it from someone who dislikes you so much? Or, were you coming to see me?"

"Well, I do like being around you...watching you...even if you are angry. I have tried to be nice to you, to show you how I feel...but I continually do everything wrong."

Elsie broke out in laughter, put her hand over her mouth and said, "Oscar, my dear Oscar...I have been so upset that you would think I am the clumsiest person in the world, because when you are around I lose complete control of myself. I drop things, fall over nothing and look like a fool. I get angry, because I want you to like me, not make fun of my awkwardness. That is why when you grabbed me up after the attack on the road, I thought you saw me as a helpless little girl."

"How could you have thought that? Without your quick thinking that day, we might not have gotten away from those thugs safely. I was so proud of you for what you did."

Elsie sat back down and folded her hands in her lap. "Well, the way you cradled me in your arms that day...and then the backdrop of me dropping those pots and pans every morning...I just did not think you took me very seriously."

"So, you were not intentionally trying to humiliate me that day when you fell in my lap?"

"Of course, not. Besides, I was a lot more humiliated than you were. I am supposed to be a lady, remember? No, I was just going to tickle your foot a little to wake you up, hoping we could visit awhile. But, then I tripped over your boot...you know the rest."

"Why did you trip over my boot?"

"Why do I drop things in the kitchen?"

"Oh, I see what you mean..."

"Honestly, I do not know why I become such a mess when you come around, Oscar. I really do so look forward to your visits every morning, but I feel like I mess them all up with my awkwardness. I am not usually that clumsy, really."

Oscar lost all of his inhibitions, grabbed Elsie's hands and pulled her into a warm embrace. Then, he looked longingly into her eyes for a lingering moment, before he began swinging her around and around, laughing with more joy than he had felt in years...and she laughed with him.

Chapter 44

Damage from the war in Charleston was not as heavy as Adam had seen in Richmond. As he rode down the streets of the city, he could see that some buildings were completely demolished, but others were only partially gone. Walls were caved in, roofs fallen into the interior of their buildings, some standing, but padlocked with CLOSED signs in the doors. He found that a few shops were open for business, however.

Adam stopped at several of the open markets to inquire as to the whereabouts of Matthew Wythe. People acknowledged knowing Mr. Wythe, but had not seen him around for quite some time. They could not confirm for sure whether or not the sea Captain had survived the war, was out to sea on his ship or even out of the country.

One man said, "I think his slaves are still living in his house down on the Battery. I know he left them there when he sailed out to sea, just before the Yankees took Charleston. You might find them there, and they may know of his whereabouts. The Wythe house is the third house from the point on East Battery Street in the Battery District, down on the harbor."

Adam thanked the man and turned to leave, but he stopped short when the man spoke again. "You know, Matthew Wythe's ship, the Phantom II, sailed out the night the Union Army reached Charleston. I don't think anyone has heard from him since. He may have been sunk outside Charleston that night. Anyway, I hope you have luck finding him."

Adam tipped his hat, but made no reply, as he walked out the door.

East Battery Street, third house north of the point, Adam said to himself. That should be easy enough to find.

The weather was dry and pleasantly warm, with a light sea breeze, as Adam rode down the street looking for a hotel with a dining room. He located the livery stable first, where his mount could be cared for while he was in town. Then he arranged for a room at a nearby hotel for himself. He paid for one night, with the option to stay another night if it became necessary.

Hungry and tired from a hard day in the saddle, Adam made his way to the dining room. He sat at a table near the window, where he could pass the time, watching traffic and pedestrians. A young black man came to the table, dressed in a white shirt and black pants. He was wearing white gloves and carried a white towel over his arm.

"Good evening, sir," the young man said with a Southern drawl. "We are serving your choice of baked chicken, roast beef, an'..."

Adam raised his hand to interrupt the young man and said with a smile, "You can stop right there...I will have roast beef with all the usual trimmings, son. I am hungry, and accustomed to meals that are well prepared and bountiful. I hope your food is as good as your service appears to be."

The young man grinned and answered, "Trimmings are a little scarce in these parts, sir. But, we do what we can to please. I do not think anyone has gone away hungry before."

"I understand. Do you have some corn bread?" Adam asked, smiling back at the young man.

"Yes, sir. I will bring you some corn bread and some coffee, right away."

"That would be wonderful," Adam said, as the young man left the table.

It was early evening, so there were not many other people seated at the tables. Adam looked around, wondering if one of them might be Matthew Wythe.

When the young man returned to pour his coffee, Adam asked, "I am in town looking for Matthew Wythe. Do you see him here this evening?"

"Mr. Wythe?" the young man asked, looking the room over. "No, I do not see him here. Do you know Matthew Wythe, sir?"

"Well no, I do not actually know him," Adam answered, "But, I have an important business proposition to offer him. Do you know if he is in the city?"

The young man shook his head. "Captain Wythe used to eat here some before the war, but I have not seen them since the war ended, sir. His place is nearby on the Battery, so you can see for yourself if he is there. The house may have been destroyed by cannon fire, I do not know. I have no reason to go to the Battery. My home is the other direction."

The young man walked toward the kitchen and soon returned with Adam's meal. He set the plate before him and poured another cup of coffee, making no further comment.

The following morning, Adam set out on foot in hopes of finding Matthew Wythe. He started toward the Battery District, looking for Captain Wythe's home address. He found that most of the houses on East Battery Street had been heavily damaged by gunfire, and the third house from the point was no different. It had suffered serious damage, also. There were some broken windows and apparently a hole in the roof, but the walls were still standing.

Adam made his way to the front door of the house on the sloping walkway. The yard was densely shaded by several live oak trees that remained undamaged,. He knocked boldly and waited. There was no answer. He knocked again, a little louder—silence. He knocked on the door a third time, waited a few moments, then knocked more forcefully. The door opened just a crack, and a black face looked out at him from inside. He was not sure whether it was a man or a woman on the other side of the door.

"Is this the Wythe residence?" he asked. "If it is, I need to speak with Captain Wythe. I have urgent business to conduct with him."

The door opened a bit further, so he could tell that it was a woman who had answered the door.

"Yes, sir, this is the Wythe residence, but Mr. Wythe is not here."

"Do you know when he will return, or how I may contact him?" Adam asked. "It is urgent that I speak with him."

"Don' rightly know, Sah. We been 'spectin' him any day now. He been in England, ever since that white man's war ended."

"Is his wife here? Perhaps I can talk with her?"

"No, Sah. Miss Laura, she went wit' him when he lef' here, just as the Yankees was comin' in."

Adam removed his hat and said, "Excuse me, I should have introduced myself. I am Adam Layne from Virginia. And you are…?"

"Ah's Nelly, the housekeeper. Ah sho' will be happy when Cap'n Wythe get back here."

"Are you staying here alone, Nelly?" Adam asked.

"Lawsy mercy, no," she replied, cupping her face in her hands. "Lija, Cap'n Matt's firs' mate, stays here wit' me. We two been wit' the Cap'n for years an' years. He very good to us."

"Is Elijah here so I can talk with him?"

She shook her head emphatically, "No, sir, he on a clean-up crew fer the city. He makes money to buy food fo' us. He'll not be back here 'til dark, Sah."

"Would it be okay with you, Nelly, if I return this evening to talk with him?" Adam asked.

"We don' answer the do' afta' dark, Sah. But, if'n yo' will knock, then wait a bit an' knock twice, we'll know it is you and 'Lije will open the do'."

"Okay, Nelly. I will see you about sundown." Adam turned and walked away.

That evening, Adam returned to Matthew Wythe's home and knocked according to Nelly's instructions. He was surprised when Nelly opened the door.

"Evenin', Mr. Layne," she said. "I'm sorry, 'Lija hasn't arrived yet. Please come in, so's I can shut 'de do' an' lock it."

Adam entered a beautifully maintained room that was elegantly furnished. There was an intricately carved walnut organ in the corner and expensive looking artwork on the walls. The seating was overstuffed with well-made tables that were adorned with china or glass vases that were full to overflowing with fresh flowers.

"Please sit down, Sah. Have yo' eaten this evenin'?" she asked kindly.

"I am not hungry, Nelly. But, thank you so much for asking. I sure would enjoy a cup of coffee, though, if you have some."

"Don' have no coffee, sah, but I can brew some tea. Would that be okay?"

Before Adam could answer, they heard a key in the front door latch, and a small black man entered.

"I see that we have company, Nelly." The man turned to Adam and continued, "I'm 'Lija. I work with Cap'n Wythe. May I help you with something, Sah?"

"Good evening, Elijah," Adam said, "I am pleased to make your acquaintance. My name is Adam Layne from a plantation near Richmond. I believe you met my father, Senator Mason Layne, during the war. I am here to talk with Mr. Wythe about making a trip to England for me. I am in the process of rebuilding the mansion on our plantation, and I need some materials and furnishings that cannot be found here in America."

Elijah reached out his hand to Adam with a wide grin on his face. "An' how is Senator Layne, now that the war is over?"

Adam hung his head, put his hands together and said, "He is dead, Elijah. He died on the operating table after being shot by a Union soldier. We miss him terribly."

Elijah nodded, and was quiet for a minute, shaking his head, not knowing what to say.

"Did Nelly tell you that we're expecting Cap'n Matt home in the next few days? We got one of them new transatlantic wires from him, telling us he would be making a delivery in Wilmington Harbor on his way here. A few days ago, he sent a telegram that they'd arrived on schedule in North Carolina. Cap'n Matt will want to get home as soon as possible, so I am sure he will be here real soon."

"Yes Elijah, she did. We've been passing the time, waiting for you to arrive. I was about to ask her to tell me a little about Matthew Wythe, when you came through the door."

"Well then, I will let y'all visit while I go upstairs to get washed up from the dirty work I've been doing today, helping to clean up the city," then he turned and started up the stairs.

After Elijah was gone, Nelly sat down in a rocking chair close to Adam and asked, "What do you want to know about Cap'n Wythe?" Then she proceeded to tell him how wonderful Matthew Wythe had always been to her and Elijah. When he escaped as the Yankees were coming, he told them they could stay in his home as long as they were comfortable doing so, even if he was never able to return himself. She lowered the tone of her voice, repeating his words to them in a very dignified way.

"Cap'n Matt, he always come back…cain't no Yankees get him, no Sah!" and she laughed as she rocked back and forth in her rocker.

Adam smiled at her candor and asked, "Is he married? I believe you said earlier today that Mrs. Wythe went with him when he left?"

"Well, Miss Laura's not his wife. She been livin' here for some time, an' Ah 'spects they got married in England when they got there. They sho' do love each other, that's fo' sho'."

At the mention of Laura's name, Adam's heart was pricked. He wondered afresh what had happened to his little sister Laura who disappeared during the war and had not been heard from since.

When Elijah came back downstairs, he asked Nelly if he could have a cup of her good tea. She jumped to her feet, put both hands over her mouth and announced that she had forgotten all about the tea, obviously embarrassed. She turned and went quickly into the kitchen, mumbling to herself under her breath.

Adam stood, ready to leave. "Please thank Nelly for me, Elijah. I need to check on my horse at the livery on my way back to the hotel, so I had better get on my way. I enjoyed visiting with you both.

"If you are sure Captain Wythe will be here soon, I will stay in town and wait for him to return. I sure need to find someone to make a trip to Europe for me right away. If he does not want to do it, I am hoping he can suggest someone I can trust to do the job for me."

Elijah assured Adam again that Matthew Wythe would be arriving very soon. "Bad weather could slow him down a little, but Captain Wythe knows the sea well, and he always keeps his word." Elijah was sure that Matthew Wythe would be a good resource for Adam, one way or another.

Nelly came back with tea cups on a tray with cookies and encouraged Adam to stay with her and Elijah until the Captain returns. She promised not to forget to fix his meals, looking down at her feet, ashamed about forgetting his tea earlier.

"Thank you both. I will stay tonight in my hotel room, since I have already paid for it. But I will come back in the morning to wait for Captain Wythe. If you will allow me to do so Nelly, I would be glad to take you to the market tomorrow and purchase some foodstuffs for all of us to eat while I am here. Elijah promised me that you are a good cook, and I intend to see if the man can be trusted."

Adam grinned and shook Elijah's hand, bowing low to Nelly on his way out the door.

Adam was getting restless, waiting for Matthew Wythe to arrive in Charleston Harbor. He often found himself walking the streets of the Battery, wishing he was back at Oaklayne with Sara Ella. This was the first time they had been separated since they were married. He was beginning to wonder if he should try to come up with another way to solve his problem. He was enjoying the hospitality of Elijah and Nelly, but did not like having to wait.

Adam arrived back at the Wythe house to find Elijah standing at the front window, looking intently at the horizon. Adam walked up beside him to see what he could see. There were several boats in the Charleston Harbor, heading up the river toward the docks to unload their cargo.

Elijah broke the silence when he said, "I still don't see the Phantom II, Sah." He did not turn to look at Adam, but kept his eyes on the horizon.

"Well, maybe this will be the day, Elijah. I sure hope so...," Adam said. "I think I will walk down to the harbor, and see what I can find out. Maybe someone down there knows something. I will be back soon." He turned and went out the door.

Down at Charleston Harbor, Adam talked with several men who were idly watching the boats going up and down the harbor to and from the mouth of the Cooper River. He walked along, inquiring if anyone knew anything about the Phantom II and Captain Matthew Wythe.

They all seemed to know about Captain Wythe, especially about his blockade running during the war, but no one had any information about when or if he would be returning to Charleston.

When Adam returned to the house, Elijah was still patiently watching for the Phantom II at the window. Suddenly, he jerked his head up and turned to Adam.

"Look! I think that's the Phantom II out there in the harbor." Now Elijah was pointing excitedly. "I would know that ship anywhere. Let's go down and meet her Adam." By the time he had completed the sentence, he was at the door, holding it open for Adam to join him. Calling out to Nelly he said, "Nelly, the Phantom II is coming in! We have gone to greet her." Adam and Elijah ran out the door, Elijah pulling the door shut and locking it behind them.

Elijah hurriedly led the way northward on foot down East Battery Street and on toward the wharf area where ships docked in the harbor to unload their cargo. It was quite a distance to go on foot in a hurry, but Elijah did not seem to notice, setting a quick pace on the road. Adam had already made this trip earlier, but that was at a leisurely pace. His bad leg started to bother him and then began to hurt quite a lot. He was limping badly now, but did not want to stop and rest.

As they drew nearer to the wharf where the Phantom II was coming in, Adam asked Elijah, "How do you know that's the Phantom II, Elijah? The name is not painted on it, and it looks just like all the others to me."

"She looks like that because of her blockade running, Sah. It kept her and the Cap'n safer that way. I am sure Mr. Matt will paint her name back on her again now. I would know her anywhere!"

Adam was out of breath as they stood watching. His leg was really aching. The deck hands jumped over the side to tie up the ship. They looked like a colony of ants, busily doing their duty in a most organized manner. Adam was impressed.

Then he saw a young woman standing at the railing of the ship. He thought to himself, *She must be the queen ant, watching the worker ants carry out their duties.* Her long auburn hair was blowing in the wind, hiding her face from Adam. He could see that she was dressed in trousers and a jacket, but there was no mistaking that she was a woman.

As Adam waited with Elijah, before long they heard someone yell, "'Lije! Is that you?"

Immediately, Elijah started running toward the place where they were already lowering the gangplank. "Cap'n! Cap'n Matt! It is so good to have you back home!"

Obviously, the man was the long awaited Matthew Wythe. Adam did not want to interfere with the joyous reunion that was unfolding before him. So he held back a bit, allowing Elijah some time to greet Matt. The young woman started running down the gangplank past Elijah and toward him.

Adam did not know what to think, when the young woman called out his name! "Adam! Oh, Adam, what are you doing here? I thought I would never see you again!"

Suddenly, he recognized his little sister, Laura, and waved frantically. He forgot all about his sore leg and ran toward her as fast as he could. "Laura! Laura!"

They both had tears running down their cheeks when they finally embraced. Adam picked her up like he did when she was a little girl and spun her around like a rag doll.

Matthew stood aside, watching as the brother and sister recognized each other and then with complete abandon, expressed their sheer delight in the unexpected reunion. Laughing and weeping with joy, they both completely forgot the rest of the world.

They both talked at once, as Laura asked questions about her other family members and Adam asked what had happened to her and where she had been all this time.

Matthew finally interrupted and asked, with a grin, "My dear, I assume you know this gentleman?"

"Oh, Matt, this is my brother, Adam Layne! I have not seen Adam since the beginning of the war." She looked at Adam and asked, "What are you doing here, Adam? Oh, how I have missed you and the family. You will have to tell me about everyone."

"I am pleased to meet you, Adam," said Matt. "My name is Matthew Wythe, and I am the Captain of this vessel. I am sure you understand when I say that I am NOT the captain of this young lady who is my wife." Matt chortled, then turned and embraced Laura warmly.

"Wife? It sounds like you have a lot to tell me as well, little sister!"

Laura put her arm around Matt and said, "If it were not for Matt rescuing me, I would not be here today, Adam. When Mother sent me back here from Oaklayne, Ham never returned. I was alone and destitute. I did not know what to do. God sent Matt to rescue a damsel in distress. I never saw Ham again, and finally learned he had been killed while on assignment for the newspaper. The rest is a long story, how we escaped the Yankees together and were married in England."

Matt looked over his shoulder at the Phantom II and said, "Let me put my ship to rest, so my men can go home for a well-deserved chance to be reunited with their families. We have been gone for a very long time.

"You go on to the house, Laura, and take Adam with you. The two of you can get reacquainted, then he and I can have some time to talk later.

"Lija, can you arrange to get our luggage taken home, please? I shall follow soon." He put his arms around Laura and whispered in her ear, "I love you, Laura. Thank you for marrying me."

Laura leaned in to whisper in Matt's ear, "And I love you, too, Matthew." Then she said openly, "You cannot know how happy it makes me to have my husband and my brother meet. Hurry to the house, so we can all get acquainted. We have a lot to tell Adam about our experiences during the war."

Laura and Adam walked slowly, arm in arm, toward the house. Finally, Laura asked, "Adam, please tell me, how is everyone at Oaklayne?"

"Well, I have some sad and some funny things to tell you, Laura. But, first, I want to know what happened to you after you left Oaklayne? I know about Mother sending you back to Charleston to stay with Ham. But then you disappeared, and we could not find you."

"Did Mother tell you that I left Ham and went back to Oaklayne, because he left me alone on our honeymoon to watch the shelling of Ft. Sumter for his newspaper? You knew he worked for the New York Times, right?"

Adam nodded and, with a wide grin, added, "Yes, and I also know that Mother did not think you were justified in leaving your new husband, just because he ignored you on your honeymoon night."

"Exactly! Mother did not understand at all. She told me I could not come back to the plantation unless Ham was with me." It was clear that Laura was still angry about her Mother's lack of understanding. "But before I got back to Charleston, Ham had already gone on another assignment for the newspaper. He was following the Army, they said, and could not be located. I was alone in Charleston and did not know what to do. I did not have any money or a way to take care of myself. Matthew Wythe took pity on me and allowed me to stay in his house, while he was gone making trips back and forth to Europe in the Phantom II.

"Later, I found out that Ham was killed in the war. I just stayed on here in Charleston with Matt. When the Yankees were converging on Charleston, Matt and I left Elijah and Nelly here and went to Europe. Matt needed to keep the Phantom II out of the clutches of the Union Navy, and we are just now finally returning to America.

"So, that is my story in a nutshell. Now, please tell me about Mother and Papa and everyone else at Oaklayne. I miss everyone so much!"

Adam knew that what he had to tell Laura would hit her very hard, so he stopped along the road and took both of her hands in his. Then he briefly told her about the deaths of her parents, her brother Goddard and his four-year-old son, Randy's blindness and his own near death experience in Andersonville Prison. He saved the news of the destruction of Oaklayne to share with her later, after she had time to deal with the loss of so many family members.

Laura sobbed uncontrollably as Adam continued to share one disaster in the family after another.

"Oh, Adam, we were such a happy family before that awful war started. Did Sara Ella ever come back to you, after that disastrous Christmas break up?"

Adam smiled and said, "Actually, it was Sara Ella who rescued me from Andersonville Prison, and brought me back to Oaklayne. We were recently married in Washington City. Oh, how we missed you and the other family members who were not there on our wedding day. We did not know if you were alive or dead."

Adam continued, "I should tell you that Oaklayne was demolished by mortar fire near the end of the war. We are currently working hard to rebuild it to its former glory, which is why I came to see Matt. Almost all the slaves are gone. Only Tom, Nathaniel and Emma Lou remain, and a very few of the others.

"Oh, I almost forgot! You will find this interesting, Lisa came to Oaklayne after Goddard and Little Goddard's deaths. You will never believe her story."

Laura was pleased to hear that her friend Lisa was still alive, but concerned about her at the same time. "Lisa? What else happened to Lisa? I would think that having her son and her husband die would be about all she could take."

Walking along down the streets of Charleston in the shade of the moss covered live oak trees, Adam shared Lisa's heartbreaking story with Laura, including the part about Angela. Laura cried, mourning the losses her friend Lisa had suffered in the years since they had seen each other.

Then Adam smiled and said, "But, you will be pleased to know that Lisa has adopted an orphan boy named Samuel who is about the same age that Little Goddard would be if he had lived. They are both very happy to have each other. She can fill you in some more when we get back to Oaklayne. You are going back to Oaklayne with me to see everyone, are you not?"

Laura looked off in the distance, wiped away a tear and said, "Well, our Mother would remind me that my place is with my husband, which I believe it is. Matt made lovely accommodations for me aboard the ship so that I can accompany him in comfort wherever he sails. If he agrees to make this voyage for you, I will need to go with him. But, we can see everyone when we deliver your cargo. I would really like that."

Adam held Laura's hand like he did when she was a child, as they walked slowly together to her home on the Battery. Nelly was waiting on the front veranda, where she wrapped Laura in her arms and welcomed her home. Nelly was concerned for Laura's obvious emotional state of mind, so Adam explained the situation.

"Ah's so sorry, Miss Laura. Ah'll fix yo' some tea right away. Maybe that will help yo, dear."

Laura thanked Nelly and turned back to Adam. She encouraged Adam to sit beside her on the couch and tell her what he needed Matt to do for him. They discussed the work on the plantation, while they waited for Matt to arrive.

Matt shook Adam's proffered hand after he had finished greeting a very excited Nelly. "Adam, how is your father. I am sure you know that I delivered a load of tobacco to England for him during the war and brought back food to feed his people."

Adam responded, "Well, that is some of the bad news I shared with Laura already. Both of our parents died during the war. She will want to tell you the rest of the news of our family herself, I am sure."

"I am so sorry for your loss, Adam...and you my dear...," as he hugged Laura tenderly. "I am sure this was quite a blow to you both."

Adam cleared his throat of a huge lump and changed his tone to business. "The reason I am here is that I need someone I can trust to make a trip to Europe for me. I am trying to rebuild our plantation home after it was demolished in the war. I need building materials and furnishings that cannot be obtained here in the states. Is it too soon after arriving back here to ask you to make that journey for me?"

Matt put his hand on Adam's shoulder and said, "That is my business, Adam. The Phantom II does not do very well, sitting in a harbor not being used. Of course, I can make the trip for you. I did not see a lot of folks waiting in line for my services when I pulled in to Charleston Harbor. Shall we go to my desk and make a list of what you need?"

Adam pulled a folded piece of paper from his pocket and said, "No need to do that. The list is already made, and I have a copy for you right here. We can go over it whenever you are ready. I would like for

Laura to be there too, if you do not mind, because I will need her to shop for furnishings as similar as possible to what she remembers was in our family home before the destruction. I can tell her what few pieces survived without too much damage and are still usable."

"Fine, we can just talk family this evening and get acquainted, then we can sit at my desk tomorrow and go over your list. Or, are you in a great hurry?"

"Oh, not a great hurry, Matt. The things I need have to do with the final finishing work, and we will not start on that right away. We hope to have the outside brick walls erected and timber on the roof this winter. We will try to finish the inside walls late this winter into spring, and finish the trim parts of the exterior walls. So, as you can see, we are not desperate just yet. But, I know the voyage will take you some time each way, and you will need time to procure what we need when you are there. So, we clearly needed to get you on your schedule."

"Sounds like we can do some business, Adam. It will be a long way around for Laura to get back to her childhood home, but I will get her there eventually. And maybe we can stay long enough for her to be anxious to come back here, now that this is her home. Now, both of you tell me more about Oaklayne and your family," then, he whispered, "especially some stories about my sweet Laura's childhood." That brought laughter from Matt, Adam, Nelly, Elijah and even Laura.

They talked until bed time, planning to arise early enough in the morning. They wanted to take care of business, so Matt could start planning the voyage to Europe before too many days passed. And Adam was anxious to return home to Sara Ella in Virginia

Chapter 45

The warm sunshine felt good on Sara Ella's face that morning, as she sat on the porch in front of the temporary house. Many of the ornamental trees in the yard were beginning to turn color, announcing that fall had arrived in Virginia. She looked down the lane of stately live oaks that had remarkably survived the awful damage the plantation sustained from mortar and gunfire during the recent war. With the limbs removed that had been broken off, she could see through the trees almost as far as the pike. Hearing a buggy coming toward the house, she stood and watched as the driver finally came to a halt in front of the house.

"Good afternoon, ma'am," the man said, as he smiled broadly and tipped his hat to her. She could not help but notice that the man was impeccably dressed in a finely tailored suit. But, she was immediately very uncomfortable, because he looked her up and down like a man would a lady of the night he ran across in a saloon.

Guardedly, Sara Ella asked, "May I help you, sir?"

"Yes, ma'am. I am looking for Adam Layne. Is he here?" asked the man.

Sara Ella was afraid to give any information to this stranger, so she simply answered, "I am sorry, Mr. Layne is not available at the moment. Perhaps, I could pass along a message for you if you would like to tell me what this is about? Mr. Layne can get back with you accordingly when he has time." She hoped the man would just leave and not come back.

Just then, Nathaniel came around the corner of the house carrying his hunting rifle, a good sized white tail deer over his shoulder. Unsure of the stranger's intentions, Nathaniel said nothing, but dropped the deer to the ground and walked over to stand beside Sara Ella. It was clear to Nathaniel that Sara Ella was uneasy about this unexpected intruder.

"I just want to talk to Mr. Layne about buying that property he is clearing over to the side of the plantation." The man looked at

Nathaniel with disgust, and said, "I am sure you know that it is against the law for that black man to have a rifle..."

Interrupting the man's comment about Nathaniel, Sara Ella said firmly, "None of our property is for sale, so there is no need for you to talk with my husband." She stopped momentarily, then continued, "What business do you have looking around here, anyway? This is private property, and it is NOT for sale."

"Oh, I think I could persuade Mr. Layne to listen to my most generous proposition," he answered, his voice becoming louder and more firm.

Nathaniel repositioned the rifle and spoke up, "I think you heard the lady, Mister. This property is not for sale – no part of it. Now, turn your buggy around and leave our plantation."

Sara Ella was shocked that Nathaniel spoke so clearly, without any hint of his usual dialect. But, she resisted the urge to look at him. They both stood their ground, shoulder to shoulder.

Looking down his nose at Nathaniel, the man responded, "I was talking to the lady, so I suggest you mind your own business. Again, what are you doing with that rifle? I thought you people were not supposed to handle guns. It is illegal for emancipated Negroes to carry a fire arm, I am sure of it."

"You heard me," Nathaniel said loudly, ignoring the man's comment and pointed the rifle directly towards him. "Go on, now. Git on out of here, RIGHT NOW."

"You tell Mr. Layne that I will be back, and I will bring some help with me next time."

Nathaniel raised the rifle and said again, "Go!"

As the trespasser hurriedly turned the buggy around and went back out the drive to the pike, Sara Ella realized she was trembling. Not sure if her shaking was from fear or anger, she turned to Nathaniel and said, "Thank goodness you showed up when you did, Nathaniel. I do not know what I would have done, if that man had gotten rough with me. I think he is one of those carpetbagger people from up North we have been hearing about. I have not seen one of them before, but the way he was dressed told me he is not a regular working man.

"When do you suppose Adam will return home? That man scared me more than I like to admit, Nathaniel. With all of you men out working every day, how can we ladies be safe here during the day? What will I do if he comes back and you are not here?"

Nathaniel put his big arm around Sara Ella's shoulders and said, "Don't worry, Missy. We won't leave you ladies alone. We will station men with guns here every day until Mr. Adam gets back." His deep voice was very solemn and reassuring. "I'll talk with Oscar and Tom right away, and we'll decide on a schedule of men to protect you while we are away from here during the day."

Nathaniel turned and headed back toward the mill, forgetting all about the deer he shot that morning. Sara Ella went inside to get help carrying the venison to a table where it could be skinned and then hung up for the blood to drain before it would be butchered.

In just a few minutes, one of the hired workers who had proven himself to be reliable and honest working with Nathaniel at the sawmill, came trotting toward the house carrying a rifle.

He walked boldly up to Sara Ella and declared, "Ms. Sara Ella, Nathaniel sent me to stay with you 'til him and Tom get here this evening. I'll keep you safe, Ma'am. I'll be sittin' right here at the front door...yes sir, I'll stay right here...," and he sat down on the ground near the door.

"Thank you, so much. That will be a relief for me. Your name is Isaac, isn't it?"

"Yes, Ma'am, but my fam'ly calls me Ike," and he grinned, ear to ear.

"I'm glad you have a rifle with you, Isaac. It might be hard to get a man like that one this morning to leave without something to persuade him."

He nodded and said, "Thank you, ma'am."

That evening after supper Tom and Oscar discussed the situation with Nathaniel. Tom sat back in his chair and said firmly. "I want to stay here with Sara Ella and the ladies during the day until Adam gets back. He left me in charge, and I think that is what he would want me to do. I am sure that Sara Ella can find plenty for me to do around here, so my time won't be unproductive. I know that the pavilion needs to be closed in before winter, so I can work on that, if nothing else. I just think I need to be here. If you can spare him, I would like to keep Ike here as well, Nathaniel."

Nathaniel and Oscar were in complete agreement with Tom's plan.

The next morning, when Sara Ella went to the front door, Ike was already sitting there with the rifle across his lap. She was relieved to see him already guarding the house.

"Tom?" Sara Ella called back to the kitchen where Tom was getting a cup of coffee, "I thought you were going to be watching us girls? So, why is Ike out here?"

"Well, I thought it might be a good idea to have a couple of us watching out for you ladies during the day, not just me. I might be in the wrong place if I am the only one here. It is a serious matter when a man frightens a lady, so I want to make sure you feel safe," Tom said.

Midafternoon, Sara Ella recognized Adam's voice out front asking, "Ike, what are you doing sitting here? Are you not supposed to be working? Are you hurt or sick?"

Ike responded, "No, I'm just fine, sir. I'm here guardin' Ms. Sara Ella and the ladies."

"Guarding? Guarding from what?" Adam asked as he dismounted from his horse.

Sara Ella flew through the front door and wrapped herself around Adam, saying, "I am so glad you are home! As you can see, we had some trouble here yesterday from a carpetbagger! Nathaniel had Ike come to guard all of us ladies, and Tom has insisted on being by my side every moment since..." she said catching her breath. "I expect that man to come back, so we will need to be prepared for it."

Adam turned to Tom and said, "I knew I could count on you, Tom. Thank you for staying with Sara Ella, it is obvious that man really upset her." Adam put his arms around her to comfort her.

Then, looking more closely at Ike, Adam was astonished and said, "Is that my rifle he is carrying?"

Tom quickly stepped up and explained, "As Proctor, I decided it was best for Nathaniel to keep his rifle with him at the sawmill, so I gave Ike that rifle from your gun collection to use protecting the ladies. I also distributed all of your remaining firearms to the other white men that I knew we could trust to help protect the plantation. Nathaniel and I are the only black men with guns. I did not want to put the other black men in a position where they would be breaking the law. I hope that is what you would have done if you had been here, Adam."

"That is exactly what I would have done, Tom." Adam reached out to retrieve his rifle from Ike and said, "You go back up to the mill for the rest of the day, Ike. I will be here now to look after the ladies. When I pay you this week, I will give you a little extra for your help here." With that, Isaac stood and started back to the mill.

"Now, my dear," as he turned to Sara Ella. "It is wonderful to be at home with you! I had a great trip," he paused, "And, you will never guess what I found when I located Captain Wythe!" He grinned a devilish grin, then said, "Shall we get a cup of coffee, and sit down? I have got some great news...you would not guess in a million years. Come on, let's go in the house, and get Emma Lou. She will be excited, too. I cannot wait to tell you all what I found. Tom you will also be amazed." Adam was so excited he could not talk in complete sentences.

"What? Adam, tell me!" Sara Ella picked up his excitement, her eyes sparkling with curiosity.

Adam grinned and shook his head, "Oh, no you don't! Not a word will cross my lips until I can sit down in a comfortable chair with that cup of coffee. Then, and only then will I tell you what I know." Then he squeezed her tightly, before picking her up and carrying her into the house. Elated to be together again, they both laughed heartily.

Emma Lou came in and greeted Adam warmly, promising him a hot cup of coffee to wash down the dust from the road. She joined them right away with the coffee pot and three cups on a tray, anxious to sit and listen to what Adam had to say about his trip to Charleston.

Adam removed his boots and sat down. Then he stretched and relaxed in the chair for a minute before beginning. Sara Ella, Tom and Emma Lou all sat on the edge of their seats, waiting to hear what he had to say.

He began, "Let's see...where should I begin?"

"Adam! Come on! Do not leave us in suspense any longer," Sara Ella begged.

"Well...when I got to Matthew Wythe's home, he was not there. I talked with Nelly and Elijah, former slaves of his who were living in his home on the Battery. They told me they had received a telegram from him that he was delivering some goods in Wilmington, North Carolina, and that he would be back to Charleston Harbor in a few days. So, I decided to just wait until he arrived." He stopped. He was having a great time, teasing them and making them wait for his surprise.

"So, I waited there and Matthew Wythe did come home after a few days, just like Elijah said he would. We...that is Elijah and I...like I told you, Elijah is a former slave who was living in Matt's house..."

"Adam!"

"Okay, okay...I am getting to the good part..." Adam put his right index finger up, tilted his head to the right and motioned for her to be patient and listen...then he continued, "When Elijah saw the Phantom II...that is the name of Captain Wythe's ship...when Elijah saw the ship coming in to the Charleston Harbor, we hurried to the wharf, so we would be there when he disembarked. I am telling you, by the time we got there, my bad leg was killing me!"

"Adam! Come on!"

"Oh, sorry...guess I got carried away..." He grinned, then continued, "Elijah and Nelly told me that he took a lady with him when he escaped South Carolina as the Yankees were approaching, but they did not say much about her beyond that."

He paused, took a drink of the coffee, and said, "Emma Lou, I had forgotten how good your coffee is. Most of the time in Charleston, I drank tea."

"Tea? But, you don't drink tea, Adam," remarked Emma Lou, still sitting on the edge of her seat.

Ignoring Emma Lou, Sara Ella poked Adam and said, "Adam Layne, if you do not tell me what this is all about immediately, I am going to dispose of every grain of coffee in this house! Now, clear up this mystery, right this very minute!"

He poked her back and said, pausing between each word for emphasis, "I...found...Laura...my...sister," he paused, "You remember Laura, do you not?"

Sara Ella gasped. "You found Laura? Our Laura? Where? How? Where has she been all this time?"

Tom jumped up out of his chair and with tears streaming down his face said, "Oh, Adam! I am so happy for you!"

At first, Emma Lou was guarded, wondering if Adam actually saw a ghost. But Adam assured her that Laura was no ghost. Then she squealed with delight that little Laura was alive and well.

"Laura will have a lot to tell you all when she comes here for a visit soon. She is now Mrs. Matthew Wythe." Adam went on to explain what had happened to Laura during the time she had been away, and told them that she would be going with her husband to England to procure what they need for Oaklayne. Then she will stay for a visit at Oaklayne when they make the delivery. "I really had a wonderful time with her, and I really like Matt. They sure love each other, and she is happy as can be."

"But Adam," Tom paused, "Why did your father not see Laura there when he hired Captain Wythe to take the cotton to England during the war? He was in Matthew Wythe's home, was he not? Did he not see Laura? I do not understand."

"Well, before they were married, Laura stayed hidden away from guests who came to Matt's home to avoid any embarrassing assumptions about her reason for being there. Under the circumstances, Matt arranged for Father to meet him in Wilmington. Had he known that Laura was his daughter, of course things would have been handled differently. It is a strange story, and Laura will tell you all about it when she gets here. I need to get this news to Lisa right away, too. She will be so excited to find out that Laura is alive and well."

"Lisa will be so surprised! I am so happy you found her, after all this time! And, I am even happier to have you home again. I have some news of my own to share with you. Perhaps, I should make you beg for it like you did us?"

Adam looked at her with a silly pouty expression saying, "You are much too sweet to put me through that, aren't you?"

"Well I do not know about that, but I have been about to burst, wanting to tell you what I know. That is one reason I was in such a hurry for you to tell me your news."

Adam sat forward in his chair now, anxious to hear what Sara Ella had to say, "So, tell me! I am not as patient as you are, you know."

Then she blurted out, "...Richard is here! He is so excited about seeing you that I am sure you will want to find him as soon as possible. They helped him get up to the sawmill to watch the operation there."

Adam was beside himself with joy at first, then he frowned and asked, "What do you mean, they helped him to the sawmill? Richard Moreland would not be watching unless...Oh, no...is he okay?"

"Adam, my love, all these questions are keeping you from him. You had better just go see for yourself. Richard is infectiously high in spirits and eternally grateful for the team you sent to rescue him. Now go!"

"I am on my way," Adam said, as he hurried to the door.

"Oh, before you go, is it okay with you if I send a message to Lisa by Brandon and Steven about Laura coming here? They go to the Callahan Plantation every evening to work on their cabins."

"That is a good idea, dear." said Adam.

"Okay, now go see Richard!"

As Adam arrived at the sawmill, the noise was deafening, as usual. Adam saw Richard and realized that he was missing a leg, before Richard knew he was there. Adam had to swallow hard and choke back tears, knowing that Richard's constant care for him in Andersonville Prison was the only reason he still had both of his legs...and his life, for that matter.

As Adam moved closer, Richard caught a glimpse of him and flashed a big smile in Adam's direction. Then he grabbed his crutch and hurried to meet his friend. The two men embraced and cried tears of joy, as the other men stopped what they were doing to watch their long awaited reunion.

Adam did the best he could to talk through his tears, "I wanted to go and find you myself, Richard. It was so hard to send someone else, but I felt I had no choice, under the circumstances our nation is facing. I hope you understand."

"Understand? I cannot tell you how grateful I am for the way I was rescued, Adam. I was near death, but August and Trevor found me. I do not know how, but they did. And they brought Doctor Ralph Fowler with them to help me get on my feet...well, you know what I mean. And, I cannot wait for you to meet Ezra and his family.

"I appreciate so much all that they and you have done for me, Adam. I cannot wait to tell you all about my trip here and all that I have learned along the way about life, family, love and how to survive insurmountable obstacles that are much bigger than losing my leg.

"Now, I cannot wait to get back home to Michigan. I left there as a self-centered boy, but now I can return as a man to help my family." Richard rambled on and on about what he had been through to be brought to Oaklayne.

Adam listened intently, wondering about so many of the things Richard said, but not wanting to interrupt the flow of his thoughts as he spoke so enthusiastically.

Adam said, "I am speechless, Richard. I am so sorry that I could not have gotten them there sooner."

Richard ignored Adam's comment and said, "I think losing this leg will be a nuisance, but I also think it will make me a bigger man than I would ever have been otherwise."

Adam was excited to see Richard, and they had a sweet reunion. But, all Richard could talk about was getting home to Michigan and his family. Adam encouraged him to stay, but understood his desire to return to his own family. So he reluctantly took him to the train station in Richmond. Adam paid his fare and gave him some money with which to help his family when he got there. Richard was hesitant to accept the money, but agreed when Adam reminded him that he owed it to his family to accept it.

"Richard, my family left me with plenty of money. Please accept this gift of my love for you and your family."

Both men embraced warmly, then Richard said, "Andersonville Prison is a strange place to begin a lifelong relationship with someone you will never forget. I will never forget you, Adam Layne." Then Richard turned and boarded the train.

Adam watched the train take Richard away, sadly wondering if he would ever see this remarkable man again.

Chapter 46

Samuel was absolutely enthralled with country living. He could not imagine why he had been so afraid to leave the city. Even more amazing was the fact that his beautiful new mother actually loved him. She had assured him time and again that she loved him from the first moment she laid eyes on him, though he knew not why. But, he would surely be forever grateful that she obviously cared so much about him.

His life had changed so much for him, since that day Lisa rescued him from the orphan train. Most of his life, he lived on the streets of New York City, stealing what he needed to survive and eating discarded, sometimes rotten food that would often make him sick. The Salvation Army helped him with warm clothes and an occasional meal. But most of the time he found things he could use in the trash and garbage cans in the alleys of the city. As he got older, he learned to pay attention to where people lived who had boys his age. Sometimes they would discard things that interested him, though he did not have a place to keep those treasures. Everything he tried to keep was inevitably stolen by one of the bigger kids on the street.

"Samuel, where are you?" Lisa called out to him from the porch, after she arrived home from her work day at the hospital.

He heard her voice and came running to tell her, "Mama, I am so glad you are here! But, we need to be real quiet, because Mr. Callahan is not feeling well today. I was reading to him like he asks me to do all the time, but he fell asleep. He has never done that before. And, then he asked me to bring him a coverlet from the drawing room, which did not make any sense, it being so hot today. You might need to help him, Mama."

Lisa hugged Samuel and said, "I am so pleased that you are so compassionate and notice when someone needs help, Son. I will do whatever I can to help Mr. Callahan feel better."

"He is a very special man, isn't he Mama?" Samuel said in a concerned tone of voice.

"Yes he sure is. Now, please go and see if Martha needs you to help her with supper in my place, while I check on Mr. Callahan."

Lisa was very concerned when she found Warren Callahan unconscious in the parlor, burning up with fever. A flush of fear caused her to tremble and feel faint, as she remembered the fever that took Little Goddard from her only a few years before. Knowing she must keep her composure if she was going to be able to help him, she gained control of her emotions and immediately called, "Samuel, Samuel, come quickly!"

Lisa took hold of Samuel by both arms, got down on one knee and looked him intently in the eyes. Keeping her voice as calm, but firm as possible, she said, "You must go find Moses, and tell him I need him NOW. Tell him that it is urgent. Please hurry, Samuel."

"But Mother..."

"There is no time for that now, Samuel. Just go."

As Samuel ran off, Martha came running into the room. What's the matter Lisa, can I help?"

"Oh, Martha. I am glad you are here. Warren is burning up with fever and unconscious. We must get him into a tub of cold water quickly. I sent Samuel to get Moses to carry him outside and help us lift him into a horse trough. Can you help me get his boots and shirt off?"

"I understand," Martha replied. Worried and not knowing what else to say, Martha added, "When he is feeling better, I will warm up some broth for him like you had me do for Mrs. Gary when she was sick."

Warren Callahan had not been feeling well for the past few days, but had not said anything, assuming that whatever was the matter was minor and would soon go away. Today he was much worse, and it had been a struggle for him, just to function. He had no energy, and his mind seemed fuzzy.

Lisa tended to Warren all night, monitoring the fever, which had now subsided somewhat. Occasionally, he would stir and attempt to smile when he saw her face, but then he would lose consciousness again.

As the night wore on, Lisa pondered how much she had grown to care for this man, who now lay dying before her. She had never known anyone like him. Lots of good men like Goddard and Adam Layne had crossed her path. But, Warren was different. He had a peace and joy about him that she had never seen before. At last, after working with damp rags all night, trying to keep his fever down, Lisa succumbed and fell asleep in a chair, with her head on the bed next to him.

As she began to stir from deep slumber, Lisa found herself praying, Thank you, Lord, for loving this wonderful man. If it is your will, please heal him....I feel your comforting hand on me, and your answer of love...Thank you..." Then, she was startled, as the hand that comforted her suddenly moved! It felt so real, so physical! Was it actually God's hand?

She reached up to embrace the hand, then slowly raised her head to see that Warren was awake and alert.

"Well, good morning sleepy head. How in the world did I get into this bed? I do not remember anything after Samuel was reading to me in the parlor. I do not remember last night at all. What has happened? Is Samuel okay?"

Lisa smiled and said, "Samuel is fine. As soon as I arrived home from work last night, he came running to tell me that you fell asleep while he was reading, and he could not wake you. We could not wake you either, so we dumped you in the horse trough and brought you to bed. That will teach you not to be bored by my son's reading!" She laughed with relief that Warren was feeling better.

"Boring? His reading is not boring! If that is the only explanation, then why are you here? Did you spend the night here with me? It seems like I remember seeing you?" asked Warren.

"Yes, I admit that I did..."

"Well, if you spent the night with me in my bedroom then, at last, maybe you will finally start calling me Warren."

"My goodness! You sure woke up cranky this morning." she said, trying to keep a straight face, while praising the Lord for this joyful answer to her prayer.

"Now, would you mind giving your bed partner some privacy to get dressed before anyone starts talking?"

"I beg your pardon, I was not your bed par....!"

Warren patted the bed where Lisa's head had been a few minutes before and said, "Your head was right here next to me in my bed, was it not? What would a court of law say, with evidence like that? Well?"

"Mr. Callahan!" Lisa exclaimed.

"That is Warren, my dear," he said, patting the bed again. "Now I have evidence to blackmail you with. So, from now on, you must call me Warren!" His blue eyes dazzled her with a teasing glint.

"This is a side of you I have not seen before," Lisa said, enjoying the moment. "Now, I wonder what was really wrong with you last night! Maybe you were not sick at all, but this was all a ploy to get me into your bed."

They both laughed heartily, as Martha came in with a bowl of warm broth for Mr. Callahan.

Two days later Warren was just about to open his front door to go sit on the porch when Steven and Brandon knocked.

"Good evening, Mr. Callahan," Steven said.

"Please call me Warren, gentlemen."

Brandon smiled and reached out to shake Warren's hand, but did not speak. Brandon always seemed to be the more serious one of the two. Warren wondered if he was ever a little boy, or just came into this world fully grown.

Warren welcomed them into his home and said, "Now, let us get this paperwork signed, so you men will be landowners. Do you have plans for how to celebrate?"

"Well," said Steven, "If you do not mind we thought we would like to start doing some clearing. Would it be alright if we make camp on our land this weekend?"

"That is a splendid idea. Please feel free to use any tools I may have that you might need. Moses can help you look through what I have available. We would love for the two of you to go with us to church on Sunday and then join in our church picnic here on my property Sunday afternoon. The women are great cooks! What do you say?"

Steven looked at Brandon and back at Warren before he said, "Well, we do not have anything to be properly dressed for going to church or a social event like that. We only have our work clothes, and they are not even clean, Mr. Callahan...I mean Warren."

"Everyone will understand, gentlemen. I will explain your attire. We do not pay much attention to things like that at our little church. We are more interested in a man's heart than his outward appearance. So, please do not let a little thing like your clothing keep you from coming."

Brandon spoke up for the first time and said to Steven, "We could take a bath before we go to bed Saturday night, and rinse the worst of the dirt and sweat from our shirts and hang them to dry by morning. That way at least we won't smell as bad as we look."

Steven turned back to Warren and announced, "We are much obliged for your kind invitation. We would be happy to accept, and will do our best not to embarrass you too much. Now, let's talk more about the settling of our property."

Warren smiled and said, "Great! Be ready to leave here shortly after breakfast Sunday morning.

"Moses and I went out there yesterday and marked off that area of the property into lots. We put your names on the two we think are the best ones out there. I think you will agree when you see them. There is a stream running along the back that is lined with some woods where you can nestle your cabins in the trees for shade in hot weather and protection from the cold wind in winter. I am sure you will find the location lovely.

"Brandon, your name is on the closest lot, because B comes before S in the alphabet, no other reason. You may not agree that those are the two best lots, or you may want to trade with each other. It is entirely up to you which lot you each claim for yourselves.

"'I' would like for you to build a road that goes down to that stream from the existing road along the north side of my property. That road will need to be shared by all the lots down there, so please allow access to each lot without having to trespass on any other lot.

"Through those woods and beyond the stream behind your property is still more crop land that I would like to do the same thing with, but that will be a project for later on. After you have looked things over, if for any reason you are not completely satisfied, come back here and we will work it out."

When Brandon and Steven arrived at the stream, they saw how the lots had been clearly marked off earlier by Warren and Moses. They dismounted and let their mounts enjoy the cool running water of the stream in the abundant shade of the big oak trees. Following the boundary line of Brandon's property they came to the place where Steven's land started. Steven looked at Brandon who had a big grin on his face, then both men, who were always so serious by nature, let out a simultaneous whoop of joy that startled their horses.

Having spent all day Saturday clearing and staking out where they each wanted to build their cabins, both men went to the cool stream and bathed. They left their clothes on to wash the sweat and dirt away as much as possible. Then wrapping themselves in a bedroll blanket for modesty, they removed their clothes and left them hanging on tree branches to dry overnight.

Looking at Brandon fully dressed the next morning, Steven said, "Not bad. I'd say you look clean enough if you would wipe the dirt off of those boots."

"Well I could say the same thing about your hat, but I won't. I think we will pass, since we smell okay now."

Steven and Brandon both enjoyed the church service. It had been a long time since either of them had been near a church, so it was quite a treat to hear the music again and be challenged by the Pastor's sermon. The picnic was bustling with people when they arrived back at the Callahan Plantation and dismounted.

"Well, boys how did you like your property?" asked Warren Callahan.

"It is so much more than I could have ever hoped for, sir. I did not expect such a beautiful place," Brandon exclaimed.

Warren shook his head and said, "I agree, it is a beautiful setting for a cabin. I am so pleased that you like it."

"I never thought I would have a place like it, that is for sure," said Steven. "I cannot wait to bring Rita Kay here to see it. You have treated us like princes, Warren, and I will be forever grateful."

Warren smiled, "I am excited about our plan for you to build cabins on that property. I am looking forward to being able to use it for tenant farming or sharecropping."

Steven pointed to the Callahan mansion and said, "Warren, won't you let us express our appreciation by finishing that roughed in wall for you? We could do it in the evenings this winter when we will need to be doing indoor work. We are so overwhelmed that you sold us those beautiful lots at such a reasonable price that we want to do something more for you in return. We can finish that wall the way it should be, and it won't cost you anything."

"Now, I am the one that is overwhelmed. I have accepted the way that wall looks, and I am grateful for all the love that went into building it for me. But, I would certainly cherish your labor of love if you finish it for me."

"We would be more than happy to do it, as thanks for what you've done for us." Steven said.

Dozens of children suddenly swarmed around Warren Callahan, cheerfully begging, as they were leading him away, "Mr. Warren! It is almost time to eat and you have not yet told us our story! PLEASE...tell us a story!"

"Sorry gentleman, duty calls," said Warren with a grin.

Brandon whispered, "Come on Steven, let's go see what's for supper. Perhaps, I can accidentally get my finger in some cake icing."

With his plate full to overflowing with country cooking, Brandon sat down on the ground. After just a minute, the young woman who had been in line behind him plopped down beside him and said, "Hi! My name is Elizabeth. You are Brandon, right? I heard Warren Callahan introducing you around, but I was bringing food out of the buggy and did not get to greet you."

"Yes, I am," he said, putting his plate down to get up.

"Oh, do not be silly. You do not have to get up for me," said Elizabeth.

"I always rise for a lady," said Brandon.

"Well, do as you please, but it is not necessary."

Nervous in the presence of such an attractive young woman, Brandon stumbled to know what to say. "So, you do not consider yourself a lady?"

"Excuse me?"

"Uhhh...I'm sorry, I didn't mean it that way."

"Well what did you mean?"

Brandon sat back down in frustration, knowing he was not making a good impression on Elizabeth. Always a practical man of few words, Brandon said, "I tell you what, let's start this over again. Yes, Elizabeth my name is Brandon, I am pleased to meet you."

Elizabeth smiled and said, "So, Brandon, what brought you to church today?"

"Well, I just bought some property from Mr. Callahan, and he invited my friend Steven and me to your church and this picnic, both of which I have been enjoying very much."

"I did not know that Warren had any property for sale."

"I do not think he does. We just happened to have some skills that he could use right now, so we worked out a great plan."

"What kind of skills would that be?" Elizabeth asked, wiping the remnants of some fried chicken from the corners of her mouth.

Hoping not to bore Elizabeth, Brandon said, "I am an engineer. I worked with the Army Corps of Engineers during the war. But, since the war is over now, Steven and I have started working as builders. I do just about anything except fine finishing, and that is Steven's specialty." Brandon was trying hard not to show how uncomfortable he was talking so much. He had not said so many words in longer than he could remember. But, he sure wanted Elizabeth to stay, so talking was the price that had to be paid to make that happen.

"Oh my, that is wonderful! With so many homes needing to be rebuilt and repaired around here, you will both be a great asset to the community."

"What about you, Elizabeth. What do you like to do?"

"Oh, I am the new teacher at the school. I am getting a good start this year with the children in this area. Many of the children are here at the picnic today.

"But, I have to tell you, Brandon. My heart is with the children of the freedmen and even their parents. I have seen how much they long for an education. I just do not know how to start something like that and still make a living, as well. I have to support myself, as I do not have a husband to take care of me."

"That is a noble thing, Elizabeth. You must be a very compassionate person to want to tackle something like that."

"Oh, it does not take much for a teacher to respond to that much desire for learning in the heart of a child. And the parents of those children want better jobs for themselves, and for their children to be able to better provide for their children in the future."

"If you have not already, you should talk to Martha about this."

"I think you are the first person I have talked to about my feelings. I guess that is because you are the first person who asked, Brandon."

Always being a man of action, Brandon asked, "Are you finished eating?"

"Wow, you sure do change the subject in a hurry!"

"Well are you?"

"Am I what?"

"Finished eating? Is that not what I asked?"

"Yes, I am finished eating. Why does that matter?"

"Come with me then." He grabbed her by the hand and lifted her to her feet, almost spilling her plate that was about half empty.

"If you insist," Elizabeth said as she dropped her plate and followed Brandon, who was dragging her as fast as her legs would carry her.

"Hi Martha, you know Elizabeth here, right?"

"Of course, Brandon, what is this about?"

Dispensing with the usual formalities of greeting, Brandon said, "Elizabeth wants to teach black children, and I knew that you and Sara Ella Layne had been talking about doing just that. I thought you ladies might want to discuss having Elizabeth help you."

"Elizabeth, why did you not tell me you are interested in teaching black children. I am so pleased. Yes, Brandon, we need to go and talk with Sara Ella about all of us working together. Adam Layne is going to build a school for them on his property. With three of us involved, there is just a chance that we could do this. I will see if I can get Moses to take us over there to talk with her. Let me...."

Brandon interrupted with, "That is not necessary. Steven and I will be going that way in just a little while. I can take her to see Sara Ella myself."

"Elizabeth, how did you get here?" Martha asked.

"I rode in a wagon with some friends from church."

Brandon spoke up again, "If I could use Warren's carriage, I could drive both of you over to Oaklayne to talk to Sara Ella, then take you all home later and pick up my horse."

Martha looked at Elizabeth and asked, "What do you think, dear? Would that be okay with you?"

"Oh yes! I am excited about it. I never dreamed it would be possible to do this so soon! How wonderful it would be!"

"Yes, it would. And I think Sara Ella has the connections we need in Washington City to get us started. I will go see about that carriage. It would be nice to get going, so it would not be after dark when we return."

Brandon listened intently to the conversation between the three women about opening a school for the black children. He had no idea how complicated starting a school could be, but he found the discussion fascinating.

Elizabeth lived in a pristine little cottage behind the larger home of a family from the church. It was a perfect arrangement for her, as well as for him, now that he found himself so interested in this lovely young single lady who came into his life today out of nowhere.

After helping Elizabeth down from the carriage and to her door, Brandon drove Martha to the Callahan Plantation to get his horse so he could ride back to Oaklayne. He asked Martha if it would be okay for him to go to church with them again the following Sunday.

"I think Steven might want to go again also. We both enjoyed the preaching and the music, both at church and at the picnic. I think Steven would enjoy playing his guitar with them sometime. He is REALLY good. I play guitar, too, but not as good as he does. Maybe we could both play with them sometime—I would like that."

Martha smiled, "You are welcome to join us any time. Those men with the guitars get together regularly to play and sing, and not only at church and church functions."

Brandon was pleased and told her so. He trotted along the road back to Oaklayne with a song in his heart.

Chapter 47

Adam marveled at the brilliant fall colors against the clear blue sky, as he emerged from the honeymoon cabin to begin his day. He thought, *It is enough to take your breath away!* Spontaneously, he thanked God for the glory of His creation. As he sat down on the front steps to drink it all in before going about his busy day, he experienced a fullness of joy that he did not know was possible.

As he was getting up, Sara Ella came through the door and saw him there. Before she could say anything, he jumped up and embraced her warmly saying, "Mrs. Layne, I sure do love you! Has there ever been a more beautiful day than today?"

"Well, let me see—perhaps yesterday?" she said sarcastically.

"No, it could not have been. I am sure I would have remembered," said Adam, returning her tone.

"You have been so busy that you just did not notice. I should be offended that you apparently have not noticed me either, because I have pointed all this out to you several times in the past few days. But, you obviously do not remember, do you?"

"It sounds to me like you are already becoming a nagging wife...."

"I am not nagging, just pointing out what you have been missing. And, I am not talking about the leaves on the trees, Mr. Layne."

"Okay! You win. I give up. You are right, I have been preoccupied. If that is what it takes, please keep nagging me. Nothing is as important as enjoying moments like this with you."

"I actually have permission to nag? Let me go get my list..."

"Now wait just a minute! Do not get carried away," said Adam, as he pulled her closer. He looked deeply into her beautiful brown eyes and said, "There is one thing even more beautiful than this day. Thank you for your love, Sara Ella. I will cherish you always."

The ringing of the breakfast bell broke the spell. Sara Ella jumped up and said, "You have missed your coffee this morning."

"Coffee could not have been as stimulating as this view and my time with you this morning. But, I am hungry. Shall we go find something to eat?"

After enjoying a good breakfast, Adam turned to Oscar and asked, "Do you think there is any way we could have the big house ready enough to use by Christmas? It would be wonderful to have the warmth of all those fireplaces burning at once that time of year."

Oscar tipped his head to one side and said, "That is a possibility. There is quite a lot to do, but if everything goes well, there is a chance we could be ready by Christmas for you to move in. I know you have to leave for Washington City tomorrow. Do you have time today to go over things with me so I can set some priorities?"

"Yes, I could do that right now, if that will work for your schedule. I have some ideas that I hope you will have time to incorporate. Then I will need to do some reading to prepare for my meeting with Stanton at the Capitol, " said Adam.

When they arrived at the train station, Tom immediately loaded their trunks onto a cart and headed off toward the baggage car. Adam congratulated himself on having Tom always know just what to do and how to handle every situation perfectly. He could not help but notice that other men all around him at the station were struggling with their luggage, without the help Adam had always taken for granted.

For the first time in his life, Adam realized that he had always taken the credit for Tom's accomplishments. Today he was suddenly aware that there was something wrong with that. He was very pleased that the slaves had been freed, but somehow his relationship with Tom had not changed, and now that troubled him. He knew that the former slave owners of the south had all been devastated by the loss of their slaves. They depended on them always being there, just like Adam depended on Tom being there. Was there any difference between him and those former slave owners? Did he really respect Tom as a free man with plans and dreams of his own? Adam did not like the answers to those questions.

As Tom walked back toward him, Adam instinctively held out his hand to him. Tom was shocked by the gesture, and did not know what to do. He turned around to see if there was someone behind him that Adam intended to greet, but found no one.

Adam smiled and said, "Thank you, Tom. I really do not know what I would do without you."

"I do not care how you do it, just get this thing stopped!" barked Stanton to Secretary of State, William Steward, as they exited Stanton's office together. Continuing, Stanton said, "I understand your concerns, but I frankly do not agree with you."

Noticing Adam waiting in the reception area, Stanton dismissed Secretary Steward summarily and greeted Adam warmly.

"Come right on in, Adam, it is good to see you. Have a seat." Without a moment's hesitation, Stanton continued, "I need your help on these blasted Black Codes! Johnson started this mess, and many of the southern state governments have decided to adopt it.

"Adam, I have talked to several key Republicans and we all agree with your assessment that the only way to keep those states from enacting this is to prevent those state representatives from taking their seats in Congress this fall.

Handing Adam a document, Stanton said, "Here is a list of all the Republicans and Democrats in Congress. I need you to investigate and bring me a list of the Republicans and any Democrats who indicate to you that they will for sure stand with us and vote to keep those secession state Congressional members from being seated who want to begin using these Black Codes. I need to know how many are still undecided. Time is running out. We must not let the freedmen be hindered under these oppressive codes. Come back when you have solid numbers."

"Yes, sir. I will see what I can do," Adam responded. As usual, Stanton dominated the conversation. As he turned to go, Adam walked out of Stanton's office into the rotunda of the Capitol Building. Looking up, he could hear the unmistakable sound of men with hammers, working on the dome—still. *Will they ever be finished?*

"He is not in a good mood today, is he?" Adam heard someone say. He turned around to see Secretary Seward standing there and shook his proffered hand.

"Just being his usual charming self," Adam remarked, somewhat irritated that he had been treated so abruptly.

Secretary Seward smiled and asked Adam to sit down for a minute and listen to a story. As the two men sat facing each other in the reception area, the Secretary began, "Let me tell you something you probably do not know about our Secretary Stanton, Adam. You may or may not know that this past April, I was thrown from a carriage and gravely injured. They tell me that I was injured so seriously that I was almost not recognizable. My face was disfigured, bruised and bloated. My eyes were swelled shut, and blood was running from my nose."

Seward pointed to Stanton's office door, and continued, "That, not so charming man in there, sat by my bedside for hours on end. He wiped my brow with a cool cloth, and blotted blood from my lips and nose. When others did not know what to do, my friend Edwin Stanton tenderly comforted and consoled me like no other. I was in and out of delirium, and my family feared that the congestion or inflammation might cause my death. Though he lived several blocks north, he even came to see me three times on Palm Sunday."

"Stanton did that for you?" Adam remarked in amazement.

"Yes, my friend. Edwin Stanton is much more than meets the eye. Lincoln could see much more in the man than most people do.

Journalist Noah Brooks said, "Stanton is known as a 'bull-head'; that is to say, he is opinionated, implacable, intent, and not easily turned from any purpose."

Secretary Seward sat back in his chair and choked back tears as he said, "I agree that Stanton is not very likable much of the time, but I personally love the man, and so did President Lincoln."

Adam felt more respect for Stanton than ever before. "Thank you, Secretary Seward. I appreciate so much you affording me this opportunity to know Secretary Stanton better."

Seward looked intently at Adam and said, "He speaks as highly of you as anyone, Adam. In fact, I expect he has assigned you the chore of trying to find votes to block the secessionist states congressmen from being seated in Congress, right?"

"Yes sir, and I am aware that you do not necessarily go along with some of his thinking."

With a chuckle Seward said, "He has been trying to win me over, but I keep telling him that it is my job to support the President. And the President has a considerably different position on these issues. My hands are tied."

Adam rose to leave, "It has been a pleasure to visit with you, sir."

"The pleasure is all mine, Adam. Perhaps, we could have lunch together sometime?" asked Seward.

Then, without waiting for an answer from Adam, Secretary Seward said, "Oh, here comes someone who might be willing to help you with your assignment."

Seward stopped the gentleman approaching and said, "Senator Kelley, I would like to introduce you to General Adam Layne, Adviser to Secretary Stanton."

Adam reached out to shake the man's hand as Seward continued, "Adam, this is William Kelley, Senator from Pennsylvania. You may have already heard that his sterling reputation is derived from his wife

Caroline's famous peach cobbler. Let me tell you, the fact that he co-founded the Republican Party, has introduced numerous bills for women's suffrage and is famous for his oratories on opposition to slavery and suffrage, these are of little consequence compared to his wife's cobbler." The Secretary grinned, then said, "I will leave the two of you to get acquainted. I must be getting along now."

"Thank you so much for taking the time to talk with me, sir. I hope to see you again soon," Adam said, shaking Secretary Seward's hand.

Turning to Senator Kelley, Adam smiled and said, "I think Seward knows I am in over my head. I expect he would not be disappointed should my mission fail, but he was generous enough to think you might be of some assistance to me, anyway."

"General Layne, your reputation precedes you. I know that Lincoln thought highly of you. He relied heavily on your insight into the south during the war, coming from a southern plantation, yet supporting the Union. If you are doing something for Stanton I would like to help any way I can. That man is on a mission to make things right with the freedmen. What can I do for you?"

Adam briefly explained his assignment, and the Senator said, "Well, I think I know someone who would be of more help to you than I could be, General. But, you will also need to talk with the Speaker of the House, Schuyler Colfax. I will warn you, do not be surprised if it takes a while to get a meeting with him.

"In the meantime, I would suggest you start with Henry Wilson from Massachusetts. He likes to be called General Wilson. He is a staunch Republican Senator as you know, who will strongly agree with Stanton on this issue. Wilson has a way of finding out what people are thinking. He sort of becomes all things to all men, asking questions without giving his own opinion. It is surprising what kind of information he can get from people. I am sure he will enjoy helping you.

"As you are visiting with him, keep in mind that he is proud of being a self-made man. He does not like aristocrats, especially those who were slave owners. So, watch how you introduce yourself. I will be glad to make a list for you of the congressmen that I already know will be supportive, like Charles Sumner, Benjamin Wade, Thaddeus Stevens and Henry Davis."

Adam heaved a sigh of relief and said, "Senator Kelley, thank you so much for your help. I know this is a very important issue, so I will set up a meeting with General Wilson right away."

306

After a long day of visiting with various Congressmen, Adam's list of supporters was growing. General Wilson had been invaluable toward that effort and had invited him to join him for supper at the Willard Hotel. Also invited was Senator Charles Sumner who was as fiercely opposed to slavery as was Senator Wilson.

At the table that evening, the three men discussed politics openly. Pounding his fist on the table, General Wilson said, "Those southern landowners who lived off the backs of their slaves for years are still trying their best to maintain control of them with these Black Codes. Freedom and slavery are arrayed against each other! As I have always said, 'We must destroy slavery, or it will destroy liberty'. Abolishing slavery was the whole reason for establishing this Republican Party."

Handsome and dignified, Charles Sumner, the scholarly senior colleague of Wilson's from Massachusetts, quietly agreed with the more outspoken Wilson. Adam was struck with the obvious differences between these two men who were so strongly allied on these issues.

Sumner rose from the table and spoke with classical allusions. Adam pictured him wearing the toga of a Roman Senator, watching him waving his hands around, giving a grandiloquent address to his subjects.

Adam stifled a laugh, as he imagined General Wilson in Roman garb. No, that thought just did not fit. He had heard Wilson described as an "earnest man who presented the cold facts of a case without flamboyant oratory". In fact Senator Boutwell said that Wilson was "not learned, not eloquent, not logical in a high sense. He was not always consistent in his political actions, and yet he gained the confidence of the people". From what he knew of the man, Adam agreed with that assessment.

"Adam," Wilson broke into his thoughts, "I am working on a Civil Rights initiative that is aimed at outlawing these Black Codes, as well as other forms of racial discrimination. I plan to present it to Congress in December. I tell you, I'm more than just disappointed in the stand that President Johnson has taken on these issues. I had so hoped he would join the Radical Republican agenda for the reconstruction of the South.

"Frankly, I do not understand his endorsement of the immediate return of the Confederate states to the Union. They seceded from the Union, and there should be penalties for that treason, not just a slap on the wrist! Why, he is not even requiring any protection for those newly freed slaves. I am getting concerned that he may even veto the Freedman's Bureau Bill that Lyman Trumbull will be presenting to the Congress."

Adam realized he was getting a headache, listening to Wilson and Sumner hash over these hot political issues. It was nothing he had not heard before, but after having his eyes opened to his own struggle with prejudice at the train station earlier that day with Tom, these issues were somehow becoming more personal than political for him for the first time.

When Adam arrived at the Layne townhouse that evening, he found Tom reading by lamplight in the library.

Tom looked up from his book and said, "Good evening, Adam." Then he asked, "Have you had supper?"

"Yes, Tom, I had supper with a couple of Senators, after a very full day. You would be surprised how many important people are working diligently to write amendments to the Constitution that would protect the rights of freedmen to give them equality, the same rights as other men. The complexity of the task is enormous. I do understand the controversy, but thought that winning the war would put an end to it all. Especially, after Lincoln's 13th Amendment was passed.

"Did you know, Tom, that since the war ended, Jefferson Davis is the only Confederate leader that was imprisoned? There were no trials for treason, and President Johnson has allowed many of those ex-Confederate leaders to maintain control of Southern state governments." Adam went on to explain to Tom how the Radical Republicans were going to try to put a stop to the Black Codes that President Johnson supported, by not allowing the congressmen from the southern states to be seated in Congress.

"There is a lot going on, Tom. And, frankly, the potential for disaster is scary."

Tom beamed with respect and admiration for Adam and his influence over so many important people in Washington City. "I am pleased that you are working so tirelessly for my people, sir. You are a good man, and I am proud to be working for you." Then Tom sighed and asked, "Since you have already eaten, may I take my leave now? I have had a full day myself, repairing harness leather in the carriage house, and I am very tired."

"Yes, of course, Tom. I will see you in the morning."

As Tom left the room, Adam picked up the book he had been reading. Examining it more closely, he realized it was the book Benjamin had been presented by Frederick Douglass, an autobiography entitled, The Narrative of the Life of Frederick Douglass, an American Slave. Opening it, Adam began to read Mr. Douglass' words:

CHAPTER I

I was born in Tuckahoe, near Hillsborough, and about twelve miles from Easton, in Talbot county, Maryland. I have no accurate knowledge of my age, never having seen any authentic record containing it. ...The nearest estimate I can give makes me now between twenty-seven and twenty-eight years of age. I come to this, from hearing my master say, sometime during 1835, I was about seventeen years old.

My mother was named Harriet Bailey. She was the daughter of Isaac and Betsy Bailey, both colored, and quite dark. My mother was of a darker complexion than either my grandmother or grandfather.

My father was a white man. He was admitted to be such by all I ever heard speak of my parentage. The opinion was also whispered that my master was my father; but of the correctness of this opinion, I know nothing; the means of knowing was withheld from me. My mother and I were separated when I was but an infant—before I knew her as my mother. It is a common custom, in the part of Maryland from which I ran away, to part children from their mothers at a very early age. Frequently, before the child has reached its twelfth month, its mother is taken from it, and hired out on some farm a considerable distance off, and the child is placed under the care of an old woman, too old for field labor. For what this separation is done, I do not know, unless it be to hinder the development of the child's affection toward its mother, and to blunt and destroy the natural affection of the mother for the child. This is the inevitable result.

I never saw my mother, to know her as such, more than four or five times in my life; and each of these times was very short in duration, and at night. She was hired by a Mr. Stewart, who lived about twelve miles from my home. She made her journeys to see me in the night, traveling the whole distance on foot, after the performance of her day's work. She was a field hand, and a whipping is the penalty of not being in the field at sunrise, unless a slave has special permission from his or her master to the contrary—a permission which they seldom get, and one that gives to him that gives it the proud name of being a kind master. I do not recollect of ever seeing my mother by the light of day. She was with me in the night. She would lie down with me, and get me to sleep, but long before I waked she was gone. Very little communication ever took place between us. Death soon ended what little we could have while she lived, and with it her hardships and suffering. She died when I was about seven years *old, on one of my master's farms, near Lee's Mill. I was not allowed to be present during her illness, at her death, or burial. She was gone long before I knew anything about it. Never having enjoyed, to any considerable extent, her soothing presence, her tender and watchful care, I received the tidings of her death with much the same emotions I should have probably felt at the death of a stranger.*

Called thus suddenly away, she left me without the slightest intimation of who my father was. The whisper that my master was my father, may or may not be true; and, true or false, it is of but little consequence to my purpose whilst the fact remains, in all its glaring odiousness, that slaveholders have ordained, and by law established, that the children of slave women shall in all cases follow the condition of their mothers; and this is done too obviously to administer to their own lusts, and make a gratification of their wicked desires profitable as well as pleasurable; for by this cunning arrangement, the slaveholder, in cases not a few, sustains to his slaves the double relation of master and father.

I know of such cases; and it is worthy of remark that such slaves invariably suffer greater hardships, and have more to contend with, than others. They are, in the first place, a constant offense to their mistress. She is ever disposed to find fault with them; they can seldom do anything to please her; she is never better pleased than when she sees them under the lash, especially when she suspects her husband of showing to his mulatto children favors which he withholds from his black slaves. The master is frequently compelled to sell this class of his slaves, out of deference to the feelings of his white wife; and, cruel as the deed may strike any one to be, for a man to sell his own children to human flesh-mongers, it is often the dictate of humanity for him to do so; for, unless he does this, he must not only whip them himself, but must stand by and see one white son tie up his brother, of but few shades darker complexion than himself, and ply the gory lash to his naked back; and if he lisp one word of disapproval, it is set down to his parental partiality, and only makes a bad matter worse, both for himself and the slave whom he would protect and defend.

Every year brings with it multitudes of this class of slaves. It was doubtless in consequence of knowledge of this fact, that one great statesman of the south predicted the downfall of slavery by the inevitable laws of population. Whether this prophecy is ever fulfilled or not, it is nevertheless plain that a very different-looking class of people are springing up at the south, and are now held in slavery, from those originally brought to this country from Africa; and if their increase do no other good, it will do away the force of the argument, that God cursed Ham, and therefore American slavery is right. If the lineal descendants of Ham are alone to be scripturally enslaved, it is certain that slavery at the south must soon become unscriptural; for thousands are ushered into the world, annually, who, like myself, owe their existence to white fathers, and those fathers most frequently their own masters."

Adam closed the book and put it down thoughtfully, with the uncomfortable awareness that he did not know who Tom's parents were. He assumed that Tom did not know, either. Why had that never bothered him before? He thought of Emma Lou and Nathaniel, realizing that they would have no remembrance of their parents, either. What a tragedy.

Unable to sleep, Adam was troubled all night by memories from his childhood. Details of how slaves were treated at Oaklayne came to his mind and kept him awake. He realized that he must have suppressed these thoughts, because they were an abomination to him now.

On the way to the Capitol the next morning, Adam stopped at the Newspaper office briefly to see Scott Bryan.

"Look at this, Adam," Scott said. "I expect it might bring you some closure on your treatment at Andersonville Prison." Scott handed a section of newspaper to Adam, then continued, "The Commandant of that infamous camp, Captain Henry Wirz was executed for war crimes yesterday, November 10, 1865. He is the only Confederate leader to be tried and punished."

Adam examined the article and said, "I had heard he would be hung, but I'd been so busy that I had forgotten about it. Thanks for showing it to me. My experiences at that camp are something I wish I could forget, but the memories still haunt me quite often."

Scott understood and said, "I sure hope those southern states leaders do not get seated. If they do, that war will have accomplished nothing."

"I know," said Adam. "Thanks for the news about Captain Wirz. Guess I had better get on over to the Capitol."

Adam was relieved when the Congressional seats of the secessionist state representatives were denied by the Republicans.

General Wilson and Senator Kelley had given him all the help he needed to supply Stanton with the information he needed to be successful.

As he was walking through the Capitol rotunda, Adam recognized Senator Kelley approaching him with his hand extended. The never ending sound of construction on the dome was deafening as Kelley said, "Congratulations Adam on the work you did to help keep those southern leaders from being seated."

Shouting over the noise, Adam said, "I appreciate all of the help that you and Senator Wilson provided."

"We were also able to get the Freedman's Bureau expanded. Those two things have been important steps forward for reconstruction, Adam. Speaking of Wilson, did you know that he is just finished introducing the first Civil Rights Initiative aimed at outlawing the Black Codes and other forms of racial discrimination to the 39th Congress? He has been bold enough to propose that the Constitution be amended to prohibit any effort to limit the right to vote because of race. I tell you, General Wilson is straight forward and relentless, a real asset to Congress."

"I concur completely, Senator. I enjoyed working with both of you. Do you know if Stanton would be in his office, yet?"

"Yes, I expect he is. You will be glad to know that he is in a good mood today. Enjoy your visit with him."

Stanton rose and motioned to a chair as Adam came into the room. "Adam, come right in. While we have them leaning our way, we are going to hurry and get the 13th Amendment on the floor of the Congress. It is important that we get it ratified to abolish slavery permanently. As we all know, Lincoln got it passed, but it will not officially become an Amendment until it is ratified. At last, I am encouraged that we might actually get that done. We will be voting on it December 6th, then after that we will go into recess until January. I am sure you will be anxious to get back to your family for Christmas."

"Yes, I am looking forward to getting home, but I must say that being here has been quite exhilarating. The issues have been so hotly debated and everyone has such strong feelings about everything."

Stanton leaned forward and almost whispered, "Until then, keep me informed if you hear anything being said about the 13th amendment. We do not want any surprises on this one."

"Yes, sir."

Before retiring, Adam picked up Frederick Douglass' book again. Turning to the page where he left off the night before, he began reading again:

I have had two masters. My first master's name was Anthony. I do not remember his first name. He was generally called Captain Anthony—a title which, I presume, he acquired by sailing a craft on the Chesapeake Bay. He was not considered a rich slaveholder. He owned two or three farms, and about thirty slaves. His farms and slaves were under the care of an overseer. The overseer's name was Plummer. Mr. Plummer was a miserable drunkard, a profane swearer, and a savage monster. He always went armed with a cow skin and a heavy cudgel. I have known him to cut and slash the women's heads so horribly, that even master would be enraged at his cruelty, and would threaten to whip him if he did not mind himself. Master, however, was not a humane slaveholder. It required extraordinary barbarity on the part of an overseer to affect him. He was a cruel man, hardened by a long life of slave holding. He would at times seem to take great pleasure in whipping a slave. I have often been awakened at the dawn of day by the most heart-rending shrieks of an own aunt of mine, whom he used to tie up to a joist, and whip upon her naked back till she was literally covered with blood. No words, no tears, no prayers, from his gory victim, seemed to move his iron heart from its bloody purpose. The louder she screamed, the harder he whipped; and where the blood ran fastest, there he whipped longest. He would whip her to make her scream, and whip her to make her hush; and not until overcome by fatigue, would he cease to swing the blood-clotted cow skin. I remember the first time I ever witnessed this horrible exhibition. I was quite a child, but I well remember it. I never shall forget it whilst I remember anything. It was the first of a long series of such outrages, of which I was doomed to be a witness and a participant. It struck me with awful force. It was the blood-stained gate, the entrance to the hell of slavery, through which I was about to pass. It was a most terrible spectacle. I wish I could commit to paper the feelings with which I beheld it....

CHAPTER II

My master's family consisted of two sons, Andrew and Richard; one daughter, Lucretia, and her husband, Captain Thomas Auld. They lived in one house, upon the home plantation of Colonel Edward Lloyd. My master was Colonel Lloyd's clerk and superintendent. He was what might be called the overseer of the overseers. I spent two years of childhood on this plantation in my old master's family. It was here that I witnessed the bloody transaction recorded in the first chapter; and as I received my first impressions of slavery on this plantation, I will give some description of it, and of slavery as it there existed. The plantation is about twelve miles north of Easton, in Talbot county, and is situated on the border of Miles River. The principal products raised upon it were tobacco, corn, and wheat. These were raised in great abundance; so that, with the products of this and the other farms belonging to him, he was able to keep in almost constant employment a large sloop, in carrying them to market at Baltimore. This sloop was named Sally Lloyd, in honor of one of the colonel's daughters. My master's son-in-law, Captain Auld, was master of the vessel; she was otherwise manned by the colonel's own slaves. Their names were Peter, Isaac, Rich, and Jake. These were esteemed very highly by the other slaves, and looked upon as the privileged ones of the plantation; for it was no small affair, in the eyes of the slaves, to be allowed to see Baltimore.

Colonel Lloyd kept from three to four hundred slaves on his home plantation, and owned a large number more on the neighboring farms belonging to him. The names of the farms nearest to the home plantation were Wye Town and New Design. "Wye Town" was under the overseership of a man named Noah Willis. New Design was under the overseership of a Mr. Townsend. The overseers of these, and all the rest of the farms, numbering over twenty, received advice and direction from the managers of the home plantation. This was the great business place. It was the seat of government for the whole twenty farms. All disputes among the overseers were settled here. If a slave was convicted of any high misdemeanor, became unmanageable, or evinced a determination to run away, he was brought immediately here, severely whipped, put on board the sloop, carried to Baltimore, and sold to Austin Woolfolk, or some other slave-trader, as a warning to the slaves remaining.

Here, too, the slaves of all the other farms received their monthly allowance of food, and their yearly clothing. The men and women slaves received, as their monthly allowance of food, eight pounds of pork, or its equivalent in fish, and one bushel of corn meal. Their yearly clothing consisted of two coarse linen shirts, one pair of linen trousers, like the shirts, one jacket, one pair of trousers for winter, made of coarse negro cloth, one pair of stockings, and one pair of shoes; the whole of which could not have cost more than seven dollars. The allowance of the slave children was given to their mothers, or the old women having the care of them. The children unable to work in the field had neither shoes, stockings, jackets, nor trousers, given to them; their clothing consisted of two coarse linen shirts per year. When these failed them, they went naked until the next allowance-day. Children from seven to ten years old, of both sexes, almost naked, might be seen at all seasons of the year.

There were no beds given the slaves, unless one coarse blanket is considered such, and none but the men and women had these. This, however, is not considered a very great privation. They find less difficulty from the want of beds, than from the want of time to sleep; for when their day's work in the field is done, the most of them having their washing, mending, and cooking to do, and having few or none of the ordinary facilities for doing either of these, very many of their sleeping hours are consumed in preparing for the field the coming day; and when *this is done, old and young, male and female, married and single, drop down side by side, on one common bed,—the cold, damp floor,—each covering himself or herself with their miserable blankets; and here they sleep till they are summoned to the field by the driver's horn. At the sound of this, all must rise, and be off to the field. There must be no halting; everyone must be at his or her post; and woe betides them who hear not this morning summons to the field; for if they are not awakened by the sense of hearing, they are by the sense of feeling: neither age nor sex finds any favor. Mr. Severe, the overseer, used to stand by the door of the quarter, armed with a large hickory stick and heavy cow skin, ready to whip anyone who was so unfortunate as not to hear, or, from any other cause, was prevented from being ready to start for the field at the sound of the horn.*

Adam had a cold chill run down his spine, as he placed the book on the table next to his chair. His head was spinning because of the similarities between Frederick Douglass' experiences as a slave and his own treatment at Andersonville Prison. The only difference he could see was that Frederick Douglass did not have the hope Adam relied on, that his situation at Andersonville was temporary.

He was relieved that Tom and the other slaves at Oaklayne were not treated so brutally. But, hearing what it felt like for a man to have no control over his own future, ever, was troubling. He realized that the slaves at Oaklayne endured knowing that they could do nothing to make a better life for their families.

What if he had felt that way at Andersonville? How could he have survived? He probably would not have survived.

His thoughts immediately went to Tom. Does Tom have plans and dreams for the future? Why had he never asked him? He did not think he had ever regarded Tom as less than any other man. But, he could not deny that Tom was never given the opportunity to make choices about his life.

Adam faced for the first time that there was definitely something wrong in his relationship with Tom. He always thought he loved Tom, but would love treat another person the way he treated him? When two people love each other, does one of them rule over the other? This cannot be right. But on the other hand, how could he manage without Tom? What if, given a choice, Tom wanted to leave? Adam knew he could not bear it if he did.

The Thirteenth Amendment was ratified on December 18th. On his way home, Adam stopped by to see Scott Bryan to give him the good news.

"Thank you Adam, I am relieved to be able to publish this for tomorrow's paper. Are you heading home now for Christmas?" asked Scott.

"Yes, Scott. I am looking forward to leaving this turmoil behind for a while." As he made that comment, he realized that the turmoil in his heart over Tom was even bigger.

Scott changed the subject when he said, "Some of those Senators are going home with their pockets full, Adam. Have you been following railroad stock investments recently? I do not know what is going on, but stock prices on a construction management company for the Union Pacific Railroad called Credit Mobilier have been steadily rising, and many of the Senators are benefiting enormously from it. Something does not smell right to me, but then what do I know?"

Adam raised his eyebrows and said, "Perhaps, I need to invest in that company myself, if it is that good. But, I think I will wait until you learn some more, especially since it sounds suspicious to you. It sounds interesting to me." Adam smiled and said, "Have a Merry Christmas, Scott. I will see you in January."

"Merry Christmas to you also Adam, see you then."

Chapter 48

It was still dark outside, but time to get up. Sara Ella lay still, listening for Adam to stir, hoping he did not have anything planned for his first day back to Oaklayne. Adam rolled over and sat up on the side of the bed, so glad to be home.

Breaking the silence, Sara Ella said, "Good morning, Darling! Do you have any big plans for your day?"

"I thought I would go up to the mill and see how Nathaniel is getting along. Why do you ask?"

"It is just that Christmas will be here soon, and we do not yet have a Christmas tree. I would like to get one, decorate it and...."

"And you would like for me to go find one for us? Why, Mrs. Layne, I would love to go find the perfect Christmas tree for our first Christmas together," he said as he lay back down and pulled her into his arms. "Tom can handle anything that comes up around here. Do you want to go with me? It would be fun to go together, what do you think?"

"Sure, I will go with you. You are right, it would be fun."

Adam's mood became reflective as he remembered, "When I was growing up, my mother would sit at the piano at Christmas time. We all gathered around her and sang Christmas carols for hours. I miss her so much, Sara Ella. Christmas will not be the same without Mother."

After breakfast, they put on coats, mittens and warm caps and headed out into the woods in search of the ideal tree for the Christmas festivities.

As they walked along holding hands, Adam smiled wistfully and said, "I always looked forward to the 'shooting of the guns' on Christmas Eve. It was our way to say 'Merry Christmas' to the other plantation owners along the James River. When I was a small child, I held Father's pocket watch, and gave the order to shoot at the exact hour. Later, Goddard took on that important responsibility, then Randy after him. After Father fired the first shot, the others would respond with a shot fired as well. It sounded like an echo, as it got farther and farther away, with the others shooting off a round as well, one at a time."

Sara Ella nodded, "That Christmas that I came here to meet your family when we announced our engagement, I so enjoyed hearing the next plantation down river respond with a shot, then the next one, and so on clear until we could hear them no longer."

His smile faded and he sighed, "I suppose those old traditions have been lost. It is great to hear guns announcing Merry Christmas again, instead of the guns of war"

Sara Ella nodded, "Yes, we are living in a different time today. But, we can start some new traditions of our own, can we not?"

Adam smiled and squeezed her hand, but did not respond verbally. There was a light covering of snow on the ground and the tree limbs still showed a little white, like blankets on the tree limbs. The snow crunched beneath their feet as they walked along the path.

As they were walking past the family burial ground, Adam stopped at the fence. Looking at the small markers that were partly buried in the snow, he shook his head, "There are no markers for Father, Mother, Goddard and Little Goddard. I think when spring comes and the ground thaws, I will have their remains moved here. We can have new markers put in place for each of them. It seems irreverent to me, not having the entire family acknowledged here."

They turned and started walking again. Sara Ella took hold of Adam's arm and said, "I agree with you, Adam. As soon as we get the mansion finished, that should be our next project. It's a small one, but it is an important one."

Adam looked up and said, "I hope we do not have any trouble finding where they are buried." Then, he made no further comment on the subject.

Together they walked a good distance further, looking for just the right size and shape of a tree. Both were enjoying the crispness of the winter cold and the scent of the more thickly forested part of Oaklayne that Adam had not investigated in years. Adam stopped several times to examine a small tree more closely, then walked on, still looking for the perfect one. He was enjoying the time alone in the wilderness with Sara Ella.

"Here," said Sara Ella, "How about this one?"

Adam shook his head, "It is nice, but too short."

They continued walking hand in hand, looking at the beauty of the forest, until Adam stopped. "This one should do, I think," He looked at her. "Agreed?"

"It looks fine to me," Sara Ella said, nodding her head.

"Okay, then let's cut her down and drag her to the house."

Adam took his saw and cut down the tree just above the ground.

"It is beautiful!" Sara Ella smiled. "I am excited, Adam. Are you going to help with the decorating?"

"Oh, no you don't! I do not do decorating, my dear. It will be much better if I do not get involved, trust me. And, that is just the way I like it! I will get Randy and Benjamin to help you after they get here. We will just leave the tree out in the yard until they come. They can bring it in for you and help decorate it."

"But, they will just be getting home from college. Do you think they will want to do it?"

"I will make sure they do," Adam said with a grin. Being out for a while with Sara Ella had cheered him up. Now he was really enjoying himself.

Sara Ella started back toward the river and the plantation housing area carrying the saw. Adam hoisted the tree to his shoulder and caught up with her. They walked back together, arm in arm. As they passed the rebuilt horse barn, Adam looked at it with satisfaction. It was built much bigger and more efficient than before. One building, with a partition down the middle, horses on one side and cattle on the other. And, the new barn had a much larger haymow for storage.

Adam remarked, "The barn should be finally ready for the stock to be housed this next week. I will be glad to get the horses in out of the weather."

Sara Ella nodded, "How many new horses will you need to start rebuilding the herd, Adam?"

"Probably around twenty-five more work horses. As you know, riding horses cannot be used for pulling wagons and buggies. We will also need a lot more cattle, enough for milk cows, stock to butcher for meat, as well as breeding cows and bulls. They will soon produce calves to boost the numbers."

Before long, they entered the Temporary House, which would still be home to them for the balance of the winter and probably all of the spring months. All was quiet.

"Emma Lou?" Sara Ella called out. "Where is everyone? We found a Christmas tree."

From the kitchen area came a voice they would recognize anywhere, "So that is where you've been!"

Adam looked at Sara Ella and she looked back at him. Then suddenly, he yelled, "Where are you, Randy, my boy?"

They heard a giggle coming from the kitchen, and ran in there. There at the table sat Randy, wearing a college sweater, with a cup of hot coffee in hand. Benjamin was with him. Emma Lou stood over by the stove, arms folded, and a great smile on her face.

"Look what wandered in while you were gone?" said Emma Lou.

Adam embraced Randy, and Sara Ella wrapped herself around Benjamin. Adam stretched out his arms, holding Randy by the shoulders and remarked to Sara Ella.

"Look at this boy, Sara Ella! And that one, too! They have changed. They are all grown up! It looks like being away at Richmond University is good for both of them."

Benjamin smiled when Adam asked, "How is school going for you, son?"

"It's just fine, Mr. Adam. I am really enjoying being there to help Randy. I am learning a lot, too. I am sure glad Randy taught me as much as he did when we were children. I do not have any trouble following along with what is being taught to the white boys in class."

"And he is really helpful to me as I study," said Randy, reaching out and patting Benjamin on the knee. "He is even letting me walk to classes without leading me a lot of the time now. It is good to know he is there beside me, so if I make a wrong turn he helps me get back to where I need to be. But, I appreciate him letting me do as much as I can on my own.

"I am learning to read better in Boston line type, Father. More and more books are being published with embossed type these days. I have heard that a blind man in Europe named Louis Braille has come up with another way for blind people to read, but it does not sound like it will work very well to me. It is just a bunch of dots instead of real letters. He actually intended it to be used for soldiers to communicate in battle without the enemy hearing them. But, now he thinks it might work for the blind. I do not know, we shall see."

He paused for a moment, then said, "Father, I have decided that I want to get my certification in English language and then go on to law school. As I explained before, there are some blind lawyers who take cases, and I know I can do it if they can.

Adam reacted exactly like Randy knew he would. "Randy, I just do not want to see you do all that work and then be disappointed. It makes sense that people who need an attorney will shy away from a blind one. Legal issues are always about very important things, so folks will not likely take chances when hiring a lawyer. Even if you graduate at the top of your class in law school and have the credentials on the wall to prove it, I do not think people will hire you."

"But Father, General Imboden says..." Adam flinched with disgust when Randy mentioned the man's name, "...several blind men have overcome their handicap and are successful lawyers. I wish you had confidence in me that I can overcome this like other men have. What would you have me do, just sit in the house and let the world pass me by? I can do this, Father...no, I must do this."

"Randy, I do have confidence in you. I have watched you overcome enormous obstacles in your short lifetime, and I am so proud of you for it. But my confidence in you will not extend to people who need your help with important legal matters. They will want a man who can look a Judge or jury in the eye when they are defending them."

"No, Father, you do not understand. The Judge or jury will be listening to my voice, not watching my eyes." Randy stood and walked to his father by following the voice that he knew and loved so well. When he reached Adam's side, he took hold of his arm and said "Father, trust me, I know what I am doing. Please, no more talk about not going to law school. I'm going, with or without your support! Is that clear? Like I said when I was a little boy, 'My head's made up'!"

Adam choked with pride in the determination Randy expressed. Obviously, he could not be swayed from his goal. When his 'head was made up' he always proved himself worthy in the past.

"You certainly know how to argue a case, young man, that is for sure!" said Adam.

Adam turned to Benjamin and asked, "What about you? Have your plans changed? Are you fed up with this lawyer business by now, or are you still wanting the same thing as your litigious friend here?"

Benjamin laughed, nodded vigorously and said, "Yes sir! I will be at Randy's side at least for the rest of this school year. I have already written a letter to Frederick Douglass. He has approved my staying in Richmond to help Randy, thereby allowing me to attend the University myself. He thinks it will be good experience for me, especially the legal work Randy and I are doing for General Imboden's law firm.

"Mr. Douglass told me that he has been working with the Radical Republicans to add a Law School at Howard University. It is a black college that he hopes will be founded in about a year. He recommended that I go back to Ashmun Institute next year and get a degree there that will make me eligible for Howard University, once it is established. He does not think I will be allowed to get a law degree from a white man's school.

"General Imboden has assured me that he knows lots of people who can help Randy if I am not there. He thinks it might be good for Randy to not have me there to depend on all the time. It would encourage him to be more independent."

"Have you talked with your mother to see if she approves of your decision to go back to Ashmun, then continue on to law school?"

Benjamin swallowed hard and said, "Uh, no...not yet, Mr. Adam...but I will." He hesitated, then added, "Probably tomorrow?"

Adam nodded, smiled at Benjamin, and then turned back to Randy. "I tell you what, gentlemen, you get your college degree, and then I will pay your Law School tuition. I will also pay whatever it costs for Benjamin to be there at the University with you the rest of this year. Then, I will pay for Ashmun and Howard University for you Benjamin...that is, if you can get your mother's approval.

"Then, as soon as you both finish and are ready to start your practice, I will set you up with law offices of your own. What do you think?"

Then, grinning from ear to ear, Adam pointed his right index finger in their direction and said, "Oh, I almost forgot. I expect you both to graduate at the top of your class in both college and law school. Absolutely, no slacking allowed!"

Randy beamed. "That sounds like the best Christmas present a boy ever had, Father! I won't disappoint you, sir."

Benjamin just stood there with his mouth open, unable to speak.

Adam smiled and changed the subject. "Now, I need your help with something, and I do not want to hear any moaning. Do you understand?"

Benjamin looked at Randy, and saw a puzzled look on his face. "What, Father? Anything you want, just ask."

"My lovely wife found a Christmas tree in the woods earlier today that I cut down and brought here for her. It is out there in the snow. Now she wants it brought into the big house and decorated. You know how I feel about being involved in such things, so I need you both to be at her disposal. Understand?"

Randy stuck his lower lip out exaggeratedly and said, "But, Father, a blind boy could never decorate a Christmas tree!" Then, stifling a giggle, Randy continued, "But, there is no reason why Benjamin cannot do it, though."

Sara Ella rolled her eyes and said, "Oh, for heaven's sake! It is just a Christmas tree! You men are impossible. Decorating the tree is one of the most enjoyable parts of Christmas. If you will help me move it inside, I will show you how much fun it is to decorate a Christmas tree. But, before we get started, I need to see if Oscar has the big house ready enough for us to move the tree inside over there. We may need to wait a few days."

Chapter 49

"Ouch!" said Martha, pricking her finger with the darning needle. "Guess I need to pay more attention to what I am doing if I am going to have usable fingers left when I get done with this sock." She was talking to herself, but Lisa overheard, as she was coming into the room.

"Do you need some help, dear?" asked Lisa.

"No, I was thinking about Christmas coming up and was not paying enough attention to this needle. I will be done in a minute if I can keep my mind from drifting off." Martha smiled, than continued, "But, thank you anyway."

"Tell me, what is Christmas like here at the Callahan Plantation? What does Mr. Callahan do to make it a special day?"

For self-preservation, Martha put her sewing in her lap and looked up to see Lisa with a curious expression on her face.

"Well, of course there is always the shooting of the guns to greet the neighbors on Christmas Eve and then again on Christmas day. He always gave us a ham or turkey and something to keep us warm for the winter. He has always been generous with all of his slaves at Christmas."

Lisa shivered slightly, remembering what Christmas was like when she was a little girl in Louisiana. Those memories of her past had been suppressed for so long that thinking of them was uncomfortable...even painful. Not wanting to linger there, she changed the subject.

"What about Mr. Callahan's family? Does he have family that comes to visit him at Christmas? Or was it just he and his wife?"

"Mr. Callahan has some family far out west somewhere, but he never talks about them. Cora Callahan had some family here in the area, back before Moses and I came, but I do not know where they are now. No, as far as I know, this family basically only consisted of Mr. and Mrs. Callahan and little Leonard," said Martha.

"Who is Leonard?" asked Lisa.

Martha smiled warmly and asked, "You have not heard about Leonard Callahan? I'm surprised Mr. Callahan has not told you about his son. It is both joyful and painful for all of us to think about Leonard.

"Leonard was a charming and bright boy, much like his father by nature. He and two of his friends who visited here from time to time, loved to go down and play in the creek. About ten years ago, when Leonard was a little older than Samuel, the boys begged Mr. Callahan to let them go play in the stream, even though he knew it was swollen from heavy rain. The rain had stopped and the sun had come out, so they were able to convince him it would be safe. He was not aware that little stream had become a fast flowing river.

"The smallest of the three boys was almost immediately swept away by the water, screaming as he was carried downstream. Young Leonard drowned trying to rescue him. The friend was able to grab hold of the limb of a tree and hang on, while the third boy ran to get Mr. Callahan. But, I am sorry to say, they did not find Leonard's body until late that evening.

"Mr. Callahan has always blamed himself for not checking the creek for himself, before allowing those boys to go down there. His wife, Cora, was devastated also. But, she did not blame him. She helped him finally give that burden to the Lord, and he has never been the same since.

"The man you know today understands full well the price that was paid for him on the cross of Christ. He knows that, while the death of Leonard was an accident, the death of God's son was not. He is proud of his son for being willing to give his life for his friend."

Lisa was solemn, taking in the seriousness of the tragic story of Leonard Callahan's death.

"Thank you so much for telling me about this, Martha. I had no idea that Mr. Callahan had a son. He told me about Cora and her death, but not Leonard."

Martha went back to her sewing, and Lisa sat looking down at her own hands that were folded in her lap.

Lisa broke the silence and said, "Can you help me think of something we could do that would make Christmas a joyous occasion for Mr. Callahan this year, or would it only bring back painful memories?"

"Oh, I am sure he would love to celebrate Christmas, but it will have to not cost anything. He is no longer suffering from the painful memories of losing his family, Lisa. He is focused on the good memories and the wonderful years God gave him with each of them. What do you have in mind?"

Lisa jumped to her feet with a big grin, clapped her hands together and said, "Oh! Surely we can come up with some natural decorations to make the house festive. Then we need to bake some goodies to make the house smell like Christmas. Can you come up with stockings for everyone for the mantle? I want Samuel to be involved with the decorating and anticipation of the joyous day. He has never celebrated Christmas before, you know."

Samuel enjoyed gathering magnolia leaves, holly branches and pine cones from around the grounds of the plantation. He was amazed to see how Lisa used them to make magnificent decorations. She placed them on the fireplace mantles, over the doors and around candles on the tables. She even made a beautiful wreath for the front door. He was astonished at her creativity, taking scraps of leftover cloth from the quilting box and tying them together to make colorful ribbons and bows. Lisa showed him how to roll pine cones in glue made from water and flour then in a little sugar to make them sparkle in the candlelight. In the daytime they looked beautifully icy.

"What is next, Mother?" asked Samuel.

Lisa responded, "Here, let's tie up the ends of our aprons around our waists, then fill them with pine cones. Now, follow me and watch."

"Hey!" said Samuel, "This makes a great pocket! I'll have to remember that."

"It does come in handy, does it not?" said Lisa with a smile.

Samuel was impressed as she nestled the pine cones like ornaments into the pretty Christmas arrangements she had already placed around the house. Next they sat down with a large bowl and pulled berries off the broken pieces of holly that were left over and the little light blue berries off of the cedar branches he had toted in earlier.

"What are we going to do with all these berries?" asked Samuel. "Can we eat them?"

"Oh, no! You must not eat them, Samuel. They would make you very sick."

"But, the birds eat them. Why don't they get sick?"

"Well, God made the birds with a different kind of tummy than he made for us. Birds would get sick if they ate what you eat. Only birds can eat these berries. We are going to string them and add them to our decorating."

Working diligently to pick berries for his wonderful mother, Samuel was filled to overflowing with joy.

Innocently, Samuel asked, "Mother, is this what you did with your mother at Christmas every year when you were a little girl?"

Samuel had no idea that his question would bring with it a cloud of bad memories for Lisa. She had never shared her past with him. Is this the time? Will he understand? She had never lied to him before, and did not want to start now. She had known the time would come eventually when he would need to know her secrets. Now, he was asking, and there was nothing to do but answer him truthfully.

"No, Samuel. My childhood was much different than you think. You see my family was slaves like Moses and Martha, so I did not have all of these nice things. My life was almost as hard as yours, when you were living on the streets in the city. I lived in a little hut with my mother. She was a cook, and I was put to work when I was about 8 years old. I took care of the master's little girl after she reached her 5th birthday. The master of the house made these arrangements, but his wife did not like it at all. I did not know why at the time, but she treated me quite cruelly."

"But I thought that slaves were always black?" Samuel said with a confused expression.

Lisa hesitated, not knowing how Samuel would take hearing that she had black ancestry.

"Samuel, I know this is confusing, but my mother was half black and my grandmother was black. My father was white, so for some reason I look white. But, your sister Angela that I often talk about and hope to find someday, looks black.

Samuel jumped up and started walking around and around in circles, then without a word he ran outside letting the door slam behind him.

Warren Callahan came out of his study, as he saw and heard Samuel run out the door sobbing. He could see Lisa sitting in the entry hall next to the little table with her head in her hands, crying. Quickly he ran up to her and sat in the chair next to her.

"What is it, my dear. Little boys can be difficult at times. Can I help? Does he need a little discipline?"

Slowly, Lisa lifted up her eyes to meet his, tears streaming down her face.

"No, discipline will not help this time, Warren. He is deeply hurt, and I know of no way to help ease his pain."

"What could possibly have hurt him so much?"

"The truth," she said, as she once again hid her face.

Warren sat there for several minutes, wanting to comfort her. He wanted to nestle her in his arms, but hesitated because he did not think it would be appropriate for him to do so. Instead he reached out and lifted her chin, saying, "The truth will always set you free, dear one. Whatever it is, Samuel is strong enough to work it out and you will be greatly strengthened by having shared it. I will be praying for both of you, as you deal with it together."

Lisa was grateful, knowing that prayer was exactly what she and Samuel needed most right now.

The next evening, after her day at the hospital, Martha handed Lisa a cup of hot coffee when she entered the kitchen.

"Oh, Martha, this is the best coffee I've ever tasted."

"You say that every evening, Lisa."

"Well, this time I really mean it," Lisa said with a strained smile.

"What's wrong, Lisa?" asked Martha.

"You know me too well, Martha. I am troubled, because I finally told Samuel about my family being black last night. He seemed okay about it, until I told him that his sister is black. He has not said two words to me since he ran out of the house last night after I told him.

"Oh Martha, I do not belong anywhere. Last night Mr. Callahan told me that the truth will set us free, but it sure does not feel like it to me right now. I know that keeping the truth from Goddard was a mistake, but then I would never have met him if he had known the truth. Now, I have accepted that I will never marry again, because I will not keep that secret anymore. Besides who would marry me if they knew? A black man would not consider me, because I am white. And a white man will never marry me because there is a possibility that I could give him black babies. I have accepted that, but now it is hurting Samuel. It never occurred to me that he would be hurt when I adopted him. I only knew that he needed my help, and I needed to get him off that train."

"Samuel will be fine, Lisa. He just needs a little time to sort this out. You will see."

"Thank you for your encouragement and the coffee. How was Samuel today? Did he perform his studies and give you the book report he has been working on? Do you know if he gave Mr. Callahan any trouble when they worked with his math?"

"He was somewhat fidgety and solemn with me today, but he did his work. I do not know how things went with Mr. Callahan."

"Thank you so much for taking the time to teach him, Martha. Between you and Mr. Callahan, he has learned so much."

"Samuel is a pleasure to work with, Lisa. I enjoy my time with him very much."

"I think it is wonderful that you are spending time with Sara Ella working up a plan to train some black people to be teachers. You certainly are a wonderful teacher yourself."

"Thank you, Lisa. By the way, your decorating is beautiful and brightens up the house so much. I expect it will also brighten Samuel's spirits, too. Do you have time to help me make a list of Christmas goodies we want to bake real soon?"

Talking to Martha helped Lisa feel better, and the list of treats they decided to make for Christmas lifted her spirits.

That evening Lisa finished stringing the berries. Warren asked where she was going to put them.

"Come and help me and you will see. I wanted Samuel to be involved, but he has made himself scarce this evening."

"I would love to," said Warren. "Lead the way, my dear."

Lisa asked him to lower the huge chandelier over the dining room table, so she could lace the berry strands through it. Then she put holly accents on the tubes and attached them there.

Warren could hardly contain himself, watching her make such an ordinary thing into a beautiful spectacle, when she had so little to work with. He could not take his eyes off of her beauty, enjoying being so close to her. He was about to burst with excitement, wanting to tell her what the Lord had revealed to him the night before.

"All right, you can pull it back up now," Lisa said.

Warren raised up the heavy light and tied it off. Lisa stepped back to look at it.

"Oh, I need to straighten that one place," she said, pointing at a particular spot. She pulled out a chair, lifted her skirt and climbed up, while precariously holding on the arm of the chair. After making a small adjustment, she tripped on her skirt as she was stepping off of the chair. Warren lunged and caught her in his arms, before she hit the floor. But, he inadvertently lost his balance and they wound up tangled together on the floor. They both spontaneously broke out in unbridled laughter.

Sprawled out on the floor together, Warren looked into her beautiful dark eyes and said, "You know, as I was praying for you and Samuel last night, the Lord spoke something profound to me."

"And what might that be?" she said, feeling remarkably comfortable, supported by his strong arms, there on the floor.

"He told me that I need to take care of you myself."

"Well, the Lord did not have to tell you that. You are already doing exactly that, and very well, I might add."

"No, Lisa. You do not understand. You see, I argued with Him half the night, because you are so young and beautiful. I never dreamed it could be possible for you to love me...and of course you may think me much too old...and oh, well...what I am trying to say is...Lisa Layne, will you marry me?"

Lisa grew pale, then pushing herself away from him, she leaned her back against the wall.

"Oh, Warren! I cannot, I wish I could, but I cannot. This is so hard for me to explain, but after I do, you will not want me, I am sure of it."

"Oh, yes I will..."

"No, wait! You need to rescind that request, before I tell you why. That way you will not feel so bad about having to take it back after I tell you why I cannot marry you."

"If it has to do with your black heritage and your daughter being black, I already know about that," Warren said matter-of-factually.

Lisa was shocked. "What? How long have you known? Did Martha or Moses tell you?"

"No, they did not tell me, Samuel did. I went out to console him last night, and we had a good talk."

"You talked to Samuel?"

"Yes, and he is coming around. You will see."

"I do not know what to say. This is just too much. I had resigned myself to never being married again. Do you understand that if I marry you, our babies might be black? Does that not bother you?"

"The Lord has given me perfect peace about it, Lisa. I do not know what the future holds, but I do know that He wants me to ask you to be my wife. But, you have every right to say no. And if you do, I will understand and never mention it again."

"I have loved you for some time now, Warren, but could not allow myself to think you would ever love me. Yes, yes! If you will have me, my answer is yes. I would be honored to be your wife. Oh! And Samuel will also have a father!" she said with excitement, as Warren lifted her up off of the floor, drawing her to himself.

Just then Samuel burst into the room.

"Did I hear right? Did she say yes?"

Startled by his entrance, Lisa was puzzled.

Turning to Lisa, Warren said, "Ask her yourself, young man."

"Is it true Mother? Did you agree to marry Mr. Callahan?"

"Yes Samuel, I did. You know, this means you will soon be calling him Father."

"Whoopeeeee!" Samuel yelled at the top of his lungs and tossed a sprig of mistletoe to Warren. Then he turned and ran as fast as he could in search of Moses and Martha to share the good news.

Warren pulled Lisa close again and kissed her passionately, then said, "That is not exactly the romantic plan I had in mind for my proposal, but I am glad it worked all the same."

Chapter 50

"That slate roof will last for a hundred years, Trevor!" Oscar said, looking around, examining the construction progress at the big house. "And, those trusses Brandon helped you and August build could support the weight of a locomotive! You men do amazing work," Oscar exclaimed.

The men were busy taking down the scaffolding and cleaning up when Oscar arrived on the scene. He inspected the finished plastering work he had assigned to Darrell and Norman, and was pleased with the results. He expected Adam to be there soon to see what had been accomplished, and hoped he would be pleased with their progress.

Adam finished a cup of coffee in the kitchen, as the ladies were cleaning up after breakfast. Benjamin and Randy had just gone out to sweep a light dusting of snow from the little porch. Adam smiled, listening to Benjamin instruct Randy to stand at the bottom and work his way up, feeling each step with the broom.

Adam got up with a sigh and asked, "Would you and Emma Lou like to go with me to see what remains to be done at the big house? That way, you will know what needs to be done to get ready to have our Christmas celebration there."

Ross greeted Adam, Sara Ella and Emma Lou at the front door of the mansion with a big smile. Ross was rarely seen without his pistol strapped around his waist, and today was no different. They could hear lots of hammering and banging around, as the crew was busy doing the finishing work on the large home.

Adam asked, "Ross, what is this I hear about you getting mixed up with a gal in town named Lorraine?"

"Oh, General Layne, I cannot wait for you to meet her. I met her in the General Store where she works as a bookkeeper. You know, we have made several trips into town to pick up supplies, and I always see her there. She is so beautiful, with thick dark brown hair and the most gorgeous hazel eyes. She's really smart, a lot smarter than me. But, I guess she is fine with that, because she invited me to have Christmas dinner with her and her parents, Clifford and Edith Scott. I think that's a good sign don't you?" Ross said with a quizzical expression.

"Ross, you are one of the smartest men I know," said Adam. "Your engineering skills are extraordinary, and the way you have that pump working in the pump house is nothing less than genius. I am sure Lorraine is smart, too. But do not put yourself down. You would be a prize for any girl. And once she hears you sing and play that Martin guitar of yours, she will be smitten forever, I am sure."

Ross opened the door of the big dining room, where the fireplace was ablaze with warmth. All of the men were standing around the Christmas tree they brought in for Sara Ella. As the door opened, they all shouted, "Merry Christmas!"

Everyone exchanged warm greetings, then Oscar gave them a full tour of the work that had been accomplished downstairs, including the added kitchen area that was a marvel to Emma Lou, and then the upstairs. Before they concluded the tour, Oscar took Adam alone to show him the new secret room in the basement.

Sara Ella and Emma Lou were filled with excitement and joy, as they went back into the dining room to consider what they would need to make this Christmas the most memorable of all.

Oscar leaned against the wall in the entry and said, "I think we are finished inside, until we get the finish wood and materials that you have ordered from overseas, Adam. If it is okay with you, I would like to send the men away for a Christmas break. Then, when we get back we will work on the porches outside. I will get the columns ordered in town before I leave."

Adam ran his fingers through his hair and looked around in amazement. "Oscar, I am speechless...you men have even thought of extra little things, like window seats that open for extra storage. You have used every little alcove to make storage or bookshelves, which will be a wonderful asset to our home.

"I am especially impressed with that room at the end of the hall with all of that plumbing in it. Sara Ella is excited about going to Washington City with me to pick out the porcelain tub and sink for that room, as well as the new water closet you described. I am glad you made us a list of the faucets and other fixtures we will have to pick out while we are there. We have never had anything like that before, so I would not know what we need otherwise.

"That big pump in the pump house that Ross engineered will not have any trouble bringing water up through all of those pipes, I am sure. And, that pipe he has going through the chimney to heat water for the kitchen sink and bath closet is so ingenious.

"Did you see how excited Emma Lou is about the porcelain sink you described to her for her new kitchen? She cannot wait to use it.

"I am also impressed with all of the pipes for the gas sconces and chandeliers, and cannot wait to see them working, lighting up the house.

"Thank you my friend. The Lord brought you along at just the right time. I am so pleased with what you have done here."

Oscar beamed and replied, "Thank you, Adam. It has been a joy to do it for you. I have had fun researching all of the latest inventions. This job was perfect timing for me and my men as well. And thank you for your trust in us.

"You did not answer me about the crew taking a Christmas break, though. Is it okay with you?"

"Of course," said Adam. "That is an excellent idea. Please give each of them a Christmas bonus from me before they leave."

"Great! They will be pleased, I am sure," said Oscar. "I know Steven's wife Rita Kay is arriving by train in Richmond tomorrow, and he wants to go into town to pick up some necessities to make it more comfortable for her in their new cabin at the Callahan Plantation. He says she will want to pick out most things herself, but he wants it to be nice for her from the start."

"I think it is wonderful how the other men are helping him get ready for her. I'm pleased that he and Brandon have decided to stay here in Virginia, and I hope you will consider doing the same, Oscar. It would be great to have you living close by."

Oscar looked off into the distance, obviously pondering Adam's words. Then he said, "I have not made up my mind about anything yet. I guess I have been mostly focused on this building project."

Adam smiled, aware that Oscar's hesitation was full of hidden meaning. "Seems to me there is something else that appears to be capturing your interest lately, Oscar."

Oscar cleared his throat and said, "...that obvious, is it? Well, you are right, Elsie is quite a distraction. And, to tell you the truth, sometimes it scares me."

"What about Elsie could possibly scare anybody? She is intelligent, beautiful, talented, has a great sense of humor and many other admirable qualities. And for some unknown reason, she seems to adore you. What else could a man ask for?"

"Exactly! That is what scares me! What if all that changes down the road? That happened to me before, and I do not know if I could endure it again."

"What do you mean, she has changed her mind about you before? I cannot believe that Elsie..."

"No, not Elsie. I was engaged before the war. But, when I came home, Sally May had married someone else. It broke my heart, and I swore I would never fall in love again."

"Elsie is not Sally May, Oscar. You cannot live your life in fear like this. I am sure you have been thrown from a horse before, but you cannot leave your horse in the stable all the time, because you are afraid you might get hurt again. No, you take the risk. You commit to it every time you get in the saddle. The journey of life is too important to miss out, because you might get hurt. I admit, I had to learn that the hard way, too."

Choking back the lump in his throat, Oscar said, "Thank you, my friend. I appreciate your advice, and I will think about it."

The men left right away, leaving a cloud of dust behind. Oscar planned to go home to Northern Virginia for Christmas to visit his family, and he wanted to ask Elsie to go with him. But, he was afraid she might think it too forward of him. He did not want to scare her off, but had no reason to think it would. Why did he want her to go with him so badly? He didn't want to consider the answer, it was too frightening. But, he was already in so deep, he was going to get hurt, even if he did not ask her. Now, that was a new thought.

Mulling over his thoughts as he walked through the door of the Temporary House, he almost bumped into Elsie and said aloud, "Oh no. Now what do I do?"

"Do about what?" Elsie asked.

"Oh, I do not know!" he barked out, not knowing what to say to her, as he ran up the stairs.

"Well, hello to you too," she said to the empty room. Why has he been so moody these last couple of weeks. It seems like the Christmas spirit would have encouraged him. I sure have not been able to...I wonder if he has just lost interest in me, or if I have said anything I should not have said, or something? She took the rugs on out the door and shook them extra hard in frustration.

After getting cleaned up for the trip home, Oscar walked to the stable. He kicked at the snow and fumed, completely unaware of how beautiful the trees looked with a light dusting of snow, as he walked along the tree lined lane.

In and out of the stable he went, but try as he might, he could not get Elsie out of his mind. It is better when I am working...at least, when I am working, I am not tortured by what to do about her. I long to be with her every minute...but when I am, I am so touchy. What is wrong with me? Fear...Adam said it is fear. I had not realized it was fear, until he called it that. If it is fear, then I know I must deal with it, one way or another. I cannot keep treating Elsie this way. I have got to be free of this torment. I cannot imagine life without her, but what will I do if she does not want me? One thing is for sure, if I do not face this fear, I will never know.

Oscar realized it was now or never. He marched toward the house to ask Elsie to go back home with him for Christmas. Cold as it was, sweat began to bead on his forehead.

As soon as he entered the house, Oscar reached out and took Elsie's hand, turning her around to face him. This startled her a bit, since he seemed to have been avoiding her.

"Please forgive me for being so grumpy lately, Elsie. It is not your fault, it is me..."

"Have I done something wrong? Have I..."

"No, no you did not do anything wrong." Oscar felt guilty for treating her so unkindly. She gripped his arms firmly, then he pulled her close, nestling her head up under his chin. He did not want her to see the emotions he was unable to control.

"I have been such a fool, Elsie. I am so selfish. All I have been thinking about lately is myself. I have been so concerned about getting my feelings hurt, that I have forgotten about your feelings. The truth is that your feelings are the most important to me. It is just that I wish I could make your feelings the same as mine. But, now I see how selfish that is..."

Elsie pushed back and said with a frown, "Oscar Baynes, what on earth are you talking about? You do not make any sense at all." Then she saw the look of fear, mixed with pure sweet longing for rescue on his face and said, "Oh, Oscar what can I do to help? I would do anything for you."

"Would you Elsie? Do you really mean that?"

"Of course, I do. What is wrong?"

Sighing deeply, Oscar said, "You make it sound so simple. Why did I not ask you this before?" After a big long breath he said, "I have wanted to ask you if you would consider going with me this Christmas to meet my folks."

Brushing the loose curl back from her face, Elsie said, "Well, why in the world would you hesitate to ask me that? Of course, I will go with you. Why in heaven's name would I want to stay here, if I can go with you instead?"

Oscar finally let out his breath and a grin began to form on his mouth. Then he could not help himself and began laughing, pulling her close to him and planting kisses all over her face.

"Dear, dear Elsie...why do I ever doubt you?"

Reaching up and putting her arms around his neck, she pulled his head down for a passionate kiss before saying, "Someday, I hope to understand you, Oscar Baynes. But for now, I will have to settle for a cup of hot apple cider..."

The next morning Steven came in for breakfast looking real sharp. He had been to the barber for a bath, shave and haircut while he was in town picking up supplies the day before. He was wearing a new shirt, trousers, hat and boots. After enduring lots of ribbing from the other men, they wanted to know when he would be bringing Rita Kay there to meet everyone.

"What? Are you all out of your mind? It has been two long years since I have seen her. Do you think for a moment that I would bring her here to meet this scruffy bunch? I am going to take her straight to that brand new cabin I built for her, where we will stay like two peas in a pod until after the Christmas break, when I have to come back here to work. Yep, I want her all to myself."

After a good laugh around the table, Steven choked down some breakfast and hurried out the door. He could not wait to get to the train station.

Elsie was nervous about meeting Oscar's wealthy family. She was glad her work had given her the opportunity to live in close proximity with the Layne family. That helped her gain some confidence in her ability to communicate with the Baynes family. She packed the nicest things she had, hoping they would be nice enough to not embarrass Oscar.

Trevor and August had tickets to ride the same train with Oscar and Elsie, as all of them traveled to their respective homes for Christmas.

Chapter 51

CHRISTMAS 1865

The Christmas tree was beautifully decorated and completely surrounded with packages. As was the Layne tradition, gifts would be distributed and opened on Christmas Eve, rather than Christmas Day.

Following a tasty meal around the table in the dining room, Nathaniel, Tom, Randy and Benjamin each took a place on the floor near the tree. Adam, Sara Ella and Emma Lou followed, sitting in chairs from around the table. Everyone had a gift or two, but the gift that drew the most attention was Benjamin's gift from Adam. When he opened the box, he found one hundred gleaming gold dollars inside. He was speechless, his mouth hanging open.

Swallowing hard, Benjamin asked, "Mr. Adam, this is supposed to be Randy's, and it was given to me by mistake, right?" He held the box out to Randy. His mother jumped up from her chair in disbelief and rushed to his side to examine the generous gift more closely.

Shaking all over in awe, Emma Lou said, "Oh, Mr. Adam! Is this some kind of joke?"

There was a quiver in Adam's voice when he answered, "No, Emma Lou, it isn't a joke. I mean it for Benjamin. He has been so selfless and helpful to Randy, not asking for any kind of payment. This is just my way of expressing my appreciation the only way I know how. Benjamin's love for Randy expresses best the essence of a man's love for his fellow man." He swallowed hard and continued, "Were it not for Benjamin, Randy would not be alive today, nor would he be so self-sufficient. There is no way we could possibly pay him for what he has done for Randy. Those gold dollars are just a token of our appreciation of your son, Emma Lou."

Emma Lou began sobbing, and Benjamin put his arms around his mother. He also had tears rolling down his face.

Through a broken voice, Emma Lou said, "Mr. Adam, yo' cain't know what it mean to us ta' be part 'a yo' fam'ly."

Benjamin wiped his eyes with his shirt sleeve and nodded. He swallowed hard and turned to look at Adam saying, "Thank you for loving my mother and me."

Swallowing hard and finding his voice, Adam looked Benjamin in the eye and said, "From now on, whether you are with Randy or not, we will meet your needs the same way we meet his. It is not pay, Benjamin. It is appreciation for what you mean to him and to us. This money is yours to do with as you choose." He reached over and hugged Benjamin warmly. "We love you, son."

Benjamin wiped his eyes again with his sleeve and said simply, "Mr. Adam, I love him, and I love you all, too."

Randy took hold of Benjamin's hand and squeezed it. A big smile brightened his blue eyes, as they filled with tears. Though Randy saw nothing, he had heard everything...and he was very pleased.

There was not a dry eye in the room, as Adam openly expressed his appreciation for each person there, individually.

"Well, then," Adam drew in a deep breath, smiled and said, "I am ready to sing some Christmas carols, how about you?"

The following week, Lisa and Warren were married. It was a beautiful, simple ceremony at their little neighborhood Church. As Lisa and Warren requested, everyone, including the bride and groom, dressed in whatever they usually wore on Sunday mornings to church services.

Leftover Christmas decorations brought from home made the church more festive than usual for the wedding. The ladies of the church located enough flowers to make a beautiful wedding bouquet for Lisa.

After the marriage vows had been exchanged and the couple was congratulated by their loving church family, Tom picked them up in a beautifully decorated carriage, arranged by Adam and adorned by Sara Ella, Emma Lou, Benjamin and Randy.

Everyone was invited to the reception at the Layne mansion, where Emma Lou stayed to put the finishing touches on preparations. When the wedding party arrived, the meal was ready to be served. After the main portion of the meal, there was a three layer wedding cake with white icing all around. The mood was festive, as Warren and Lisa fed cake to one another in the traditional ceremonial way.

Just then, there was a sharp knock at the door.

"Who can that be, coming to our house on Sunday?" It was nearly dark outside, when Adam opened the door.

"Mr. Layne?" inquired the stranger.

"Yes," Adam answered. "As you can see, we are in the middle of a celebration here. If you are here on business, I have no time to talk."

The well-dressed man did not introduce himself, but said, "I am here to purchase that cleared plot of ground on the other side of your plantation."

"It is not for sale, sir." Adam was abrupt and started to close the door.

"Just a minute," the man said, and stuck his foot and leg inside the closing door.

"Everything is for sale for the right price. I would like to make an offer on it."

Adam was now irritated and subsequently discourteous, because the man had the audacity to force himself into his home. "Number one, we are having a celebration here at this time, and do not want it to be broken into by strangers. Number two, the property is not for sale, to anyone at any price. Do I make myself clear? The land is NOT FOR SALE!" and he closed the door forcefully. The foot was quickly drawn back, before the door closed on it.

The man continued knocking repeatedly, getting louder and louder. So Tom, Nathaniel, Moses and Warren got up to go stand beside Adam.

"You do not have to open the door to him again," Nathaniel suggested, very firmly.

The men were all accustomed to carrying a fire arm, with all the trouble they had been having at the plantation, lately. But, they had removed them for the wedding reception. Adam instructed Tom and Nathaniel to go get their guns and his from the cloak room where they had left them earlier. Now, the pounding on the door sounded like it was coming from a club rather than a fist.

Adam looked at Benjamin and said, "Be ready to protect the ladies if necessary, boys." Randy and Benjamin went around the table to stand next to the women and Samuel.

Tom and Nathaniel returned with guns for Adam, Warren and themselves. With guns loaded and ready, Adam opened the door again. Moses stood with Tom and Nathaniel behind Warren and Adam. Rifles and pistols were pointed and ready.

Adam stepped forward and said in a low, firm voice, "I am only going to say this once, Mister. Leave now and do not come back. Not an inch of this property is for sale at any price! Now, leave before I count to five, or we will see to it that you are no longer able to do so. ONE, TWO, THREE....," Adam counted loudly.

"I will be back," the man spouted off with some superlatives added for emphasis. Then he left.

Sara Ella turned to Adam and asked, "Who was that man? And what if he had come here another time, with you up at the mill? What should I do?"

Adam rushed to her side, put his arm around her for comfort, and then raised his voice for everyone to hear, as he said, "Under no circumstances should any of the ladies be without protection. Ladies, do not open the door to anyone, I mean anyone, from here on. Understood? Keep the rope latch fastened at all times."

Warren, who had been standing directly behind Adam at the door, shook his head. "I have had carpetbaggers come to my place, but they have never been as rude as this man. Sometimes they actually appear to be sincere, wanting to help me out, knowing I cannot support myself. But, I have never had them be belligerent like that, trying to force me out. Wonder what the motivation is to act in that manner? Surely they know that they cannot be rude and expect you to listen to them."

Adam shook his head in agreement and said, "Sara Ella and Nathaniel had a bad encounter with a carpetbagger while I was gone to Charleston recently. Since then, I have had at least one man staying with the women for protection. We have also had trouble on the road with people being accosted by strangers."

Samuel asked a thousand questions, worried about the safety of his mother and new father if he was not there to help protect them. He knew he was supposed to spend the night with Randy and Benjamin who seemed so brave and strong when he stood together with them to protect the women. Moses assured Samuel that he would keep watch over his family for him, as he needed to watch his own family as well.

On horseback, Nathaniel and Tom escorted Lisa and Warren in the wedding carriage, as Moses and Martha drove them home. They all watched the tender moment when Warren swept little Lisa off her feet and carried her across the threshold of the Callahan Plantation home for their wedding night together.

"Good night, everyone," Adam announced. "I think we have had enough excitement for tonight."

Sara Ella clung to Adam more tightly than usual, as they made their way to their little cabin to go to bed. Frightened for her, Adam asked, "Have you ever fired a gun, Sara Ella?"

"No," she answered, "I have never had a reason to do so. You know I do not like guns, Adam."

"Well, first thing tomorrow morning you are going to learn to shoot a pistol and a rifle. My mother and my sister were proficient with a rifle and a hand gun, so there is no reason you cannot be, as well. I want you to keep the pistol with you at all times, especially when I am not with you. With all that is going on around here, you simply must to be prepared to defend yourself."

Sara Ella was very reluctant, yet she knew this was a good idea. The plantation was in a remote location, with no neighbors very nearby. She knew that she was very vulnerable if she was ever alone for any reason.

Early the next morning, Adam introduced Sara Ella to his 1858 Remington hand gun. As he explained the operation of it to her, she held it in her hand.

"It is heavy! I did not expect it to be so heavy..."

"Yes, it is," Adam responded. Then he explained to her that she would only have six shots until she would have to reload the revolver. She would need to learn, not only how to shoot well enough to hit her target, but how to reload quickly as well.

Listening intently, Sara Ella said, "Just let me shoot it once, so I know what it feels like."

"All right, he said, showing her how to hold the gun with both hands. As instructed, she pulled the hammer back on the .44 caliber Remington pistol and reluctantly pulled the trigger. Fire belched from the muzzle. Smoke from the powder that covered the area seemed to blot out everything. The loud report and jerk of the gun almost made her drop the weapon in fright.

Trembling and almost blinded by the smoke, she cried, "Oh, Adam, will it always do that?"

Not wanting her to be overcome with fear of the weapon, Adam nodded without emotion and encouraging her to try again. Sara Ella pulled the hammer back and very cautiously repeated the shot. After nearly an hour of doing that over and over again, she began to feel more at ease. As her fear of the weapon subsided, she began hitting her target occasionally.

"Adam, will I ever feel comfortable pointing this thing at someone and pulling the trigger?"

"You may never have to shoot anyone, Sara Ella. But, you must be comfortable and confident enough holding the gun that your enemy assumes you know how to use it proficiently. Hopefully, that confidence alone will prevent you from having to fire the weapon at anyone. Remember, you must have it with you at all times. Understand?"

Sara Ella nodded soberly, as they turned and went back to their cabin. Adam continued instructing her as they walked along. "From now on, both of us will have our gun under our pillow when we sleep, and we will take them with us wherever we go. Do you understand? Not just for today, but for a long time. Until our country has settled down and we can live without fear." She nodded, but said nothing.

As Adam closed the door behind them, Sara Ella put her arms around him, and said, "I am so glad you are my husband, Adam Layne. I love you."

He smiled, picked her up and kissed her passionately. "I love you too, Sara Ella Layne, not just for today, but forever. Celebrating Lisa and Warren's wedding with them reminded me of the journey our love has taken us down through the years. From the day we met at the church picnic to the day I first put the ring on your finger that Christmas day so long ago...and then our wedding at the train station...I have never stopped loving you, and I never will stop loving you. I am so grateful for everything you are to me."

Chapter 52

Adam reached up and took Sara Ella's hand to help her down, as they disembarked from the train in Washington City. He was so grateful to have her with him this time. Oscar had given her a list of bath closet and kitchen fixtures he needed for the mansion, so she planned to meet with plumbing suppliers to pick out everything. Tom went to collect their luggage, as Adam mused about how it could already be the year 1866. His stay at Oaklayne for Christmas had been much too short.

Realizing there were too many bags and trunks for Tom to handle alone, Adam suggested that Sara Ella hail a cab, while he went to assist Tom.

Once Sara Ella was finally settled at the Layne townhouse, Adam left and headed to the newspaper office to see his friend Scott Bryan. On the way there, he was assaulted with the terrible stench of the city, reminding him of another reason he loved Oaklayne. *They need to find a way to get plumbing into this city, so this odor can be taken care of, once and for all. It takes your breath away!*

The young man at the front desk of the newspaper office recognized Adam and waved him on back to see Scott Bryan.

"Adam, come on in! It is good to see you. What are you up to this chilly day?"

"Hello, Scott. I am on my way to a meeting with Stanton, so I thought I had better have you fill me in on all of the latest news."

"Well first, everyone knows that big decisions must be made soon at the Capitol about the Reconstruction. And, of course, they are all standing firm on their own political agendas.

"However, the biggest thing everyone seems to be talking about is the stock hikes that just keep climbing on Credit Mobilier, the construction management firm for Union Pacific Railroad. You will remember my bringing that up the last time you were here. Look at these statistics, Adam. They are even a lot higher than they were when I told you about them last time you were here. I tell you, it is just going through the roof. This all has to do with a transcontinental railroad they are building to go all of the way to the west coast. I am still suspicions about it though. I do not know what is going on, but it seems to be growing too fast. Keep your ear to the ground, Adam, and let me know if you hear anything about it. I will keep you up to date as I hear more about it."

"Thanks, Scott," said Adam, scratching his chin. "Sara Ella is with me this trip, so maybe we could get our families together one evening, while we are here. I guess I had better be on my way. It is best not to keep Secretary Stanton waiting, you know," Adam said with a silly grin that he knew Scott would understand.

"Hey, it would be a great idea to get together. Perhaps, it would be best for the ladies to make a plan? See you soon."

As Adam climbed up the steps of the Capitol, something seemed different. He could not quite put his finger on it, but it was very strange. Once inside, the rotunda seemed very different, as well. Looking up, instead of watching where he was going, he bumped into someone.

"Oh, excuse me," he said, recognizing Senator William Kelley.

"Well, hello Adam! Is it not great to be finished with all that racket? I was beginning to think they would never get finished rebuilding that dome."

"That is it! That is what is different. When I bumped into you I was trying to figure out what was different. You are right about the quiet. That noise was obnoxious."

"Are you on your way to Stanton's office?"

"Yes, just reporting for duty. By the way have you been keeping up on the Union Pacific Railroad stock? I have heard that it is really going up."

"I am aware of it and know that there are a number of Congressmen who have purchased it and seem excited. Are you interested? I could give you some names of those who have invested in it, if you would like to talk with them about it."

"It might be interesting to talk with them, if you do not mind giving me their names."

"I will make a list and get it to you later. I have a meeting with General Howard right now about some revisions to the Freedmen's Bureau Bill."

Secretary Stanton greeted Adam with his usual lack of warmth and immediately started hammering away at the issues. "Adam, soon the Radical Republicans will present the expanded version of the Freedman's Bureau Bill for a vote. You may already know that Wilson's Civil Rights Initiative was defeated. As a result, he has now proposed that the Constitution be amended to prohibit any effort to limit the right to vote because of race. Soon, Lyman Trumbull will be presenting his Civil Rights Bill to the senate. It seeks to grant citizenship to the freedmen. That one should be interesting. You might want to sit in on it, since you are here."

"I would like that, sir. Do you have any idea when it will come up?"

"Hard to say. I expect it will be by the end of January or first of February," said Stanton.

"I will be there," said Adam. "By the way, have you heard anything about the Union Pacific Railroad's construction management company, Credit Mobilier?"

"Funny you should ask. One of the Congressmen was just telling me I should buy some of that stock. He pointed out how steadily it has been going up in price. I know that the Federal Government is subsidizing Union Pacific to build a railroad that will continue from Missouri, all the way to California. Why do you ask, Adam?"

Adam sat back in his chair and said, "Well, I am not sure, frankly. It is just that I have a friend who is suspicious about it, that is all. I might do some snooping around if it is okay with you."

"I do not have anything particularly pressing for you to do right now, so go ahead and ask around. Keep me posted on what you find out."

"Thanks, I believe I will look into it."

Adam left the Capitol and went directly to the Washington Examiner. He was waved on by with a smile from the young man at the front desk. When Adam entered Scott's office, he found him conversing with John Kendall, their mutual friend.

"Adam!" John called out as soon as he saw him. "It is so good to see you. Scott was just telling me about Credit Mobilier and Union Pacific. He said he mentioned it to you earlier."

"Yes, Scott seems to have some misgivings, so I asked a few people about it at the Capitol this morning. They only had good things to say. In fact, I came here to see if Scott would tell me exactly what he is concerned about."

John spoke up and said, "Scott has good reason to be concerned, Adam. So am I. Do you know anything about the scoundrels who are in charge of Union Pacific?"

Scott broke in, "I knew that there was something fishy going on, but, I had not put it all together until John reminded me about Doc Durant. You remember him, Adam. Dr. Thomas Clark Durant owned the Missouri & Mississippi Railroad. He made a fortune smuggling contraband cotton from the Confederate states with the aid of General Grenville Dodge."

"Yeah, I am very familiar with that story. I do not think the South or the North profited from that arrangement, but Durant pocketed a fortune. He wound up cheating both the North and the South. What does Durant have to do with the Union Pacific Railroad or Credit Mobilier?"

"Keeping in mind his lack of scruples," Scott said, "You will understand why I am concerned about Union Pacific when I tell you that the Union Pacific Railroad is owned by Durant. Lincoln hired him to build the Transcontinental Railroad, because years ago Durant had hired the young Lincoln as an Attorney to defend him in a lawsuit. Some boaters did not like a bridge he built for his M&M railroad, the first bridge across the Mississippi River."

"I met Durant when I was on a mission in St. Louis. Arms and ammunition were being smuggled up North by way of the Mississippi River, and I was there to find out how it was being done. I remember coming across some of that cotton, but could not do anything about it because of my mission.

"Dr. Durant was in town, but I did not find out about his involvement with the cotton smuggling until later. The man was boisterous and very impressed with himself. When other men attempted to advise him, he humiliated them, treating them like mere children. Distasteful as his morals are, I had heard he became a very wealthy man during the war.

"Now, I understand why you would question his involvement, but do you know of anything in particular he is doing that is criminal or even not above board?"

Scott wrung his hands and grimaced as he said, "Well, John and I were just talking about that. Currently, neither of us is aware of anything specific."

John broke in and said, "There is another man involved in this scheme with Durant, Adam. George Francis Train is his name. He is a charming, very charismatic and adventurous man. Everyone seems to like him, unlike the pushy tyrant, Durant. I cannot imagine how the two wound up doing business together."

Adam rubbed his chin with a puzzled expression, and said, "The name sounds a little familiar to me, but I cannot say that I know him."

"If you have ever met him," John interjected, "I do not think you would forget him. He makes a big impression on folks. He used to own a finance company called Credit Foncier of America, before he became involved with the Union Pacific Railroad. He is making a fortune from real estate as a result of the transcontinental railway. The railroad is opening up access to land out west, making it necessary to build new settlements and developments. In 1864 the Credit Foncier of America became Credit Mobilier."

"Hmmm..." said Adam. "So, there is the connection. Learning about Durant being involved arouses my suspicion. I will give this some thought. There should be some way to find out more. Thank you gentlemen, for your thoughts. If you hear any more, please let me know."

Back at the townhouse, Adam found Tom stocking the kitchen cabinets with groceries.

"Hello Tom, where is Sara Ella?"

"She is at the plumbing store looking at samples and a big catalog the proprietor showed her earlier when I was there with her. She confessed to me that she is overwhelmed, knowing it will take some time, working with the shop keeper, before she will be ready to make any decisions. I told her I would go to the grocery store, then pick her up there at about 4:30. I will need to go get her shortly."

Adam sat down at the table and watched Tom putting the groceries away.

"Tom," he asked, stretching his legs under the table, "you have never shared with me your dreams. What would you like to do with your life? Where would you like to live? Do you want a wife and kids, or would you prefer to remain single? Would you like to have your own business, maybe a stable? Would you like to have a house in the country or in the city?"

Tom looked at the floor, hesitant to discuss this subject with Adam.

"You have been a good man to me, Adam, and I am pleased to serve you in any way that I can. Is that not enough?"

"Surely there are things you dream about, Tom. I am interested to know about your dreams. Would you like to visit France someday? Or, maybe live out in the wild west?"

Tom looked at him and laughed. "That is ridiculous! I think you would be surprised if I told you what I have dreamed about..."

"Try me. I really want to know, Tom."

Tom sighed, looked down at the floor and said, "Well, I would really like to have a wife and lots of children, even more than Moses and Martha. I think it would be perfect to live in a city, where I could get to know lots of people. I wish I could walk in the front door of a store or restaurant and receive a friendly greeting from the owner, instead of always having to go around back to the kitchen."

Adam was speechless, as if the wind had been knocked out of him.

Tom stepped back and said, "I told you..."

"I...I had no idea, Tom," said Adam. What have I stolen from this humble man that I care so much about? His dreams have been squashed by the color of his skin and his service to me all these years. Adam was crushed by the simplicity of Tom's longing for what white men take for granted. He was stunned and frozen to his chair, while Tom returned to the menial chore of putting away the groceries.

Tom noticed that Adam looked sullen and distraught, so he sat down at the table beside him and said, "Adam, listen to me. I came into this world to be your slave. We have had some hard times, as well as some wonderful adventures together through the years, you and me. I do not deny that I have thought about freedom at times, but never seriously considered what it would be like.

"When Mr. Lincoln gave me my freedom, you were quick to explain it to me. I have known I am a free man ever since. You are such a good man that I have never known any physical need, before or after slavery. And, you continue to care for me in very generous ways. I am in no hurry to realize any of my dreams if they mean leaving you behind, my friend."

At that point Tom got up, and went back to putting away the groceries. Coming to his senses, Adam told Tom that he would go get Sara Ella himself. All the way to the store he could not get his conversation with Tom out of his mind.

When Adam arrived at the plumbing store, Sara Ella was glad to see him. She showed him several fixtures she was interested in, and asked his opinion on several others she was not sure about. It took longer than he expected and it was obvious she would have to come back the next day to settle on which of two sinks she liked better for the bath closet. Everything would be ordered and sent to Richmond for them to pick up there.

About a week later, Adam was encouraged when Congress renewed the Freedman's Bureau Bill.

Investigating Credit Mobilier and Union Pacific for the next few weeks, Adam found out that James Garfield, Schuyler Colfax, James Patterson and Henry Wilson, men from both political parties, owned stock in both Credit Mobilier and Union Pacific. They were known to be ecstatic about its growth, but none of them were personally willing to give him any information. Oddly, the only facts he was able to gather came from an associate of the opposing political party.

"Adam," Stanton said gruffly, pacing back and forth and tugging on his long beard, "I think you are onto something with this Union Pacific thing. But, we are going to have to be discreet to find out exactly what is going on. Let me know what you find out."

"Yes, sir," said Adam, "I will keep you posted. I am sorry that President Johnson vetoed the Freedman's Bureau Bill. I understand that even the media is upset with him, and the Conservative Republicans are so shocked that they are leaning into an alliance with the Radicals Republicans against him. I read an article in the paper written by Johnson's friend, John Forney, rebuking him."

"Yes, we were all surprised that Forney took a stand against the veto. This President continues to confuse me. His actions are not at all consistent with his position when he ran for office along-side of Lincoln."

"That is my understanding as well."

"If you do not get on over there, you are going to miss hearing Senator Lyman Trumbull proposing his Civil Rights legislation. He is the leader of the Moderate Republicans, you know."

Adam looked at his pocket watch and exclaimed, "Oh my, it is time! I had better get over there."

The Senate Chamber was nearly full as Adam searched for a seat. Senator Trumbull was already talking as Adam found a seat with a good view and hurried right to it.

"I tell you that the abolition of slavery is empty if laws are to be enacted and enforced depriving persons of African descent of privileges which are essential to freemen...A law that does not allow a colored person to go from one country to another, and one that does not allow him to hold property, to teach, to preach, are certainly laws in violation of the rights of a freeman...The purpose of this bill is to destroy all these discriminations..."

Later Adam was able to read the bill which said:

"All persons born in the United States...are hereby declared to be citizens of the United States; and such citizens of every race and color, without regard to any previous condition of slavery...shall have the same right in every State...to make and enforce contracts, to sue, be parties, and give evidence, to inherit, purchase, lease, sell, hold, and convey real and personal property, and to full and equal benefit of all laws and proceedings for the security of person and property, as is enjoyed by white citizens, and shall be subject to like punishment, pains, and penalties and to none other, any law statute, ordinance, regulation, or custom to the Contrary notwithstanding."

On February 2, 1866, Adam ran into the townhouse, grabbed Sara Ella in his arms and exclaimed, "It passed! The Civil Rights Bill passed the Senate!"

"That is wonderful news, Adam. Tom is out in the carriage house getting our trunks, so we can start packing to return home."

"I will go tell him! I brought him a copy of the Bill. I am sure he will want to have it. The House still has to vote on it in the middle of March, but this is a big first step."

Chapter 53

Though the paper was quite brittle and delicate, Miles Cutler's original plans for the Oaklayne mansion proved to remain in good enough condition to follow. Both Adam and Oscar spent a good deal of time pouring over them, during the course of rebuilding the house to the original specs. Of course, upgrades were made to make it more efficient and modern than when it was built nearly a hundred years before, but the appearance was to be as much like the original mansion as humanly possible.

Adam was pleased with the progress, and anxious for Matt and Laura to arrive from Europe with the finishing wood and windows. If the Phantom II was on time with the supplies, the house would be finished in the early Spring. Adam expected them to arrive in the next few days, a week at the most.

He was so pleased that Laura would be the one looking for furnishings like she grew up with when she lived at Oaklayne all through her childhood. Hopefully, shopping for those items would not slow down their departure from Europe for their voyage back to Virginia. Laura would have good taste if she had to compromise on some things that were not exactly the same as the original.

He was eager to start construction on the Oakville cabins he planned to build for Tom, Nathaniel and Emma Lou. After his talk in the Townhouse with Tom about his dreams, he wanted to get a chance to find out what each of them really wanted, rather than assuming he already knew. If Tom preferred a place of his own in town, then that is what he should have.

Sara Ella was still pressuring him to build the school building right away, so she, Martha and Elizabeth could begin teaching the black children what the white children were studying. They were already holding classes for many of the black adults, hoping they would be able to become teachers soon, as well.

351

Chapter 54

It was a cool evening when Randy and Benjamin entered the Richmond University Dining Room. Randy leaned over to Benjamin and asked, "Do you see Samantha anywhere?"

Benjamin looked around the room, and spotted Samantha Imboden sitting nearby.

"Yes, I see her, and she is waving at us to come to her table," said Benjamin.

When Randy met General Imboden's niece, Samantha, they immediately became fast friends. She accepted Benjamin, which went a long way with Randy. Samantha's parents were killed during the war, so her Uncle John took her into his home and took care of her as if she were his own daughter.

"You are late tonight," remarked Samantha, "What have you boys been up to?"

Randy rolled his eyes and told her that some white boys were harassing Benjamin again, assuming that he should not be on campus.

"I am so sorry. People can be very ugly sometimes, when they are trying to adjust to change. I hope that they will grow to accept it better someday," said Samantha.

The three young people went on to enjoy an evening of light conversation. But, just as it was about time to depart, a man came rushing in calling out, "Randy Layne, please raise your hand, so I can find you."

Randy looked at Benjamin and asked, "What is going on, Benjamin?"

"I do not know, Randy. Just do as the man says," Benjamin said quickly.

Randy raised his hand, and the man came hurriedly toward him. "Mr. Layne, there is a buggy waiting for you in front of the dining room. You are to go with the driver immediately. They say your mother has been shot, and is in the hospital." As Randy got up, the man continued, "I am sorry, I do not know how serious it is."

"Shot? What happened?" Randy asked.

"I do not know anything more. I was only told to come and get you immediately."

With no time to allow him to find his own way, Benjamin quickly grabbed Randy's arm and guided him hurriedly to the door. They did not even take time to say goodbye to Samantha, but knew she would understand why.

When they reached the buggy, they found Oscar waiting for them. Randy asked what had happened, as they both climbed inside. Oscar explained that he and Adam were going over some things at the big house when they heard gunshots, and Tom came racing toward them yelling, "Sara Ella's been shot!"

"Adam and I got there as fast as we could. We loaded her in the carriage and brought her to the hospital," said Oscar, as he pulled away from the campus Dining Room and raced toward the hospital. "I will get you there as quickly as possible, boys."

"Is she going to be alright?" asked Randy.

"She is in bad shape, Randy. I just do not know. She has lost a lot of blood. Your father needs you." Oscar swallowed hard and continued, "When he saw Sara Ella there on the ground, he collapsed beside her. She looked dead, Randy." Oscar choked back tears and said, "Adam cried out in anguish and held her in his arms. I reached for her pulse and found that she was alive.

"When Tom brought the carriage around to take her to the hospital, we had to literally pry her from your father's arms. She was bleeding profusely, so we told him to hold a towel firmly over the big hole in her chest, while I drove us to the hospital.

"Randy, I have never seen him fall apart this way. I hope you can calm him. He asked me to come and get you once we had her settled at the hospital."

With blood stains all over his shirt, Adam grabbed Randy into his arms as soon as they stepped into the waiting room Benjamin stood at Randy's side.

"What happened, Father?"

Finding it difficult to talk, Adam did his best to explain to Randy and Benjamin that Sara Ella had lost a lot of blood and was in critical condition.

"Tom said he was in the stable when he heard her scream from in front of the Temporary House. I do not know why Tom was in the stable, he was supposed to be protecting her. Tom grabbed his rifle, not knowing what he might find. Running as fast as he could, he heard a gunshot and smelled gunpowder as he arrived on the scene.

"The man was close to where Sara Ella lay injured on the ground, bleeding from a gunshot wound to her back. The man had his pistol pointed at her like he was going to shoot her again, so Tom raised his rifle and shot him. He fell dead, and Tom raced toward the big house where he found us running toward the sound of the gunshots. He told us what had happened. Randy, the shooter is the same man who has been at the house twice before wanting to buy land.

"Oscar and I raced here to the hospital with her, then I asked him to get you. I do not know where Tom went. I have not seen him since he brought the carriage and helped us load Sara Ella in it to bring her here."

Pausing for a deep breath, Randy asked, "When will we know something?"

Adam shook his head in despair. Randy did not think he had ever seen his father so despondent. He put his arm around Adam and sat quietly by his side.

Benjamin touched Randy's arm, signaling that he needed to speak with him privately. "Randy, I am concerned about Tom. No one knows where he is. He shot a white man, when he is not even supposed to have a gun. White people will not care why he did it. He is in big trouble, Randy. I do not know how to help him out of the spot he is in now. What should we do?"

Randy was so consumed with his father and Sara Ella that he had not considered what this situation would mean for Tom.

"You are right. We need to get General Imboden to help Tom right away. I need to be here to comfort my father, so you will need to get Oscar to help you deal with Tom's situation. Hurry!"

Randy considered talking to Adam about Tom's predicament, but decided instead to take charge of the situation himself, rather than giving his father another heavy load to carry. Oh, how he wished he were already out of law school, so he would know what to do. He knew enough to know that he had to do everything possible to keep Tom from being jailed. Without any witnesses the authorities could charge him with murder, and probably would. He trusted Benjamin to be able to convey everything that happened to General Imboden, and he would know what to do.

Chapter 55

After helping load Sara Ella into the buggy for the ride to the hospital, Tom hurried back to the body of the carpetbagger. He found the man lying right where he shot him, the bullet passing through his heart, killing him instantly. To help Tom, two of the men who had been working in the big house soberly picked up the body of the man and carried him to the barn area.

Horrified by what had happened and worried about Sara Ella and Adam, Tom hitched a horse to the buckboard and loaded the bloody corpse into the back. He felt compelled to take the body to the Police Station in Richmond as soon as possible, so Adam would not have to deal with it when he returned.

A crowd of people gathered around the buckboard, as Tom came into town. It had not occurred to him that he would need to be careful how he worded his explanation to the authorities for why he had the body of a dead white man in his wagon. His plan was to simply tell the truth about how the man shot Sara Ella and would have shot her a second time if Tom had not stopped him.

The crowd began to murmur and follow the wagon down the street. The murmuring grew louder, as he got closer and closer to the Richmond Police Station. Questions rumbled to the surface, with some of the followers shouting expletives about Tom's color and his heritage.

"What is going on here, boy? Who is this dead man in the back of your wagon? Why is that white man dead? Who are you? Who killed him? Where was he killed?"

Tom pulled up in front of the Richmond Police Station and climbed down from the wagon. As he entered the building, he was relieved to finally be under the protection of the authorities, who could keep him from being mauled by the mob in the streets.

Just inside the door, he was met by a young man dressed in a Union Army Captain's uniform. This military man was part of a contingent of the Union Army that had been assigned to keep the peace in the former Confederate States who had not yet rejoined the Union. These men were tasked with keeping order and governing until every Confederate soldier, whose home of record was in the State where they were assigned, had taken a pledge of allegiance to the United States of America. Only then would the State be allowed to make their pledge of allegiance and be admitted back into the Union. Consequently, the citizens of Virginia felt as if they were living under martial law, and they were not at all happy about it.

With lightning speed, the man grabbed Tom's left wrist and forced it behind him. Before Tom knew what had happened, both of his hands were behind his back and in handcuffs.

"Sergeant, hold this man in custody until I see what is going on here," the man said abruptly.

Then he walked outside to the source of the rumbling voices that had disturbed his otherwise quiet afternoon. Approaching Tom's buckboard, the Captain climbed into the back and examined the bloody body of the carpetbagger. Concerned about the state of mind of the crowd, he was wary and did his best to maintain composure and control of the situation.

He carefully got down from the wagon and shouted over the noise of the ruckus, "Does anyone here recognize this dead man, or the one who brought him here?"

The Captain's inquiry was ignored. The crowd became even more belligerent and aggressive. When he opened the door to go back into the office, a rush of men almost knocked him down, pushing their way inside.

In a chaotic instant, the mob of men grabbed Tom from the Sergeant who had him restrained and turned their guns on the Captain and his men. Warning the law enforcement officers not to interfere, they dragged Tom outside, as he struggled to free himself. Tom knew there was no sense in trying to explain to the unruly mob that he was innocent and justified in killing the carpetbagger.

They dragged Tom down the street, followed by the noisy crowd. They stopped in front of the livery stable. A noose was thrown over Toms head and tightened, as he valiantly resisted. The other end of the rope was quickly thrown over the extended arm of the beam that supports the hay loft. Now in a frenzy, several men grabbed the end of the rope and together pulled Tom up, with the rope around his neck, until his feet were dangling.

The crowd stood and watched as Tom jerked and convulsed. Gradually, his movements became weaker and weaker. Then, finally his body stopped thrashing around, and he hung lifeless.

The crowd was exuberant. They had seen to it that justice prevailed, Satisfied with what had been done, they began to drift away from the scene. After all, this black man had shot and killed a white man.

Tom's lifeless body was left hanging as a warning to other black men that they must never accost a white person in any way for any reason.

Chapter 56

"Mr. Layne, I'm Doctor Hill," said a kindly looking gentleman wearing hospital garb and a stethoscope around his neck. "I am pleased to report that your wife is most fortunate. The bullet hit just under her left shoulder blade and went all the way through barely grazing the bone. She was clearly shot in the back where there is a small hole, then the bullet tore its way through to the front, leaving a wicked exit wound in her chest.

"I expect her to be in the hospital for some time, before it will be safe for her to return home. She lost a lot of blood, and is having a bit of trouble breathing right now. We will have to watch her wounds closely for infection for the next several days. But, barring any complications, I expect her to have a full recovery. However, she will be weak for several months. She is lucky to be alive."

Adam broke down, as his knees gave way. Sobbing and shaking the doctor's hand, he awkwardly expressed appreciation.

Randy turned to the doctor and asked when they would be allowed to see Sara Ella. The doctor suggested they wait close by, so the nurse would be able to let them know when she had gained consciousness. Relieved that she was going to be okay, Randy was anxious to ask Sara Ella some questions that might help in Tom's defense if it was needed down the road.

As they waited impatiently, Randy asked Adam question after question, "I wonder why Sara Ella was alone? Was not someone supposed to be with her at all times, after that man had been so aggressive before? Why was Tom in the stable, instead of with her? Did she fire her gun in an attempt to protect herself?"

Adam kept answering, "I do not know, Randy. None of it makes much sense. All I could think about was getting her here to the hospital as quickly as possible. I do not know what I would do if I lost her, Randy. All I know is what Tom told us, that she was shot by the carpetbagger who had been at the house earlier. He did not have time to tell me anymore. We will have to wait and ask Tom and Sara Ella more details later."

Randy continued with questions, "Are you sure that Tom shot the man? Or, could it have been someone else?"

Exasperated, Adam said, "I do not know, Randy. Tom said he shot the man to keep him from shooting Sara Ella again. That is all I know. We will just have to wait until Sara Ella and Tom can tell us more. Right now, it really does not matter much, does it? We will sit and wait until the nurse tells us we can go in, all right?"

Randy knew it did matter a lot, but he did not want to give his father any more reason to worry. So, he sat quietly in the waiting room all night, waiting for Sara Ella to wake up. He and Adam both struggled to get comfortable, squirming and sleeping sporadically, as time passed slowly.

As dawn broke the early morning sky, the sun began to peek into the window of the waiting room. Adam got to his feet and stretched, wondering about Sara Ella's condition. He made his way to the nurse's desk and inquired about her. The nurse told him that she was just beginning to show signs of consciousness, but was not able to communicate yet.

He asked if it would be okay for him to go sit with her, and the nurse reluctantly agreed. "Talk with her. It will help her wake up to hear your voice. She may not be able to respond for a while, though."

"Thank you so much!" responded Adam. "Would you mind sending someone to the waiting room to tell my son Randy of my whereabouts. Tell him that I will report to him as soon as she is conscious enough for him to see her."

Benjamin found Randy in the hallway and reported that he and Oscar were able to contact General Imboden about Tom.

"General Imboden said that we need to see if we can find the bullet that passed through Sara Ella's chest. We also need to find her gun to see if it was her or Tom who shot the man. He needs to ask Tom for his account of what happened, and exactly who the man was. Maybe he will have some identification on him?" Benjamin was still concerned, but encouraged after visiting with General Imboden.

Chapter 57

It was early March, when Adam, Randy and Benjamin arrived at Oaklayne by hired carriage. As they pulled up in front of the house, Adam could see the Phantom II docked on the James River, indicating that Laura and Matt had arrived on schedule. Tired and emotionally drained from their ordeal at the hospital with Sara Ella, the three men gathered enough energy to run toward the Temporary House, excited to see Laura again.

Laura burst through the door when she heard them coming. "Adam! Randy! It is so good to be home." She flew into Adam's arms, then turned to Randy and embraced him warmly saying, "Look at you! You are a man now, and so is Benjy! The last time I saw the two of you, you were just little boys. My, how you have changed. I was so sorry to hear about your injury, Randy. Please let me know if there is anything I can do to help."

Then she turned back to Adam and said, "Oscar told us about Sara Ella being shot, and that you sent word that she is going to be okay. What a relief!"

"Yes, she will have to walk down a long road to recovery, but she is going to be fine," said Adam. "I am so glad you are here, Laura."

Adam introduced Matt to Randy and Benjamin, then turned to Laura and said, "I guess you have seen the devastation that the Union troops left behind when they marched across Oaklayne. We are following the original plans for the mansion house to make it as much like before as we can. But here, let me walk you over there and show you."

Rather than going with them on the tour of Oaklayne, Matt excused himself to oversee the unloading of the Phantom II.

Adam asked Laura if she and Matt would be able to stay at Oaklayne awhile, and was disappointed when she said they would need to take a load of cotton to Boston after the harvest for a customer in Savannah. But, they should be able to stay long enough to see Sara Ella get well enough to return home. And, of course, she wanted to see Lisa.

"We will just stay on the ship, so you will not be inconvenienced any by our being here. The Stateroom that Matt set aside on board for us is well equipped and lovely. Besides, that way we would not have to pack and unpack our clothes."

"It will be wonderful to have you with us again for however long you can manage to stay," said Adam. "I have missed you so much." He hugged Laura tenderly, then turned to Benjamin and said, "Please see if you can find Tom, Benjamin. It is strange we have not seen him and that he has not come to greet Laura."

Benjamin was relieved to be able to excuse himself to go in search of Tom.

Randy spoke up and said, "Wait, I want to go with you." Then, when they were out of earshot from his father, he said, "I am really concerned that something terrible has happened to Tom, Benjamin. We simply must locate him right away."

The two young men searched everywhere, but found no sign of Tom. The construction crew told them about Tom loading up the body of the dead man to take it to Richmond, shortly after Adam and Oscar left to take Sara Ella to the hospital, explaining that he wanted to take care of it before Adam returned. They said he felt awful for letting Sara Ella talk him into leaving her alone to go get manure from the barn. They explained that she had him helping her transplant some crocus bulbs to a spot in front of the honeymoon cabin where they could enjoy them more. They had not seen Tom since he left.

"Benjamin, we simply must tell my father. We cannot wait any longer. I do not like involving him one bit, but it is time he knows the situation. We also need to go see General Imboden. Someone will need to find Tom and make sure he is okay. It sure does not look good...," said Randy.

When the two young men returned to the Temporary House to report to Adam, they learned that he had returned to the hospital to be with Sara Ella. So, they decided to follow him.

Arriving at the hospital, Benjamin escorted Randy to Sara Ella's room to check on her condition. They were pleased to learn that she had been moved to a private room. When they located Room 229, they found Adam asleep in the chair beside Sara Ella's bed. He woke up and smiled, as they entered the room.

Randy asked about Sara Ella's condition, expressing his delight upon learning that she had been moved into a private room. Then, in a grave voice he told Adam of his concern for Tom, explaining that he had not returned after taking the dead man's body to Richmond.

"Father, he placed himself in mortal danger, taking that white man to the authorities alone. I am afraid for him," said Randy.

Adam's face grew grim. "Tom is a law-abiding, honest man, boys. I am sure he told the police exactly what happened. They might have put him in jail for having a gun in his possession, even though having it helped him protect Sara Ella. You are right, we need to find out what is going on. Tom should not be in jail. He protected Sara Ella, and they need to understand that."

As they rode together in the wagon to the Police Station, they discussed what they knew of the circumstances. None of them knew the identity of the man who accosted Sara Ella. Randy told his father what the men said about the situation.

"Who is in charge here?" Adam asked, as he walked through the door of the Police Station.

"That would be Captain Duprey, sir," said the young Union soldier who was standing behind the high counter inside the office.

"I need to speak with him immediately. One of my most loyal employees is missing, and last I knew he was on his way here with the body of a man who shot my wife and nearly killed her," said Adam. "She would be dead for sure if he had not been there to protect her."

"Just a minute, sir. I will get him for you," the young soldier said nervously, as he left the counter and returned in a few minutes with a man he introduced as Captain Duprey.

"You are General Adam Layne, are you not?" said the man, meaning it more as a statement than a question. As Adam nodded impatiently, he said, "I thought I recognized you."

Adam did not smile, but asked crisply, "What can you tell me about my man, Tom? He left our plantation yesterday to come here with the body of a man who had just shot my wife. She would be dead if Tom had not defended her."

"Come in my office and sit down, please. We need to talk," said the Captain.

They followed the Captain into his office, and he offered them seats.

"Now, let me see if I can explain...," the Captain began, "Yesterday, Tom came here to the office with the body of a white man in the back of his wagon. He told me who he was, and that the white man had shot Mrs. Layne in the back. After he admitted shooting the man himself, a large mob of white men forced their way into the station. There was nothing we could do to hold them back, there were too many of them. They took Tom from our custody and rushed him out of the building. I am sorry to say, they hanged him at the livery station."

Adam was shocked and horrified! He began shaking violently in unbelief, jumped from his chair and pounded on the Captain's desk, "How could you let that happen? How could you allow them to come into the station and take a man out and lynch him, without doing something to protect him?"

"I am sorry, General. There simply was not time for me to prepare before the crowd broke in. They held me and my men at gun point— there was nothing we could do."

Adam slumped into his chair and wept bitterly. His emotions were so raw from his ordeal with Sara Ella's situation that he could not contain his grief over hearing of Tom's savage death. Randy and Benjamin were numb with shock, but had sense enough to ask where Tom's body could be found.

Sheepishly, Captain Duprey said, "He has not been taken to the burial ground yet. The sexton only digs once a week. Tom's body is in a wooden box behind the office. It should be buried early next week."

Adam collected himself and coldly said, "Do not bother. We will be taking Tom home with us. He will be buried with honors at Oaklayne, the only home he has ever known. He was like a brother to me, and I will not have him buried in a potter's field like some common criminal."

"Again, I am very sorry this happened, General Layne. I can have my men bring the body to you at Oaklayne if you like."

"NO! You have done quite enough already," Adam said, gritting his teeth. He was infuriated at the incompetence of this man who should have known better how to do his job. "Just show us where he is and we will take him with us."

Adam, Randy and Benjamin picked up the wooden box that contained the remains of their lifelong friend and comrade and somberly carried it to the wagon. They placed it there tenderly, as though the contents were their most valuable possession.

"Benjamin, will you please drive the wagon back to Oaklayne for us?" asked Adam. "I want to ride in the back with Tom."

Randy and Benjamin understood completely when Adam laid in the back of the wagon next to Tom, crying openly all the way home. With his heart broken, they could hear him talking to Tom and apologizing over and over for not making sure Tom's dreams come true for him.

"It was always about me, wasn't it, Tom...right to the end..."

Chapter 58

With tears in his eyes, Nathaniel said, "Massa Adam, Ah'll get some men to dig a grave for Tom right away."

"No, Nathaniel," said Adam, "I appreciate your offer, but I want to do this myself. It is the least I can do, after all that Tom did for me through the years." He went immediately to pick up a shovel and started toward the burial ground. "I will finish as soon as possible, then I want everyone to gather around to have an opportunity to show their last respects before we put him in the ground." Adam could hardly speak for the lump in his throat.

"Massa Adam, Ah loved Tom, too. He was a good frien' to all o' us."

"Please spread the word and tell everyone they are welcome to come, Nathaniel. Before Tom is laid to rest, I would like a few minutes to talk with the former slaves, while we have all of them together."

While Adam worked the dirt with the shovel, he reminisced about Tom's life, the fun they had as children, the mischief they got into together, the years at West Point, Tom's faithfulness and dedication throughout his life. And, he could not get his mind off of the discussion they recently had about Tom's dream of having a family of his own. He knew he had let his best friend down, allowing his life to be taken in such a degrading, unjustified way.

When Adam was about half finished with his solemn chore, Laura brought him a tall glass of lemonade and sat quietly and patiently as he drank it. Then she interrupted the silence with a message from the hospital that they had agreed to release Sara Ella to Lisa's care at Oaklayne. Lisa learned about Sara Ella being in the hospital from some of the Oaklayne workers, and she volunteered to be her private nurse, if they would let her go home. Laura suggested that Adam consider letting Nathaniel see to finishing what he was doing, so he could go get Sara Ella.

"She will want to be here with you as soon as possible, Adam," said Laura, putting her arm around him and pulling him close. "The rest of us can get everything ready for you here, if you will allow us to do so. Now, go and get your wife, my sweet brother."

Adam was torn between finishing the work of preparing Tom's final resting place and going to the hospital to get Sara Ella. Laura assured him that Tom would want him to have Sara Ella with him, so he reluctantly agreed to put down the shovel.

Lisa rode in the carriage with Adam and Sara Ella, as Adam told them both about what had happened to Tom. Sara Ella cried, telling Adam about her last few minutes with Tom, before he obediently went to the stable for her.

"If he had not come when he did, I am sure I would be dead, Adam. I do not know what we will do without Tom. I can only imagine how you must feel, my darling."

Lisa and Laura both cried tears of joy when they arrived at the plantation. As they embraced, Adam was aware of another piece of their family being restored.

Since Sara Ella was not able to attend the grave side ceremony, Adam made his way there alone. The pain was almost unbearable, as he stood before the crowd of mourners who had gathered to celebrate Tom's life. He offered everyone hope with Jesus' words in John 14:2, "In my Father's house are many mansions: if it were not so, I would have told you. I go to prepare a place for you, that where I am you may be also."

After sharing some stories from his own life of Tom's faithful friendship and selflessness, he told everyone how Tom saved Sara Ella's life, then subsequently, gave his life in loving service. Together they sang, "Shall We Gather At The River", then Adam offered a prayer of commitment of Tom's body to the Lord and the short funeral service was over.

There were very few dry eyes present. Every person in attendance had known Tom as a friend and had been served by him at one time or another. Then four of the men set the wooden box on two ropes, lifting it quietly and carefully, then reverently lowered it into the grave.

After the crowd dispersed, Adam approached the small group of former slaves that Nathaniel had asked to stay. Standing before them, he thanked them for their faithful service to Oaklayne through the years. Then, he laid out his plan for Oakville to them, explaining that he had assumed that they would all want to stay and work for him, living on their own land at Oaklayne.

"But, recently I learned that Tom had always dreamed of living near the city with a family of his own. My plan for him to have his own place at Oakville was not his dream, but mine. I had no idea, because I had never asked him what he wanted.

"I do not want to make that same mistake with you, so I am giving each of you two options. You can have a plot of ground of your own at Oakville, or if you prefer, I will give you a settlement of equal value that you can take elsewhere to start a new life for yourself and your family. It is entirely up to you. This is not a gift, it is something you earned.

"Again, this offer is only for former slaves of Oaklayne who faithfully served our family through the years. If you know of any who are not here, please help me contact them. Please give me an answer as soon as possible, so I know what each of you want to do before we start building Oakville.

"Thank you for taking the time to hear me out. I hope all of you know how much I appreciate you."

As Adam turned to walk away, the group broke out in applause. Adam understood the gesture. But he continued to mourn deeply, wishing he had given Tom the home near the city he had always wanted.

Chapter 59

"When can Sara Ella manage well enough to be moved to the mansion, Lisa?" Adam asked. "We can move all of the furnishings that Laura and Matt brought with them from Europe into the house now, or Matt said he can store them on board the ship for as long as they are still here visiting. There is still some finish work to be done both inside and out, but it is possible to move in now. Will it be better to leave her in the cabin for a while longer? Or, would she be more comfortable in a bigger room with a nicer bed? I will have to trust you to tell me what is best for her, Lisa."

"How exciting, Adam! I have to say, the extra room would be nice, but I am concerned that she will not be able to rest well during the day while the work continues. I think it is probably best to leave her here in the little cabin for a while longer."

Adam was disappointed, but understood the situation clearly. He certainly did not want to do anything that might slow the recovery process for Sara Ella.

"I wish she could see how wonderful it looks now, but I understand completely why that is not a good idea yet. You will have to check it out yourself, when you get time. The circular staircase with the English walnut banister and balustrades is now finished. Most of the walnut door and window frames are in place, as well as the fireplace mantles. The wide plaster and horse hair intricate crown moldings are perfect! And, I especially like the egg and arrow style molding in the grand foyer. I think Sara Ella will be in awe, as I was, when she sees what a beautiful job the men have done.

"The only thing missing from the original Oaklayne mansion is the painted border around the tops of the side walls of each room...and, of course, some of the people who lived there before. Try to take time to go see it when you can. I expect that walking through will bring back fond memories for you of Goddard and Laura."

Lisa smiled and said, "It will be a blessing, Adam. I will let you know when I think it is a good time to move Sara Ella. She is recovering nicely. She is a very strong and determined patient!"

Chapter 60

Hearing a horse coming down the lane at a good clip, Adam was alarmed and told Sara Ella to stay out of sight.

"Who could be coming this early in the morning, he said as he strapped on his pistol and then picked up his rifle.

Sara Ella groaned, "Oh, why do we have to be afraid of everyone that comes down our lane. I hate this! It never used to be that way."

"I do not know, dear. But, I do know that I am not going to let you get hurt again," he muttered under his breath, as he marched out the door, a man to be reckoned with.

Oscar, Nathaniel, and Ross, along with Darrell, Norman, Trevor and August were stumbling out onto the lawn half dressed, as the man on horseback rode up.

"My goodness! This is not the friendliest welcome I have ever received," the man said, looking at eight stern faces glaring back at him.

"State your business, then be on your way," Adam barked.

Swallowing hard, the man said, "All right, then. Which one of you gentleman is General Adam Layne?"

"That would be me," Adam said, spreading his legs for more stability, should he need to shoot his rifle.

"General Layne, I was sent here by Sergeant Clifford O'Reily to inform you that your son Randall and his friend Benjamin are incarcerated at his facility in Richmond. I would be happy to escort you back there if you would like to accompany me?"

Adam frowned and glared at the man in shock, having trouble digesting what he had just heard.

"Excuse me? Ah, my son is in jail? What for?"

"I am not at liberty to discuss it, but Sarge told me to come and get you. He did not even want me to take time to get into my uniform."

"I will saddle my horse and be right out," was all that Adam could think to say.

Sergeant O'Reily was stern and clearly unhappy when he said, "Sir, I caught these boys snooping around in the middle of the night near the old train station, where a group of no account scoundrels hang out. I have a man working undercover, trying to gather information. He brought them here to me before they were seen. All I can get out of them is that they are trying to solve a case. When I found out who they are, I sent for you right away."

"Thank you, Sergeant. I am glad they were not hurt."

Adam turned to Randy and Benjamin and said, "What were you boys doing? You might have been hurt or even killed!"

Randy was clearly anxious and said, with his voice low, "We overheard a man talking about being paid to hurry to the Police Station the day that Tom was lynched. We followed him to that shack and heard them all laughing about getting Tom hung. It did not just happen, Father, it was planned somehow. We were not able to find out who paid them, before we were caught and brought here."

Sergeant O'Reily said, "Wait a minute, boys. How is it that you just happened to hear someone talking about this?"

Benjamin answered, "Well, when we reviewed all of the facts surrounding Sara Ella being shot and Tom's hanging shortly thereafter, we realized that something was up. It seemed odd to us that there were so many people assembled near the Police Station when Tom arrived there with the body.

"So, we decided to dress up in these old clothes and go to some of the bars in the area around where Tom was murdered to see what we could learn. Randy's heightened hearing allows him to pick up people's voices from quite a distance away, without them knowing about it. And tonight we finally got lucky and heard this one drunk fellow bragging about it."

Adam looked at Clifford, then back at the boys. "Are you sure about this?"

"Yes, Father, there is no mistake. We also know that the dead carpetbagger's name is Thaddeus Flanagan. But, none of the other carpetbagger's we talked to seem to know him. He is not from around here."

Clifford O'Reily scratched his head and asked, "Adam, what is going on here? Is it your Tom that was hung?"

"Yes, Clifford. I thought it was just an unruly mob, who did it out of prejudice. But this sounds like much more. Tom had no enemies that I know of. He did not even know many people outside of our family."

Sergeant O'Reily pointed his finger at Randy and Benjamin, saying, "I do not want to encourage you boys to do something foolish like this again...but, I think you may be on to something here.

"For example, Thaddeus Flanagan is no carpetbagger. He is a felon that we had been trying to apprehend. A ruthless man with a long list of charges against him. His so-called friends called him Teddy. That might be one reason you had trouble finding out anything about him.

"I cannot imagine what he was doing at your place, Adam. But, it is definitely not a good idea for either of you young men to be in the company of any of his acquaintances. They are a bunch of scoundrels, that's for sure."

Adam was glad to have Sergeant O'Reily involved. "Thanks Clifford. You have been most helpful. Now, if you would not mind releasing these boys into my custody, I would like to give them both a stern talking to about their judgment. Then, we are going to go see General Imboden."

Chapter 61

APRIL 1, 1866

By the time Adam finally arrived at the Layne Townhouse, it was late and he was exhausted. He went to bed despondent about not having Tom by his side, and wondering why Stanton wanted him in his office so early the next morning.

Sleeping fitfully all night, Adam was somewhat surprised that he was still awake before Tom's alarm clock sounded. He was glad, because the awful sound of it would wake a bear in winter, and he dreaded hearing it go off.

Immediately craving his usual cup of coffee, he slumped in despair when he realized he would have to make it himself. He decided to see how well he could get along without coffee. Then his stomach growled and he realized he would not have any breakfast, because he did not go to the store for the supplies last night before he retired. He had skipped supper last night, because he was too tired, so he was really hungry.

"Oh well, maybe I can find something to eat and some coffee somewhere on my way to see Stanton," Adam said to himself.

He bathed and shaved, then opened his trunk to get dressed. That is when he remembered that Tom had always unpacked everything immediately upon their arrival.

"I do not have time for this! I must be in Stanton's office in an hour! Good thing I do not have to wear my uniform today—civilian attire is more suited to wrinkles than military. Maybe Stanton will not notice...."

"Adam," Stanton barked, "I have never known you to be late to anything—except your wedding, that is. Is everything alright? Why are you dressed like that?"

"It is too complicated to explain, sir. Suffice it to say that I am both embarrassed about my appearance and sorry for keeping you waiting."

371

Stanton frowned, but sensed that Adam did not want to be pushed for any further explanation, so he dropped it. "Well, sit down, Adam. I have some good news and some bad news to share with you.

"The good news is that on March 13 the Civil Rights Bill passed in the House. The bad news is that on the 27th, President Johnson vetoed it.

"Can you believe it? This man continues to baffle me and a lot of others. Even Moderates urged him to sign the bill, but he vetoed it instead. Wait...let me read to you the summary of his excuse...," the Secretary searched through some papers on his desk. "I have it here somewhere...oh, here it is. Johnson said he vetoed it 'because the Bill gave citizenship to the Freedmen at a time when the Southern states, eleven to be exact, were unrepresented in Congress.'"

Adam was shocked and appalled. "Why would the Union want those states represented in this vote on Civil Rights? This issue is why they rebelled in the first place! We won the war—we do not need to fight it again!"

"Oh, that is not all—listen to the rest of this. He also said he objected to the measure, 'because the other twenty-five states attempted to establish by Federal law a perfect equality of the white and black races in every State of the Union.' He also thought that the bill 'invaded Federal authority of the right of the States, and should not be in the Constitution', but here listen to this—he said it was a 'stride toward centralization and the concentration of all legislative power in the national government.'

"Adam, the Democratic Party felt empowered and proclaimed itself the party of white men, northern and southern Democrats are supporting Johnson in this."

"I do not think any of us realized Johnson was such a white supremacist," Adam said shaking his head. "I am sure Lincoln had no idea about that when he agreed to run for President this last time with Johnson on the ticket for Vice President."

Stanton shook his head in agreement adding, "Stevens and Sumner are fired up, my friend. I tell you, they are working all hours of the day and night on this. We simply must keep Johnson's veto from blocking the Civil Rights Bill and prevent him from overriding the Freedman's Bureau Bill. Lyman Trumbull of Illinois is working with us, too. He ushered the Freedman's Bureau Bill through Congress, remember?"

"Yes, and it was not easy."

"Right! Trumbull is a persistent man and will not give up easily, Adam. He is already working on another amendment that will be comprehensive in scope. His 14th Amendment is designed to put the key provisions of the Civil Rights Act into the Constitution and go a step further. If enacted, the 14th Amendment will extend citizenship to every person born in the United States (except Indians on reservations) and penalize states that do not give the right to vote to freedmen. Most importantly, it will create new federal civil rights laws that will be protected in federal courts. It will also guarantee the Federal war debt and void all Confederate war debts. Best of all, if the 14th Amendment is passed and submitted to the states for ratification by Congressional joint resolution, it will not be subject to Presidential veto."

"That would be fantastic, Mr. Secretary. Let's pray that Congress passes it."

Adam sat forward in his chair and said, "Is that why I am here? Do you want me to help with that?"

"No, Adam. There is something else I need your help with. I have been doing a little asking around about this Union Pacific stock and it seems legitimate. However, the odd thing I found out is that Credit Mobilier is not a finance company, as we formerly assumed. It is a construction company. I do not know what all of this means, but I thought you might be interested in finding out more.

"Could you go undercover for me as a government auditor and check out both the railroad company and the construction company? I cannot say I even know what we are looking for, but I think it bears some scrutiny. What do you say?"

Adams eyes glistened and a smile was playing around his mouth. Stanton did not realize it, but Adam's first thought was that he would not have to worry about wearing wrinkled clothes to do the job. He could do the kind of work he liked best without worrying about his appearance—perfect.

"Yes, of course. I would love to go on a little fishing trip for you. I will update you with what I find out, after I get a look at their books."

A week later, Adam found himself in a hotel room in Pittsburgh, Pennsylvania looking over figures from the records of the construction company, Credit Mobilier. Scott Bryan had helped him research both companies before he left. It took a great deal of compulsion on the part of Secretary Stanton before Credit Mobilier finally agreed to give him access to the records, and company people watched him very closely whenever he was in their Business Office.

On his way out of the office one day, he heard someone pleading, "But Doc, the Board voted against it."

Another voice gruffly answered, "I don't care what the Board did, we are doing it my way! It's my railroad. Do you understand?"

Just then the gruff man's eyes met Adam's, and with an already red face, he demanded, "What are you doing here? I don't know you."

The clerk next to Adam answered meekly, "Mr. Durant, this here is Adam Sheldon. He's an Auditor from the government."

"Get him out of here! We do not cater to auditors around here! I do not like auditors, never have." Adam was interested to know why Thomas Durant would be in a position of authority at Credit Mobilier. He was the owner of the Union Pacific Railroad, which was supposed to be a completely separate company.

Adam knew Thomas Durant would not be happy that tomorrow he would be going to Council Bluffs, Iowa to audit the records of the Union Pacific Railroad. He only wished he knew what he was looking for.

Getting off of the train in Council Bluffs, Adam noticed someone looking at him who was disembarking from another train car at the same time. *Why does that man look familiar? Strange...somehow, I do not think it was an accident that he looked this way. I wonder if he is following me.*

Dusting off his shoes, Adam entered the Union Pacific Operation Center first thing the next morning. He ran into the same treatment there when he requested access to the books that he received with Credit Mobilier. But, eventually he was able to recover figures and information consistent with what he had found at Credit Mobilier.

As he was leaving, Adam saw the man from the train station entering the building. Suddenly, he remembered where he had seen him before. It was on his first day in Pittsburgh, as he was entering the Business Office there.

Adam scowled, scratched the stubble on his chin and thought, Interesting...why did he follow me here? I wonder if he came here yesterday afternoon to warn them that I was coming. I do not like this.

Walking back to his hotel in the bustling little town, Adam decided to go up to his room, change into his riding clothes and head down to the restaurant to see what he could learn from eavesdropping and conversation.

His attention was peaked when he overheard a man say, "Hey Charley, when's it goin' to warm up around here? It's almost April, and I'm getting tired of working on those rails in the snow. I've got to head back tomorrow and help unload some more supplies from Cartwright Truss."

"Excuse me," Adam interjected, "Did you say Cartwright Truss?"

The wiry little man was hesitant to give information to a stranger. "Yes I did, who's askin?"

"I'm sorry, I was just thinking how it is a small world. My name is Adam Sheldon, and I am supposed to meet that shipment and verify that it agrees with the invoice. We want to be sure that you get all that you are supposed to receive."

The little man smiled, "That is a coincidence. Name's Joe Wright. So, are you ridin' the early bird special in the mornin'?"

"Yep, 'fraid so, how about you?"

"Yeah, and it's cold back in the baggage car."

Adam leaned close and whispered, "Why don't I let you know as soon as the conductor has taken our tickets. You can sit with me in the passenger car with the potbelly stove. It would be a shame to waste all that warmth, now wouldn't it?"

The scrawny man smiled an almost toothless grin and said, "You'd do that for me?"

"Sure, why not? It's no skin off my back."

"That's sure gentlemanly of you. Thanks. I'll take you up on that."

"I will see you in the morning, then. I have some errands to run, so I will be getting along now. Nice meeting you, Joe."

Adam stopped in the General store and purchased some warm outdoor work clothes, some work boots and a hat suitable for a company Inspector. Then he went a roundabout way to the train station to buy Early Bird Special train tickets for himself and for Joe.

At one point he suspected he was being followed, so he ducked into the Barber Shop. Going out the back of the shop, he made his way down the alley and saw the man who had been following him earlier across the street.

After supper Adam stepped out for some fresh air. Suddenly, he saw movement to his left, then felt the cold hard muzzle of a pistol on his neck. "Let's take a little walk around the corner. I have some friends waiting there with some advice for you, stranger."

Just as they rounded the corner, Adam felt a hard blow to his head. He immediately fell to the ground, feigning unconsciousness. He was stunned, but alert. He could see there were two men, besides the gunman. To his right there was a wooden barrel, with a shovel leaning against it. He rolled in the direction of the shovel, acting like he was recovering from the blow.

The gunman said, "The boss said for us to either kill him or make sure that he's senseless enough to load him on that eastbound freight train tonight. I don't know what he's done, but the boss doesn't want him snoopin' around anymore."

Adam groaned, then quickly turned over, grabbed the shovel with both hands and, in one continuous movement, he knocked the gunman's arm so hard that the gun hit him in the head rendering him unconscious. The gun hit the ground with a thud, followed by the in cognizant gunman. Instantly, Adam's shovel connected with the other two thugs, and they also fell to the ground in pain.

Adam snatched up the pistol and, while holding them at gunpoint, said, "Gentlemen, I know there are some folks around here who could use those work boots you are wearing. I sure appreciate your generosity in giving them away. Why don't you just take them off and line them up nicely in front of you there. Please tie the laces together, so I can carry them more easily. Oh, and those trousers you are wearing would be helpful as well. So, just pile them neatly with your boots. Now hurry up. Oh, it seems your friend with the bad hand, the one who is napping over there, is having trouble getting his boots and trousers off. Would one of you be so kind as to help him?"

One of the conscious thugs whined, "You can't just leave us out here in this snow to freeze!"

Adam responded sarcastically, "Well now, just why not? Considering what you had planned for me, I think I have been very gracious..." Then he squinted his eyes, pursed his lips and said, "But I would not push it if I were you. You hurt my feelings, and just when I thought we could be friends. I tell you what, if you are real nice to me, I just might take you over there to the livery stable, where you will be nice and cozy. Otherwise, I will just leave you out in this snow.

"Now, we both know that boss of yours would not be pleased that you did not eliminate me as he ordered. But, if you see him, tell him I am looking for him."

As Adam made his way to the Early Bird Special the next morning, he wondered if the goons he met the night before had ever gotten loose from their bonds and found some clothes and boots to wear to escape from their boss.

Shortly after boarding, Adam found Joe in the baggage car and brought him into the warmth of his coach. Joe liked to talk and impress Adam with all he knew, so it took very little prodding to get a lot of information from him. Joe knew the wages of almost all levels of railroad workers, and how many workers there were, including the large number of Chinamen, who received only a pittance for pay. He even knew what the workers had to pay for the rations the railroad sold to them, as well as the cost of tents and other items the workers needed to survive. Joe knew all this, because he was in charge of unloading it all.

"Joe, when we get off at Grand Junction in Nebraska, why don't you have lunch with me? Then I will go out with you to check on that load from Cartwright Truss?"

"Sure, that would be great," said Joe.

After Adam checked the invoice for the trusses and spikes, along with some tools that were included, he wrote down the name of the man who made the delivery, the cost of the materials and the delivery cost. Then, he said goodbye to Joe and went back to Grand Junction. There he caught the first train back to Washington City.

Entering Stanton's office the next morning, Adam heard the Secretary say, "Well it is about time!" Also in Stanton's office was Thaddeus Stevens, the Radical Republican, who jumped up and fervently shook Adam's hand.

"We have good news, Adam!" said Secretary Stanton. "While you were gone, the Republicans in Congress overrode Johnson's veto of the Civil Rights measure and it became law on April 9th. They have also passed the Freedmen's Bureau Bill over Johnson's veto."

"That's wonderful news," said Adam, glowing with excitement. "What a relief for the freedmen to now be declared citizens of the United States. Now they will have the same rights as all men. This has been quite a battle for the Republicans, and I am so relieved that they won. I believe this is a historical landmark decision that will be remembered throughout the future of this young nation."

Thinking of Tom and the other freedmen he loved, Adam had a lump in his throat as he spoke. Oh, how he wanted to race back to the townhouse and tell Tom the wonderful news.

Adam was jerked back to reality when his thoughts were interrupted by Stanton clearing his throat and asking, "Well, what did you find out about the railroad, Adam?"

"Well, we were right to be suspicious, Mr. Secretary. Credit Mobilier is in charge of building the railroad, then they bill Union Pacific for their services. Union Pacific bills Congress, supported by the invoice from Credit Mobilier, with Union Pacific's overhead added on.

"Credit Mobilier is assumed to be owned by George Francis Train, but I overheard Thomas "Doc" Durant, owner of Union Pacific Railroad, arguing with a board member there, in a manner that indicates that he is also an owner of the construction company.

"The Union Pacific Railroad is supposed to be owned by Thomas Durant, but I found George Train's name suspiciously on documentation throughout that company.

"The financial figures at Credit Mobilier were consistent with those at the Union Pacific Railroad. I was followed from CM to UP however, so I do not know if the figures at Union Pacific were changed to make them agree before I arrived.

"On the actual job site, I found that expenses were considerably lower than the figures I found at both Credit Mobilier and Union Pacific Railroad.

"I had some research done on the Baltimore and Ohio Railroad to get an idea of the legitimate cost to build a railroad. It is substantially lower than what Congress is paying Union Pacific. It is also a lot less than what Union Pacific is paying Credit Mobilier. There is definitely something going on there. I do not understand it all, but it sure needs to be investigated further for criminal activity."

Secretary Stanton wheezed, as he stood up and declared, "Adam, it looks like you are onto something very big here. Thank you for this report. I am going to look into this further."

Chapter 62

It was a beautiful "May Day" when Lisa announced to Adam, "I think Sara Ella is ready to be moved into her new bedroom in the mansion," said Lisa with a big grin. "She will have to stay upstairs for a while yet, because she is very weak. She still faints whenever she tries to stand or sit upright for long periods, because of the excessive blood loss she suffered. Recovery from anemia takes a long time, Adam. But, it will still be better for her to move to her new bedroom in the plantation house, rather than staying in the little honeymoon cabin. I know you are anxious to carry her over the threshold of your forever home, and I cannot think of a better time than now, can you?"

Adam let out a whooping holler that could have been heard all over the county. "You bet! May I go get her now?"

Laughing out loud at Adam's display of enthusiasm, Lisa said, "Hold your horses, cowboy...your little filly is still very delicate. Moving her will need to be a process. For example, do you not need to have the furnishings brought in from the ship before we move her in there?"

"Oh, yeah...I forgot about that," said Adam, running around in circles with excitement. "I will go see Matt right now!" he said, muttering under his breath as he retreated from the room, "Wonder how long that will take?"

Adam knew that all the finishing touches on the mansion were nearly done, so Sara Ella would not be bothered much with construction noise. The realization of his dream of sharing his home with her was about to come true, and he could not hardly think straight. *Where is Matt?* As he rushed toward the Phantom II, looking for Matt, he mused.

I am so glad we could finish before Matt and Laura had to leave. Laura will be so happy to see the furnishings she located in Europe placed throughout the mansion. She did a very good job of finding things that are much like what we had before. I cannot wait for Sara Ella to be able to enjoy everything. It is so wonderful! It will be so much like I remember.

The blessing of having Oaklayne restored to her former glory is much like the reconstruction of our nation after that horrible war. No matter what we do, things will never be like they were before, because so many loved ones are gone now. But some things will actually be better than before. We have many new family members as a result of the war, and some modern conveniences have been built into the reconstruction. Our nation has a long way to go, but we are making progress toward restoring a lot of what was lost with new ways of doing things that should be better than before.

"All right, every man down to the dock!" Matt called out to his crew and the construction workers who had been working at Oaklayne for the past several months. Every wagon and team had been hitched together to expedite the transfer from one location to the other as efficiently as possible.

"Let's get this thing unloaded, gentlemen!" Grinning at Adam, he added sarcastically, "The man's quite anxious to have his furniture, for some reason—I do not know why it is suddenly such a big deal now, when it has been sitting here for so long."

Matt was very pleased for Adam and Sara Ella that they would finally be moving into their home. "I need every hand to get this ship unloaded before it starts to rain. It looks like it could pour any time now. Come on y'all, step lively! Handle with great care, but get the ship unloaded as quickly as you can." This was Matt's way of managing the men when they arrived in port with freight. His constant verbal push kept the men moving. He swung his arm in a sweeping circle, getting the workers to move more hurriedly and trotted ahead of them, urging them on.

As quickly as the men arrived to make another trip, Matt gave orders concerning particular pieces. "Do not unwrap this until you get it into the house. Put everything in the ball room and dining room for now. We will find out where everything goes inside after we get the ship unloaded."

The men asked very few question, only nodded their heads in agreement.

Adam stood at the door of the mansion, talking with Laura about the purchases she had made. "I am so pleased with everything, Laura. Thank you so much. I am sure this was a lot of trouble for you."

Laura smiled warmly and said, "It was a joy for me to do, Adam. I tried to get everything as nearly as possible to what our great-grandfather purchased when the house was furnished so many years ago. Thank you for including me. It was such fun! Sometimes I found myself getting carried away, with so many wonderful things to choose from," Laura explained.

"Not everything is the same style as before, especially in the upstairs bedrooms," remarked Adam. "But, that is okay. I remember Mother telling me that Great-Grandfather George Layne was quite a miser when it came to spending money on the house. So, some of the things he acquired for the upstairs bedrooms were of lower quality than downstairs. But, according to Mother, Great-Grandmother Samantha Layne was able to bewitch, beguile and persuade him in her own feminine way to make some improvements a little later."

Laura laughed, "Yes, she must have been quite a character. Mother often said I am just like Samantha Layne—I always figure out a way to get what I want."

Adam's eyes brightened when the hunt table was brought in. "This piece had to be handmade, Adam." said Laura. "I could not find one anywhere in Europe. It is sixteen feet long with eight legs and made entirely of mahogany. Everywhere I went looking for a hunt table to replace the one we had, they did not know what I was talking about. I explained to each shop I visited that a hundred years ago, a game table was used during a game hunt. They placed it along one wall of the hall leading to the ball room and put food on it. People coming in from the hunt, still dressed in their riding clothes, fill their plates themselves from the food on the hunt table and go sit down to eat, usually in the ballroom. It saved them from having to clean up so much mud and dirt brought in by the hunters."

Both Adam and Laura choked back tears when the men carried in a beautiful grand piano. She turned to Adam and said, "This is to replace Mother's piano. This just would not be Oaklayne without Mother's piano."

"Thank you, Laura. You thought of everything."

Adam could see that the ballroom and dining room were becoming quite filled. Next came the bedsteads, wardrobes and chiffoniers. Bedroom furniture is what he was the most anxious to see, because that is what would be needed for Sara Ella to be moved into the mansion.

"Great! Please take two sets of bedroom furniture upstairs, gentlemen. One set will need to go in the master bedroom and the other in an adjoining bedroom for Lisa. Laura, if you know which set goes in the master, perhaps you could point those pieces out for these men?" asked Adam.

When the last load of furniture, carpet rolls and boxes had been delivered, Adam expressed his appreciation to the men. Just as they finished, it started to mist, then suddenly turned into heavy rain. As they were leaving, Adam thanked each man personally, and assured them they would receive a bonus for their hard work.

First thing the next morning, Adam carried Sara Ella across the threshold of the Oaklayne mansion. He did his best to control his emotions, not wanting to drop his sweet bride in her delicate condition. Lisa had already prepared the master bedroom for her upstairs, but she wanted Adam to carry her around throughout her new home before he carried her up the stairs, where she would have to stay for a while until fully recovered.

Adam showed her as much as he could, without putting her down. Then he told her she would just have to wait until she was completely well to see the rest. "By then, I will have all these furnishings unwrapped and put where they go."

Sara Ella looked over Adam's shoulder at Laura and said, "Please do not get away without showing us which of these beautiful fabrics are for each room, Laura, and what you intended each to be used for in particular. I am not very good at that sort of thing, so I will have to have someone do all that for us if you are gone by then. You did a beautiful job for us, Laura. How could you remember all the many different rooms and how they were each furnished before?"

Laura laughed. "Remember, Sara Ella, this was my home from the day I was born. I always had the run of the house. Actually, I never paid much attention, but today I can close my eyes and see each room as it was in my childhood. It was great fun to go into stores and buy, without having to worry about the cost. I wanted to make each room come alive again. I appreciate being asked to help."

Sara Ella giggled and said, "People who were here before the war, will think the mansion was never damaged. Oaklayne has truly come alive again, Adam."

Adam carried Sara Ella upstairs to the master bedroom and left her with Lisa to get settled, because she was exhausted from exertion. Pleased, he walked slowly back down the stairs, looking around and admiring everything he saw. It had taken a year, but the mansion was virtually finished and even more elegant and beautiful than Adam could have hoped, while still maintaining the style and ambiance of his childhood home.

At the bottom of the grand staircase he turned and looked up. In his mind's eye he could see his mother descending toward him in her usual graceful way. He knew she would be very pleased, and so would his father, if they could see it restored. Adam fell to his knees in gratitude for all that God had done. He was reminded of the scripture in Joel 2:25 about God restoring what the locusts had eaten. He was content with what remained of his loving family, Sara Ella, Randy and yes, Benjamin. He was so blessed.

Chapter 63

Adam lay in bed and looked at the ceiling, thinking about all the things they had accomplished over the past year. Except for some work the ladies were doing to make draperies for the windows, the mansion, outbuildings and food cellars were finished. The barns were erected, stock had been purchased, chicken houses had been completed and there were new hens and baby chickens, including a pair of feisty roosters. And, he was pleased that even some of the cabins at Oakville had been completed.

He sighed and looked over at Sara Ella. Moonlight was streaming through the sheer drape, casting a soft light over her sweet face. She was sleeping soundly, exhausted from the ordeal of recovering from her injury. Adam was ready to get a good night's sleep himself, but found himself having trouble relaxing.

As he turned toward the window, he noticed that the sky above the trees had an orange glow that he had not seen before. He could not remember the moonlight ever previously having that strange hue. Suddenly, he was wide awake and ran to the window. Looking toward Oakville, he realized that the glow was coming from a fire! Remembering that Oscar and most of the other men had gone into Richmond to celebrate the finishing of the mansion, he jumped up, pulled on his trousers and grabbed for his boots and pistol. Then he ran as fast as he could to the temporary house, yelling for Nathaniel.

"Nathaniel! There's a fire at Oakville! Let's go!"

Nathaniel was startled awake and leaped from his bed. "What? Fire at Oakville?"

"It won't surprise me to find out that someone set fire to those cabins we're working on, Nathaniel. Come on, let's go see what we can do. Maybe, we can save some of our work. Bring your rifle and some shovels with you. With just the two of us, we will have to throw dirt and gravel on the fire. That's our only hope of extinguishing it." He turned and ran toward the cabins. Nathaniel was already on his way to the barn to get shovels.

When Adam reached Oakville, one of the cabins was engulfed in flames and another was less involved. He and Nathaniel worked valiantly to save what they could of the two cabins, trying to prevent the fire from spreading to any of the others. Suddenly, it occurred to Adam that someone might have set the fire at Oakville to lure him and Nathaniel away from the house, leaving the women unprotected.

"Nathaniel, I am worried that someone knew the men are in town and we have been drawn away to tend to this fire on purpose. I must go back to make sure the women are safe. I am not willing to take any chances on Sara Ella or any of the women.

"Just do the best you can to fight this fire. When I get back, I will see if any of the men are back from town yet, and send them here to help you. I am fairly sure someone who does not like it has gotten wind of what we are doing for our former slaves."

"Do you think that could be it?" Nathaniel said, panting.

As Adam made his way back to the house, he saw movement beside Nathaniel's cabin and ducked behind a pile of lumber. He could see that someone was carrying a torch. Adam raced around to the far side of the lumber pile.

With pistol drawn, he ran out in front of the perpetrator and yelled, "Hold that torch up real high, or I will shoot!"

Just then, Oscar and his men rode up on horseback. Adam's gaze was distracted by the noise of the horses, enough that the man threw the torch at him and ran for the cover of the darkness in the trees behind the cabin. Adam shot, but did not think he hit his mark.

"I must check on the women to make sure they are alright," said Adam, as he turned and ran toward the house.

"I saw him, Adam. It was Burt," said Oscar with his voice raised so Adam could hear him. "You know, the man I fired when he refused to work for Nathaniel."

The men continued to throw dirt on the fire, but it was too late the cabin was completely engulfed in flames and could not be saved.

"Thank goodness you got here before he could burn the others, too," Oscar said to Nathaniel.

"Thanks for coming Oscar," said Nathaniel. Do you know if the women are safe?"

"No, I do not. We saw the glow of the flames as we were coming home, and rode straight here."

Adam returned on horseback and reported that the ladies were all safe from harm, but concerned.

Oscar said, "You and Nathaniel go on back to be with the women. I will stay here to make sure the fire burns out safely. I will also look for clues as to exactly what happened."

"My first thought when I saw the fire was that it was started by a disgruntled former slave who is angry because he is not being included. But, that was before I saw Burt with a torch," said Oscar.

Adam brushed black soot from his pants and said, "Well, it does not make sense for Burt to do it either. We saw him once on the road with those hecklers, which I thought was because he did not like black men taking a job he wanted. Truth is, I really do not think he is smart enough to plan something like this and then carry it out.

"You know, I mentioned several weeks ago that we are going to have to put a guard in Oakville, and now I am sure of it." Panting for breath, he continued, "We sure cannot have this kind of thing happen after people are living in the cabins."

Adam was furious. "Oscar, why do people not let you do what you want on your own land, without destroying it? I am glad I thought to pick up my pistol when I ran out of the house. I am relieved that the ladies are okay."

The cabin walls fell in, as the roof fell to the ground in a smoking heap of burning timbers. Wiping the sweat from his forehead and the smoke grime from his face, Adam said, "We need to be alert, Oscar. Double check carefully around the other cabins for any sign of incendiary materials left there. There may be more of those scoundrels who ran off when I started shouting. Hopefully, they left tracks by the other cabins. If you see anyone who does not belong here, shoot—and do not miss like I did!

"This pile of ashes was to be Tom's cabin, Oscar...," Adam said with a lump in his throat. "I am exhausted, so I think I will just sit here a spell and catch my breath." He watched as Tom's cabin smoldered, knowing that eventually it would be rebuilt for someone else. But, not any time soon...

Oscar sighed and said, "Perhaps you should consider letting Nathaniel go ahead and move into his cabin? It is almost finished, and was not one of the ones damaged tonight. If the cabins were occupied as they are finished, they would be less vulnerable."

"I guess you're right. I had hoped to wait until after we finish the school, the little church and the playground, but we probably don't have that luxury."

"Sometimes you have to change plans for safety reasons. This is not a perfect world we live in. It sure looks like someone is out to get you Adam."

Nathaniel walked up to Adam and heaved a great sigh of relief. "Well, Massa Adam. Guess Ah'll go see if'n Ah kin git some of this black off 'o me so's maybe Ah kin git some sleep tonight."

Adam reached out to Nathaniel, looked him in the eye and said, "Nathaniel what would I ever do without you? You have always been there when I needed you. You fought a good fight tonight. We will talk tomorrow about starting a watch service down here to protect your cabins. Okay?"

"Yes, Massa Adam."

"Tomorrow morning I want you and all of those whose cabins are finished to move into them. I have decided not to wait until after the rest of the village is complete. It is too dangerous. We will supply guards to protect everyone until you are all settled in and able to form your own neighborhood watch."

Nathaniel smiled from ear to ear, but Adam could not see it in the dark. Before he left, he approached Adam with a request. "Ah've been fixin' to ax yo' 'bout this for a while now, Massa Adam..." Then he explained that the fire made it more urgent in his mind to do what he had been meaning to do for a long time.

Adam's eyes widened. "What on earth are you trying to say, Nathaniel?"

"Well, Massa Adam...do yo' think it'd be okay fer me to ax Emma Lou to share my cabin wit' me? Her cabin was one o' dem dat was damaged, so she might want to jus' move in wit' me...maybe...least Ah hopes so...."

"She can't just come and live with you, Nathaniel! What would people say?"

"Oh, no sah! Ah didn't mean that. Ah wants ta know if'n it be okay wit' yo' if'n Ah ax 'er to marry me? Ah'm an old man, so she may not want me..., but Ah'd like to ax her. If'n it's okay wit' yo'?"

Adam smiled broadly and slapped Nathaniel on the back. "Nathaniel, I had no idea. After all of these years...why did you wait so long? You don't need my permission to marry whomever you wish. I have to tell you that I'm very pleased you want to ask Emma Lou. And, I sure hope she says yes.

"I am so sorry, Nathaniel, for not taking more time to help you understand your freedom. As far as I am concerned, you can marry Emma Lou or any other woman who will have you. And you can live in one of the cabins at Oakville or anywhere else in the world you want to live. You have been faithful to my family and I am eternally grateful. You choose your life, and I will set you up. You will always be a trusted friend and so will Emma Lou.

387

"Now, you swallow hard, and go ask her. I will be here praying that she will say yes!"

"Yes, Massa Adam. Ah'll ax 'er firs' thang in the mornin'! Ah don' wanna' ax her while she upset t'night." Nathaniel hurried off to the Temporary House to get some sleep.

Adam turned and immediately located Oscar to tell him, "First thing in the morning, I will need to go to town and report what happened here tonight. Sergeant O'Reily may need your testimony about seeing Burt last night, so I would like for you to go with me. I know you and your men were planning to leave tomorrow, since your work is done here. But, we would sure appreciate any help you can give us. If possible, could your men help Nathaniel organize the move into the cabins that are ready for occupancy before they go?"

"No problem, Adam. Glad to help."

Sergeant Clifford O'Reily paced the floor, shaking his head, as Adam and Oscar explained the events of the night before at Oakville. "I'll need to bring Burt in for questioning, since you both saw him with the torch last night. I tell you, he must be working for someone. There are strange things going on out at your place, Adam."

Adam shook his head in agreement and said, "Maybe we can find out who is behind all this when you interrogate Burt."

One of Sergeant O'Reily's men overheard Adam's remark and interjected, "We won't be interrogating Burt, gentlemen. I just learned that he was found this morning on the road with a bullet hole in his head. I guess he won't be talking to anyone about anything."

"I shot at him last night," said Adam, "but I am sure I missed. So, how can he be dead?"

"We'll look into it, Adam. I suggest you go talk with that lawyer you were telling me about. We will all work together to gather and analyze the information we have. Maybe, it will start leading to some answers."

Later, leaving General Imboden's office Oscar asked, "So, what is it that you do not like about this man, Adam? It is obvious that something is going on between the two of you. The man seems very competent to me. He figured out that the carpetbagger who shot Sara Ella worked for Colonel Hatfield. I would think that you would want to put that peacock of a man away for a very long time."

"You are right on all counts, Oscar. I do want to get Hatfield, but the idea of working with John Imboden is hard to swallow."

"Why? What has he done?"

"He is a traitor."

"That is a serious charge, Adam. What do you mean?"

"Well, John was a friend of the family, or so I thought. He even had an eye for my sister Laura at one time. But, then he fought against our country."

Oscar was shocked to hear Adam say such a thing. "Are you telling me that you are holding a grudge against him, because he was a 'Johnny Reb'? The war is over, Adam. You live in the South, so a lot of your neighbors were Confederate's. You cannot live your life resenting everyone who fought for the South. It is time for some forgiveness, do you not agree?"

"I know that what you say is right, Oscar. But, when I am with him I just cannot seem to forget."

"Well, he can help you, Adam, and clearly wants to do all he can. So, give him a chance."

Changing the subject, Adam said, "So, you are taking Elsie with you when you return to your home, right? She is a really nice girl, and I am sure you will have a wonderful life together. Are you excited about it?"

Oscar smiled and looked off into space, as he imagined the lovely face of his sweet Elsie. "You have no idea how much Elsie has brought into my life, Adam. We will be married right after we get there. Her family is already there helping my folks with the planning.

"I will start rebuilding my own plantation right after we are married. There is a little caretaker house there that we can live in while we are building. The soldiers who are going with me will help us. By the way, Trevor and August have decided to stay and help Nathaniel build Oakville. They will just stay in the Temporary House until the work is done, then they will travel back north to visit us and see their family. Brandon and Steven, of course, will be staying here in their own cabins at the Callahan Plantation."

Oscar shared his plans for his future with Adam all the way back to Oaklayne, but Adam was distracted. He was struggling with his feelings toward John Imboden, and Oscar's words of wisdom, as he confronted him about it. Adam knew he needed to forgive the man, but it was not easy.

As they pulled into the yard, Adam turned and asked Oscar if he would follow him into his house. "There is something that Sara Ella and I want to talk with you about before you leave, but she is not well enough to come down the stairs just yet."

Sara Ella rose from her chair, as Adam held the door to the master suite for Oscar. "Oscar, please come in," she said warmly. "I cannot wait to tell you both the good news! Emma Lou said yes! Nathaniel and Emma Lou... can you believe it?

"Elsie told me that Emma Lou was stunned at first, but then she smiled from ear to ear and ran into his arms. Everyone cried, including big tough Nathaniel. He suggested to her that they go to the preacher right away, so Emma Lou handed her apron to Elsie and they left, hand in hand. Is it not wonderful? They were married early this afternoon, and are setting up housekeeping as we speak."

Adam slapped Oscar on the back and said, "See, you are not the only one whose life is coming together, my friend! And while we are on the subject of your life, Sara Ella and I have a wedding gift for you and Elsie."

Sara Ella got up from her chair, walked carefully over to Oscar and handed him a soft leather pouch with a drawstring closure. He smiled and helped her back to her chair before opening the pouch.

When he looked inside, his eyes filled with tears. His lower lip quivering, he said, "Adam, you already paid me handsomely while I have been here! You do not owe me anymore. I cannot accept this. It is too much!"

Adam put his hand on Oscar's shoulder and said, "This is a gift for you and Elsie to start your lives together. The Lord brought you to me at just the right time, and you have been like a brother to me while you have been here. Now, with this gift you can rebuild your own plantation home for the two of you. This will also help you employ all those men who did such a great job for us here."

"I do not know what to say. Thank you both from the bottom of my heart. Just as soon as we have finished, I want you to be our first guests."

Chapter 64

"We are expecting a little one!" said Laura, blushing with excitement. "I cannot wait to find out if it is a girl or a boy!"

Adam swelled with family pride as he patted Matt on the back. "Congratulations, Matt!" The he embraced Laura and kissed her on the forehead.

Laura ran to Sara Ella's side and hugged her warmly, saying, "I wish we did not have to leave so soon." Sara Ella was doing well enough to come down the stairs with help, but she still had to move very slowly and conserve her energy.

Matt looked at Laura and smiled. Then he turned to Adam and said, "I have been giving a lot of thought to your suggestion that we move our home here instead of staying in Charleston. You are right, Richmond is big enough to support my shipping company. If you would allow me to build a more suitable docking facility, with some room for storage, I believe I could make a go of it here."

Laura jumped into his arms and squealed with excitement. "Whoa! Wait just a minute, dear. I still need to pick up that load of cotton in Savannah and deliver it before we can do anything about pursuing this any further. But, I will do what I can to make it happen, eventually."

"Oh, thank you Matt!" Laura said with tears in her eyes.

Suddenly there was a loud knock at the door. Adam opened it to find a well-dressed man standing on the porch, surrounded by several of the men whose job it was to guard Oaklayne from intruders.

One of the guards said, "This man says he has a contract he must present to you."

"Thank you, men. You may go. I will handle this." Then turning to the guest he said, "My name is Adam Layne, what is this all about?"

Extending his hand, the man said, "Frederick Larson, Attorney for Colonel Herbert Wade Hatfield of Royal Hatfield Plantation. I have this contract ready for you to sign, Mr. Layne."

"Let me see that," Adam said, taking hold of the document. The contract was a sizable offer for the purchase of Oaklayne Plantation.

Adam was furious, but he tried to keep his emotions in check so Hatfield's lawyer would not see his anger. He wondered how Hatfield could come up with the kind of money he was offering. He also knew the Colonel had no way of knowing that he had almost unlimited resources at his disposal with the gold bricks his great-grandfather left him. *He obviously assumes I would sell for this great a sum of money. Well, he is wrong!*

"I already informed the Colonel that Oaklayne is not for sale at any price." Then, hesitating a moment, he continued, "However, his offer is very generous, so I would like to keep this contract for a few days to consider it further, if that is okay."

"Adam! You cannot be serious!" Sara Ella shrieked.

Turning to look at her, he made a face and said, "It is okay, dear. I will explain when this gentleman has gone." Then turning to the lawyer he said, "Now, Mr. Larson, I must bid you farewell. As you can see, I have guests."

"But, I was told to have you sign this tonight."

Adam smiled, took the man by the arm and ushered him to the door. "I am sure Colonel Hatfield will be happy to know that I am considering his offer. Good day, sir."

After closing the door behind the man, Adam turned to Sara Ella and said, "I am going to take this contract to John Imboden first thing tomorrow. He has reason to suspect Colonel Hatfield of being responsible for you being shot, Tom's lynching and the other misfortunes we've been having at Oaklayne. But, he needs more evidence. This contract may be a big piece of the puzzle."

Early the next morning, John Imboden was not in his office. So, Adam asked for his address and found him at home. "Come right in, Adam," he said. "Have a seat." He turned to his niece and said, "Samantha, this is Adam Layne, Randy's father. Adam, this is my niece Samantha. She knows your son, Randy, and his friend Benjamin quite well."

Samantha asked, "Would you like a cup of tea or coffee, Mr. Layne?"

"I have heard a great deal about you from Randy, Samantha. It is nice to finally meet you. I do not need anything, but thank you for the kind offer. I have some important business to discuss with your father."

Adam showed the contract to John. He read it over quickly, but carefully, then looked at Adam. "We need to gather everyone who knows anything about this case and show them this document. Sergeant

O'Reily, Detective Avery, and anyone else they can think of. We need to get all of our heads together, and see if we can solve this case."

Samantha interrupted and said, "Do not forget Randy and Benjamin. They have worked very hard on this case, Father."

"We will meet in my office in an hour. You can come too, Samantha. You have been involved in the work Randy and Benjamin have done, so you may have some thoughts that could help," said John Imboden.

"I will find them myself," Samantha said. "I think I know where they will be this time of morning."

"Okay, everyone," said General Imboden. "On this table are all the documents relating to this case, as well as transcripts of the depositions I have taken from each of you and anyone else I have run across who might know something. These are all pieces of a puzzle. We need to look at everything with fresh eyes and see how the pieces fit together."

Looking over the documents, they saw information about the fire at the sawmill; Burt and others harassing workers setting fire to one of the Oakville cabins and then being shot; Hatfield's visit to the pier, then trying to buy Oaklayne and the recent outrageous offer; the attack on Oscar and Elsie; carpetbagger persistence; Sara Ella being shot and Tom lynched.

Then there was information about Sara Ella's attacker, Thaddeus Flanagan, being a felon wanted in several states and reportedly found murdered in Pennsylvania; Burt being seen with scoundrels at the railroad shack; scoundrels paid to lynch Tom; complaints from Adam's neighbors who had been forced from their property by Hatfield's unscrupulous offers.

Also included was documentation that Hatfield was seen with both Milton Littlefield, a tycoon from North Carolina, and Thaddeus Flanagan, as well as being overheard talking with "Doc" Durant about questionable business practices.

There was even a map that had been produced by Randy, Benjamin and Samantha, showing property owned by Hatfield adjoining Oaklayne in a line to Richmond.

Adam was impressed that Imboden had collected so much information. The table was covered with papers.

John said, "Now, I want each and all of you to examine each piece of paper on this table. Then, start talking."

After a few minutes, everyone started talking at once, and the roar made each voice indistinguishable.

"Wait! I cannot understand any of you. Shall we each take turns here? Adam, you first."

"I find it interesting that Flanagan had dealings with Hatfield..."

"Yes," Detective Avery responded. "And, there appears to have been an exchange of money between the two men. I have been trailing Hatfield for some time."

Randy spoke up, "What about this new offer contract from Hatfield to buy Oaklayne? How does that fit in?"

Adam remarked, "I cannot imagine how Hatfield could come up with that kind of money, or even why he wants Oaklayne so badly."

"Let Benjamin show you the map, Father. You will notice that Oaklayne is in line with other property that Hatfield has purchased recently. Why would he want all of those properties in line like that? I think Oaklayne is in the way of something he wants if he does not own it."

Adam rubbed his chin for a moment, then said, "Wait a minute...I think I remember seeing somewhere in this information that Hatfield had dealings with Doc Durant...yes, here it is." Adam held up a piece of paper and continued, "I have met Thomas Durant. He owns the Union Pacific Railroad, as well as some other under the table holdings. I tell you he is a tyrant of a man. Do we know what he and Hatfield talked about?"

Avery said, "I overheard Hatfield and Durant arguing. Durant told Hatfield that the deal was off if he did not have the river front. It did not mean anything to me at the time, but now with this map, it all makes sense."

Randy spoke up again, "Do you not see, Father. If Durant builds railroads, Hatfield must be trying to sell him property for building another one across Oaklayne to Richmond. Look at the map again. Everyone knows that Oaklayne is the closest place to Richmond to bring in large ships with cargo."

At first, Adam was speechless, wheels of thought turning furiously in his head. Then smiled and said, "John, this young man is my son. I think he might make a good lawyer someday. What do you think?"

"That is what I have been trying to tell you, Adam. I concur wholeheartedly," said John. Then he turned to Randy and Benjamin and said, "But now, how do we prove what we know in court? That is the ultimate test of a good lawyer, you know."

Adam interjected, "I would still like to know how a simpleton like Peacock Hatfield could come up with the finances to pull this off?"

"Tell him, Randy," said Benjamin. "I tell you, Randy is able to hear and remember, word for word, things that are said even in a crowded room. He does not have the visual distractions that occupy our thinking so much of the time. We knew that Milton Littlefield always wore a flower in his lapel, so he was easy for me to spot when he came into the bank. I helped Randy identify the sound of each of the men's voices, so he could listen to anything that was said. Tell them, Randy."

"Wait a minute, what were you doing in the bank?" someone asked.

"Well, Detective Avery told us that Hatfield had an appointment with some wealthy individuals at the bank, but he did not have a way to find out any more details," said Samantha. "We asked Father to make arrangements with the bank Manager to let the three of us use their conference room for a school project, which he was able to do with some difficulty. The bank's conference room is in close proximity to another area where we hoped the meeting would take place. And, it turned out we were right."

Randy said, "Father, this man has no scruples, nor do most of the people he met with. That being said, I will boil down what information I heard that is pertinent to this case.

"Long story short, Herbert Hatfield is involved in railroad fraud in North Carolina where he contributed about $200,000 that was used to bribe the North Carolina legislature. He made a lot of money on that deal. Milton Littlefield and George Swepson defrauded the state of North Carolina to the tune of $4 million, after the North Carolina Legislature granted $27.8 million in state money for railroad bonds. In their meeting, they boasted that no railroad construction has ever begun, nor do they expect it to ever be built. Now, those funds are being used to speculate in bonds to further defraud the government.

"In the case of Hatfield, he wants to sell his property to them so they can start another lucrative, but fraudulent, railroad building scheme. I overheard Hatfield tell Littlefield that he only had one more piece of property to acquire, then he would have access all the way from the river to Richmond. Durant said he could get a sizable payment for him from the government, but not if it did not include access all the way to the river."

John looked at Adam and said, "This is bigger than any of us could have imagined. But I ask again, how can we prove his guilt enough to get him convicted and incarcerated for a very long time?"

Sergeant O'Reily sheepishly spoke up, "It didn't seem important until now, but I happen to know that Burt is alive. I intended to pass along that information to you, John, but haven't had time. I only found out about it yesterday."

"Where is he Clifford? I will go and drag him in myself," said Adam, his face red with anger.

"Now, let's just calm down here," said Imboden. "This has to be done carefully, or we could lose our only hope of proving what we know. Burt is very valuable to us right now." Turning to Sergeant O'Reily, he said, "Tell us everything you know about him Clifford."

"Well," said O'Reily, "Yesterday, one of my Detectives heard some of Burt's friends say they were paid to fake Burt's death. It seems that some street bum was dressed in Burt's clothes and shot in the head so he wouldn't be recognizable. They also said that Burt probably wishes he were dead, considering where he is."

John Imboden turned to Adam and asked, "How would you like to become a scoundrel for the next few days and hang out with me in some dark places?"

Adam did not hesitate when he responded, "When do we leave?"

"You will need to work with the undercover detective who gave me this information," Clifford said. "We will need to take time to do some planning. You cannot just go barging in on something like this."

The detective's undercover name was Leo, and Adam immediately thought he really looked the part. Heavy set with predominant nose and bushy eyebrows, he was so dirty you could not distinguish the natural color of his skin. The stench emanating from the man was horrendous.

Adam did not realize he was their contact until he closed the door to the little back room where they were playing cards. After the door was closed, Joe stood up straight with perfect posture and said, with a cool frankness, "This is no game gentlemen. What we are about to do can get any or all of us killed. Do you understand? Are either of you getting cold feet? If you are not willing to trust me with your life, then you are not welcome to accompany me to the places we must go. Please leave quietly, and no questions will be asked."

Both Adam and John cleared their throats, then Adam said, "John, this is my problem. You do not have to take the risk."

With a wry smile, John answered, "Adam, Hatfield is a menace to our city, our state and even our nation. I cannot risk losing him now that we are so close. This is why I became a lawyer, to put people like Hatfield behind bars."

"Well gentlemen, it seems you have more fortitude than I had expected. Here is the plan. You must do exactly as I instruct you, or it will put us all in danger. First, and of utmost importance, I will do all of the talking. Is that clear?"

"What if we are asked a question?" asked John.

Leo barked his answer abruptly, "If that is your attitude, you will not come with me! I said, I will do all of the talking! This is non-negotiable. Got it?"

In unison, both men said, "Got it."

"These men do not like strangers. They will be very suspicions of you. You," he pointed to Adam, "will be Chuck, and you will be Dutch," pointing to John. "Chuck and Dutch are the names of a couple of men that work for Hatfield in Maryland. Some of the men here have heard of Chuck and Dutch and their ruthlessness. Since you will not be talking, I will take care of introductions. Chuck, you are known for snapping people's necks, then just leaving them where they fall to be eaten by rats and other vermin. Chuck is known to walk with a bit of a limp in his right leg. Dutch, you do not like for people to stare at you, and have been known to jab men's eyes out with your fingers for it. Hopefully people will steer clear of both of you."

"Have any of the men ever been to Maryland?" John asked.

"Let's hope not," Leo said and continued. "Now, what I need your help with most is manpower. We are looking for Club. You will recognize him easily for obvious reasons. Teeter is always with Club, and he is the man we need to help us.

"But, we do not want Club around. Teeter's a little dimwitted and Club kind of looks out for him. Teeter is the one who slipped with the information about Burt.

"We will not waste any time when we find them. I will accuse someone of staring at you Dutch. You must jump up in a rage toward that man, which will provide a distraction. Chuck, you grab Teeter. He has wild red hair and he is very skinny, you cannot miss him. Take Teeter to the little shed down the road that I will point out to you along the way.

"I will detain Club, then Dutch and I will get there as soon as we can. Do you both understand? There will be no deviation from this plan. Is that clear?"

"Clear," said Adam and John in unison.

On the way to another dingy saloon, Leo pointed out the small shed to Adam. Leo swaggered up to a sweaty man at a table and asked, "Buster, can we sit here with you?"

Adam noticed a bushy headed man with an obviously deformed foot sitting at the table next to Buster. The red headed Teeter was with him.

Joe continued, as he took a seat at Buster's table, "I'll bet you already know my friends, Chuck and Dutch. They just got here from Maryland. We need to be real nice to these fellers.

"They work for Colonel Hatfield, bustin' up folks who get in the way of his business, you know. Why, you probably already know that Chuck here is real good at snappin' folk's necks with his bare hands, even if he doesn't have a good reason. And, we need to be careful not to look to closely at Dutch there. He don't like it much, so he will poke your eyes out quicker than you can blink! Yes sir. Be real nice to these fellers."

Buster's eyes were wide with fear when Leo leaned over close to him and said, just loud enough for all to hear, "Thanks for lettin' me sit next to you. I'm afraid I'll accidentally look at Dutch, and I really don't want to do that." Then Leo looked at Dutch, and Buster, sure enough, followed his gaze.

"No Buster! Don't look at him! He's...."

Chairs started flying, as Dutch jumped up with a howl that would scare a mother grizzly bear away from protecting her cubs.

Adam instantly had Teeter in a death grip, and he was determined not to let go. Pulling him up and out of his chair quicker than he thought possible, he ran with him to the shed before they could be discovered.

Before long, Leo arrived. He came in with a pistol pointed at Adam saying, "I stopped Dutch from gougin' out Buster's eyes, and now I'm here to protect little Teeter there. Now, git on outta' here, you mangy Yankee!"

Adam jumped up, and made a run for it.

When they met back at the office awhile later, Leo had all the information they needed to rescue Burt from his captors. Burt was expected to be fully cooperative when they had him in custody.

"Colonel Peacock Hatfield will have a new address real soon," thought Adam, a smile crossing his face. "And, John will have lots of questions for him, as he files a case against those who perpetrated the North Carolina Railroad fraud."

Chapter 65

JULY 20, 1866

"Randy, what a wonderful gift you have given me. I do not know how you found them and arranged to have them brought home, but I am so glad you did. Now that your grandfather and grandmother are here in our own family cemetery, the rebuilding of Oaklayne is finally complete. I love you, son. You are a remarkable man."

As they stood together in the family cemetery, they could hear music in the distance. Today, everyone involved in the reconstruction project in any way was invited to the House Warming celebration. It was wonderful to hear Steven, Brandon, Ross and Clifford playing their guitars, with Michael and some of the other men singing along.

"Samantha helped me find them and arrange to have them brought here," said Randy. "We are still looking for the graves of Uncle Goddard and Little Goddard. I expect we will find them eventually. It is eerie how Samantha seems to read my thoughts. Anyway, she went with me when I questioned people and did the research that I was unable to do. I do not know how many obituaries we read, but it was quite a lot."

As they looked toward the gathering crowd, they saw Aaron and Isaac arrive and join the instrumentalists.

Matt and Laura were busy discussing the final touches on their plans for a new home near the river front at Oaklayne. Matt had to leave tomorrow to pick up the load of cotton he had promised to deliver for a customer. He was relieved to be able to leave Laura at Oaklayne, since she was now pregnant with their new baby. They were both excited about relocating to Oaklayne.

Samantha grabbed Randy's hand, just as Samuel, chasing Leah and Dinah, almost knocked him over. Moses scolded them, asking them to be more careful. Martha and Lizzie sat and visited comfortably, each enjoying a glass of lemonade.

John Imboden shared with Warren about the arrest of Colonel Herbert Wade Hatfield of Royal Hatfield Plantation, including the new charges against him on the North Carolina Railroad fraud. "In the trial, we learned that Thaddeus Flanagan shot Sara Ella in a failed attempt to kidnap her for Colonel Hatfield. I guess he did not expect her to have a gun and fight like a tiger to resist him. Flanagan was a professional, so he would have known it was impossible for her to be protected constantly. He hid out and watched, waited patiently for an opportunity to snatch her. He wanted to use Sara Ella as a hostage to force Adam to deed the property over to him, so he could sell it to Hatfield without anyone knowing that Hatfield was behind the conspiracy."

Warren said, "Well, I am glad the man is behind bars, and Thaddeus Flanagan cannot hurt anyone else, ever again. But, I wish Adam's friend Tom had known there was nothing he could have done to prevent it from happening. Is it not wonderful that Sara Ella is doing so well!"

Even Oscar and Elsie came for the House Warming celebration. Scott Bryan, from Washington City, brought his wife Marie and their three sons Dean, Sterling and Ross. Walter Beasley rode the train with them so he could visit Benjamin and give him the latest news about his work with Frederick Douglass and the others.

"Look at this spread," Oscar said, as Elsie ran over to join the ladies setting up the food.

Sara Ella looked up and smiled at Adam, with a twinkle in her eye. Putting down the dish she was carrying, Sara Ella turned to Elsie and invited her help in the kitchen. Jessica's husband Dominique was following her around in the kitchen, just like always. Lisa, Emma Lou, Martha and Beverly Jean were all busy bringing big trays of food to the tables that had been set up outside on the lawn.

Nathaniel was directing the show as usual. Benjamin called him "Pop" with obvious pride, respectfully carrying out his new father's instructions. Adam offered Benjamin a room in the mansion next to Randy if he wanted, but said he preferred to stay with his mother and new father in their cabin instead.

Steven's wife, Rita Kay, and Brandon's wife, Elizabeth, busily discussed plans for their new babies, who would soon be arriving. Ross was explaining to his new bride, Lorraine, how the pump he engineered works to provide water indoors to the mansion.

As everyone quietly gathered to share the bountiful meal together, Adam addresses them all. "On this beautiful occasion, my heart is warmed, as I see all of you here. Each of you contributed in your own way toward the reconstruction of Oaklayne Plantation. You have all given your best, and it shows.

"Please consider Oaklayne your home away from home. Any and all of you are welcome to be our guests at any time. I want you to know that I am eternally grateful that the Lord chose to bless me through you..." His voice broke, and he stopped to gather his composure before continuing, "I am indebted to Him and to you, for your love and faithfulness in making this dream a reality."

Everyone cheered and clapped. Then Adam held up his hand to quiet them.

"I have here a telegram from the Secretary of War, Edwin Stanton," he said, waving the telegram in the air. "In it he tells me that the Senate passed the 14th Amendment on June 8th, 1866. Then, the House passed it on June 13th, 1866. We have every reason to believe it will be ratified."

A jubilant applause erupted all around. Some in the group jumped up and patted others on the back.

"Wait! That is not all!" continued Adam. "It says here that the Freedman's Bureau Act was presented a second time, and again the president vetoed it."

The crowd immediately started grumbling, and murmuring. But, Adam interrupted the gloom and said, "But, listen! On this occasion, the veto was overridden and the bill passed, finally being enacted on July 16th 1866!"

Everyone responded with a cheer of delight, then Adam continued, "I tell you, the Reconstruction of these United States is well underway! And, without further delay, we shall now give thanks to the Lord for what He has done in our lives and our nation, and for this food He has provided."

While Adam prayed, they could hear a covered wagon coming down the lane. Adam wondered who else could be coming to the House Warming celebration.

As the wagon approached, Adam recognized Ben and Naomi, sitting in the front. Then, when the wagon stopped, two little girls about the same size jumped out the back, followed by Ruth.

Lisa immediately started toward the wagon crying, "Angela! Look, it is my sweet little Angela!"

Adam hurried to Lisa's side and caught her in his arms. "Lisa!" he said, holding her and trying to calm her. "Listen to me, Lisa. Nathaniel was able to locate Ruth so we could offer her one of the cabins at Oakville for her family. I thought it best not tell you so you would not be hurt if they decided not to come. They are naturally hesitant to bring little Angela here for fear she might be hurt. Remember, though she is your daughter, you remain a stranger to this little girl, my dear. Please, do not scare her away. Give her time to know you before you rush her to accept your love. If you handle this encounter carefully, there is a good chance Angela will be living near you at Oakville with her new family."

Lisa knew Adam was right. So she offered him a controlled smile of appreciation, swallowed her tears of joy and composed herself before approaching Ruth, Naomi and Ben. She knew that the circumstances would require a lot of time and considerable wisdom if her relationship with Angela would ever be restored. Both Warren and Samuel rushed to her side to rejoice with her.

Sara Ella put her arm around Adam's waist and said, "I was going to wait for a quiet time to tell you this, but I think now is a good time for you to know..." She looked into his face and said, "You are going to be a Father again, my love."

Notes from the Authors

HUMAN RIGHTS

Slavery was abolished when the American Civil War was over, but the passionate struggle for civil rights had only just begun. The Reconstruction Era was a tumultuous time in our nation's history, However, much was accomplished for human rights during those years, both politically and socially.

Following Reconstruction, progression of the civil rights movement was stymied by white conservative Democrats and other insurgent groups. They used force to regain power in the state legislatures where they passed laws that effectively disfranchised most blacks and many poor whites in the South.

At the turn of the century, from 1890-1910, many southern states passed new constitutions, completely disfranchising blacks. Early Supreme Court rulings on these provisions upheld many of these new southern constitutions and laws. Therefore, most blacks were prevented from voting in the South until the 1960's. Full federal enforcement of the 14th and 15th Amendments did not occur until after the passage of legislation in the mid-1960's, resulting from the African-American Civil Rights Movement (1955-1968).

Progress for civil rights continues today as we work together to truly become The UNITED States of America.

CREDIT MOBILIER

The Credit Mobilier fraud began in 1862, ultimately costing America's taxpayers many millions of dollars. It continued until the scandal broke in 1872, during the Ulysses S. Grant administration.

Look for the previous book in the Oaklayne Series, entitled

Oaklayne, A Civil War Saga

Now available for purchase in print or in your favorite e-book version
from all major bookstores and online.

The year is 1860. Conflict is threatening to dissolve the country in bitter strife if North and South cannot peacefully settle their controversy. Not only does the country face problems, but families and relationships are also vulnerable.

Oaklayne Plantation has been a very successful tobacco enterprise and home for generations of the Layne family for nearly 100 years. But now the family faces devastation as the calm, serene, stately plantation is torn with a passionate quarrel over the North-South friction.

Adam Layne is devastated, as he remains strong in his loyalty to the Union, despite being banished from the plantation by his father. The balance of the family stands strong with his father's Southern allegiance.

Called into the White House to personally meet with President Lincoln, Colonel Layne is intimidated as he accepts the tremendous responsibility of "Intelligence Support Officer" for the President, studying the arms situation of both the Union and Southern troops and learning where the South purchases or manufactures ammunition. Many times, in his incognito travel for the President, Adam faces perilous situations, finding himself at last in Andersonville Prison, the most notorious, ominous prison of the Civil War.

Oaklayne, a Civil War Saga is about a man struggling to serve both his family and his nation in a time when those things are in conflict.

Karen C. Shriver and Maurine R. McCullah

USA
KY
02 August 2014